PRAISE FOR
ROBERT LIPARULO'S NOVELS

"*Deadfall* is a brilliantly crafted thriller with a terrifying premise and flawless execution. I loved it."

— Michael Palmer, author of *The Fifth Vial*

"Another brilliantly conceived and terrifying thriller from Robert Liparulo. *Deadfall* will leave you looking over your shoulder and begging for more."

— David H. Dun, author of *The Black Silent*

"In *Deadfall*, Robert Liparulo gives us a fresh, fast-paced novel that instills a well-founded fear of the villains and an admiration for the people who refuse to be victims. It deserves the name 'thriller.'"

— Thomas Perry, author of *Silence*

"What if Mad Max, Rambo, and The Wild Bunch showed up—-all packing Star Wars-like weapons—in a small Canadian town? You'd have the thrilling adventure novel *Deadfall*. Robert Liparulo reminds us that small town life is still the scariest, and man's inhumanity to man is still The Most Dangerous Game."

— Katherine Neville, *New York Times* best-selling author of *The Eight*

"High-octane thrills are Robert Liparulo's specialty, and boy does he deliver in this ultimate tale of survival."

— Tess Gerritsen, author of *The Bone Garden*

"Inventive, suspenseful, and highly entertaining. An engrossing and imaginative tale that sticks in your brain and makes you wonder about its real possibilities. Robert Liparulo is a storyteller, pure and simple."

— Steve Berry, *New York Times* best-selling author of *The Alexandria Link*

"Very rarely does a writer come along who can entertain at the highest level while exploring human character so effectively."

— *Bookshelf Reviews*

"Robert Liparulo has written an edge of the seat thriller—complete with characters you truly care about. *Deadfall* will keep you turning pages long into the night."

—Joan Johnston, *New York Times* best-selling author
of *The Price* and *The Rivals*

"Liparulo's dialogue is smooth and competent, and he throws in just enough twists to keep the pages turning."

—*Publishers Weekly* review of *Germ*

"Great characters and literate writing, a compulsive read. I loved it! Truly."

—Douglas Preston, *New York Times* best-selling author
of *Relic*, *Tyrannosaur Canyon*, and *The Book of the Dead*

"Exceptional writing . . . Brilliant plot . . . Terror at its best."

—inthelibraryreviews.net review of *Germ*

"...comes a well-crafted page turner mindful of *The Da Vinci Code*."

—*Tampa Bay Tribune* review of *Comes a Horseman*

"Prophecy and murder run roughshod through *Comes a Horseman*. From the mountain peaks of Colorado down to a labyrinth beneath Jerusalem, mystery and adventure abound in a read that will keep you up to the wee hours of the morning. Not to be missed!"

—James Rollins, *New York Times* best-selling author
of *Sandstorm* and *Map of Bones*

"Frightening and fiendishly smart, *Comes a Horseman* is a must-read! Robert Liparulo's intense thrill ride will keep your nerves frayed and your lights on."

—David Morrell, author of *Creepers* and *The Brotherhood of the Rose*

"*Comes a Horseman* is an ambitious and original debut thriller by a fine new writer. Robert Liparulo deserves an audience, because he has something meaningful to say."

—C.J. Box, Anthony Award-winning author of *Out of Range*

ROBERT LIPARULO

THOMAS NELSON
Since 1798

NASHVILLE   DALLAS   MEXICO CITY   RIO DE JANEIRO   BEIJING

Published in Nashville, Tennessee, by Thomas Nelson. Thomas Nelson is a trademark of Thomas Nelson, Inc.

Thomas Nelson books may be purchased in bulk for educational, business, fund-raising, or sales promotional use. For information, please e-mail SpecialMarkets@ThomasNelson.com.

Publisher's Note: This novel is a work of fiction. Names, characters, places, and incidents are either products of the author's imagination or used fictitiously. All characters are fictional, and any similarity to people living or dead is purely coincidental.

Library of Congress Cataloging-in-Publication Data
Liparulo, Robert.
  Deadfall / by Robert Liparulo.
    p. cm.
  ISBN: 978-0-7852-6179-7 (HC)
  ISBN: 978-978-1-59554-476-6 (IE)
  1. Businessmen—Fiction. 2. Terrorists–Fiction.
  3. Saskatchewan—Fiction. I. Title.
PS3612.I63D43 2007
813'.6--dc22

                                                                2007032736

Printed in the United States of America
07 08 09 10 QW 6 5 4 3 2 1

For Jodi

This is as much your story as mine.

Thank you.

If you are going through hell, keep on going.

—WINSTON CHURCHILL

A lifetime is a flash of lightning in the sky.

—BUDDHA

The most dangerous of enemies are the ones who hide in plain sight.

—PROVERB

When you are unsure of a man's character, look at his friends.

—DAVID RYDER

1

FIDDLER FALLS, SASKATCHEWAN, CANADA
*On the north shore of the Fond du Lac River, thirty miles from
the Northwest Territories*
Population: 242

The people trying to kill Roland Emery quickly closed the distance behind him.

"Back off!" Roland yelled at his rearview mirror, where the big front grille of their truck loomed.

This rutted half-road was as familiar to him as the ever-increasing contours of his face. He knew every bump, every bend, every place where the trees stepped in closer to slash at your paint or, if you really were not paying attention, kick a dent in a side panel or door. Still,

1

the newcomers stayed on him, falling back on the turns, then roaring forward when only rough terrain stood between them. Their truck was one of those big fancy jobs, those pseudo-military monsters that ate ruts and boulders like granola.

A jolting bump gave him a glimpse of his own face in the mirror: red-rimmed eyes, bulging in fear. One of his shaking hands came off the wheel, fluttered to his face, and wiped at the oily sweat on his brow.

What do they want? he thought. No, no, no . . . That wasn't the question. The question was *why?* Why did they want to kill him?

Steering around each tight curve, he tried to get hold of his frenzied mind. What appeared to him, calming him, was his wife's face. Lizzie. What would happen to her if he died? Fine lady, tough as the wolverines they trapped together; but she always said what kept her going through the cold mornings checking traps and the long days guiding hunters into the hills was knowing Roland would be there at night to stoke the fire and fix a cup of *Nahapi* "sit down" tea just the way she liked it.

He pushed his lips together and cranked the wheel, taking the car down through a shallow stream and out the other side. He felt his panic pulling at him, trying to make him do something stupid. He squinted and forced Lizzie to fill that place in his mind instead of the terror.

He wished they had put some money aside so the old gal wouldn't have to work so hard by herself if these guys after him got their way. Thank heaven she wasn't with him now.

Oh yes, at least there was that.

She'd risen with him at five, as usual, but moving a little more slowly, with a little less spunk.

"Just a little tired's all," she'd said. "Ain't nothin'."

But he knew her. "Just a little tired" for Lizzie was "I'd better go see the doc" for most people. So he had insisted on checking the traps alone.

Which is what he had been doing when the big truck appeared, as bright yellow as a birthday balloon. He soon realized that the color had nothing to do with the owner's fun-loving disposition. Rather, it was ironic or sarcastic or one of those words that meant "you can't judge a fellow by the color of his car."

Roland had been coming back from checking yet another empty trap when he'd spotted the truck. He'd left his old Subaru right on the rutted trail since travelers in these hilly woods were nearly unheard of this time of year. The big yellow truck had been farther up, as though returning from camping. But he had seen it parked in front of Ben Mear's B&B on his way out of town. Fiddler Falls was too small for visitors to go unnoticed, let alone a group with a fancy machine like that.

Sure enough, he'd seen where the vehicle's wheels had pushed down the grass and some saplings on its way around the Subaru. The driver must have realized there was nothing to see but more trees along that route and turned around. He had stopped fifty yards away, as though waiting for Roland.

A man and a girl had appeared to be standing in the bed of the truck, but straps crossed over their shoulders and chests, so they must have been sitting in chairs. The chairs positioned them high enough to see over the cab's roof. And that was just weird.

He had waved, but the strangers had not waved back. Instead, the man seated in the bed had pointed at a tree between them.

The tree had exploded.

There had been the sound of thunder, a blinding flash, a wave of hot air, and the tree had disappeared. It hadn't been blown out of the ground or knocked off its trunk. It hadn't fallen into the woods or across the path. It had just . . . *disintegrated*. Needles and splinters and dirt had shot straight up, then rained down. The branches closest to the destroyed tree had ignited, burning like a thousand tiny torches.

Roland had fallen back into the brush, then staggered to his feet. The man's finger had swung slowly toward Roland. Roland had run around the car, hopped in, and reversed off the trail. He had turned the Subie toward town and punched the accelerator. The station wagon had coughed and sputtered, and he'd slapped his palm against the steering wheel and cursed himself for not giving it the tune-up it had wheezed for since summer.

Now it was moving pretty good, bouncing over rocks and ruts, but it was no match for the newer, bigger truck on its tail. Every now and again he'd catch a glimpse of the two heads bobbing furiously over the cab's roof. They would duck under branches hanging over the trail, and Roland thought the trees must have batted them a few good times. Still, they appeared to be laughing. When he squinted for a better look, he almost went off the road.

Finally he came out of the heavy woods and onto the dirt road that became Shatu' T'ine Way a quarter mile up: town, people, Constable Fuller. No way his pursuers would follow him there, not into the heart of Fiddler Falls. Small as it may be, witnesses were witnesses.

Weaving from side to side, too many thoughts crowding his driving etiquette, he saw the truck plow out of the trees and grow larger in the mirror.

"Not here!" he yelled out loud. "Not in town!"

He flew past the B&B, where he'd seen the truck earlier. Approaching the town's main street, he braked. The car's rear tires tried to slide out from under him. He gave it more gas, bumping up onto Provincial Street's blacktop. The avenue was barren. Most of the town was only now waking up. The autumn sun was still burning off the gray haze of morning twilight.

"Be there, be there," he said, speeding past the community center on his left.

His pursuers swung into view behind him. As he crossed Fife Street, he swerved to the left curb. The RCMP substation was dark. The CLOSED sign Tom used to inform folks he was out and about leaned against the big front window. Tom made it a point to tell everyone that he, as constable, never really closed; they simply needed to find him somewhere else.

Home, he thought. *I'll go to his—*

He saw Old Man Nelson sweep a plume of dust out of the general store's front door across the street. He cranked the wheel and shot to the opposite curb, but the old man had stepped back inside.

Roland grabbed for the door handle, flicking his eyes to the mirror as he did.

The truck had stopped at the intersection.

The man in the cab was pointing at him.

Everything happened at once, but for Roland, it seemed to take a lifetime. Metal ripped and tore. Glass shattered. Roland burst into flames. It wasn't that part of him caught fire and quickly spread. No, he was instantly engulfed. His arm spasmed. His fingers caught on the handle, and the door opened. He rolled out and stood, thinking what he needed to do . . . thinking . . .

His hair singed away, his flesh blistered, his blood boiled.

He was blinded by agonizing pain . . . then by the physical destruction of his eyes. He stumbled, may have fallen; he did not know. Every nerve—head to toe, skin to marrow—cried out for relief.

A thought, an image occurred to him. He was *frying*. He tried to scream.

He flailed his arms . . . or thought he did.

He—

2

Tom Fuller sat at the kitchen table, a plate of pancakes and link sausages half gone in front of him. He was listening to Dillon complain about an older boy, a sixth grader who'd been taking kids' snacks and threatening to pound anyone who told.

"Aren't you afraid of getting pounded?" Laura asked, turning from the counter with a fresh pitcher of orange juice.

The question in Tom's mind was *Who is this punk?* Leave it to Laura to explore their son's thought process instead.

Dillon shrugged. "What's he gonna do? My mom's the teacher and my dad's the law."

Tom laughed. "Is that what I am?"

Dillon grinned and nodded enthusiastically. At nine, and with the encouragement of a stack of video Westerns he had received for his birthday, he was just realizing how cool it was for his dad to be the town's only cop.

"So what are *you* going to do about it?" Laura asked, eliciting a perplexed expression from Dillon: wasn't telling his parents *doing* something?

Tom stopped the arc of his fork traveling toward his mouth so he could give Dillon a smile and a wink. The kid was cute without resorting to puppy-dog expressions. In puppy mode he could soften the stoniest heart. Sometimes Tom felt sorry for him. Tom and Laura shared a love of knowledge and learning; wanting their child to also appreciate erudition, they tended to turn their conversations into teaching opportunities. Couple that with an outdoorsy lifestyle in a region where the weather battled the terrain to see which would wear a man down the most, and you'd end up possessing both brains *and* brawn. At least that was the idea. Indeed, Dillon was philosophical beyond his years but still very much a young boy. Tom didn't want him growing up too fast.

Tom said, "You could always kick him in the—"

From outside, a *boom!*—as loud as an exclamation point, as brief as a period—rattled the windows. Dogs began barking.

Dillon's face instantly reflected shock-worry-fear. Laura mirrored his expression and looked more like her son than ever. The OJ sloshed against the clear pitcher, settling from the shake she had involuntarily given it.

"What—" she started.

"Stay here," Tom said. He dropped the fork and pushed back from the table. He grabbed his gun belt from a hook and yanked open the rear door.

"Dad?"

"Don't worry," Tom said, forcing a smile. "I'm sure it's nothing.

Just . . . just stay in the house." His eyes locked with Laura's. "Don't head to school until you hear from me."

She nodded.

He pulled the door shut, jogged around the house, and saw black, billowy smoke snaking into the sky from the center of town. Strapping on the gun belt, he ran up Camsel Drive. A door opened. Lars and Barb Jergins, owners of the Elder Elk Diner, stepped onto the porch. Their eyes rose up to the smoke as their mouths dropped.

Tom raised a hand. "Lars! Barb!" he called.

"What happened, Tom?" Lars asked.

"Don't know. Stay here. I'll come tell you when I find out."

They went back inside.

Tom rounded the corner onto Provincial Street. This was Fiddler Falls's main thoroughfare, though it consisted of only four short blocks of businesses, including an Elks Lodge, a combination town hall and community center, and Dr. Jeffrey's big Victorian house-cum-office. At the street's southern terminus was Dirty Woman Park, a half-moon swatch of grass, trees, playground equipment, and redwood picnic tables and benches.

Tourists chuckled at the name until they learned its literal meaning. Despite living right on the river, Becca Nahanni was said never to have bathed. Never. Her stench and a patina of grime that covered her skin, caking in her wrinkles, had supported the rumor. When she had died in her nineties, she willed her small shack to the town. It had been so odorous and foul, the town had razed it and created the park in her honor.

Beyond Dirty Woman lay the Fond du Lac River, half a mile wide where the town touched its banks. In the other direction, due north, Provincial Street passed, among other businesses, a restaurant, a boardinghouse, St. Bartholomew's Church, and finally a small school that serviced forty-three students, K through 12. Just beyond the school, the community's only paved street crumbled into dirt. Before long it devolved into grassy ruts, marking the passage of hunters, fishermen, and other souls brave enough to venture into Canada's northern backcountry. It was the town's widest street, one lane north, one lane south, with room at both curbs to parallel park. Townies rarely bothered to drive, since a mile walk connected any two points in Fiddler Falls.

Tom saw that Provincial was occupied now. A block and a half from where he stood, directly in front of Kelsie's General Store, a car sat twisted and burning. It looked like the newscast images he'd seen of car bombings. A few people—likely everyone in the vicinity at that hour of the morning—had come out of the stores and businesses to watch from the sidewalks. Others were closer, in the street.

Hurrying forward, he yelled to the people standing around it. "Back away!"

The asphalt around the rear of the car appeared to be burning with a low blue flame. He guessed that meant the gas tank had already ruptured, but he didn't want another explosion to prove him wrong and take out the closest spectators in the process.

The first scent he recognized was ozone, a powerful sterilant that destroys bacteria, viruses, and odors. Lightning strikes and fastflowing water create the chemical, which accounts for the fresh smell after thunderstorms and around waterfalls. In a drug enforcement course, Tom had learned that affluent pot users were known to use ozone generators to eliminate the smell of the drug. Ozone always reminded him of freshly laundered sheets.

As Tom inhaled, the ozone gave way to the pungent odor of gasoline, burning rubber, and a putrid reek he could not identify. It stung his nostrils, drawing tears from his eyes.

He coughed and yelled, "Step back!"

No one did. He realized that those nearest the car were not townies but the group of six young people who'd arrived by floatplane the
previous day. They'd picked up the bright-mustard Hummer, which
had been sitting at the service station since the week before. According
to Lenny Hargrove, the station's owner, the driver had been from a
transportation service and had hitched a ride on an outfitter's plane
back to Saskatoon. The Hummer's appearance had caused a flurry of
speculation about who was coming. The group had moved into the
B&B on Shatu' T'ine Way.

Tom spotted the Hummer just beyond the wreckage. One of the
visitors stood at the curb opposite Kelsie's, in front of the used-book
and curio store. Maybe twenty, he was sloppily dressed in a Rolling
Stones T-shirt that skimmed over a fat belly and hung straight down.
Pudgy, sweatpants-clad legs appeared from under the stomach's over-
hang. Wisps of hair clung to his cheeks and chin in patches. A baseball cap was turned backward on his head. He lifted a professional
video camera up to his eye and pointed it at the burning car. Another
man—bald, black, young—nudged the cameraman, spoke to him. The
camera panned to take in Tom's approach.

A teenage girl clung to the arm of a man in his late twenties.
Flawless skin, freckles, and short-cropped brown hair could have con-
spired to make her seem more youthful than she was. Still, he didn't
like the idea of a girl so young paired with such an older man. It was
an observation he would not have made had the contrast between
adult and child not been so acute. While the man appeared smug and
insouciant, the girl bounced excitedly. She bore a broad, open-mouthed
smile, which she reined in by biting her lower lip when she saw Tom
appraising her.

A glance around revealed smiles on all of the visitors' faces. Except
one: a young boy with ruddy cheeks not yet ready for a razor stood

away from the rest. Frowning, he fidgeted from one foot to the other and went from clasping his hands to crossing his arms and back again.

"What happened?" Tom asked, eyeing the car. Instead of the outward rending of metal he had expected, the roof had been crushed in by something circular, as though a peg-legged giant had nailed it as he strode past. The four corners had buckled upward. The wheels and tires—the two in Tom's view were ruptured—canted out, as if they'd experienced an unbearable weight before rising with the fenders. The vehicle rested on its undercarriage. Every window had shattered onto the street. Thousands of tiny squares of safety glass sparkled with reflected fire like diamonds. Flames filled the roof's concavity, reminding Tom of the cauldron that held the torch fires during the Olympic Games.

"This looks like Roland's Subaru," he said to no one in particular. Roland was a local hunting guide and trapper. His all-wheel-drive station wagon boasted more dings, bangs, and chips than a space shuttle after reentry. He peered into the passenger compartment, through the slits that once were side-window openings. Flames owned that space as fire did a crematorium's furnace. Heat radiated out with more intensity than seemed right to Tom; he wondered if an acceler-ant had doused the interior. Bending at the waist, he sidestepped around to improve his view.

"Was anyone—" he started. The next word jammed in his throat. On the street behind the wreckage, the charred remains of . . . of what appeared to be a smoldering human body. It looked like tightly packed ash over burnt wood, positioned to somewhat approximate the shape of a man. One arm jutted up out of the cinders, as though in a final grasp for salvation. Its fingers were gone.

Tom backed away. The evidence of violent death sent his hand automatically to his holster. He unclipped the retaining strap but did not withdraw the weapon.

"Musta been lightning, Sheriff."

He turned his head. The cradle robber was watching him. His twisted half smile seemed calculated to either intimidate or provoke. The man wore gray denim pants, tight on his legs and hips, flaring a bit where they covered the tops of gray-and-black boots. The boots were square-toed and made of some scaly reptile hide. A black T-shirt clung to his torso, accentuating his physique: sinewy muscles, no fat. He wore an expensive down vest, black and unzipped. It was insufficient protection from the fall climes in northern Canada. A twisting chain of black gems hung around his neck, and another necklace made, it seemed, of old rotting teeth. A big watch clung to his wrist like a pet beetle. Resting against the watch and rising three inches up his arm was an assortment of bracelets, some metal, some thread, braided and knotted. More bracelets adorned his other wrist, stopping before they reached a colorful Oriental dragon tattooed on the underside of his forearm. His hair, the brownish color of spruce bark, appeared coifed into an intentionally messy tangle. A faint golden shadow hued his cheeks, chin, and upper lip. To Tom, he could have been one of those grunge models he'd seen in magazine ads: fashionable, edgy, not quite groomed to perfection.

This guy said lightning? Tom thought. He had detected ozone, but the sky was cloudless. No way lightning. He straightened.

"What do you know about this?"

The man shrugged. "Where are the wieners and marshmallows when you need them?"

Someone laughed.

"You were in the Hummer?" Tom's head inclined toward the big SUV. His pistol's grip felt solid under his palm. He considered freeing it from its holster, despite these visitors' lack of threatening gestures. Tom was even more disturbed by their nonchalance. But equanimity was no reason to draw a weapon.

The man turned his head to look at the Hummer, as if there were so many of the expensive vehicles in town, he wanted to make sure.

"Yeah," he said slowly, "that's ours."

"Let me see some ID."

The man reached behind him. Tom tensed. The hand reappeared holding a money clip. The man slipped a driver's license from the folded bills and handed it to Tom.

"Declan," Tom read, giving the name a sharp *e*.

The girl snickered. "Deck-lan," she corrected.

"Declan Gabriel Page." Tom eyed him. "Seattle?"

"The Emerald City," Declan agreed.

Tom returned the license. He scanned the scattered visitors, then gestured to them. "All of you come on over here. If you came into town with Declan, step over, please."

No one moved.

"Come on now!"

Tom's eyes moved to Declan's. They were flat, emotionless.

Declan's smirk bent up slightly. Keeping his gaze on Tom, he called out, "Come say hi to the nice sheriff, boys!"

They shuffled closer.

Declan extended his hand to Tom. "I didn't catch your name."

Tom gave a curt nod. "Constable Fuller, RCMP." He added, "Royal Canadian Mounted Police."

"Ahhh," Declan said. "A Mountie." He turned to the girl. "See, I told you we'd run into them up here."

The cameraman—still filming—and the black man stepped beside Declan. A teenage boy he hadn't seen earlier appeared behind the girl. His thick dark hair fell to midear, curling up at the ends. Gold loops pieced an earlobe and the left side of his bottom lip. A gold rod, bent into a rectangle at the top like a sardine-can key, harpooned his right eyebrow.

Tom wanted to know everything at once. What were their names? Why were they in town? What did they have to do with Roland's car exploding, with Roland's death? He wanted to tell the fat kid to get the camera out of his face. But because everything at once was a bit beyond his pay grade, and because he was already looking at the teenager, he asked, "Shouldn't you be in school?"

"We're tutored," the boy said. "We have flexible schedules."

The girl giggled, and Tom wondered how deep this weirdness was going to get. He took in the gathering of visitors. Missing one: that other boy, the youngest of the bunch.

"Where's—"

"Tom!" someone yelled—*screamed*—to his left. It was Old Man Nelson, who'd named the mercantile after his daughter. He stood in the doorway of the store, looking as if he might have seen Roland, burnt beyond recognition, get to his feet and skip into the ice cream parlor. He pointed, but Tom had already caught the object of Nelson's concern in the corner of his eye and was spinning toward it.

Looking straight into it, the diameter of the gun barrel appeared as big as a tank's. The boy pointing it at Tom looked as terrified as Tom felt. Big eyes, quivering bottom lip. The pistol wavered and shook, but at a distance of three feet, any shot at all would have taken off Tom's head.

"Now, son," Tom said. "This isn't the way to—"

Fingers gripped his wrist, firmly lifting his hand away from the butt of his gun. Declan. That nasty little smile.

Declan pulled Tom's service pistol from its holster and moved to the boy's side. "Good job, Julie."

The boy lowered his weapon, obviously relieved to do so. Sweat had broken out on his brow beneath long bangs. He closed his eyes. He said, "It's Julian. Don't call me Julie." He strode off toward the Hummer.

Tom expected a wisecrack from Declan: *Guess you're done asking questions*, or even a simple *Well, well, well*. But the man only watched him, seeming to read his thoughts and intentions in the contours of his face. After a moment he called out, "Bad, round up these people. Put them where we talked about. The community center."

The black man—had Declan called him "Bad"?—brushed past Tom, beckoning to Old Man Nelson, who was backpedaling into the shadows of the general store. Bad held a pistol high above his head, as if to say, *I got the power now. Listen to me!*

"Cortland, you and Julie put out this fire," Declan said. "Kyrill, get the phones."

The older teen jogged toward the store. He stopped to let Nelson and Kelsie exit, prodded from behind by Bad. Then he disappeared into the store.

Tom's stomach knotted. *The phones.* He was certain Declan was referring to the town's satellite phones, their only means of quick communication. This far north, in a part of the world too sparsely populated to warrant a major investment by any corporation not mining for uranium, there was no mobile phone service, no landlines, no cable or satellite television, no Internet.

This isolation, this snub at time's technological force-feeding, was part of Fiddler Falls's charm. On Thursday nights the Elks Lodge hosted a movie night on its big-screen TV. Trouble for the movie hero often originated or was compounded by a cell phone or e-mail, and inevitably a townie would pipe up with "Wouldn't happen here!" or a "tsk tsk." Few residents wanted the telecommunication revolution to find Fiddler Falls. Even the businesses that would benefit from selling their goods online or touting their services on a Web site recognized the negative sea change to the community's appeal that technology would bring. Several businesses had contracted with a company in La Ronge to host their Web site or online store.

Tom knew of only four satellite phones in town. One he had left charging in the storefront that acted as the RCMP's substation—so close the Hummer was stopped in front of it. Janine Red Bear, the conservation officer, maintained another phone. She had left two days ago on a weeklong trek through the district. Old Man Nelson kept a phone in his store. He charged a buck a minute to use it, which was low enough to prevent townies from investing in their own phone. John Tungsten owned one. He ran Tungsten's Outfitters and Fishing Lodge outside town. Tom had not seen John; John's wife, Margie; or Billie, their part-time cook/part-time guide, for a few days. Most likely, they had taken advantage of the change-of-season lull to make repairs on their wilderness cabins or travel to Wollaston for supplies.

The kid named Kyrill hurried out of the store, brick-sized satellite phone in hand. He navigated around Roland's metal pyre and jogged directly to the RCMP office across the street. Finding the door locked, he used the phone to smash the front window. At the sound, a woman screamed. She was part of a group of about a dozen people Bad was herding toward the community center, which occupied an entire block on the RCMP side of the street. The teen kept striking at the glass until only the top crown of the force's logo was visible on a shard clinging to the upper molding. Then he stepped through.

These visitors knew precisely where to find the phones. They knew what was needed to cut the town off completely. Even the time of year aided them: fall, after the summer tourists departed; when rainy weather made the long, unpaved roads between communities all but impassable; before the winter freeze, which paved the roads, lakes, and rivers with ice, making them more traversable than any other time of year.

A grim realization came to Tom: this had been researched and planned, this—what was it?—*taking* of the town, holding its citizens hostage, terrorizing them, *murdering* them.

He closed his eyes, then opened them to the visage of Declan's devil-may-care attitude. The man acted as though he did this sort of thing every day. *No big deal. I'm in control, and there's nothing you can do. So just relax and enjoy the ride.*

Tom's gaze dropped to the Sig Sauer semiautomatic he knew so well, now turned on him like a recalcitrant Doberman pinscher. He recalled the words Laura had directed at Dillon less than ten minutes ago.

So what are you going to do about it?

What are *you going to do about it?* he thought. With that, he could go no further. Mental constipation, his mother had called it. A puzzle so confounding, options so numerous, the mind simply paused. And paused.

Declan's eyebrows rose as though he understood Tom's predicament and wondered how he would resolve it . . . as though *any* resolution Tom considered was fine by him. *I'm in control, and there's nothing you can do.*

Think! Tom told himself. But unable to grasp how his world had changed in ten minutes—six hundred seconds!—with the odor of Roland's burning corpse in his nostrils and the cries of the citizens he had sworn to protect in his ears and his own service weapon pointed at his head, he stopped trying to think.

He took action.

He just did it.

He leaped for the gun.

4

Chin resting on his chest, John Hutchinson—"Hutch" to just about everyone—had let the drone of the helicopter's engine lull him into a fitful half-sleep when he felt a hand on his shoulder. He ignored it until the nudging became hard raps. He emerged into full consciousness to find Phil's arm reaching around from the seat directly behind him with firm and insistent fingers. He twisted to face his friend.

"Look!" Phil called out, pushing his soft lips into a big grin. His cheeks lifted wire-frame glasses off the bridge of his nose. He nodded toward the side window.

David, seated behind the pilot, had his forehead pressed against the glass. Next to him, in the middle rear seat, Terry was unbuckled and half standing to see past David.

Hutch looked. As perfectly as a mirror, the lake below reflected the sky and, around its edges, Precambrian granite cliffs and staunch evergreens, like fairy-tale sentinels. Hutch watched a breeze ripple the surface, making the clouds below appear to dance in air currents unfelt by those high above. Green and brown and gold wilderness, unscarred by man, fanned out from the lake as far as he could see; it rolled over the terrain like a rumpled blanket, upon which rested a flat, glistening gem.

The Bell JetRanger glided between water and sky, and for only the fourth time in his life, Hutch felt beauty snatch his breath away. The first time it had happened, he had been shocked to realize that the concept wasn't simply the province of songwriters, but that it really, physically, literally happened. His eyes had followed the long aisle and caught sight of his bride stepping through the church door, her arm hooked through her father's. She had been halfway to him before he had remembered to breathe again. The first sight of his children, each just seconds old, had been breath-stoppers two and three. That it happened here, now, caught him off guard, not only because it was the first time the love for a human had not elicited the response, but mostly because he had been so downright ornery lately. How could anything, let alone *landscape*, have penetrated his sour disposition? It validated his decision to come up here, to get away from it all and just *be*.

He smiled at the pilot, but the man was an automaton behind mirrored Ray-Bans. Hutch consulted the topographical map in his lap, then turned and hooked an elbow over the seat back. "Black Lake!" he yelled over the din of the engine and rotors.

"Beautiful!" Terry pronounced.

Phil slapped Hutch's elbow and beamed. "So we're almost there?" he asked.

Under Phil's mask of elation, Hutch recognized fatigue and road-weariness. They all felt it. Even Hutch's butt was numb from riding in Terry's van so long: twenty-seven nonstop hours on paved roads from Denver to Lac La Ronge, Saskatchewan, then nine more grueling hours on a potted, rutted dirt road to Points North Landing, where they chartered the helicopter.

After so much discomfort, Hutch wondered if Phil could appreciate spending the next two weeks living out of tents in the deep wilds of northern Canada. The trade-off—at least for Hutch, and he hoped for all of them—was the isolation. Not just the *feeling* of getting away from it all, but getting away from it all for real: no e-mail, no cell phones, no television or DVDs or video games, no golf courses, no restaurants, no work emergencies. And no way to get to any of them, even if they wanted to. Just the thought of that kind of seclusion calmed him. Since Janet had found another man, filed for divorce, and taken the kids eleven months ago—in that order and that quickly—there had been times he thought he was going to explode—not in rage or frustration, but literally—or at least stroke out. And at thirty-eight, he was too young for that.

Maybe it was true that rotten luck struck in threes, because life had recently battered Phil and Terry as well. After fourteen years at the same company, Phil had been passed over for a promotion. Passive-aggressive to his marrow, instead of confronting his boss, he opted to express his displeasure by letting his physical appearance go out the window. Anything but lithe at the start, he had gained twenty pounds in thirty days.

"If Robert DeNiro and George Clooney can do it for movies, I can certainly do it in protest!" he had said when Hutch noticed the sudden gain.

"Yeah, but Phil . . . they got paid millions, were probably under a doctor's supervision, and got back in shape when filming ended."

Phil had grumbled something Hutch didn't catch.

"Besides," Hutch had said, "I don't think your boss cares much about your weight."

Mistake, saying that. Not only had Phil kept the fat; he'd started shaving only every third day and changed his gait to a shuffle and his watercooler chat to barely audible mumblings that compared his boss to Brutus (as in *et tu*), Benedict Arnold, and, inexplicably, Rosanne Barr. At one of their monthly poker nights, he had given the guys a demonstration. Terry and David had laughed, but Hutch hadn't thought it was so funny. He suspected his friend was suffering from depression, but he didn't know what to do about it.

"Well, if you're trying to get fired," Hutch had told him, "that'll do it."

It *had* done it, much to Phil's surprise, which in turn had puzzled Hutch. That was four months ago, and Phil was still jobless. In the insult-to-injury department, Phil's weight gain and job stress had sent his blood pressure shooting out of control and gave him what his doctor called "borderline type II diabetes."

Then there was Terry: Realtor, businessman, playboy. His trouble had begun with a slump in the housing market and had grown worse when a former sales assistant and girlfriend started her own company with the specific intent to take as much business from Terry as she could. Confident of his position on the food chain, he had been slow to respond. Dwindling sales and high overhead had driven his company to bankruptcy. Three months later denial coupled with a high-flying lifestyle had pushed him back into court, except this time one door down, in the personal bankruptcy division. He now worked as a sales associate for his ex-girlfriend.

Of the four friends, only David seemed to have avoided a crisis during the previous year. Hutch prayed his friend's good fortune would continue, but he had the impression David would get by all right even if it didn't stay smooth for him. Blessed with movie-star good looks, he had never played the handsome stud. He was in fact the humblest man Hutch had ever known. David had married his high school sweetheart and had gone to work for her dad, managing a Furniture Brigade store. Once he had appeared in his own store's television commercial, pointing out the great bargains there. Sales spiked the following weekend. When someone had suggested it was David, not the bargains, that drew the customers, David stopped appearing before the cameras. Now he and Beth had a son and a daughter, and his life was simply hunky-dory, if not—as Hutch, Phil, and Terry said—"Fantastic with a capital *F*."

Every fall for the past seven, the four friends had packed up Terry's ratty van and headed to Canada for a weeklong fishing excursion. Usually they'd hit La Ronge and canoe into the finger lakes north and east of that vast water park—largely Nun, Keg, and Otter Lakes. By summer, Hutch had known it would take a better getaway to decompress from their recent trials. And ten days in the wilds between Lake Athabasca and the Northwest Territories sounded about right.

It was in extreme northern Saskatchewan, which remained much as it was one hundred, two hundred years ago; where the weather was unpredictable—something about that appealed to Hutch's mood—but rarely fatal; and where barren-ground caribou from the Beverly and Qamanirjuaq herds still roamed that time of year. Hutch was the only hunter of the four. He had always wanted to bow hunt for caribou. They were fast, mobile animals, with senses keener than those of deer—a challenging trophy to take. He felt his skills were up to the task, and a victory here would mean more than bagging a deer or elk, which he had done since he was fourteen.

He had convinced the others that ten days sans *everything* would do

them a world of good. Perhaps it would not offset the year's setbacks—
no way, nohow—but he was sure it would prove to be a much-needed
respite. Upon their return, their troubles would probably not appear less
awful, but he hoped their confidence in being able to handle them
would have improved. Each of the men had been able to adjust his vaca-
tion dates. Almost giddy over it, Hutch had made arrangements to
arrive in No Man's Land—a term Terry had used and the others had
adopted—on October 15: today. Archery season would begin tomorrow.

Phil slapped him on his elbow again, jarring him out of a day-
dream. He believed he may even have fallen asleep for a few seconds;
he had done the bulk of the driving, and it was catching up with him.

"Hmmm?"

"We're almost there, right? No Man's Land?" The blue sky and
clouds shimmered in Phil's glasses, as though on tiny television screens.

Hutch brought the map around.

"I'd say another half hour or so."

Phil's smile pushed wider. He elbowed Terry. "Half an hour," he
informed him.

Terry passed the word to David.

Hutch took in their smiles. Good to see, good to see. He faced forward in his seat again, and through the copter's footwell windows,
watched the trees and hills and ropes of blue water whipping past.
Suddenly the landscape turned black. The trees became scant, limb-
less poles rising from dark, barren fields. He rapped the pilot on the
arm. "What's that?"

"Fire. Last year. Five thousand acres burned. We were tasting the
ashes all the way down to Points North. They evacuated a handful
of towns—Fond-du-Lac, Fiddler Falls, Black Lake—but a rain came
and saved them." He smiled. "Don't worry. I'm taking you away
from it, eh."

Hutch leaned over a knapsack, pulled out a lukewarm can of Monster energy drink, and downed half of it in one long swig. Phil tapped his shoulder. He turned to see Terry drinking from his thumb, then gesturing to the three backseat comrades. Hutch handed a Monster to each of them, making sure Phil got the low-carb version. Tops popped, they touched cans in a silent cheer and drank.

Hutch realized he was smiling again. He nodded and thought, *We're not going to want to leave, not to go back to our pitiful, stinking lives. Someone's going to suggest staying longer.* He wondered who would be the first to bring it up, but he knew. He was ready to say it now.

5

Tom Fuller sprang forward, his hands darting out to grab the pistol and turn it away, then wrench it out of Declan's grip.

Declan deftly sidestepped out of Tom's path. He swung the gun hard into the back of Tom's head as he sailed past.

Tom crashed heavily to the road, cracking his chin, but his mind was focused only on the raging pain that had erupted in his skull. Declan came to mind, and the gun. He rolled, expecting to hear the crack of gunpowder, almost indistinguishable from the crack of the slug breaking the sound barrier: the last sounds he would hear.

Declan squatted ten feet away. He rested his forearms on his knees, letting the pistol dangle in his hand between them.

Propped on one elbow, Tom now noticed that the man's gray jeans had patches of elasticized fabric sewn into the sides, crotch, and cuffs.

Declan was prepared to move quickly. Tom reached around to the back of his head, grimaced in pain. His fingers came back bloody.

"Your eyes telegraphed your intention to go for the gun," Declan said. "Maybe even before you were conscious of it yourself. Then your shoulders and hips."

"Why are you doing this?"

Declan rolled his eyes. Clearly, it wasn't the question he'd expected. He answered as if it had been. "Fifteen months at the Shaolin Temple Tagou School under the personal tutelage of Grandmaster Liu." He nodded, pleased with himself. "That's where this one comes from." He fingered one of the braided bracelets on his left arm, above the watch. He saw Tom squinting at the collection. His finger rose to a red bracelet. He said, "Kabbalah." He touched a white one. "Satin cord . . . Hamsa. This one's *kuri-chiku* from Africa." He brushed the tips of his fingers over the rest of them as if playing a stringed instrument. "Each one wards off evil."

"*Evil?*"

"It's everywhere," Declan said, scanning the skies. "Every culture has its idea of what fends it off." He crossed himself. "There's a lot going on the eye can't see. If something invisible can hurt you, who am I to say wearing a strand of material, kissed by a shaman, blessed by a priest, doesn't have power?" He stroked the bracelets again. His hand rose to the black-jeweled necklace. "Black diamonds. From outer space. They impart wisdom." He touched the string of molars. "Basalt lightning teeth from the island of Siquijor. These things magically appear at the base of trees that have been struck by lightning."

"What . . ." Tom was dumbfounded. Declan was a walking contradiction, a boogeyman afraid of the dark. "What do they do?"

"What *don't* they do? Heal, strengthen, keep demons at bay." He held up his arms, turning them slowly. "I can't say for sure all of these work. I mean, come on." He shrugged. "But it can't hurt to cover your bases, right?"

All Tom could do was stare.

Declan stared back, until his eyes shot up to take in something behind Tom.

Tom craned to see. Sylvia Blackstock stood on the sidewalk, having rounded the corner five or six steps earlier. Two girls, one in Dillon's grade, the other slightly younger, trembled at her side. Their mouths hung open.

"Tom . . . ?" Sylvia said finally.

"Run!" he yelled.

Sylvia gripped a shoulder of each girl and took a step back.

Casually, Declan raised the pistol. "Don't," he said flatly. Then: "Kyrill!"

A distant "What?" came back.

"Got some ladies for you!"

So this is the way it's going to happen, Tom thought. *As the townies reveal themselves, Declan and his gang are going to scoop them up.* He wondered if Declan knew how suddenly his harvest would grow over the next fifteen minutes, as Fiddler Falls children made their way to school. Forty-odd students plus maybe a half-dozen parents. Fifty. With the ones already in the community center, a quarter of the population would be captured before eight in the morning.

He prayed that Laura and Dillon would follow his instructions to remain in the house until they heard from him. He believed they would do that . . . at least for a while. If he never returned, would Laura venture out to find him? *Yes,* he thought with weight growing heavier on his chest, *she would.* With guns blazing, if he knew anything about his wife.

A loud whooshing noise startled him. Julian and the girl—

Cortland—were aiming household extinguishers at the burning wreck-age of Roland's car and corpse, releasing great plumes of mist. After a minute, the car and the teens were hidden by a cloud. After another minute they reappeared, sans flames.

The Kyrill kid had already hustled Sylvia and her daughters to the community center when three boys appeared on the street, closer to the school. They had no reason to pass this way, but when they saw the smoldering car, one of them said, "Whoa!" and sprinted toward it. His buddies followed. They stopped twenty feet from Tom and stared down at him.

"Hey, Mr. Fuller, what happened?"

Tom glanced at Declan. "Little accident, Adrian," he said.

Another boy pinched his nose. "What's that smell?"

Tom said, "Look, you boys do what this man says and everything will be all right. You hear? Don't do anything except what you're told."

"Mr. Fuller, where's—"

"Adrian! Do only what this gentleman or his friends ask you to. Do you hear me?"

The boys nodded.

"Julie!" Declan called.

The boy was inspecting the front grille of the trashed Subaru and did not respond.

Declan shook his head. "Julian!"

Now he looked.

"Go relieve Bad at the community center. Send him and Kyrill back here. Take these three with you." To the boys, he gestured toward Julian. Reluctantly, Adrian and his friends shuffled past Tom.

"It'll be okay, guys." After they had disappeared into the building, Tom said, "So what now?"

"We're not done collecting," Declan said. He rose and extended

29

each leg out to the side in turn, stretching it, and rotated each foot at the ankle. He pushed his hands into his lower back and bent backward, groaning. "And just think how many lives you're saving."

"Saving?"

"You're their protector, right? The guy with the gun. The man with the plan. And here you are, bruised and broken. In the dirt. Who's gonna say they can do better? Who's gonna try to fill your shoes?"

At first Tom had thought Declan's cockiness stemmed from stupidity, as most cockiness did. Tom had found that arrogance belied poor self-esteem, and people with poor self-esteem often rashly defended against any perceived risk of getting knocked down a peg, because they were already so low. Rash behavior meant stupid behavior.

But he didn't think Declan was stupid. Far from it. On Tom's mental Cartesian graph of personality types, the intersection of high intelligence and grossly immoral behavior—oh, say, murder and kidnapping—was marked with a single word: *evil*. And evil people were a lot harder to outfox, outmaneuver, and outguess than people who were simply ignorant. He was going to have to do a lot better than simply lunging for a gun, which he admitted was both stupid and rash.

"What are you going to do with these people?" he asked.

Declan smiled. "Have a little fun."

"Like you did with Roland?"

Declan looked perplexed, then he got it. "The car?" He thought about it. "Yeah, something like that." He scanned the street in one direction, then the other. "I feel like I'm waiting for the doorbell to ring on Halloween. Where is everybody?"

Bad and Kyrill were cutting across the grass in front of the community center, which was set farther back from the street than the stores and businesses on each side of it. Both held handguns.

"What's your goal here?" Tom asked. "What are you trying to—"

Declan raised a hand to stop him. "Shh, shh, shh."

Tom followed his gaze. A group of eight or nine kids and parents had come onto Provincial and were slowly approaching, murmuring among themselves. He had yelled for Sylvia Blackstock and her daughters to run because they were close to the corner and he'd thought they could make it and hide. He had not factored in their confusion, which slowed their reaction time. Of course, with their constable lying bloody in the road, near a crushed and smoldering car, any townie who stumbled onto the scene would spend precious seconds puzzling over the sight, if they didn't outright do what Adrian and his friends had done and run straight for Tom. If they eventually determined the situation warranted a quick retreat, Tom had no doubt any one of these visiting fiends would shoot them in the back.

As if his thoughts had given it permission to exist, he heard a sound that sent a cold spark streaking down his spine: it was the metal-sliding-on-metal and *click-chink* of a bolt-action rifle receiving a bullet into its firing chamber. "Locked and loaded" was the military expression. He looked and saw Bad and Kyrill at the open back door of the Hummer. The teenager had the rifle, a long, tightly constructed weapon. He'd seen something similar only twice before. The first time was at RCMP's Special Emergency Response Team training, before the unit had become Joint Task Force Two. It was the firearm of choice for the snipers there. Took a six-inch-long .50-caliber Browning machine gun load. Tom had seen his second BMG rifle when an affluent hunter brought one to town, keen on bringing down a caribou from a thousand yards. Evan MacElroy had guided him backcountry. Later Evan said the man had shot from one basin ridge to another, about twelve hundred yards, and dropped a big bull with one round.

"The thing just toppled over," he'd said. "When we got over there, I coulda stuck my arm in the hole that bullet made."

Kyrill yanked the stock to its full extension, seated it into his shoulder, and peered through the scope at the sky.

If this gun was anything like the others Tom had seen, it was too powerful to shoot like a normal hunting rifle, a .30-06, say. The manufacturer provided a bipod at the base of the barrel, designed to stabilize the heavy weapon and minimize its recoil. He wondered how experienced this boy was with it. He hoped not to find out.

Showing a toothy grin, Bad was appraising a weapon even more exotic. It looked like something from a space movie: a plank of rectangular metal with a grip and trigger extending from the center of one of the narrow sides; on the other side, opposite the trigger, was a handle that appeared to contain a built-in scope. Bad looked up. He saw the group of townies and stiffened. He pulled the weapon in close to his chest and turned his torso so one end of the gun pointed at them.

Declan waved his pistol at the kids and adults, as if in greeting. When they stopped, Tom said, "You better come on over. Do what they say."

"What have you done to Tom?" one of them yelled.

Declan sauntered to the woman, who took a step back. He leaned his shoulder against hers, whispered in her ear. Her eyes widened and her skin paled noticeably in the brightening morning light. Declan kissed the air between them, then took in each face, one at a time, making sure they understood his intentions. He ordered the group to the community center. He watched them go, one hip cocked, apparently feeling pretty good about himself.

The girl approached him, affecting the same sauntering gait, and she put her arm around his waist. They kissed. When their faces parted, she melted into him, notching herself into the shape of his side.

"A place like this, you guys must play a lot of video games," Declan told Tom.

"We find better things to do. Lots of outdoor things."

Declan looked surprised. "Like what?"

"Family outings . . . touch football, picnics, hide-and-seek. Hiking, camping, boating, off-roading, bird watching, fishing, hunting . . ."

"I like hunting," Declan said.

Tom studied his face. "Animals," he clarified.

The younger man nodded.

"Rabbit, coyote, sheep, caribou."

Declan gazed south down Provincial, seeming to cast his vision beyond Dirty Woman Park, over the wide span of water, to the rolling green and gold hills on the far side.

"Yeah," he said. "That's something I could do. What do you think? Wanna try that, Cort?"

"Sure."

"Later," he said. "After we take care of other business."

The way Declan looked at him made Tom's guts feel like soup.

6

The pilot brought the JetRanger down in a meadow of tall green and yellow turf. Hutch watched the grass sway in the propeller's downdraft like the hair of a girl swimming in a strong current. The way it strained away from the helicopter in a large, vibrating circle, he could imagine it trying to flee from the bellowing contraption invading its peace. In the distance a rabbit bounced up and disappeared into the woods.

The pilot—named Franklin, Hutch remembered—switched off the engine and inverted various other toggles on the center console. The roar and bluster they had grown accustomed to diminished like a dragon's dying breath.

Hutch patted Franklin's shoulder and gave him a thumbs-up. The man returned the gesture.

"Yeah, baby!" Terry said in a passable imitation of Austin Powers.

David opened a rear door. Cool wind blew in, bringing with it swirling bits of grass, leaves, granules of dirt—and something else, a fragrance. Musky and floral and clean, Hutch didn't know if it was earth or trees or water or animals or more likely a sort of aura derived from all of them over eons, but he did know it was wonderful. It smelled like freedom, the way the world must have smelled when it was new. All of them sensed it. They were taking in lungfuls through their nostrils. David sniffed the air like a dog, his eyes closed, the mere hint of a smile on his lips. Terry and Phil leaned toward the open door, seemingly unconscious of their posture.

Then the dying engine backfired. A plume of smoke, reeking of oil, blew in.

Terry coughed and waved his hand in front of his face.

David hopped out. He moved twenty paces into the meadow, out from under the slowing blades and away from the engine's fumes.

Phil found the handle that opened the door beside him. He slid down, leaping the last twelve inches. He tumbled, rolled, and sprawled in the grass, face up, as though he were making a snow angel.

Hutch climbed out of his own door, laughed at Phil, and laughed at being here. He leaned back into the cabin to shove the map into his pack. He withdrew an empty Monster can from a cup holder, and Franklin touched his hand.

"I'll get those," the pilot said. "You'll have enough trash to haul out in ten days."

"How far are we from that area where you suggested we camp?"

"Three, four hundred yards. That way." He pointed over Hutch's shoulder.

Hutch wondered if he truly looked as glum as his twin images appeared in Franklin's glasses. He felt lighter, happier than he had in months. Maybe the emotion was only a tiny swing in the right direction, but it felt good after the long months of near-constant stress and depression. The thought made him realize his heart still ached, heavy in his chest.

Give it time, he told himself. *We just got here. If simply flying over No Man's Land could nudge my happy meter up even the slightest bit, imagine what ten days of surface dwelling, river fishing, caribou hunting, campfire storytelling, and peeing like a bear is going to do.* Speaking of peeing . . .

"You good with the gear?" he asked. "I've gotta get rid of two cups of coffee and an energy drink."

"Just step away from the bird, eh?" Franklin said.

Hutch grinned and moseyed over to where Phil lay. He looked skyward, treeward, anywhere-ward but Phil-ward, acting like he didn't see him down in the grass. He adjusted his waistband, unzipped his fly.

"Hey, hey, hey!" Phil yelled. He rolled away, then rose to his knees. "What're you doing?"

"Oh, Phil, man, I didn't see you. Sorry." He turned away and relieved himself.

"You're still too close," Phil scolded.

Hutch chuckled. Every trip up north, they all took a day or two to get used to the freedom. There was something about living in a civilized, restroom-abundant world that made relieving yourself outdoors feel as wrong as swearing in church. He recalled taking his son, Logan, on his first camping trip six years ago, when the boy was five. Phil, David, and Justin, David's son, had been there too. As kids his age do, Logan had waited until the last moment to ask where the bathroom was. He had been holding himself, legs crossed, bobbing up and down. Hutch had pointed to the nearest tree.

"I can't go there," he had protested.

"Why not?"

"It's outside."

"Where did you think we were going to go?"

Logan had shrugged and bounced, worry etching his smooth features. Finally he had dashed behind the tree. By the next morning he was attempting to put out the campfire in the way only boys can, shooting off boulders into the lake and generally proving that inhibition crumbled fast.

Pleased he had gotten into the swing of things quickly, Hutch zipped up and smiled. "Just don't douse our campfire the way Logan did that time, remember?"

Phil laughed. "That was classic." He looked off toward the trees a moment. "Should have brought him. Logan."

"Think he's old enough to hang with us?"

"Sure. Justin too." David's boy was now twelve.

Hutch shrugged. "I did run the idea of bringing Logan up here past his mother. She said no way. I checked with Harris"—a friend and Hutch's divorce attorney—"and he said no magistrate would approve taking him out of state, let alone out of the country, if she fought it. Not with the custody thing going on."

"I'm sorry," Phil said. He rolled back onto his butt, his knees up and his legs spread in front of him. He looked even fatter like that.

Hutch didn't like the way he and his buddies seemed to be falling apart. Family, finances, health—it was as though the angels who were supposed to be looking out for them had gone out for a smoke and never came back.

He stepped to the starboard cargo hold, unlatched the door, and swung it open. His hunting gear was on top: a bow case, which also contained six aluminum arrows with Muzzy broadheads and urethane vanes. A waterproof duffel held his Realtree camouflage clothes and makeup, utility belt, canteen, binoculars, compass, and knife. Two more duffel bags stored a sleeping bag, a tent, a change of clothes, extra socks, thermal underwear, a tarp, freeze-dried food, pots, pans, cups, utensils, a water purifying system, a first-aid kit, a Coleman lantern, an isobutane stove, biodegradable soap and toilet paper, and various other knickknacks designed to ease man's encroachment on nature.

Terry appeared at his side.

"I'm missing a green duffel," Terry said.

Hutch hefted his last bag from the hold, revealing a green duffel behind it. "There it is," he said. He moved away to deposit his gear a good distance from the copter and grant Terry access to the hold. Terry pulled out the bag and immediately began rummaging through it.

Phil moaned. He rolled over, got himself standing, hitched up his pants, and ambled to the other side of the aircraft where his gear was stowed.

"What the hey?" Terry whined. He tapped at a device in his hand, then raised it over his head, glaring. He put it to his ear.

Hutch shook his head. "I told you, Ter, no mobile phones up here."

"You did? No wait . . . I thought you meant we *shouldn't* bring any, not that it didn't matter even if we did." He appeared devastated. "I got deals pending. I get the Multi-Listing Service on this. E-mail." He showed Hutch the face of his phone. It looked like a small computer.

"Not up here you don't."

"But I used it in La Ronge."

"That's La Ronge, four hundred miles south." Hutch went to his friend. "Look, we all agreed. No business."

"But I'm . . ." Terry was crestfallen. He appeared ready to weep.

If he starts bawling, Hutch thought, *I'm going to carry him all the way to the river and throw him in.*

"I'm . . . putting my life back together."

Hutch put an arm around him. "I know. This is part of it. Really."

David came around the back of the helicopter, burdened with bags. Straps crossed over both shoulders, his neck, and a forearm. "What's up?" he asked.

"Terry thought he'd be able to use his mobile phone."

"Well, I was glad to leave mine home. But I did remember this." He set down a bag and pulled something out of a breast pocket. An iPod. "Self-contained," he said. "The White Stripes, Coldplay, Third Day." He pulled earbuds out of the same pocket and began untangling them.

"Wait'll the battery goes," Terry grumbled.

"Grouch," David said, smiling. He squinted at a knot in the white cable.

Phil trudged up, dragging a duffel. He dropped it and went to fetch another.

Franklin ducked under the tail boom from the copter's port side, pulled the last bag out of the cargo compartment, slammed the lid down, and latched it.

"Hey," Terry said. "What if I climb a tree . . . or hike up one of those mountains? Maybe I can get a signal there."

"Not with that," Franklin informed him. "Not up here."

Terry gazed sadly at the phone, a child with the best Christmas present in the world but no batteries to run it.

"Now *this* . . ." Franklin said and reached around his back. He produced a decidedly unattractive hunk of plastic with what could have been a black foot-long hot dog protruding from one end. "E.T. could phone home with one of these."

"That?" Terry squinted for a better look.

"Satellite phone. Only way to talk up here. 'Less you're First Nation."

"What?" Phil said, returning with another duffel. "Smoke signals?"

"Well, maybe. I've seen strange columns of smoke. Could be them doing that, I don't know. But I meant the animals. They say some First Nations can talk to a lynx or bear or hawk. Then the animal goes and tells another First Nation what it heard."

"For real?" Phil asked.

Franklin laughed. "I don't know! That's just what they say. But I tell you"—his voice grew conspiratorial—"weird things happen up here. An animal goes into a cave, a man comes out. A First Nation gets his leg crushed in one of the mines—I mean pulped meat and broken bone—shows up next day fine. Strong magic in these parts, eh."

"You believe that stuff?" Hutch said with more sarcasm than he'd intended.

"I'm just saying . . ." The satellite phone disappeared behind him again.

"Hey, wait a sec," Terry said, reaching for his back pocket. "How much for the phone?"

Hutch stopped him. "Save your money, Ter. We agreed . . ."

Franklin said, "Can't do it, buddy. Belongs to the company, eh. If I went back without it, it'd be my job."

Terry bowed his head.

Hutch patted him on the shoulder. "Good man. It'll work out. You'll see." He turned to Franklin. "Okay. The river's over there."

"The Straight River."

"Right. Now, where's my best bet for caribou?" He had convinced Franklin over the phone and with a wad of twenties when they had met in Points North Landing to let him go on a DIY hunt—a do-it-yourself hunt, without a guide, though his nonresident license required one.

"Here's my guiding to you, should anyone ask," Franklin said. He pointed in the direction opposite the river, toward the hills. "That way."

The landscape sloped almost imperceptibly toward the Fond du

Lac River, which shimmered like a hot wire four miles south. On the other side of the river, the earth rose again, softly. They were in a shallow valley roughly forty miles wide.

"Not toward the Fond du Lac?" Hutch clarified. Experience had taught him that lots of water meant lots of animals.

Franklin shook his head. "Right here, we're at the very southern edge of their range. Some stragglers get on down farther, but . . . nah, you'll find more up here. Besides, town of Fiddler Falls is right there, on the river. I thought you wanted to steer clear of folk."

"We do. Appreciate it."

"All right, then, you boys have fun, eh." Franklin shook Hutch's hand and climbed into the cabin. Two minutes later, the helicopter was a speck against the blue canvas and the four friends were standing in the meadow, awed by the vastness of the landscape, its beauty and serenity. None of them wanted to break the silence, so they stayed that way a long time, happy finally to be alone and together.

7

Turned out, Declan's other business did include hunting. After rounding up forty-seven people, by Tom's count, Declan grew increasingly fidgety. He checked his watch and frequently told Bad to give him a "status report." It was a task that required Bad to return to the Hummer for minutes at a time. He allowed Tom to sit on the curb while he paced. Bad and Kyrill roamed Provincial, weapons at the ready. They checked doors, looked through windows, and disappeared up side streets, occasionally returning with new prisoners. Tom hoped these new captives had ventured into the gunmen's line of sight and weren't pulled from their homes. As long as Declan's gang targeted only people outside their homes, Laura and Dillon stood a chance.

He yearned for them now, for the love in their eyes, even when they were only glancing at him or listening to his ramblings about some trivial town event or how the car needed new brakes. He wanted to feel the pressure of their bodies against his, their arms around him, their warmth. When he hugged them and they hugged back, he felt more than mutual affection; he felt . . . *privileged.* That they were giving him their time, allowing him to know how their bodies were constructed. Letting him feel their musculature and bones, their breath on his neck, the ebb and flow of their chests against his as they breathed. His favorite hugs were tight and sustained. Then if he concentrated, and he often did, he could feel their hearts beating. He wished he had insisted on that kind of hug before he'd rushed out this morning. He wished he had insisted on *any* hug.

A shout drew his attention. Kyrill was standing outside the ice cream parlor and had called to Declan.

"This place got arcade games!" he said. "Ms. Pac-Man and Galaga. Let's move them to the community center."

"Not now!" Declan called back. He continued to pace.

Kyrill peered through the store's window again, then moved on. His and Bad's gun-wielding presence instantly turned Fiddler Falls into an occupied territory, under the constant threat of sudden and arbitrary violence. The cameraman—whose name Tom learned was Pruitt—spent most of the time in the community center. When he emerged he would film the buildings on each side of the street in slow pans, then lock on the movements of one of the gunmen.

The girl had found peroxide, cotton balls, and bandages in the general store. She knelt beside Tom and began to dab gently at the wound on the back of his head. Every touch was like a hammer knocking on his skull. The first dozen cotton balls turned bright red, the next ones less so. She pushed deeper through his hair. He winced and sucked in a sharp breath.

"Sorry," she said.

43

He lowered his head to whisper. "You don't have to do this." Not meaning the first aid. When she didn't respond, he continued, "No one is worth going to jail for. If you help me—"

She jabbed a fingernail into his wound. It felt like a spike. She tilted her head to look into his eyes. Their lashes were almost touching. Her hair smelled vaguely of oranges. Her voice was low, seductive.

"Don't think for a minute you know me. I'm here because I want to be. I'm with Declan because I want to be. If he wants you gone, I'll pack your bag." She pulled back slightly. She gazed into his right eye, then his left, as though each told a different story. "If he wants you dead, I'll pull the trigger."

Without another word she finished dressing his wound, gathered the spent and unused supplies, and disappeared into the store.

Finally Declan circled around to him. He said, "Here's the deal. Remember what I said about how your being beaten down in the dirt helped everyone else from getting too confident and getting themselves killed?"

Tom didn't like where this was heading.

"Well, what really works is taking that concept as far as it can go. Know what I mean?"

"No." But he did.

Declan eyed him, cold, emotionless. "In World War II, the Nazis, man, they were conquering town after town. What do you think they did to keep the townsfolk in line?"

He thought the question was rhetorical, but Declan waited.

Tom said, "The Nazis were willing to do things good people weren't willing to do."

Declan thought about it. "True, but that's more of a *how* than a *what*, isn't it? *What* things were they willing to do?"

"Atrocities."

"Rape? Murder?"

Tom watched the other man. As organized as he seemed, as much as he appeared to possess inside knowledge of the town—as his quick confiscation of the satellite phones suggested—as well planned as this operation was, Tom believed Declan was making this part up as he went. He was drawing from his education, from his knowledge of history, not from experience. What did that mean to the town, to Tom? Inexperience led to mistakes, maybe ones that Tom or someone else could exploit. Then again, not every mistake would necessarily favor Fiddler Falls. *Oops. I guess we shouldn't have killed everybody. Kyrill, next time remind me to keep some hostages.*

"Did you know," Declan continued, "that most of the rapes and murders were not random? The Nazis were cunning. They used scouts and informers to find out whose rape, whose murder would best break the citizens' spirit of rebellion. In one town, maybe they needed to take an old lady, sort of the town matriarch. In another place, maybe it was a little girl, someone whose innocence and beauty represented the townspeople's values. Every place was different, but the person selected was always someone whose agony or death cut to the bone, broke their hearts. Sometimes they would shoot the town priest or the old wise man everyone turned to for guidance. But most of the time they chose the strongest, the toughest, the most outspoken. Someone who not only had power and skills, but also knew how to motivate people. He was a leader."

Tom gave in. "I'm that leader?"

"That's what I've heard."

"What do you mean, what you've heard?"

"A little bird told me."

Tom remembered. A few months ago, a man had come in on a floatplane. Stayed a few days at the same B&B Declan and his cronies now occupied. Took pictures, asked questions. He had said he was doing research for a series of articles on quaint small towns for Canada's leading newsmagazine. He'd stopped by the RCMP substation to ask Tom about the town's police services, its medical facilities, and its ability to call in emergency help in the event of a fire, weather-related catastrophe, or serious hunting accident. Other townies had said he'd asked questions of them as well. He closed his eyes. How many of them had unwittingly helped Declan plan this invasion of their town? It was painful enough that *he* had contributed. He pictured the spy. Mousy guy, kept pushing his thick-framed glasses back up his nose. His name was Jonathan Bird.

Opening his eyes, he said, "No article in *Maclean's*, then?"

"Sorry. Jon's a good man. A top-notch researcher. Used to be a journalist, but I pay better. His report told me that Black Lake is bigger. More people. More visitors. More cops. Too big for our purposes. And Fond-du-Lac's too small. Just a campground, really, for a bunch of Indians."

"We call them First Nations up here. Or Dene."

Declan shrugged. "I have a binder this thick about your village." He made a four-inch-wide *C* with his hand. "Says the town manager spends more time bellied up to the bar than his desk. You have a conservation officer who sometimes packs a piece, but her expertise is forest fires and hunting licenses. Ben at the hotel says she's out in the backcountry right now. I love small towns." He rolled his eyes. "Not really. Then there's you."

Tom's eyes dropped to the pistol in the man's hand.

As if to show he had other plans, Declan turned away and tucked the weapon into his pants at the small of his back. He lifted his tight Under Armour shirt and let it fall back over the gun's grip.

He said, "We—me and the guys—are competitive by nature. Business, extreme sports. We don't mind people trying to best us, because it makes besting them that much sweeter."

At his sides, his fingers began to waggle, fast, more Beethoven than Mahler. He faced Tom, stepped toward him, turned away again. Pent-up energy, anxious to do whatever it was he had planned.

"Bad? The black guy?" Declan said. "One of the best skateboarders in the world. We're developing a game that'll make Tony Hawk's look like Pong." He turned a squinting eye on Tom's blank expression. "You know Tony Hawk?"

"Sorry."

Declan sighed. "Okay, Pru . . . Pruitt? Major Unreal player. Up there on Quake too. You *do* know Unreal? Quake?"

Tom shook his head. He was thinking of Laura. Dillon.

"Online shooter games. Hundred thousand players worldwide. Really big deal outside of Podunk towns like this. Get this . . ." Somehow, his face reflected even more self-satisfaction. "The guy's a geek, working for, I don't know, Radio Shack, right? Rushes home every day and gets on the computer. I'm watching the stats. He's good. So I call him, say, 'You wanna real job? come join my posse. See the world. Be all you can be.'" He laughed, a dry, humorless sound.

Tom didn't know why, but he thought it was a good idea to keep the man talking. Maybe he'd give something away Tom could use. He nodded toward the kid who'd wanted the Ms. Pac-Man and Galaga games. "And him?"

"Kyrill . . . just a young kid, right? Seventeen. The guy wrote a video game that's about to outsell Halo 2, another game you wouldn't know. Exclusive to Xbox, but it still sold 3.5 million copies. By year's end, Kyrill's will have that beat. And he's working on another one. I'm telling you, the kid's brilliant. This next one's gonna blow everybody away. It'll change gaming forever."

Tom met his eyes. "What do *you* do?"

He smiled. "I run the company that makes Kyrill's games. I sponsor Bad, Pruitt, some others. I'm the money man and the mastermind."

He said it without irony.

Seeming to take Tom's silence as an incitement, he said, "Funny thing is, the most valuable people aren't always the ones with a single extraordinary talent. It's the person who knows how to bring them together, orchestrate them into achieving something much bigger than their individual skills could do on their own. It's the person who recognizes talent, nurtures it, makes it work for him. Henry Ford didn't know how to design a combustible engine, but he knew how to bring together the people who did. Vince Lombardi never played pro ball, but what a coach, huh? He knew how to motivate players and taught them how to reach their potential and work together to make great teams. My father . . ."

He stopped. His jaw tightened, and he turned away.

Something there.

"Your father?"

"Forget it."

His father . . . in the context of that speech, with everything else Tom knew about Declan: Seattle, moneyman, video games. His last name . . .

"Brendan Page?"

Declan faced him. "Yes, *that* Page."

Self-made billionaire, many times over. Into just about everything: software, telecommunications, entertainment, publishing, military equipment. Tom wasn't into following the sordid lives of tycoons or celebrities, but you'd have to live with bears to avoid running into

Brendan Page's name. It was usually associated with negative news: allegations of price-fixing and unfair competition; outcries from family organizations because one of his companies had planned a particularly distasteful book or a movie that pushed the limits of decency; it was often his company's weapons that slipped into embargoed countries. True, such examples accounted for a miniscule percentage of the products Brendan Page's companies produced, but Tom thought it interesting that so many accusations of impropriety were directed at the holdings of one man's empire. Said something about that man. He knew nothing of Brendan Page's family, his children. They had kept a low profile, as the children of the outrageously rich often do.

He asked, "How does someone with your money, your family, come to . . . to *this*?" He gestured at the Hummer, at the town.

Declan stared at him. "You want the George Mallory answer or something more profound?"

When Mallory had been asked why he wanted to climb Mount Everest, his famous answer was "Because it's there." Tom thought Declan meant "Because I can." If his motivations were that crass, how could any answer satisfy Tom's curiosity?

Declan continued. "Now, do you want to know the rules of the game? Or do you want to talk family?"

That Tom definitely did not want to do. If Declan's research was as thorough as he had implied, he must know about Laura and Dillon. Was the question a threat to bring them into the equation, not in conversation but in person?

"What rules?" Tom asked.

"Actually, there aren't any. You run, we try to kill you. No, wait. We do kill you, but you run as though you have a chance."

"And if I get away?"

"You won't."

"If . . ."

Declan sighed heavily. He waved to Kyrill, the brilliant game programmer, and Bad, champion of the board. From opposite ends of the street, they obeyed, moving toward him, lugging their weapons. To Tom, he said, "Do you recognize their guns?"

Tom eyed them again as they approached. He tilted his head toward Kyrill. "Fifty-cal sniper's rifle. Some hunters use it."

"And the other one?"

Tom shook his head.

"It's a variation of the Gewehr G11. Uses casingless ammo. That means it weighs the same as a fully loaded M16, six pounds, but it holds three times as many rounds."

Bad stepped in, heard Declan's words, and pulled a long rectangular magazine off the top of the weapon. He held it up for Tom to appreciate. The bullets inside were square pegs. It reminded him of a PEZ dispenser.

"When it shoots a bullet," Declan continued, "the slug comes out of the barrel and the rest of the cartridge ignites and is gone. There's nothing to eject in preparation for the next round. That makes it an extraordinarily fast-firing gun. The designers studied the dynamics of firing bursts of three rounds, a common pattern for automatic weapons. They found that the first shot's recoil causes the next two bullets to go high."

Declan spoke in such a deadpan voice, Tom wondered if the man was capable of emotion. More troubling was his suspicion that Declan did indeed experience feelings, but the events required to tap them were both extreme and intense. He wouldn't want to be around when Declan needed a jolt of emotion.

Too late, he thought.

Bad slipped the magazine back onto the gun. It ran the length of what Tom assumed was a barrel.

"This thing fires at a rate of two thousand rounds a minute. That's three rounds in one-tenth of a second. Three rounds before the shooter even feels a recoil, so each bullet hits its target."

He gestured to Bad, who glanced around, spotted a target, and aimed.

Tom realized the gun was pointed at Beggar, one of the town's innumerable stray dogs. The bony mutt was a block away, sniffing at the curb. Before Tom could protest, the weapon coughed, a quick, throat-clearing sound. Beggar spun and flipped, much of his motion lost in a mist of blood and fur. He hit the curb and didn't move, not even a twitch. Tom had no doubt all three bullets had found their mark.

Bad continued to hold his aim on the animal, ready should a fresh burst prove necessary. After a few seconds he lowered the gun.

Declan said, "This weapon alone narrows your chances to somewhere between zero and none." His smile was a wire drawing taut. "And it's nothing. A Super Soaker next to what else we have."

Tom's eyes moved to the burning car.

Declan asked, "Still think you have a chance?"

Tom looked hard into his eyes. "Always."

"Okay. If you somehow manage to elude us, to hide where we can't find you or you actually make it to civilization, then you're free. We won't kill anyone in retaliation. Promise."

"What kind of head start do I get?"

He looked at his watch. Instead of answering, he called to the girl. She came to the doorway of the general store, a folded magazine in one hand, a bitten Ho Ho in the other. There was a smear of chocolate on her lips.

"It's time. Go get the others. Tell Pru and Julie to make sure nobody can get out. They should have it all secure over there by now."

She gamboled past Tom, not offering him even the briefest glance.

A minute later, the community center door banged open, releasing Julian, Pruitt, and Cort.

"A head start?" Declan said, as though no time had passed since the question. "How does five minutes sound?"

"I think an hour's fair. You want to be fair?"

"No, I like five minutes."

He swiveled his head to make eye contact with each of his five sycophants, standing in a semicircle around them. Each gave a nod, apparently already apprised of the game and its rules.

"Ready?" he said to Tom with a wink. "Go."

8

Hutch, Phil, Terry, and David found the area where Franklin had suggested they set up camp.

"Yeah," Terry said approvingly.

There was a flat, grassy patch, which Hutch thought of as the *stage*. It was here they would make camp. Surrounding it on three sides, like side and rear theatrical curtains, were tall evergreens, mostly fir, with a smattering of birch to make it more richly textured. These trees clothed a low berm that nearly encircled the camp area, protecting it from the wind. Stage right was an opening in the trees, a trail that converged with the path leading to the helicopter meadow.

On the open side of the campsite or stage, which faced northwest, boulders paved a gentle slope down to the Straight River. The water here was not much more than a wide, fast stream. At the base of the slope, a natural pool had formed, ideal for cleaning fish, their clothes, themselves. Upstream and downstream, the current rushed over steps of rocks, serenading the campers with one of nature's finest songs: the low susurration of moving water.

Adding to his appreciation of the bivouac, Hutch didn't see a bear trail anywhere near. He did spot a few widow-makers—standing dead trees that could blow down on them if they camped too close—but the area was large enough to avoid them.

As usual, they had brought only two tents, which cut down on gear, helped each tent stay warm at night, and ensured that a bear couldn't drag off one of them without the others knowing about it. Hutch selected a spot to pitch the tent he and Phil would use and started clearing it of twigs, pinecones, and rocks. Phil pulled their tent from its pouch and began snapping together the flexible poles that would arc over it, giving structure to the material. Terry and David debated the merits of three possible locations.

A scorched circle where grass and dirt gave way to rock showed the spot where previous campers had laid a fire. Following the rules of Canadian backwoods camping, the last users had broken up the pit, redistributing the perimeter stones into the surrounding landscape. Even the ashes and unconsumed wood had been scattered, either by the campers or the weather.

Having camped together for seven years, the four men worked mostly in silence, but efficiently. In forty minutes they had erected the tents, built a fire pit, gathered kindling, and hung the food from a high branch away from foraging animals.

Phil headed for the naturally refrigerated river, a case of beer in hand. As he descended the slope, he opened a can.

"We heard that!" David called. He had draped his earbuds over his shoulders.

"Hear this," Phil answered, but no sound followed, thankfully.

Hutch knelt before the pit and wedged a thick branch into the rocks so it angled up over the center. He dug into a nylon sack, removed a well-used teakettle, and hung it off the tip of the branch.

Phil came huffing back up the slope. "I'm not looking forward to those freeze-dried meals," he said.

"I think you'll be surprised," David said.

"Man, even that crap's good eating for me these days." Terry shook his head sadly. "Used to eat at Elway's twice a week."

"Oh yeah, they got good grub," Phil agreed. "Pricey, but *man* . . ."

Terry smiled. "The valets knew my Jag. They'd run in to tell the maître d' I'd arrived before I'd even get to them. I tipped them a twenty and they'd keep the car right there, outside the door. The bankruptcy trustee wouldn't let me keep that car, too much equity. I don't think Elway's would keep the car I'm driving now right out front."

"Could be worse," Phil said. "Look at *me*."

Terry gave him a dismissive wave. "Buy an exercise bike. You'll be fine."

"I don't have a *job*," Phil reminded him. He pulled off his glasses and began cleaning them with his shirttail. "I'm in debt up to my eyeballs. Fat and broke. Does it get any worse?"

"Lighten up," Hutch said. He returned to the loose tree stump he had found earlier to sit on. "Who said, 'Where there's life, there's hope'?"

"Terence," David answered.

He had turned Hutch into a quotation geek back in fifth grade. It drove the other two batty.

"Terry?" Phil said, an unsure smile on his face.

"The ancient Roman playwright."

"Yeah, but you know the kind of plays *he* wrote?" Hutch asked.

David nodded, knowingly.

"Comedies," answered Hutch. "He never wrote a tragedy or drama. You can't quote a comedian to make a serious point about life. May's well quote George Carlin at your mother's funeral."

David ignored him. "How about 'All the world's a stage, and all the men and women merely players,' or 'Love all, trust a few, do wrong to none.' Profound, right? Probably close to the way things really are." He raised his eyebrows at Hutch, looked to Terry and Phil. "Shakespeare— from his *comedies*."

Terry jabbed a finger at him. "I got one for you: 'The ability to quote is a serviceable substitute for wit.'"

Everyone laughed.

David said, "Okay, okay, I've heard that before but I just can't remember . . ."

Hutch rubbed the stubble on his chin. "So who is it?"

Phil dug into another duffel and produced a collapsible canvas chair. Hutch had asked him to leave it home, but Phil said life was too short to do without some things. Besides, he had purchased it from Cabela's, which proved the thing's camp-worthiness. He unfolded it and eased down. The aluminum frame groaned. He said, "Hutch, didn't you interview George Carlin?"

"Nah, that was Dane Cook, before he got big and before I started focusing on locals."

Twice a week Hutch profiled people who exemplified the spirit of Colorado. Housewives, entrepreneurs, celebrities, ranchers, farmers, average Joes. The only criteria were residency; an achievement illustrating tenacity, resilience, or the prevailing over great odds; and a story that piqued Hutch's interest. For what turned out to be one of his most popular columns, he'd interviewed a man who'd spent twenty-three years erecting towers and running power cables through the Rockies' most treacherous terrain. The guy had survived four separate bouts of frostbite, cumulatively losing only three toes, two fingers, and part of one ear. He'd fended off a mountain lion and two bears. And tumbled over three cliffs, one of which had plunged him into the North Platte River. He'd traveled through three miles of rapids before a whitewater rafting guide snagged him and pulled him out.

Most stories were not as dramatic but were nevertheless inspiring. One chronicled a woman's fight against an ill wind that was battering her life. After her husband's untimely death, she'd faced foreclosure and bankruptcy. By sheer elbow grease and a previously untapped business mind, she had turned her property into what a half-dozen travel publications agreed was the nation's premier dude ranch. Then there were the Eagle Scout who'd fought off a Bigfootlike creature— probably a bear—and saved a troop of Cub Scouts . . . the restaura- teur who'd battled street thugs and naysayers to ignite a revitalization of Denver's East Village . . . the Palmer Lake woman who had created a thriving business selling hand-painted trash baskets on eBay.

The variety had given Hutch an appreciation for the struggles, both catastrophic and trivial, every breathing soul faced just to get from one day to the next. It had also educated him in countless fields of endeavors. Some knowledge had proven to be immediately practi- cal: the dude ranch had given him, Janet, and the kids one of their best vacations ever; a contractor he'd interviewed had also been an avid fly fisherman and had pointed Hutch to some of the greatest holes he'd ever fished; and he'd switched from a compound bow to a recurve after profiling a renowned bow hunter. He'd bagged his first bull elk on his next hunting excursion, a feat he credited to the recurve's lighter weight and quieter release.

A pebble struck his cheek, snapping him back to the present.

Terry was grinning at him. "Looked like you were dozing," he said. Sitting, he stretched his body up, rolling his shoulders back. He had the lean, athletic body of a cyclist. He swam at the Y—*not* at the Denver Athletic Club anymore, he'd pointed out more than once—and played an occasional game of racquetball, but the build was largely genetic. "Can't have that."

Phil huffed. "All the way here, and we *still* have to deal with *you*."

Terry shrugged. "Such is life."

Hutch and David grinned at each other. In unison, they said, "And it's getting sucher and sucher."

Terry tossed pebbles at both of them.

9

He'd been on the run an hour now—though "running" was not really what Tom Fuller was doing. More accurately, he had darted from one hiding place to another. At first he had zigzagged west, then tacked back around to within a block of Provincial Street, thinking he'd find a lone gunman to ambush with a crack on the head or . . . or *something*. But the few times he'd spotted them, between houses, through bushes, they'd been in pairs or in threes. For the most part, they had seemed content to mill around Provincial, as though they expected him to remain in some imaginary arena that kept them from having to venture too far. He'd considered commandeering a vehicle. Any of his neighbors would have accommodated his request. But then he'd remembered Roland Emery. His car had not saved him. Besides, the roads out of town made doing somersaults a faster proposition. A car would do nothing but make him a bigger target. He had not sought refuge in a house because he didn't want to put the residents in jeopardy. If Declan modeled his town-taking on Nazis—*What do you think they did to keep the townsfolk in line?*—chances are he'd make examples out of anyone who helped Tom.

He kept a pistol and a rifle in his office, but they could just as well have been at the bottom of the ocean. Years ago, the rear of the sub-station had been retrofitted with a holding cell, which had hosted more drunks than felons. Consequently, there was no rear door and the rear window was barred. Going through the front window open-ing, as Kyrill had done, was too risky, especially with his hunters mak-ing the street outside his office their de facto base of operations. If he did make it in and they converged on him while he was inside, he'd have no place to go. There would be a standoff, and they'd probably wheel out whatever it was that had gotten Roland, and that would be the end of that.

He also kept a second pistol in his home. As much as he wanted that weapon and, more important, as much as he yearned to see Laura and Dillon, to hold them and warn them, he could not risk leading the killers there.

So now he rested on damp sod, his back pressed against a cold headstone in the cemetery behind St. Bartholomew's. He was less than a hundred yards from Provincial, only two blocks from where Declan had used Roland Emery to announce his invasion of Fiddler Falls. Tom didn't know what to do.

Black spruce surrounded the cemetery. A few had bravely marched in to stand among the gravestones. Their scraggly branches and needles dappled the sunlight, casting the area in a gloomy twilight despite the midmorning hour. Tom thought the atmosphere was per-fect for the setting. The only element missing was tendrils of fog. A light breeze hummed softly through the trees. It *was* peaceful here, and Tom felt his blood pressure ease a bit. He pulled in a deep breath, let it out slowly.

Having been flayed alive before his crucifixion, Saint Bartholomew is considered the patron saint of trappers and tanners. In Michelangelo's *The Last Judgment* on the wall of the Sistine Chapel, Bartholomew holds the knife of his martyrdom, along with his own skin. The Fiddler Falls church bearing his name was constructed in 1923, as the town grew from a Denesuliné First Nation village into a bustling burg of supply stores, saloons, and brothels. Back then the town serviced primarily miners, trappers, and adventurers intent on exploring the vast wilderness to the north, as far as the Artic. The fur and leather trade was so profitable and animals so abundant that outside every business were racks of drying furs and skins. But as far as anyone knew, none as hideous as poor Bartholomew's. Over the years, the church had closed and reopened four times, reflecting the citizenry's waxing and waning spiritual interests. It now hosted two Sunday morning services: Catholic Mass at eight and a nondenominational Protestant service at ten. Its cemetery continued to accept new residents, though their plots extended farther from the church each year.

Tom sat near its center. The headstone directly across from him bore a date from 1965:

Here lies John Wood
Enclosed in wood
One Wood
Within another.
The outer wood
Is very good:
We cannot praise
The other.

He had never strolled the graveyard, reading last words and pondering long lost lives, as Laura sometimes did. He was surprised to find so much wit here. Another headstone proclaimed:

Oh, NOW you come and visit me!

And if not wit, then poignant solemnity. One epitaph marked the resting place of an eight-year-old girl:

The Gardener cried,

"Who picked my most precious Rose?"

The answer came,

"The Master took it Home."

Funny that he should begin to understand the appeal of ambling among the buried dead when it appeared he was so close to becoming one himself. He wondered what his epitaph would be. Was that something he was supposed to have already selected, or did that task fall to survivors? Maybe John Wood should have left instructions; he hadn't seemed too well liked. Tom hoped for something about his family and the outdoors he had loved so much.

Had loved so much!

He was already referring to himself in the past tense.

No . . . no . . . no . . .

He pushed himself up.

Not dead yet.

He turned in a circle. Woods on all sides, except where the church stood. The church. He could hide in there, decide what to do, when to do it. He moved toward it, then stopped. The roar of an engine reached him first. He lowered himself behind a headstone. The Hummer appeared on a thirty-foot stretch of Provincial, visible between the church and rectory. It screeched to a halt. Tom could see nothing through the black-tinted windows. The vehicle rolled out of sight, blocked by the church. If they inspected the church and continued into the graveyard, they would catch him for sure. He bolted north, into the trees. He paused and crouched. The Hummer appeared on the other side of the church, still rolling slowly. Had they seen him? Could they see him now, even in the shadows of the evergreens? He wondered if they were using high-tech tracking tools, something like infrared goggles or a GPS device they'd hidden on him.

Last week, when the Hummer had been parked at the service station, Tom had inspected it. In design, it resembled an extended-cab pickup: two doors on each side, servicing two rows of seats, an open bed in back. Two chairs were bolted to the floor of the bed. The pedestals appeared hydraulic or pneumatic, enabling the seats to rise and go down. Handgrips were mounted to the bed sides and cab roof. The setup reminded Tom of the trucks hunters and photographers used on safari in Africa. The windows, which appeared opaque, granted a dim view of the interior when he pushed his face up to them and cupped his hands to block out exterior light. The dash and center console were arrayed with gadgets that could not possibly be stock equipment.

The engine died and the front doors opened. Pruitt emerged from the passenger's side, the bulky video camera clutched in one hand. Bad came out of the driver's door and clanked the machine gun down on the hood. Pruitt looked past the church to the cemetery, scanned over to the woods, then up at the sky. He spoke to Bad, shaking his head. Tom imagined his complaints about how the shadows made for poor lighting conditions. Bad waved him off, picked up the G11, and walked around the front bumper. Together, they strode toward the cemetery and Tom's position in the woods. They spoke normally, like two guys just heading to a buddy's place.

"Man, I can't wake up," Pruitt said. "I don't know why we had to get up so early."

"Shut up, Pru. You know the plan was righteous. What else we gonna do, try to round up the whole town at once? Divide and conquer, dude. Who's up and who's not is a natural division. Props to Declan."

"So what? We let 'em just walk into our net? I bet not everyone comes out every day."

"Nah. We'll go get 'em after this first batch. Take our leisure, you know?"

A staticky voice issued a sharp command.

The two stopped. Bad pulled a walkie-talkie out of a breast pocket. Spoke into it.

The words coming through the tiny speaker were too fuzzy for Tom to make out.

Both men returned to the Hummer and climbed inside. The SUV roared to life, made a tight U-turn, and sped away.

Tom felt nauseated. *We'll go get 'em after this first batch.* They were going to go door-to-door, gathering the town into their makeshift prison in the community center. He had to get to Laura.

He continued through the woods another thirty feet, where the trees gave way to a big open lawn. Trudy Thatcher's property. Her house lay at the far end. It was only forty yards away, but it felt like miles and miles of exposure to Tom. Halfway across was a copse of white birches. He ran and didn't slow until he was in the center of the circle of trees. They weren't much coverage, a dozen arm-width trunks holding up a cloud of thin leaves. Still, he hoped the angles would obscure his human form and make him more difficult to spot. At least until he gathered nerve enough to cut across the rest of the yard. He scowled up at the autumn sun, no friend in a time like this.

He crouched and ran his hands along the ground. He took some comfort from the reality of the dirt sifting through his fingers, the clumps of earth, the tiny pebbles. He leaned sideways, touching his shoulder, then his head against a tree trunk. Solid objects in a world that had become unreal, nightmarish.

Movement caught his eye. Trudy was looking out a window at him, one hand holding aside a curtain. She was the town curmudgeon. At community meetings, it was Trudy who would point out the foolishness of using Fiddler Falls's meager Northern Improvement Plan proration on pothole repairs when it was a new plow the town needed. And if the council agreed, she would ask how they could even consider such an extravagant purchase when the perimeter firebreak so obviously required widening.

Eighteen years a widow, she was as tough as the caribou jerky she cured and delivered personally to stores as far south as Saskatoon and by mail to consumers "all over the stinkin' world," as she often reminded listeners. But the visage at the window was not the indomitable scowl of which Tom had grown fond for its sheer longevity and predictability, as you might a particular lump in a favorite chair. Her eyes were wide with fear, her mouth slack, as if to pull in sharp gulps of air or let out a scream.

Tom held a finger to his lips, making sure she understood to be quiet. The curtain fell back over the window.

He glanced at her front garden, a living quilt of black currants, dewberry, fireweed, and bog violets as aesthetically pleasing as Trudy was disagreeable. Most mornings she could be found there, pruning and planting, glowering at the schoolkids walking past, admonishing them against picking her flowers, even though not a single townie young or old would dare risk her wrath for a mere bouquet. Tom had always suspected that her gardening at that time had less to do with the morning glow or the crispness of the air than it did with the steady stream of children to accost. He looked over his shoulder, back the way he had come. St. Bartholomew's blocked his view, but from

Trudy's garden she would be able to see straight up Provincial Street all the way to the park.

The timing would have been perfect: Trudy had witnessed everything, maybe even the event that had ended Roland Emery's life.

So she is already involved, Tom thought. He hoped he wasn't simply justifying his desire to seek help from her. He didn't know how she could aid his cause, but he desperately needed fresh ideas. And if she didn't already realize how awful these visitors were, he should warn her. If she tried to leave town or reach a phone or, knowing Trudy, give them a piece of her mind, they would spare her no mercy. He shot forward, out of the trees, across the yard, and leaped onto a concrete pad that served as Trudy's porch. He tried the handle. Locked, as he knew it would be. He pressed himself against the door and rapped gently. Then again, harder.

Come on, Trudy.

He thought about kicking in the door. Thought about the noise it would make. He jumped off the porch and sprinted toward the rear of the house, staying under the shadow of the eaves. He tripped on a low bush, crashed down, felt his ankle twist under him. Nerve endings jangled up his leg. He rose and hobbled around the corner. He pushed his back against the clapboards. His ankle throbbed. Just what he needed. Raising his foot relieved some of the pain, but he would have to ignore the injury to run. He would have to.

10

This was insane.

Maybe it really was a dream, a nightmare.

I'll wake up any minute now, Tom thought.

But the throbbing in his ankle and the ache radiating from the back of his head told him the truth. The clapboards were hard behind his head and shoulder blades. He pressed his palms against the wood and raked his fingertips across the rough surface. He felt splinters breaking off. One slipped under his fingernail, shooting a needle of hot pain as far as his wrist.

No dream.

How did this happen? Where did the men hunting him come from?

Men? he thought.

How old was the one named Julian? Thirteen, maybe fourteen.

Five years older than his own son, no more. Only a boy. The girl wasn't much older, and Declan had said Kyrill was seventeen. Children. How could that be? How could kids that age go so wrong?

A few years ago Laura had attended a "Future of Education" conference in Montreal. She'd returned mostly disgusted by the speakers' determination to "prepare" children for life by turning them into little adults at increasingly younger ages. Among the insanity: teaching sixth graders about sensual, not just biological, sexuality; giving fourth graders their own credit cards and mobile phones; advocating a secondary-school model for elementary schools, where the children— specifically not parents—selected their own courses of study. An article Tom had recently read warned that video and computer games gave preteens knowledge of hand-to-hand fighting, weaponry, battle strategies and tactics, and a tolerance of violence that was once the province of adulthood.

Tom had never paid much attention to extreme naysayers. He'd always thought if they had their way, *nothing* would ever change—no medical advancements, no improvements in transportation, no expansion of democracy. And to them, anything other than the firmest hand and five hours of reading per day would result in the moral decay of today's youth.

Declan's gang was enough to sway him to the naysayers' side. He supposed an overpowering personality like Declan's would add to the process of growing up too fast, the way sugar accelerates fermentation. Tom suspected Declan sought out youths whose dispositions inclined toward his and whose minds he could mold.

But still . . . so *young?*

He pushed aside these thoughts. All he had to think about was warning Laura, then getting away. He would either take Laura and Dillon with him or, more probably, sequester them in the attic of their home, telling them not to move or make a sound regardless of what they heard.

If he escaped, he could bring help. Never mind that the nearest town was Fond-du-Lac, thirty-two rugged miles west. He would get there. He would bring help. Or . . .

His thoughts tumbled in his head like clothes in a dryer, flipping and tangling with each other.

An idea began to form, to become clear among the chaos.

He'd already ruled out using a land vehicle, but what about a boat? As far as he knew, all of the regular boats, including his RCMP MirroCraft Striker, had been dry-docked in expectation of an early freeze. Still, it would take only an hour or two to get one into the water.

Wouldn't the killers have considered that?

Only one way to know.

Should he wait for dark? Only Dirty Woman Park lay between the end of Provincial and the river. From the shore, a good mile of water was visible in each direction. Plenty of time to shoot at a boat. But at night, he could drift past until he was out of sight, then start the engine.

Okay, then. Night.

After ensuring Laura and Dillon's safety, he would slowly make his way toward the dock. The nearest building was Tungsten's Outfitters and Fishing Lodge. He would wait there until it was dark enough to safely move the boat and drift away.

His throat tightened. Could he really leave without Laura and Dillon? He couldn't help but feel he was preparing to abandon them. To get help, yes, and only for a short while, a couple hours away from town at most. Still, it was leaving them.

He squeezed his eyes tight. Today was Monday. Yesterday seemed like ages ago. Laura had wakened him by caressing his cheek, as she did most Sundays. She had kissed his temple and said, "Shhh." More kisses and nibbles on his earlobe. His heart had quickened, anticipating the words she would whisper. Sometimes they were funny— *Mouthwash, Tom, it's a good thing*, or *I like my eggs over easy . . . and soon.* Sometimes it was a simple *I love you.* Occasionally, most often when the sky had not lightened much, it was more intimate. He had opened the eye she could not see and rotated it toward the window. A band of yellow sunshine cut through the thin drapes.

Oh well. Regardless of what she said, her voice was a sweet song in his heart.

Her words, soft and sexy: "I was thinking . . ."

The door had crashed open and Dillon had burst in with the sort of energy only a nine-year-old boy could muster first thing in the morning. He had jumped onto the bed and wedged himself between his parents.

"Bear Canyon today?" he had fairly yelled.

"We'll see," Tom had answered.

"Come on! Before it gets too rainy and snowy."

"Right after church?" Laura had suggested. She had been making little figure eights with her fingernail on the top of his head. She knew her boys cherished fishing together and that getting to areas they seldom visited was special to Dillon.

"Pleeeeaaase," the boy had whined, and Tom had looked into his eyes, feeling the last of his resistance crumble as he did.

"Dad!"—sharp and pleading and not a memory.

Tom hitched in a breath and held it, listening.

"*Daaad!*"

Tom's chest hollowed as his heart dropped into his stomach. Dillon's calls were coming from a couple of blocks away. Tom had no doubt where Declan was holding him: the very spot from which Tom had started running. That was Declan, showing he was so smart, he could pay out the line and reel you back in.

A scream. Laura's.

Tom pushed away from Trudy Thatcher's home and went back the way he had come. He limped but felt only a vague pain in his ankle. It felt numb. He felt numb. His soul was numb.

Atrocities.

Murder.

Rape.

Always someone whose agony or death cut to the bone, broke their hearts.

Declan's words.

Tom cut diagonally across the lawn, then through the strip of woods separating Trudy's property from the church.

He walked toward the street, along the length of St. Bartholomew's, absently brushing his fingers along its rough-hewn stone blocks. He could not simply run now, could not hide and wait. Declan would not wait for victory. He would not be patient in his quest to break the spirit of this town.

Tom stepped onto the sidewalk, where the sun was brighter. Off the curb onto Provincial. When he turned, he saw them. Three blocks away, in front of Kelsie's General Store. Dillon was tugging, struggling to free himself from Kyrill's grasp. Laura stood motionless, Bad's arm around her neck and his eyes peering over her shoulder, as though he assumed Tom had armed himself and was about to start blasting.

If only, he thought. He saw neither the .50-caliber nor the machine gun.

Holding himself as erect as his ankle allowed, he limped toward his family. The Hummer loomed directly behind them. Declan sat in one of the safari chairs, his stomach level with the cab roof. He was fiddling with some sort of handheld device. His thumbs flicked over knobs, pushed buttons. Dillon had asked for a Sony PSP last Christmas, and Tom had looked into it before deciding it was too expensive. The game console was self-contained with a small screen flanked by thumb controls, small versions of what used to be called joysticks. Leave it to Declan to strive for the height of coolness by playing a video game while destroying human lives.

The girl, Cort, came out of the general store holding a can of Dr. Pepper. She spotted Tom and stopped. She looked at Declan . . . Tom . . . Declan.

"Wait a minute!" she yelled, running up to the Hummer. "Declan, what are you doing?"

He continued playing the game.

Cort threw down the soft drink. "Declan! Not with them here!" She waved an arm at Laura and Dillon. "I mean it!"

His jaw hardened. He rotated his face toward her. Glared.

She returned it.

His shoulders lifted and fell in an exaggerated sigh.

"Bad! Kyrill!" When they turned, he gestured with his head.

"But, Dec—!"

"Hurry!" Declan snapped.

The two acolytes dragged Laura and Dillon back and away, in the direction of the community center.

Laura began kicking the air. "No! No!"

Dillon reached out. "Daaad!"

"Wait!" Tom called. He tried to run.

Declan rose, standing on an unseen rail or platform. He pointed a pistol at Tom. "You wait!" he said.

Tom stopped. He called out, "Laura! Dillon!"

"Tom!"

"Dad!"

He felt as if a bullet had already struck his heart. What could he possibly say? Could he tell them it would be okay? He was pretty sure it wouldn't be. Could he say good-bye? Not without terrifying them even more. So he yelled the truest thing he knew. "I love you!"

Then Kyrill pulled open the building's door.

"I love you!" Tom repeated.

The four of them entered.

"I—"

The door banged shut.

Tom stared after it, then brought his vision around to Declan. He had remained standing, gun in hand.

"This is competition?" Tom said through clenched teeth. Tears spilled from his eyes.

"Why not?"

"What chance did I have? Why'd you let me go at all?"

"You didn't have to show yourself."

"My family—"

Declan shrugged. "You didn't have to show yourself," he repeated. "Your call. Your Achilles' heel."

Bad and Kyrill pushed through the door, alone. They jogged to the Hummer.

Declan lay the handgun on the Hummer's roof and sat. He lifted the gaming device, and Tom realized it was not, in fact, a gaming device.

Flicking his eyes between Tom and whatever he held, Declan developed a true from-the-heart smile, the first one Tom had seen. He raised his arm and pointed at Tom.

Tom turned and ran, faster than he had ever run, faster than anyone had ever run—straight between John and Harriet Larson's tackle shop and Pat Kramer's boardinghouse and straight out of town . . .

If desire alone made things happen, that's precisely what he would have done.

What did happen was Tom took a step toward, the breezeway between the two buildings. Then another, coming down on his injured ankle. It buckled under him and sent him tumbling to the street. As he fell, he glanced at Declan—his tongue was bent over his lower lip, like a child trying his hardest at a difficult task—then back at Bad and Kyrill, looking straight up into the sky. Tom looked too. Beautiful blue, as far as the eye could see. And a flash, a silver glint directly overhead.

What the—

"Ohhhh!" Kyrill yelled, holding his ears, squinting.

Bad laughed, a loud *whooping* sound. "Declan! Yo, man!" He danced in a circle, pointing.

Julian climbed out of the SUV, shut the door, and leaned against it. He didn't feel so hot. After a few moments he stepped away and looked up at Declan. He was standing on the chair's foot rail, gazing over the cab. In this unguarded moment, Julian witnessed his brother without the Mask of Coolness, a rare sight indeed. Declan's mouth was frozen in a sort of shocked smile. His eyes were wide, not held in that droopy-lidded squint of perpetual apathy.

Julian shuffled to the front fender. He jumped when something clattered onto the pavement in front of the car.

"What's that?" Declan asked. "Julie, see what that is."

Julian wasn't sure he wanted to know. He approached the smoking thing, bending toward it when he was close. His heart tightened, but at least it was nothing that turned his stomach. He poked at it, test-ing its temperature. He lifted it with two fingers and tossed it onto the hood of the Hummer.

Declan rose to see it. He laughed and said, "Ooh yeah. Sheriff Tom's *badge.*"

Julian watched his brother's reaction, then dropped his eyes to the gold shield the sheriff had worn over his breast pocket. It was twisted, blackened, and smoldering.

"Pru, make sure you get a shot of this," Declan called out.

Julian's heart inched up into his throat. Almost a block away, where Sheriff Tom had been, he was there no more. In his place was a four-foot circle in the road, defined by an inch-deep depression in the asphalt. Cracks radiated out from the indentation. Heavy gray smoke wafted up and dissipated in a breeze Julian could not feel.

Kyrill slowly moved closer. Bad did what Julian thought might have been a jig toward the smoking depression. Pruitt cruised past him the way cameramen do, in fast mini-steps. The camera extend-ing from his face pointed like a bloodhound's snout toward the scene of the crime.

Julian's breakfast of eggs, bacon, and toast tried to come up.

Scene of the crime. That's what it was. Not that this was the first to which Declan had treated him. The guy in the car had been just a few hours ago. But this was . . . different. He felt he knew this guy. Sort of. And he had witnessed his destruction. The other guy had been nothing but a silhouette seen through a murky rear window. Faceless. Nobody. Until the door had opened . . . but that's when Julian had turned away and refused to look.

Not wanting the others to witness his reluctance, to tease him about it later, he stepped forward. The asphalt had melted. The tar had separated from the gravel, boiling to the surface, leaving slick patches and shiny globs. Only not all of it was tar. As he moved closer, Julian realized what the rest of it was . . .

"Oh!" Kyrill cried out again, but this time in disgust or maybe excitement. "Is that . . . *his foot?*"

Then Julian's breakfast did come up, and he didn't care who saw.

11

"I'm itching to get going," Hutch said, rubbing his palms together.

He watched the fire crack and pop. Embers sailed off into the night, dying too soon. He sat on a stump near the fire pit, Phil beside him on the canvas chair, his glasses reflecting the flames.

Terry sat on a stump like Hutch's, directly across from him. David occupied a rock that was too low for him, his knees rising up to chest-height in front of him.

"Caribou?" Terry asked.

Hutch nodded. "S'posed to be good hunting."

Using gloved hands, David picked the kettle off its perch over the fire. He sniffed at the spout and said, "Cup of joe, anyone?" He poured the steaming black liquid into a metal camp cup at his feet.

Terry and Phil lifted their cups, and David obliged.

"I'll pass," Hutch said. "I've gotta be up before dawn."

David returned the kettle to its spot above the fire. The four of them gazed into the blaze as into a hypnotic talisman. Their eyes flashed bright, their faces glowed.

Hutch saw the children they once were. There was innocence in David's sparkling blue eyes and almost perfect features. In Terry's muscular, lean countenance; his dimples and tight, coy smile held him at a younger age than his thinning hair and high forehead suggested. And in Phil's round cheeks, stubbly as they were, and wild auburn hair.

Hutch's wife had pulled him into a divorce as painful as rolling over broken bottles. And yet he ached almost as much for the trials his friends were enduring. In years past, when one of them stumbled over life's enumerable obstacles, the others had always been there to help him up. Moral support, financial aid, sound advice: among them, they'd always found what another needed. This year, however, three of them had not only stumbled but had crashed and burned.

David, the only one not scathed and scalded, had done everything he could for his friends. Not a day would pass when he didn't call each in turn with words of encouragement and offers of help. Hutch was sure David's resources and resolve were stretching thin, but his friend would never say so. The others were no good for themselves, let alone for anyone else. Hutch felt deeply for Phil and Terry's problems, but he found it next to impossible to break the surface of his own troubled waters long enough to be of any use. A drowning man was no good to another drowning man.

The wind kicked up in the trees, whispering to them. They all heard it and smiled at the same time.

"Better than the cooing of a woman," Phil said.

Terry made a noise with his mouth. "I wouldn't go that far."

"I don't know," Hutch said. "Nature's fairly predictable, if you know it. And it won't leave you for another man."

They nodded. Hutch knew they were waiting for him to pursue or drop the topic. They weren't embarrassed for him. They had known each other long enough, and to varying degrees had participated in each other's victories and defeats. Hutch hesitated, hearing words in the wind's whispers. He knew what it told him, so he said, "I want you guys to know . . . I'm glad to be here with you, and I'm blessed to call you friends."

Terry aww'd.

"Feeling's mutual, man," David said.

"Of course," agreed Phil.

Terry said, "Okay then . . ." From his jacket pocket he withdrew four cellophane-wrapped cigars. He stood to hand them out with the deference accorded to Medals of Honor.

Phil said, "Are these—"

"Cubans," David finished, rolling his cigar between fingers and thumb.

"Bolivar Royal Corona," Terry said with careful enunciation.

Hutch slipped it out of the wrapper, smelled it. "Wow. But how?"

"In La Ronge. Little tobacco shop next to the diner. Canada, man. They're legal here."

"Never a bad time for a good cigar," Phil said.

"Cutter?" Hutch asked, anxious to light up.

Terry made a face. "I knew I forgot something."

David stood, reached into his pocket, and produced a folding knife. "We don't need no stinking cutter," he said and neatly sliced off the tip of his cigar. He handed the knife to Terry, who did the same and passed it on. Together they leaned their faces to the fire and lit up.

Phil blew smoke into the sky, watching the wind catch it. "Yeah," he said.

"I detect a hint of chocolate," Hutch said authoritatively, tasting the smoke, eyeing the cigar in his hand.

"Leather," Phil added.

"Coffee," David said, licking his lips. "How in the world does all that add up to something that tastes so . . . can I say *exquisite* without sounding like a total pansy?"

The other men nodded in agreement.

"The magic of a good cigar," Terry said.

They blew the smoke over the fire, watching the powdery silver plumes swirl through the coarse gray column of smoke from the spruce logs.

Hutch scanned the sky. "Terry," he said, gesturing.

Terry stood. A ribbon of green and blue rippled overhead. It appeared to stretch for miles. It fluttered and disappeared just as another came into view. This one was orange, turning red, turning green; a rose-colored curtain rippled, faded. The men stepped around the pit to get the blaze out of their eyes. From the top of the slope that led to the river, they gazed in silent wonder.

The Aurora Borealis. Northern Lights. "*Revontulet,*" David said. "It means fox fires. That's what they call them in Finland. My grandfather used to tell me this old folk tale about an arctic fox running through the snow. Whenever his tail touched a mountain, sparks would fly up and illuminate the sky. *Revontulet.*"

He pulled at his cigar. Its tip flared red. He let the smoke drift out as he added, "Boys, does it get any better than this?"

At that moment, Hutch thought that it didn't. Out of the context of their lives, out of time, this was pretty good.

12

Dillon had finally stopped crying. He had fallen asleep with his head on Laura's lap.

She sat cross-legged on the concrete floor in a storage room. Anything she could have used to escape or attack her captors had been removed. The metal shelves bolted to three walls around her now contained only boxes of envelopes and reams of paper that, judging by the quantity, the town of Fiddler Falls obviously felt were of vital importance. Most were blank sheets preprinted with holiday borders—Christmas, Easter, Halloween, one with trees and deer for the start of hunting season, and another with rolled diplomas and mortarboards for sixth grade and senior graduations. Roughly once a month, the town manager paid kids two cents a pop to deliver to every home in town notices of community events, printed on these festive flyers. Laura had never considered that somewhere thousands of handbills awaited printing and distribution. By her estimation, she was surrounded by a ten-year supply. A paper-jacketed ream of any design was hard enough and heavy enough to cause a severe headache to anyone clobbered with it. But a headache was insignificant compared to what her captives deserved, and it would not help her and Dillon escape that room.

Had there been a window or big air vent, as rooms like this always seemed to have in movies, she would stack the reams to reach it, but this room had neither. Nor did it possess a working light, through no fault of the architect's. When they had brought her and Dillon in, she had put up so much of a fight, kicking her legs and flailing her arms, that in order to throw her down and make his exit, her captor had lifted her high. She had broken the bulb with her head. Their only light came from the crack under the door. At first it had been the yellow-white radiance of the sun through a window in the office beyond. Now it was the sterile whiteness of fluorescents. By it, she could make out the room's dimensions, roughly eight feet by twelve. She could see the room's absence of anything that would assist an escape.

And she could see the dried tracks of Dillon's tears on his face. She slid her fingers into his hair, over his scalp. She prayed that he was finding peace in sleep.

"Shhhh," she soothed, believing her voice would reach his dreams. She brushed the hair off his forehead and smoothed an eyebrow with her finger.

His anguish had broken her heart even more than what she suspected had happened to Tom. She knew the feeling was only temporary, a coping mechanism; focusing on someone else's grief helped you avoid your own. She had never before seen Dillon—or for that matter, anyone else—weep as wretchedly or for as long as he had done.

She wondered if it had been an intuition that was more attuned or a logic that was more developed than she had previously given him credit for that had given him the conviction that his father had been murdered. True, the men who had seized them from home that morning had displayed all the characteristics of bad men as Dillon would have learned from television shows and his own parents' stern warnings. True, when Dillon and Laura had seen Tom in the street, the girl had told the man named Declan "not in front of them." And true, after they had been dragged inside and thrown into this room, a loud explosion had shaken the floor.

But could a nine-year-old boy put all that together to become absolutely convinced of his father's death?

Despite Laura's attempts to console him, he had cried and wailed ceaselessly.

She had been reminded of too many funerals for children she had seen on the news. A parent—either the mother or the father, but for some reason never both—hysterical in grief, lamenting to God, pleading to the child, tearing at his hair and clothes. Without question, she would have acted similarly had she lost Dillon, and probably had she witnessed Tom's death. But not having witnessed it, she held on to a thread of hope as thin and fragile as a spider's silk.

Dillon's instant and certain grief made her believe that a bond between father and son had been violently broken, and that unlike the mere emotional bonds of psychiatric journals or the metaphoric bonds of poets, this one had been somehow as tangible as the umbilical cord that had once connected mother and child. The boy had cried and moaned until she was sure no more tears could possibly come, but they did. He had fallen into fits of ragged, desperate breathing. She had thought he would hyperventilate and pass out.

The room's darkness seemed to have added to his panic, but Laura had thought it was appropriate, a representation of the evil that had invaded the town and the bleakness of losing Tom.

Laura would have liked to check her watch by the light slipping under the door. But with Dillon finally in the slumber of exhaustion, she dared not move. When she last checked, it had been 4:12 p.m., six hours since they had last seen Tom. Six hours in the storage room. She guessed it was now somewhere around seven o'clock, but it could be much earlier or much later. Time flowed differently in moments of terror and grief. Watching her son sleep, the rise and fall of his chest, the barely discernible movements of his eyes under his lids, she tried to imagine his life without Tom. She couldn't. He had always been as much a friend as a father. Teaching Dillon how to fish, camp, work on the car, build a birdhouse, Tom had been as entertained as Dillon had been. She touched her son's chin and ran her finger along his jaw. She brushed the hair back from his temple.

"I'll try to fill his shoes," she whispered. "I'll try to be what he would have been for you."

A tear landed on his forehead. His eyes fluttered; then he was back in his dreams.

She pulled in a deep breath and raised her head. She wiped the unfallen tears from her eyes. She had not realized she was so close to giving in to the grief. She looked into the gloom and thought about being strong. Her fingers again pushed into Dillon's hair and lifted. She felt the fine strands brushing her palm.

"I'll still be me . . . and I'll be him too. But right now I have to get you out of here. I have to make you safe. That's what he would have—"

Shadows moved under the door. The lock rattled, and blinding light burst in. She blinked against it as hazy silhouettes filled the doorway.

Someone walked around her and stood at the back wall, in the dark. Two others entered. They remained in the light. One was the older teenaged boy. The other was Declan. He looked down at her. Half his face was awash in bright light, the other in shadow. His cool indifference did not so much radiate from him as it clung to him like a cowled robe. He squatted to be level with her, casually draping his arms across his legs.

"Do we have a problem?" he asked.

She glared. A dozen responses, from the shrill to the sarcastic, flashed through her mind.

Dillon stirred, groaning quietly. He adjusted his head on her lap.

Finally she said, "Where's my husband?"

He closed his eyes, appearing exasperated. "So we do have a problem."

"Only if I can't see my husband. Where is Tom?"

"Sweetheart, I'm afraid you're going to have to join Matchmaker.com. If you have that up here in Hicksville."

Every muscle in Laura's body tensed; she wanted to scream, to cry, to fight, to do so many things. This man had provided confirmation of Dillon's conviction and her fears. Keeping them all in her head would drive her crazy, so she pushed them all aside, except one: fight. She felt as though she could fly at him—just fly without benefit of using her legs to spring—and crush him by the sheer power of her hatred. But she sat, her sleeping son's head in her lap, unable to do anything.

The right side of Declan's mouth edged up, but his eyes remained black and cold, reflecting, she was certain, the state of his soul.

"Now here's the problem," he said. "I killed your husband, nice guy that he was. You're the wife of a cop." He caught himself. "Excuse me, you're the wife of a *dead* cop. Probably pretty tough yourself. Know a thing or two about weapons. And I'm hearing from these good folks"—he pointed a thumb out the door toward the large community room beyond the offices, where he was holding many of her friends and neighbors against their wills—"that you're a feisty one." His smile grew broader. "Now, don't get me wrong, I like my ladies feisty. But there's a time and a place for everything, and this ain't it for any heroics from you."

She stared and conjured the image of breaking his arms and legs. She didn't know how she'd do it. She surprised herself even thinking it, but it had come to her, the way an appetite suddenly does when you smell fresh-baked cookies.

"Nothing personal against your hubby. Like I said, he seemed like a nice guy. But I needed to squash any thoughts of resistance in these folks before they thought them. I explained it all to Tom, and he was down with it." He winked. "We don't need anyone trying to fill his shoes."

The man behind her laughed at that. The teen snorted, suppressing the laughter inside. Declan glanced over her head and then at the teen.

"Inside joke," he explained. "I hope you can appreciate the difficult situation I'm in. How much show of force does one need to control a town of two hundred and forty-two people?"

The man behind her corrected him, "Two hundred forty." He snickered.

"Oh yeah. Two-forty. How much power to break their fighting spirit but not drive them to rebellion? See, there's a fine line between scaring people and making them angry. You're more angry than scared, and that can mean trouble. So what do I do to change the equation? I can kill you next . . . or your son."

She put her hand over Dillon's chest.

Declan shook his head dismissively. "People tend to get weird when whole families are murdered, and I don't want anyone getting weird . . . yet. Besides, as a lifelong resident of this fine town and wife of the sheriff, you probably know things I might find useful. So I'd rather keep you around." He paused. "I could take your son, hold him somewhere. Keep you in line. But that could get messy and more work than I want to put into this. We might forget to feed him . . . and we'd be right back at your breaking point between scared and angry."

He stood and nodded at the man standing in the shadows. She felt hands on her arms, yanking her up. Before Dillon's head hit the ground, the teen stepped forward and grabbed him with both hands by the shirt. He pulled the boy to his feet.

"What?" Laura said. She twisted her shoulders, pumped her arms. The man's grip was solid. She tried to kick him, but he was fast as well. He dragged her several steps backward.

Dillon was instantly awake. Confusion etched his face. His sore eyes blinked. "Mom?" he said.

She stopped fighting. "It's okay, honey."

Declan reached behind him and came back with a long knife. It was thick and heavy looking. A military weapon or something hunters were getting into nowadays. He turned it in the air, letting light glint off it. He stepped closer to Dillon.

"No!" She wanted to scream, but it came out a hoarse whisper.

"You can keep your boy," Declan said. "But I want you to know something."

He brought the knife to Dillon's face, pressing the tip to his cheekbone. Dillon's eyes flared wide. He sucked in a sharp breath, as he had in September when he got his Hep B immunization.

"Don't," Laura said, straining against the powerful hands.

Declan drew the blade down, leaving a thin red line, then he pulled it away. The cut on Dillon's face grew thick with blood. It stretched to his jaw as a rivulet leaked out.

Laura hissed.

"I want you to know that I'm not above hurting a child. So be quiet. Be good. Don't cause trouble, and we'll get along. Understand?"

Her eyes flashed at him. She showed her teeth, thinking she would say something. Nothing came out. She hoped her expression was enough. Enough to let him know that he would pay for harming her son. Enough to warn him against trying it again.

"I'll take that as an agreement," Declan said. He pursed his lips and kissed her through the air. He left, followed by the teen. The man holding her turned her around, walked backward to the door. She knew he would shove her hard into the room. By the time she recovered, the door would be shut and locked again. Instead, his hands came off her like a vise coming undone. She stepped away and glared back. It was the black man, Bad. She gave him the same fierce expression she had given Declan.

He returned it and growled. Then he laughed, stepped through the doorway, and locked them in.

She dropped to her knees before Dillon. She hugged him tightly. Whenever Tom had approached Dillon to hug him, he'd say he was going to squeeze him like a Go-Gurt, a yogurt treat that you had to squeeze out of its packaging. She tried to hug him that way now.

"I'm so sorry," she said. She leaned back to examine the long vertical line on his face, black now in the dim light. Gently, she wiped at it. "Are you okay?"

He nodded. "Are you?"

She laughed, relieved. At least for now he seemed himself, always so concerned about other people.

He said, "They want us to obey them."

She braced him between her hands, looked into his eyes. "Well, they don't know us very well, do they?"

13

Hutch woke to the gentle but insistent chime of his watch. Quietly, he unzipped his sleeping bag to retrieve the clothes he'd put inside it the evening before. He maneuvered past Phil. The man had taken up snoring since their last camping trip, probably the result of his weight gain. He emerged from the tent into the cold, dark morning. Plumes of breath formed in front of his face as goose bumps popped up on his arms and thighs under his long johns. His muscles contracted in an effort to fend off the cold. It was four o'clock, still three hours before dawn.

He set his clothes on a rucksack near the tent. Standing outside the shelter in only his skivvies, he surveyed the campsite by the light of a quarter moon; the campfire had gone out hours before. He saw no evidence that animals had come to inspect their presence, that humans had made a covert visit, or that anything unsavory had fallen or blown, slithered or crawled into camp.

Fog filled the ravine, at the bottom of which the river gurgled and sluiced out of sight. Moonlight illuminated the gently swirling mist, reminding Hutch of the dry-ice fog that churns from the witches' cauldron in stage productions of *Macbeth*. It climbed the banks and sent tendrils snaking into the campsite and surrounding forest. It billowed away from him as he made his way down to the bank of the river. He dipped his hands into the freezing water and splashed his face. The cold wetness shocked him into a higher level of wakefulness. His heart raced.

Returning to his clothes, he used a towel to dry off. He shook out a pair of camouflage pants and slipped into them, instantly appreciating the extra layer of material—the extra-warm layer, thanks to sleeping with the clothes; he'd forgotten to do it plenty of times. He tugged on a shirt and jacket, then pushed into his boots. He donned a camouflage baseball hat and applied streaks of black, olive, and beige makeup to his face and neck. Since he would track his prey through the woods, his clothes and the pattern of his camouflage makeup resembled trees and leaves—not so much to look like foliage but to break up the pattern of his body.

He pulled a spray bottle from the sack and misted a few areas on his torso and legs. It was the fragrance of earth, which would mask his own scent. Many deer and elk hunters preferred to spray themselves with the urine of a doe in heat. It was a product available at retail, though not usually at the same counter as Old Spice. In Hutch's experience, earth was equally effective, less expensive, and possessed none of the *eeewww* factor, should he share his escapades with nonhunters. His clothes had been washed with a scentless detergent. Even his deodorant was specially formulated to keep big game from catching a whiff of Bambi's mortal enemy.

He snapped on a utility belt and attached a small flashlight, a canteen, and a hip pack loaded with energy bars, spare bowstrings, and other things he might find useful in a pinch. He slipped into a binocular harness, which held the glasses firmly over his sternum until needed. Kneeling beside the tent, he opened his bow case and lifted his recurve bow, to which he had already mounted a quiver of arrows. Leaning the bow against the tent door, he reached again into the sack. He withdrew the topo map he had consulted in the helicopter, folded it, and inserted it into an inside pocket of his jacket. The map had been printed on vinyl, making it waterproof and silent. He stood with his bow and slung it onto his shoulder, letting the bowstring's tension hold it in place.

He checked his bearings on the Suunto watch/compass he'd bought for this trip. (Suunto called it a "wristop computer," but Hutch thought that exaggerated its features and sounded way too nerdy) He took a moment to gaze at the river of mist, at the trees, at the distant hills as if committing them to memory for the purpose of reeling back to that spot when his day of hunting was over. He filled his lungs with cool air.

It tastes better up here, the air, he thought. The ashy smell coming from the fire pit, the tang of pines, the crisp fragrance of the water—individually and combined, these were olfactory pleasantries matched by few things back home. Two popped into his head: fresh-brewed coffee and newborn babies. He could brew coffee up here, and would have done so this morning had he not been so excited about the hunt, and the baby smell was rare no matter where you were. So olfactory-wise, as in other subjects, northern Saskatchewan won again.

He climbed a small embankment and entered the woods. Kicking away the thin covering of mist, he began looking for the game trail that would, if Artemis, Greek goddess of hunting, favored him, lead him to a great bull caribou. Over the next hour Hutch located two trails, neither with fresh tracks. He identified a high ridge that promised an excellent vantage point of the entire valley and headed for it.

The sun was scalding the horizon by the time he stood on that ridge, an outcropping of rock that did indeed overlook the broad valley. Through his binoculars he panned the terrain, gliding his glass over streams and marshes, trees and meadows. After fifteen minutes of methodical sweeps, he saw them: five brown-and-beige animals grazing in a field beyond a thick patch of forest. He made note of their compass bearings and map location.

Moving quickly now, he came down off the ledge and the small mountain that supported it and moved into the trees. He bounded over bushes and blowdowns, ducked under branches, and pushed off of trees as he careened past. Having located his prey, there was no need for stealth until he drew closer, which he did faster than he had expected. Nearing the meadow where the caribou were grazing, he slowed. His feet became more sensitive to the noise potential of the brush under them; his eyes found passages around reaching fingers of tree limbs, beds of dry leaves, soil that concealed twigs as brittle—and loud—as snapping bones.

Attuned to the wind, he headed diagonally away from his quarry, hoping to come at them against a breeze. When he finally made it to the clearing, no animals were visible. He glassed the area, disappointed. Then a shadow shifted beyond the meadow, where the forest picked up its march north. Dapples of light, shades of blackness moved too steadily to be caused by mere wind, and he panned with them until they coalesced into a caribou. Though the caribou was the only animal in the deer family in which both male and female grew antlers, the monstrous rack on the head of this animal told him he had found a bull. It was moving deeper into the woods. Hutch knew he had to move parallel with it until the woods came together and he could approach under the cover of trees.

Two hours later he stood on a game trail with fresh tracks. He followed the spoor pessimistically, remembering that caribou were fast travelers and hard to pursue. Before long, he lost the tracks. Reversing, he found where the caribou had veered off the trail. He moved into the brush to follow it. The caribou's movements through the virgin wild puzzled him, since most game followed the paths emblazoned by thousands of animals that had come before. Then he stepped into a clearing and had his answer.

Before him rose a thirty-foot-high sloping wall of golden sand and ashen dirt. It was an esker, a twisting serpentine ridge formed by meltwater streams beneath the ice of retreating glaciers. Sometimes called animal highways, eskers allowed wildlife to travel great distances quickly. He saw the tracks of his bull climbing diagonally to the flat top of the esker. The ground had crumbled under its hooves, forming an almost perfect flight of steps. Hutch had no hope of catching the animal by following it. He pulled out his map and found the esker and his current position. The esker weaved for several miles in a mostly eastern direction before arcing north and petering out.

Examining the terrain along the esker, Hutch thought the caribou was heading for a meadow at the confluence of two streams about a mile distant. The esker would take the caribou away from the spot before bringing it back. By heading straight for this meadow, he thought he could arrive there first. Lying in wait for a fast animal was always better than trying to overtake it. Hutch returned the map to its pocket and jogged back into the forest. High up, a hundred chickadees chirped to themselves. Despite their apparent numbers, he rarely witnessed one perched on a branch or flitting between trees. They were masters at hiding. Not so good at keeping quiet.

As much as he enjoyed the victory of a successful kill, he realized again the pleasure of pursuit. Moving through the trees the way an animal would, spotting their killing grounds and beds exhilarated him. He loved the fragrance of trees and moss and the dew as it misted off the leaves. His boots trod silently over the soft cushion of needles and sphagnum and crunched over dead branches. As he moved, he found himself falling into a familiar pattern in his breathing and the movements of his legs, arms, and body. Getting from one point to another in the woods became effortless, automatic, as though he'd done it every day of his life. Shadow and light, which at first had fooled him into seeing branches and leaves and obstacles in his path, forcing him to weave and duck and expend energy, once again became only shadow and light. Now he leaped when there was something to leap over and dodged when there was something to dodge. His breathing seemed to become harmonious with the woods and the wind. In this state, Hutch's mind wandered. He imagined parts of the wilderness he could not see: animals darting away before he approached, others watching him from a distance—all of them accepting him as part of their world.

The troubles of home seemed far away. Perhaps because of this, he was able to think about them without the familiar, paralyzing grip of panic and grief. Only nine months ago, his life had seemed as David's was—fantastic with a capital *F*. Picture a Hallmark card depicting a couple walking hand in hand through the surf, a pair of happy children running ahead. Add some credit card debt, make the beach a mountain trail, the couple a little older—you get the idea. Then Janet had slammed him in the head with a baseball bat. Well, not really, but it felt that way. Instead of "Louisville Slugger," the bat she used read "Petition for Dissolution of Marriage." She had left it on the breakfast table beside a sectioned cantaloupe and a glass of cranberry juice.

She'd taken the kids to school and hadn't returned. She had not answered her mobile phone until after two o'clock that afternoon, providing Hutch plenty of time to go out of his mind.

"Talk about out of the blue," he'd said.

"Hutch," she had replied, insanely calm, "it's been a long time coming."

She'd launched into a litany of Hutch's offenses: too much time at work, too little affection at home, too committed to his friends—that's the term she used, "too committed." The grievances had taken him by surprise. He'd kept regular, maybe even fewer-than-normal hours on the job. He'd often left little notes and gifts around the house professing his love for her. And he had certainly not seen as much of David, Terry, and Phil as he would have liked.

Of course, she'd had an answer for everything: he'd disappear into his home office for "at least an hour" after the kids had gone down, his notes and gifts were a poor substitution for genuine feelings, and he'd be with his buddies mentally when he wasn't with them physically. She had not wanted to try any of his solutions: counseling, changing his job, changing everything, separation. He'd felt he couldn't win, and of course that was true: "The heart in ascension is blind to faults; in decline, it's blind to reason."

He'd found out later through a friend that she had been seeing another man since well before her grand slam to his head. No wonder she'd been so unwilling to work it out. She had been swept up in the affections of a man who had been free to focus on romance— flowers, poetry, long gazes into each other's eyes—without the anesthetizing grind of daily life—getting the kids to soccer practice and violin lessons, calling AAA for a tow when the car craps out, planning for retirement. He had heard that to some women even the dangers of illicit affairs heightened the experience, as though equating it to riding with the Hell's Angels or kayaking Tibet's Tsangpo River. More like trying to catch a bullet with your teeth, Hutch had thought.

Despite the revelation, he had continued to love her through the divorce. He had admitted there were things he could have done to express his love more and to limit outside distractions. He'd begged, pleaded, and generally behaved like a teenager who had become invisible to his first crush. When she asked him to move out, he had agreed. That had been his biggest mistake. In attempting to finagle sole custody of Logan and Macie out of the deal, she'd claimed that his moving out constituted abandonment. He'd made his second biggest mistake upon hearing that: he'd displayed anger in court.

Now she had temporary custody, and he could see his son and daughter only five hours, once a week—under court-ordered supervision. It was as though she'd deliberately aimed her venomous arrows at the softest part of his heart. She used to tell her friends that he was a loving and attentive father. Suddenly, she could not tell enough people how terrible he was. As though emerging from a cocoon instead of a marriage, Janet had become a different person from the one he'd known for fifteen years. But her metamorphosis had not resulted in a butterfly but a beast. She was devious and cruel. She lied to the courts and her own kids. He sometimes wondered if her attacks were an attempt to make him hate her as much as she had apparently grown to hate him, so she could get on with her life without the guilt of watching him suffer. If that were the case, it had worked. He still loved the woman he had married, but not the woman she had become.

The loss of his wife and children had taken its toll on the perpetually reticent but upbeat John Hutchinson. In a fit of self-pity worthy of a country music award, he had declared Sting's ode to divorced dads, "I'm So Happy I Can't Stop Crying," his favorite song and played it ceaselessly for five hours.

A few months ago David had pointed out that his columns had taken a dark turn. While continuing to profile heart-of-Colorado archetypes, his articles' emphasis slowly shifted from triumph over tragedy to the tragedy itself, from the Phoenix to the ashes. One column chronicled the saga of a woman who'd been injured when a police cruiser in a high-speed chase had crashed into her car. Sheer determination had gotten her through years of physical therapy and college to become a choreographer for the Colorado Ballet Company. The accident had robbed her of her dream of becoming a ballerina, but not of making valuable contributions to the field she loved so much. Hutch's column consumed an inordinate amount of ink describing the extent of her injuries and the culpability of the police department. The woman's inspiring achievement became a mere footnote. In another column, a rancher's valiant and successful efforts to secure more state funding for mountain-road safety after his son was killed by a falling boulder became a heart-wrenching dirge of the family's grief.

"Write a book," David had suggested. "Get it out of your system."

Hutch had not believed he had a book in him, especially one that was either sufficiently direct or sufficiently dark to purge his angst. That's when he had the idea for this trip. Experiencing his friends and facing himself in a place without guile or unreasonable demands seemed like just the thing. If he returned to Denver with a chip the size of Canada on his shoulder, his prognosis would be hopeless. He'd have to resort to drastic measures—moving to the Keys or something. Of course that would distance himself even further from his children, geographically and emotionally, but he was beginning to wonder if trying to stay in their lives was a lost cause. And at the rate she was going, Janet would have them completely poisoned against him within the year. As he had finally realized about his marriage, perhaps it would eventually dawn on him that his relationship with his children was gone as well.

He didn't want that. He'd rather lose his arms and legs. He simply did not know how to fight anymore.

14

Forty yards ahead, sunlight pierced the gloom. It came first in slanting rays; beyond that lay a consistency of brilliance that indicated Hutch had reached the meadow. Craning his head around, he tried to peer into that openness, but the land there must have sloped away. All he could see were hazy mountains in the far distance. Cautiously, he crept forward, like a cat on the prowl. His eyes flicked from the open space beyond the woods to the land directly before him. He watched for twigs or dry leaves that would give away his presence.

A clump of bushes between two trees shielded his approach. Maybe they were chokeberry trees; he was never very good at identifying flora. Near the bush, he crouched lower. When it seemed he would step right into its branches and leaves, he lowered himself to his knees.

He pushed one hand silently into the bush and levered the foliage down. The meadow lay before him, but not the caribou.

Either he had guessed wrong about the animal's destination or he had arrived before it. He waited. A noise came to him, faint and so foreign to the area he could not be sure he was really hearing it. It was an engine, something big like a truck or a powerful ATV. It revved once or twice, then rumbled steadily as though it was idling or cruising slowly. Then it cut off. *Must be a road up here somewhere. Maybe hunters from Fiddler Falls.* He thought the vehicle had been far off, the rolling hills amplifying and distorting its sounds. He listened more intently, yet heard nothing but the wind through the trees.

He slipped the bow off his shoulder and studied its simple beauty. Sixty inches long and two inches wide, it was made of laminated walnut. It was cocoa in color, with a black grain pattern. The center part of the bow, called the riser, was straight and shaped to fit a hand. Above the handgrip, a nub of wood formed an arrow rest, over which the shaft of the arrow slid when being drawn back or propelled forward by the string. Above and below the riser, limbs arced toward the shooter. Each tip curved away from the archer, giving the bow its name: recurve.

A bow's power was described in draw weight. A twenty-pound draw was good for children shooting at paper targets, but the arrow would never generate enough velocity to penetrate an animal's hide and muscles. Hutch's bow required sixty pounds of pressure to pull the string back to full draw. His arrows flew fast. The arm strength necessary for recurves forced users to learn *instinctive* shooting: all the aiming took place before drawing back on the string. When it was time to fire, they would quickly pull the string back to the jawline and immediately release, giving their muscles no time to shake under the strain of the draw weight.

This was different from compound bows, which used pulleys and cams to alleviate the strength needed to hold the string at full draw. Compound shooters aimed *after* drawing and stayed at full draw until the best shot presented itself. But compound bows tended to be noisier than recurves, alerting the animal to the hunter's presence, and they were nearly impossible to restring in the field. Once Hutch switched to a recurve, he wondered why he'd ever used a compound.

The bowstring itself was made of Dacron fiber. It ran from the upper bowtip to the lower bowtip. Near the center of its length, Hutch had clamped a small copper ring. To nock an arrow, he put the V-shaped notch in the end of the arrow, near the fletching or feathers, below this ring so the bowstring ran through it.

Mounted to the right side of the riser, opposite the arrow rest, was a quiver. A soft rubber form gripped the aluminum shafts of eight arrows. Each arrow's razor tip—called a broadhead—was pushed into a plastic cup containing rubberized grips. The arrows ran parallel to the bow's riser, with the broadheads pointing skyward.

Movement caught his eye. At the south end of the meadow, the caribou trotted out of the woods, into the open.

Hutch froze, slowing his breathing, afraid to move even his eyes.

The caribou came closer. Hutch heard a noise he had previously only read about: a clicking and popping of the animal's leg joints, distinctive to this species. Intermittently, its hooves *clopped* against exposed rock. It huffed and snorted as it searched for a meal of lichen. One hundred yards . . . eighty . . . sixty. It was outside of his comfortable target range, though he had successfully practiced at that distance. The animal paused, looking around. It pawed at the ground and leaned over to nibble the grass.

Meticulously, excruciatingly slowly, Hutch pulled an arrow from the quiver and nocked it onto the string. He leaned slightly to view the caribou between two branches. He had removed the middle three fingers of his right-hand glove so his fingertips could feel the bow-string and slide smoothly over it. Now he held those fingers on the string, two below the arrow, one above. He sighted along the arrow past its broadhead to the caribou.

The animal stepped closer. It was beautiful, husky and muscular. It possessed a thick, powerful neck draped in a white scarf of long fur. Its body was dark brown. It wore beige socks. An antler rose from beside each ear, then split into a forward clump and a backward branch that climbed higher before fingering out. At their highest point, the antlers were a full three feet above the caribou's head.

Hutch avoided looking at the caribou's eyes. Hunters believed animals sensed when other eyes lay upon theirs. Skeptics were new hunters who hadn't tested the taboo in the field. The caribou lifted its head and sniffed the air. Then it trotted closer to Hutch and stooped to graze again. Forty-two yards: close enough.

Hutch took a bead on the animal's torso, just above its front leg where its heart would be. The tips of his forefinger, middle finger, and ring finger felt the pressure of the bow's taut string. In one quick motion he pulled back until his thumb nearly touched the hollow in his jaw below the earlobe.

Before he could release, the animal exploded.

15

The air boomed with the sound of thunder as the earth erupted. Dirt, sod, caribou billowed straight up.

Hutch fell back, hitting the ground hard. He blinked, confused. High above, branches formed a canopy over him, blue sky beyond. Birds streaked across his vision. Smoke and dust blew past. The smell of ash and meat reached his nostrils. He lifted his head, seeing only the bush and the smoke rising beyond it. His left hand was holding the bow, but he'd lost the arrow.

He rose to his knees again, parted the branches. Silt was still dropping. Along with it, his arrow thumped down in the meadow. It vibrated, then held still, a feathered marker halfway between Hutch and what was now a smoking crater.

Larger chunks of earth and probably caribou rained from the sky.

What appeared to be part of an antler landed behind him and spun off into the woods. A wave of warm air pushed through the leaves of the bush, washing over him. He squinted against it. Then it passed, and his skin cooled.

A sound came to him. He flinched, expecting another explosion. It was the revving of an engine, growing louder. From the other side of the meadow, a large SUV roared into view. Moving fast, it reached the crater in seconds. Hutch recognized it as a Hummer, bright yellow and caked with a day's worth of off-roading. A man sat harnessed into a chair in the bed of the truck.

The Hummer braked at the crater. The man's head flew forward, then back. The doors opened and people clamored out, laughing, hooting, hollering.

The driver, a black man, danced to the edge of the crater and peered in. "Whoa, Declan," he said. "I guess you *did* crank it up."

Coming around from the passenger side, a fat kid, maybe twenty, turned on a large video camera and held it to his face. He pointed the lens at the crater, panning to take it all in.

The hole the explosion had made was roughly ten feet in diameter and four feet deep at its center. A boy and a girl edged closer. They were both young, sixteen or seventeen. The boy's face was pierced in all the currently hip places: earlobes, top of the ears, lip, eyebrow. He grinned and said, "It was there, and then it wasn't! Holy cow!"

"Holy caribou," corrected the man sitting in the bed of the truck. He watched the celebration emotionlessly, a smirk on his face and nothing in his eyes. He could have been a bystander at the birthday party of a stranger.

Another boy, perhaps in his early teens, walked slowly around the crater. He studied it objectively, as a pupil. He wasn't reveling in the destruction.

The driver knelt, holding his palms up to the smoke as if warming them. The guy with the camera slowly sidestepped in an arc around the crater, filming it from all sides. The girl skipped up to the bed of the truck and said something to the man, who nodded without looking at her. He was watching the youngest boy, who, Hutch realized with a start, was walking toward his arrow in the field.

When he looked back, Hutch saw the man in the truck staring directly at the bush behind which he hid. His guts felt cold and amorphous, a churning mass.

What had drawn his eye? The camouflage, from boots to hat, from his facial makeup to his gloved hands, should have rendered him practically invisible among the foliage. His eyes would gleam, but barely. The shadows of the trees fell over him, helping complete his disappearance. Had he moved? Had he twitched? Was the man looking only because the bush had shuddered? Did he think it was the wind? Or had he extended his gaze out from the arrow in suspicion? The arrow, with its bright orange fletching and aluminum shaft, obviously had not spent much time in the field.

The man squinted. He examined something in his hands. He peered at the bush, then again at the object in his hand, as though marking the spot or seeing it by different means, the way a movie director watches a scene with his own eyes, then through a camera lens.

Hutch's arm was parting the bush. Could the man see his face through the gap? Hutch dared not lower his arm, back away, or move at all. The human brain is attracted to movement even more than color. That's why a turn signal flashes, why friends wave their hands in greeting.

The man in the truck scanned the woods to Hutch's right. His attention came back to the bush. He eyed the woods to his left and once again returned.

Hutch blinked.

The man squinted. "Julian," he called.

The boy approaching the arrow looked back. "There's something here!" he said.

"Get back here."

Ignoring the order, the boy reached the arrow. He knelt to examine it. A finger flicked one of the three vanes. Gripping the shaft, he yanked it out of the earth. He whacked the broadhead on the ground, dislodging a clump of dirt. He ran a thumb along one of the razor-sharp blades. He hissed—loud enough for Hutch to hear—and snatched his thumb away. He looked at it, then pressed it to his lips. Hutch had sliced himself plenty of times on broadheads. The boy stood, holding the tip close to his face, rotating it.

The man in the truck eyed his crew. His age and demeanor signaled his authority over them. His eyes snapped back to the bush.

There was no doubt: he'd seen something. Okay . . . so, was being seen the end of the world? True, these people had used a weapon much more powerful than Hutch's bow to kill the caribou. Did that make them more dangerous than other hunters he would encounter in the field? Enough that he should fear them? Probably it did, Hutch decided. Dynamite, a land mine, a bazooka for all he knew, was not legal in this context. Then again, neither was Hutch's hunting without a native guide. They were all breaking laws. What made these interlopers so fearsome?

The answer, of course, was the sheer devastation at their disposal. Their attitudes as well. From the gleeful celebration of the driver to the stoic coolness of the man in the back of the truck. Something wasn't right.

Hutch had always been intuitive about people. He seemed to instantly recognize sincerity and kindness or guile and selfishness. And these were people he did not want to meet.

Without taking his eyes off the bush, the man in the truck called out to his comrades. "Bad! Kyrill! Pru! Get in the truck! Julian, now!"

The girl, standing near the bed, peered around, puzzled. She spoke to the man.

He shook his head and gestured for her to get into the cab.

The driver stood and looked back at the man. "Declan!" he called.

Declan, Hutch thought.

"Declan!" the driver repeated, trying to get his attention. When he did, he held his palms up and apart as if to say, *What's up?*

"Just get in," Declan said. His fingers were at play on the device in his hand.

One by one, each of the young people returned to the Hummer like children called in from recess. The boy named Julian had been farthest away and walked slowest, as if hesitant to embark on whatever new adventure the man had in mind. He carried Hutch's arrow in his hand.

Hutch suspected this marshalling of troops to the vehicle meant bad news for him. The driver's door slammed shut, as did a door on the other side. Finally Julian reached the rear driver's side door. He looked back at the crater, then at the arrow, as if making some kind of connection between the two. He climbed in and pulled the door closed.

The twisted smirk on Declan's face changed to a grin, and Hutch knew the time for stealth was over.

He jumped back from the bush, letting the branch spring into place, leaves shaking. He spun, rising as he did, and ran all out into the woods, following the path the spinning antlers had taken. Within seconds, he leaped over those very antlers, a fallen tree, and a tangled mass of branches. His forehead made sharp contact with a branch, knocking him off his feet. He landed hard, crushing the wind from his lungs. Hitching uselessly for breath, he got to his feet and stumbled deeper into the gloom, trusting his lungs to kick back into gear at any moment.

From behind him came a whoosh of air, the crack of thunder, and a deafening explosion.

A shock wave of heated air and bits of twigs and dirt and rock smashed into his back. He flew forward, furiously pedaling his legs to keep from crashing down again. He glanced back to see a crater where he had hidden behind the bush. Sunlight was catching smoke wafting from the hole. But he had been in shadow. He looked up to see that the branches and leaves that had been above him were gone; others swung from thin threads of bark. Foliage floated down. The destruction in the trees appeared more or less circular, directly above the crater, as though something had exploded straight up or slammed straight down. Stunned by this vision, Hutch tripped over his own feet, striking his elbow on a rock, his knee on a branch. Pain flared from those areas, but he pushed it back, rolled, and was up again.

16

He expected to hear the roar of the Hummer's engine as it pursued him. He didn't believe even a four-wheel-drive as hearty as it was could plow into the forest, but it could certainly follow the tree line until a gap allowed it to shoot closer. The woods were splotchy, sharing the terrain with open meadows and boulder fields, the way brown and white shared the hides of overo pintos. To his left, another *whoosh-crack* explosion. Not even close. A thick pillar of sunlight beamed down, as though a door in the leafy canopy had opened.

The explosion's far-miss encouraged him to pause. Bent at the waist, he put his palms on his thighs and sucked in air. He could not see the Hummer, so how could they see him? Were they simply shooting in the dark, if shooting was what they were doing? Were they lobbing grenades, using a mortar, some kind of rocket launcher? He wasn't going to stick around to find out. Taking one more deep breath, he continued running, though not at the all-out pace he had been. He still clutched his bow in his left hand. He checked it to ensure he had not lost any more arrows. The quiver was full, less one, giving him seven. He wondered if he would need them or even have a chance to use them.

Sunlight ahead. Another meadow. The Hummer could have circled around this patch of forest to wait for him in the meadow. He stopped again. He had been heading back toward camp. That was stupid. He couldn't lead these people there. Not to Phil, Terry, and David. He ran deeper into the forest. The tree trunks were not thick, not like Virginia's oaks or the redwoods of the Pacific Northwest. They stood close to one another, their branches intertwining into a heavy canopy. Hidden in the gloom, roots, gnarled blowdowns, and loose, moss-covered rocks became enemies, trying to twist his ankle and throw him down. He touched the trees as he passed, steadying himself. Before long he came to another meadow. At its edge he scanned left and right. Then he held his breath to listen. Nothing.

More woods lay a hundred, a hundred and twenty yards across the clearing. He darted into the sunlight, swiveling his head back and forth as though he were crossing a freeway.

A *whoosh-crack*, directly before him. The ground exploded. Dirt and gravel pelted his face, and he tumbled backward. Even as silt fell down upon him, he rose and ran around the new crater, continuing toward the woods. Birds rose from the treetops, speckling the sky. His ears rang from the explosion's thunderclap. Even so, he heard the deep rumble of an engine. He glanced over his shoulder. The Hummer rounded the far end of the forest, from which he had departed.

He realized there had been no line of sight when the explosion had nearly killed him, and he wondered about the targeting mechanism on this fearsome weapon. He could see the man, Declan, jostling in his perch that raised him head and shoulders above the roof of the truck. Sensing the need to do it, Hutch suddenly broke to his right just as the ground erupted.

Whoosh-crack.

He broke left again and sprinted for the trees. The Hummer drew closer. Where the trees began, he leaped over a bush, caught his foot, tumbled, was up again, moving deeper. He zigged right, zagged left, moving farther away from the clearing. He heard the Hummer behind him. It stopped at the tree line. Loud thumps made him think Declan was pounding on the roof of the cab. The click of latches. Voices.

"Go, go, go!" Declan's voice.

Sharp calls. Confused queries. Then branches broke and leaves rustled as his pursuers entered the woods on foot after him.

Hutch crouched behind a tree, listening. The men called to one another, communicating which areas they had cleared. More than a few times, they reminded one another not to shoot unless they were certain the target was not one of them. This told Hutch several things: First, they were armed, obviously with weapons other than the cannon-rocket-bomb thing. Not good. And second, they were inexperienced. Not bad.

His advantages were that he was comfortable in the woods, knew how to move quietly, was covered in camouflage, and possessed a weapon of his own. He'd rather not have to use it. Evasion was a better strategy.

By their calls and clumsy passage through the forest, he believed that three people had followed him on foot. That left three in the vehicle. Leaning around the tree and rising on his haunches to peer over a bush, he saw the driver and wondered who had taken his place. Was this man more of a hunter, more of a killer than the others? Is that why he now had in his hands not a steering wheel, but some kind of space-age firearm?

To this man's left came the teenaged boy, the one he thought was about seventeen. He, too, carried a weapon, but not so confidently. Someone to the driver's right called out. Hutch could not see him. At least now he knew of the man's presence. If Hutch stayed where he was, they would be on top of him in less than five minutes.

Staying low, he shifted and moved away. Scuttling from tree to bush, bush to tree, he put ground between them. Rising behind a tree, his legs stiff and cramped from crouching and duck-walking, he rubbed his thighs.

He could hear his pursuers but could not pinpoint their locations or judge their distance. The woods played with sounds, muffling and echoing, making noises seem to emanate from places they had not.

He peered around the tree. The driver was fifty yards away, pointing his gun directly at him. The muzzle flashed and bullets whizzed past, striking trees behind him. Then bark ripped in splintered threads from the tree he leaned against as the shooter adjusted his aim. The tangy odor of fresh-cut wood touched his nostrils. A second gun fired, this one different, a single sharp *crack!* A huge divot of earth jumped into the air ten feet away.

The driver had a machine gun. The other, some kind of hunting rifle. Big-bore by the sound of it, .45- or .50-caliber. The kind of rifle police snipers used. He hoped this kid was much less proficient with it than a SWAT team member.

On a personality assessment twisted enough to field the question, Hutch would have listed exposing himself to volleys of machine-gun fire as the least enjoyable way to spend an afternoon, even if snake handling and skydiving without a parachute were also contenders. But now, as the gunmen drew nearer, he realized that hiding behind the tree was worse. At least by running he stood a chance. He pushed off and darted away. He expected any second to feel, even if only briefly, a slug penetrating his skull or piercing his spine. One round came so close to his ear, he heard it whining through the air like a mosquito, here and gone. In front of him, bark exploded, branches split, leaves sprang into the air.

The stuttering, maraca sound of the machine gun and the *crack* of the rifle went on and on and on.

An image of the driver came to mind: standing over Hutch, who was splayed dead in the grass, his booted foot resting on Hutch's hunched shoulder. He pointed the machine gun to the sky. In Hutch's mind, the hunter laughed and said, "Yup. It was the very last round in the magazine that bagged him."

One bullet, Hutch thought. *Only one bullet to end it all.*

Ahead, shadow gave way to light as he approached another clearing. Maybe it was the gunfire or the crunching of his own feet through the forestscape or his pulse pounding in his ears, but he did not hear the Hummer's engine at all. It simply appeared, a yellow blur in the clearing directly in front of him. It slid to a stop. The front passenger door opened. He did not wait to see who emerged. Instead, he veered right and ran parallel to the edge of the woods.

The machine gun and hunting rifle finally stopped. Either they had emptied their magazines or the shooters had realized they were firing in the direction of the Hummer. This was his chance to get away, despite the nearness of the hunters and the vehicle. He suspected these inexperienced shooters would not angle toward his new trajectory. Instead, they would go to the Hummer for fresh orders, maybe more ammo. The time it took them to do that was all he needed to covertly change directions or find a place to hide.

Hide, hide, hide.

The word gave him an idea.

17

He angled closer to the edge of the woods and peered out into
the clearing. The meadow ended a hundred yards farther along in the
direction he was heading. The woods banked around in an L shape.
That would allow him to continue north without having to risk traversing an open area. He guessed that the hunters, after hearing from
Declan, would reenter the woods where they had last seen him.

No problem. He had all the lead he needed.

He looked back along the edge of the meadow. The Hummer was
nowhere in sight. He moved deeper into the woods, into the shadows.
The forest consisted mostly of spruce trees, tall, heavily needled evergreens. A few firs offered variety, along with the tree that would best
suit his purpose: birch. While birches tended to grow together, usually
in areas where fire had cleared out the evergreens, some old ones had

remained after the spruces had reclaimed their ground. He saw one of these now and stopped at its trunk. He scanned the canopy above him: heavy with foliage, which was doubly effective for his plan because of both leaf coverage and the resulting dark shadows. The birch's leaves were yellow-green with tinges of orange. Soon they would fall away, but for now the tree was fully clothed.

Hutch slung his bow over his shoulder. Gripping the back of the tree, he pushed his toes against the front and climbed. It was a skill kids acquired and adults lost, unless you were a hunter looking for a vantage point from which to shoot. He hoisted himself higher and higher until heavy branches stopped him. He swung a leg over a branch and pulled himself up onto it. He turned, pressing his back to the trunk. The branch itself was too uncomfortable for an extended wait and failed to provide a stable firing position.

From a pouch on his utility belt, he withdrew a spare coil of bow-string. He listened for his pursuers. When no sounds reached him, he leaned out to a long, rope-sized branch coming out of an adjacent limb on his left. He bent it down and under his perch, then pulled it up on the other side. He used string to tie it to another limb on his right. The looping branch gave him a thin but solid place to rest his feet, taking some of the weight off his rump and stabilizing his entire body.

Hutch had once hunted in the Rockies with a man named Max. This man was much more serious about the sport than he was at the time. Max, camo'd the way Hutch was now, had set out on an early-morning hunt. After a leisurely breakfast, Hutch had gone to their appointed meeting place and found no Max. He had searched for an hour before hearing Max call his name. Still he could not spot his hunting partner.

"In the tree . . . not that one. To your left . . . there. See me?"

He had not. Max waved, and only then could Hutch make out the vague shape of a body sitting in a camouflaged tree stand. Hutch believed the setup he had just rigged was even more invisible than that tree stand had been.

Stably seated, he once more got his bow in hand. He removed an arrow from its quiver and nocked it onto the string. As the shaft passed the hand that held the bow, he used a finger to hold it there. He knew from practice that from this position he could draw and release with fair accuracy in three seconds.

He wasn't a killer, though he did believe he could kill in self-defense. After all, he hailed from Colorado, the "make my day" state. It was a common joke, but he wondered if even 10 percent of the people who said it could truly kill someone in the heat of the moment. He had even heard of police officers and soldiers who couldn't pull the trigger.

Wouldn't self-preservation kick in? He could not imagine enduring an attack without fighting back.

He waited.

He closed his eyes and concentrated on slowing his racing pulse and his too-quick breaths. He was the tree, ageless and unaffected by the events around it. He sat still, hearing not his own exhalations or even the slightest creak from the branches upon which he sat. Not vying for attention against the actions of survival, his injuries now made themselves known. His elbow throbbed, his knee felt swollen, and his forehead radiated waves of pain into his skull.

Still, he sat silent and unmoving. The now-shallow rise and fall of his chest, the bead of perspiration that dripped over his temple and found his jawline—the only movements he allowed. The leaves around him fluttered as a breeze passed.

He wanted to ponder exactly what he had seen, to figure out what was going on. But anything that distracted him meant the difference between life and death.

So he waited.

And they came.

He heard them first, crunching over the ground cover—more quietly than they had moved before, but still not silently enough to call themselves hunters.

Though hunters they were. Hutch did not want to make the mistake of thinking of them in any other way. They were hunters hunting him.

The driver came into view. The weapon he carried was like nothing Hutch had seen before. Hued olive green, it was a metal rectangle, the height and thickness of a hardcover book and three times as long. A handle and trigger assembly jutted from the bottom in the center of its length. It was a mean-looking weapon.

If the hunter continued on a straight path, he would walk within twenty feet of Hutch's tree. The man's head rotated like a searchlight, scanning, but he never looked down where Hutch may have left tracks. And he never looked up. If he did, Hutch would loose an arrow into his chest. He thought about doing it anyway, reducing his enemies by one. But depending on where—

There: another hunter. The teenage boy. So young, but appearing much, much older because of the sniper's rifle he carried. He passed through a ray of sunlight. The metal studding his face glinted. He would pass on the other side of the tree, closer. Hutch wondered how they had come to be so close. Perhaps they spotted some sign of his passage, or they had instinctively patrolled the darkest part of the woods. Maybe it hadn't been instinct but the correct assumption that he would stick to these areas.

If he shot one of these men, either in self-defense or as a preventive measure, the other would blast him out of the tree before he could draw a second arrow. Unless . . .

Think it through, he told himself.

Unless the surviving hunter witnessed only his fallen partner and not Hutch, not the place from which he struck.

I can do it, he thought. *Just take them out, right here, right now.* Why not? They were killers. They wanted him dead. Who knew what other crimes they had committed, what other people they had terrorized . . . or what people they *would* yet terrorize.

Another man came into view.

No, not a man. It was the boy, the one who had retrieved his arrow from the field. He carried a pistol, but it seemed heavy in his hand. He swung it lethargically beside his leg.

"Bad," the boy whispered. "*Bad.*"

The driver snapped his head back. "What?" he said harshly.

"I gotta pee," the boy said. He tucked his pistol into the back of his jeans.

"Now?" the man named Bad asked.

"Yeah."

Bad jabbed a finger at him. "Hold it."

The man passed directly under Hutch. The metal-faced teen shrugged at the boy and followed.

The boy watched them leave, his shoulders slumped. There was no way Hutch would be able to put an arrow in that kid. But if he were forced to shoot one of these people, he did not know how he could avoid going after all three. As soon as one went down, the others would certainly start firing. If his arrows found Bad and the teen, could he convince the boy to run away? Would he run on his own? Remembering Declan, his smirk, the coolness that was really icy cold, the authority he possessed over the others, he believed the boy would not want to return to him empty-handed and unharmed.

The boy walked to a tree and unzipped.

Hutch turned to find the teen and Bad. They were directly behind him, moving off. Gently, he shifted on the tree limb to follow their departure. The branch he had tied slipped out of the knot. It whipped back into place. He nearly fell but reached back and grabbed the trunk. Panicked, he looked down.

Still in the posture of relieving himself, the boy was looking up at him. His eyes were wide, his mouth open in astonishment. Hutch stared back, feeling the weight of his bow in his left hand, feeling the nocked arrow under his index finger. Camouflaged and clinging to a tree high above, he must have appeared gnomelike to the boy.

"What was that?" Bad said, a loud whisper.

The boy looked at his companions. "I stepped on something," he said.

Hutch rotated his neck enough to see the man shake his head.

"I told you, hold it. Now come on." He walked on.

The boy's eyes returned to Hutch. He had regained his composure. His face was unreadable, implacable. He was only now outgrowing childish cuteness, and he wasn't quite handsome. He would be someday, Hutch thought—if he lived long enough.

The kid zipped up and started to walk away. He stopped, glanced up. Almost imperceptibly, he shook his head. "They won't stop looking," he whispered, so faintly Hutch may have misheard. He moved on.

Hutch lifted a foot and put it on the branch. Slowly he stood, turning as he did. He leaned his chest against the tree and peered around it to watch the boy. He extended the bow past the tree and, with the other hand, slipped his fingers onto the string.

The boy caught up with the other two.

Here it comes, Hutch thought. He would shoot Bad first. He seemed the most dangerous. Then the teen. He'd decide what to do about the boy when the time came.

But nothing came. The boy apparently held his tongue. The three fanned out and slowly disappeared from sight, swallowed by shadow and the shattered geometry of a thousand branches.

Hutch waited a long time, thirty minutes or more. He listened for their return. Listened for someone trying to circle around him. He glassed the vicinity three hundred and sixty degrees. He spotted a fox, a coyote, two rabbits, and a squirrel. But no men, no boys.

18

Hutch descended from the tree. On the ground, he cast one last long gaze after his hunters. No sign. He headed in the opposite direction.

He had expected to make a wide circuitous arc through the woods and over the hills to eventually return to camp without these men on his trail. Or to run until the hunters gave up and then make the long trek back to camp. Hiding in the tree and allowing his pursuers to pass had saved many hours and miles. He wound back through the trees, stopping frequently to listen for human sounds—walking, talking, the roar of their vehicle.

When his route required him to cross open areas, he sprinted through them, ready to drop into the tall grass or suddenly tack in another direction. He kept an ear tuned and an eye peeled for the

Hummer. Part of his mind listened for the *whoosh-crack* that preceded the explosions. Of course, it preceded them by nanoseconds; hearing it would not save him, if this time Declan's aim was right on.

The morning's hike to the spot where the caribou exploded had taken hours, mostly due to the slow progress of finding prey and then stealthily approaching it. Getting back to camp should take only a fraction of that time, especially if he didn't need to evade the men in the Hummer. He passed familiar landmarks: a marsh of rushes and cattails surrounded by red willow shrubs and swamp birches; a rocky creek running like a liquid spine down the center of a grassy meadow; a steep ravine that forced him a quarter mile out of his way. He found a game trail that he had followed for some time earlier, heading the other direction. Traversing the trail was as much a reprieve to his legs and lungs, after slogging through the untamed wilderness, as a sidewalk would be after pushing through miles of heavy surf.

He was making good time.

Then he heard the Hummer, just a ghost of its engine, maybe near, maybe not. Perhaps to the south or to the north. It was impossible to tell.

Hutch came off the trail and pushed through the woods until they thinned out, eventually becoming a wide open area that sloped steeply toward the Fond du Lac River.

There it was. Across a half-mile span of grass. It was coming up from farther below, closer to the river, as though it had already passed this area once. It moved slowly, like a territorial beast searching for intruders. Hutch stepped back, deeper into the gloom, and crouched. He glassed the vehicle. Declan was harnessed into one of the pedestaled chairs, gazing into the woods on that far side. The girl occupied the other chair in the truck's bed. She appeared to be reading a magazine. With the tinted windows up, Hutch was blind to occupants in the cab; he knew, however, that they were not blind to him. He did not believe he was visible in the shadows, in the woods, camo'd as he was. His binoculars sported antiglare ruby lenses. Still, these assailants seemed preternaturally sensitive to his whereabouts.

How, for instance, had they known to reverse direction and look for him here? Had the boy finally told them about seeing him in the tree, and from that they figured he'd have headed away from them? He had no clue what the boy's relationship was with the older man, but Declan had seemed belittling and hard to please. And the boy had acted dejected. It was difficult to imagine him subjecting himself to Declan's wrath for not having alarmed them earlier. Besides, looking down from the tree, he had detected two distinct emotions in the boy's eyes after the fear and surprise had passed: weariness and defiance. Neither led Hutch to believe his decision to keep quiet would be temporary or a ploy.

How they had come to this area was not as important as the fact that they were here. Camp was not far off. Just over a ridge. The midday sky, even in autumn, was bright, so he didn't think smoke from a fire would be easily seen. But it could be smelled and possibly honed in on, depending on wind conditions and the tracking abilities of his pursuers. On this last point, he had been optimistic that they were neophytes; now that they had come this close after heading in the wrong direction, he wasn't so sure.

Half standing, he crept backward, feeling the ground's stability before putting his weight into each step. When he felt he was sufficiently hidden by foliage, he turned and hurried back to the game trail. He followed the path around the ridge. On his left, he passed a trail of beaten-down grass made yesterday by him, David, Terry, and Phil as they carried their gear from where the helicopter had dropped them off to the campsite. He suddenly recognized the berm over which lay their site. He raced up the hill, through the trees, now seeing campfire smoke undissipated this close to its source.

Terry squatted beside the campfire, attending to a frying pan. Its contents smoked and sizzled. He looked up at Hutch's approach.

"Hutch!" he yelled. "Look! I caught two grayling."

Hutch rushed up to him, a finger to his lips. "Shhhh, shhhh."

"What?" Terry said, standing, reacting to his friend's panicked expression.

Hutch kicked the grate from over the fire. The frying pan tumbled into the dirt.

"Hey—!"

Hutch grabbed Terry's arm and pressed the gloved palm of his other hand to his friend's mouth. "I'll explain in a minute," he whispered. "Just keep quiet. We have to get out of here."

When Terry nodded, Hutch released him, tugged off his gloves, and threw them down. He stretched one foot into the fire pit to break up the pyramid of kindling, then he stepped in and began stomping the fire out.

"What's going on?"

He turned to see Phil on his hands and knees in the tent, his head pushed through the opening.

"Shhhh," Hutch said, but Phil was already talking.

"Some kind of First Nation thing? Do you do that when your hunt is successful or when it's not?"

Hutch leaped out of the fire pit and dropped to his knees in front of Phil. In a harsh whisper he said, "Listen, some people are after me, bad people, really bad. They're nearby, so be quiet. We have to go now."

Phil's soft cheeks rose, pushed up by a big smile. "Yeah, right," he said. "I suppose you violated some ancient burial ground, and now they want to—"

As he had done with Terry, he slapped his palm over Phil's mouth. "I'm serious, Phil. These guys shot at me with a machine gun and a rifle. They want to kill me and anyone else they find, I think."

He did not mention the weapon that had caused the caribou to explode. Phil would not have believed him and would have continued to resist Hutch's plans, not wanting to feel duped if they were revealed as an elaborate joke.

"Now come on. We have to go. Do you have your boots on?"

"No, I—"

"Get them on. Now! Grab a jacket."

He turned to Terry. "Get your jacket, Terry." He quickly scanned the campsite, the edge of the woods around it, the slope down to the river. "Where's David?" he asked. His level of panic ratcheted up, a feat he had not thought possible.

Terry pointed. "He's still fishing. We found a great—"

"We gotta get him. We gotta go."

Phil had not emerged from the tent. "Phil!" he called.

"My shoes," Phil answered.

"Now!"

Hutch tried to think. If they could not make it back to the campsite, what would they need? Everything, really, he thought. It was not as though they had brought luxuries. The tents and sleeping bags were required gear in the far north in autumn. The nights could get deathly cold, but lugging them now, while running from killers, seemed more than stupid.

He grabbed his rucksack beside the tent and handed it to Terry. "Put some stuff in here. Only essentials."

Hutch leaned into the tent. Phil was tying his second boot.

"Hand me the first aid kit," Hutch said.

Phil did. "This is for real?" he asked.

His expression told Hutch he had started to believe it.

"Very real." He gripped his friend's knee. "We can do this, Phil. These guys, they're mostly young. They're punks. We can beat them. Right now, we just have to go somewhere they can't find us. Then we'll figure out what to do next. Okay?"

"Yeah," Phil said, unsure.

"Got your pills?" The last thing they needed was for Phil to stroke out.

Phil rummaged around, pushing aside candy bar wrappers, beer cans, a paperback novel. Then he held up a waterproof plastic cylinder.

"Put them in your jacket," Hutch instructed. "Let's go."

Terry was coming out of his and David's tent. Hutch reached for the sack.

"I'll carry it," Terry said, slinging it over his shoulder. "You got your bow?"

Hutch handed him the first aid kit. "Thanks. Ready? Let's get David." He looked from one man to the other. "No talking, okay? If you see a yellow Hummer or anyone on foot, hide. Drop straight to the ground if that'll get you out of sight. Then, if you can, signal the rest of us. Quietly."

"What's this about, Hutch?" Terry asked.

"I don't know, Ter." He shook his head. "Weird stuff. Definitely. But I do know these guys are killers. They won't hesitate to take you down. And, Ter, I told Phil, some of them are just kids. Don't let that fool you."

"What do you mean, kids?"

"Kids. Teenagers. One boy looks twelve or thirteen. I think he's in way over his head, doesn't want to be here but is. There's a girl who looks fifteen or so. Another boy seventeen, eighteen. The rest are adults, in their twenties."

"How many?"

"Six that I saw. Could be more." He turned to leave, but Terry stopped him.

"And what are they doing?"

"Killing things!" Hutch said in a stage whisper. He was growing frustrated, anxious to put ground between them and Declan's gang. "They shot at me. They gotta be insane or on drugs or hiding something pretty big. Honestly, I hope I never find out. If I do, I hope it's by seeing it on Fox. Know what I'm saying? Now . . . *where is David?*"

Terry hesitated only a few seconds longer. Absorbing this information, his face reflected puzzlement, then concern. Then it hardened in a fierce display of resolution. He was a terrible poker player but a good man to have on your side in a pinch.

"About a half mile from here, the river cuts into a deep valley," he said. "Looked like some nice, deep pools down there, so we checked it out. Good fishing. That's where I left him." Without waiting for a response, he brushed past Hutch and charged up the berm.

Hutch patted Phil on the arm. "Keep up," he said and ran after Terry.

19

Over the berm, Terry cut left, opposite the direction Hutch had taken to hunt that morning. In a single file they followed the terrain as it rose and fell, twisted and turned, sometimes catching a game trail, other times on near-virgin turf. The only evidence of humans were tracks and broken branches from the few times Terry and David had trodden through. When it felt that they had jogged considerably farther than a half mile, Terry turned up an embankment and stopped.

Way below them the Straight River churned through boulders, draped over small falls, and eddied into calm, glistening pools. Under Hutch's feet, the ground sloped steeply, but not impassibly, to the water. The earth here appeared to be mostly gravel and sand. Hutch wondered if the hill on which he stood had been formed by an esker. Eskers often acted as filters, eliminating clay and soil to eventually deposit the kind of granules they found on this slope.

At the bottom of the gorge and to their left, where the river narrowed and calmed, stood David. He was on the far side of the river, whipping a rod back and forth, making the fly dance along the water. The line looped up, catching the wind and fluttering down again. David's movements were those of a master choreographer; the rod and line seemed somehow poetic, artistic, a painter with his brush, a ballerina perfecting a *grand jeté*. He was turned sideways from them, intently watching for the strike that would land his lunch.

Behind him lay the mirror image of the slope under Hutch's feet. His eyes followed it up to where it plateaued at his own elevation. A glint caught his eye. He looked farther left, and his heart stopped. The Hummer was parked at the top of that opposite slope, parallel to the edge; visible to Hutch were its front grille and right side.

The husky cameraman knelt at the front bumper, filming into the river valley, filming David. Behind him stood the black man the boy had called Bad. He appeared to be dancing in place, gyrating his hips and shaking invisible maracas. Declan was leaning as far sideways in the safari chair as its harness would allow. His head was beyond the side of the bed. The smirk Hutch had witnessed earlier had been replaced by concentration and calculation. He was holding the device he had fiddled with before the explosion that had almost taken out Hutch behind the bush.

"No," Hutch said under his breath. Then a loud scream: "No!" He waved his arms and yelled again.

Declan spotted him. Now a grin stretched his lips. He returned his attention to the device and to David.

"David!" Hutch yelled and leaped off the edge. His feet hit the gravelly slope. He slipped, landed on his back, started sliding. He gained his feet and continued his graceless jaunt down. Sand and gravel slid out from under his boots in little avalanches. Again he yelled to David, who was oblivious to the danger above him and to Hutch's warnings.

The iPod, Hutch thought, cursing it.

Running-sliding-tumbling, Hutch continued to yell.

Finally David noticed him. He smiled and waved.

"Run, David, run!"

David tugged an earbud out of his ear. "What?"

"Run!"

At the Hummer, Declan had lost his smile. He was holding the device up and looking between it and David intently.

"Don't!" Hutch yelled. "Don't—"

W*hoosh-crack.* David exploded.

Water and sand and gravel flew up. Hutch covered his eyes with his arm. He slid farther down the embankment. Pebbles pelted him. Hot air washed over him, carrying the scent of scorched earth and ozone.

The dust and smoke settled, and there was David. He was intact, half in, half out of the river. His legs and most of his torso were on the stony bank, as though he'd lain down to quench his thirst. He was lifting himself with one arm from the river, stunned, bleeding.

"David!" Hutch leaped farther down the slope, almost there. He stopped.

Declan was staring at that device, down at the injured man. He was not finished here.

"Stop, no!" Hutch yelled.

Another explosion. Water geysered up. False rain sprayed up, down—along with bits of rock and sand and what else Hutch didn't want to know. Squinting through mist, steam, smoke, he saw the river rushing to fill the void the explosion had left. The swirling waters were opaque with mud and a rich scarlet. The boulder on which David had lain was scorched and cracked. Hutch glared up at Declan. In his heart, white-hot hate wrestled with shock and loss.

A camera had grown the body of a man and was kneeling, watching.

Hutch's stomach rolled. This was beyond murder, beyond depravity. It felt as wrong as ritual human sacrifice.

He recognized a pattern to Declan's movements, to the way he fiddled with the device, to his facial expressions. He was still not finished here.

Hutch was next.

He reached behind him to unsling his bow. As he did, he glanced up to see Terry frantically rummaging through the rucksack. Phil was not visible, but his cries of anguish and bewilderment poured down from over the edge. Hutch swung back to face Declan, plucking an arrow from the bow's quiver. He nocked it, knowing the Hummer was too far, the angle too impossible for an arrow to hit its mark. Still, he would not die without at least trying to stop his killer. If he was to join David, he wanted his last vision to be of an arrow sailing at the man who sent him there.

He took a bead on Declan's head as the man's eyes snapped from him to whatever he held. He plucked the bowstring. The arrow sailed straight toward Declan. Then it dropped, thunking into the slope. It kicked up a puff of dust and loosened a trickle of gravel. The man-camera twisted to catch the arrow's pathetic landing. After a moment, it turned its attention back to Hutch.

Declan had paused to watch. Now he smiled and returned to his work.

A shot rang out, then another and another. The window of the Hummer's rear passenger door shattered. Briefly, the startled face of the girl appeared in the opening before dropping out of sight.

Declan's head snapped up. Hutch followed his gaze to the top of his own slope—to Terry, who held a pistol in two hands. He was screaming and pulling the trigger as fast as he could.

At the Hummer, Declan pounded his palm on the roof. Bad ran around to the driver's side. The man-camera suddenly morphed into a man with a camera at the end of his arm. He disappeared through the passenger door.

Two bullets plunked into the vehicle's metal, both on the side of the bed. Declan was rocking back and forth in the chair, secured by the harness, yelling, "Go, go, go!" In a flash, the Hummer was gone.

20

Shots continued to ring out. Hutch wondered if the fleeing Hummer was still in Terry's sight. He looked up. The gun fired.

Terry, in his rage and enthusiasm, stepped off the edge. The gun went off and flew out of his hands. He tumbled and tumbled. Finally his hands flailed out, slowing his descent. On his back, head down-slope, arms out in a posture of crucifixion, Terry slid, pushing sand and gravel ahead of him. A deep groove trailed behind. When he stopped, he didn't move. He appeared dead.

"Terry!" Hutch called. He slung his bow. He dug and crawled up the unstable slope to his friend.

Terry opened his eyes. "David," he said, slow, sad.

"I know," Hutch said, then added, "You saved my life."

Terry smiled weakly. He shrugged and slid a foot before Hutch stopped him. "Least I could do," Terry said.

Hutch stood. He pulled the other man up by his jacket and kept holding him until his feet found a way to maneuver on earth that was as unearthlike as quicksand. Together they trudged up the slope. The climb required more steps than the distance seemed to call for because of the slope's insistence on bringing them down one step for every two they took. Hutch broke off from the two-man team they had formed to retrieve the pistol. He rotated it in his hands. It was a Colt 911 semi-automatic. The slide had locked in the open position, meaning it had spent every round.

When he and Terry reached the top, they collapsed in exhaustion. Down the short embankment on the other side, Phil sobbed. They were great racking cries no man should ever hear, let alone produce. Hutch felt that Phil was expressing grief for all of them. Hutch himself was numb. He ached for David and knew that a time would come when he would express it as thoroughly as Phil. But that time was not now.

He sat up, and Terry joined him. Hutch handed him the gun. "Where did you get that?"

"Snuck it in."

"You brought it into the country?" He knew he had. Except for Terry's clandestine diversion to the tobacco store in La Ronge, when the rest of them thought he'd hit the bathroom, the four had been together since leaving Denver. "You know how serious Canada takes its gun laws?"

"You're kidding, right?" Terry thumbed the lever that snapped the slide back into its resting position. He ejected the magazine, examined it. He slapped it back into the grip. He said, "What I care about now is that I'm out of ammo."

"You brought only one magazine?"

"Didn't think I'd need even that. I figured maybe we'd have to scare away a bear or something—not stop a bunch of mad youths from blowing you to kingdom come."

"Well, keep it," Hutch suggested. "They don't know we're out, and we might be able to get more ammo."

"In town?" Terry asked.

Hutch nodded slowly, thinking. "We gotta get help. And after what just happened, I don't want to be without protection until we're either back home or those guys are in jail."

He slapped Terry on the arm. He rose, feeling every bruise and cut and mile of running, every tumble he took. He scampered down to Phil, whose sobs had subsided into hitching breaths. He was curled up in a fetal position, facedown. His head was lowered and his arms covered it, as though he expected blows from heavy fists, maybe godly fists. His glasses lay in the dirt. Hutch knelt beside him and rubbed his back.

"I know," he said gently. He caught Terry's eyes to include him in the conversation. "Listen. I interviewed a guy who ran a survival school. I even went through it—not the whole thing, but I got the gist."

"I remember that," Terry said.

"Yeah. Before he started this outdoor training course, he was a federal accident investigator. Plus he wrote about these dramatic rescues and stuff for, I don't know, *National Geo* or something. He spent like years reading accident reports from all sorts of things: shipwrecks, people lost in the wilderness, hostage situations. He identified what traits survivors had in common—who lived, who died, and why."

Phil lifted his head. His flesh was red, his eyes redder. Tears and sweat misted his entire face. Bits of dirt and grass clung to it. Snot soaked the three-day-old stubble on his upper lip.

Hutch nodded. "The first thing survivors do is they recognize they're in a life-or-death situation. Sounds stupid, I know, but apparently people either acknowledge it way too late, or they immediately deny it. You know, 'No, no, no, this is normal. Planes are supposed to crash on deserted islands.' That sort of thing. Doesn't work. You gotta know you're in survival mode. The sooner the better."

He looked from Phil to Terry. "Gentlemen, we're in survival mode. These guys want to kill us. What we do from here on out, *everything* we do, will determine whether we get away alive . . . or not."

Phil uncoiled. He sat up on his knees. "Oh, I think David would agree that we're in a life-or-death situation." He ran the sleeve of his coat over the bottom of his face, sniffed. "But, Hutch . . . tell me what he did wrong. What did David do to not survive?"

Hutch frowned. "That's different. You can't help what you don't know about. They sucker punched us, that's all. That won't happen again."

Phil's face reddened further, from apple to chili. "How can you say that? You don't know." He waved a hand toward the river valley. "What was that? Do you know what that was? I didn't see them actually shoot anything, did you? So what was that?" He snatched up his glasses, stood, and glared down at Hutch.

So many emotions were raging through Phil, through all of them, that Hutch wouldn't be able to sort them out if he had an hour to do it.

Phil climbed the embankment and looked down to where David had ceased to be. He glanced at Terry, sitting at his feet, then back to Hutch. "Like you said, we can't defend against something we know nothing about. You can't say it won't happen again."

"So, what?" Hutch said, standing. "We lie down and die? We find those guys and turn ourselves over to them? What, Phil? What do you think we should do?"

Faced with having to define action and not simply ramble about the odds against them, Phil had nothing to say. He stood there ready to spew wisdom, wanting to, but in the end, he simply sighed and sat down. He brushed at the dirt clinging to his glasses.

After a minute, Terry said, "Beth. Justin and Dianne."

David's family. Hutch's guts twisted anew.

"How are we going to tell them?" Terry said. "What are they going to do?"

They didn't have even a body to bring back.

"We should all tell her," Hutch said. "We all saw it."

"If the authorities let us," Phil mumbled, not looking up from his lap.

Silence. Hutch broke it with, "They'll be okay. We'll see to it, right?"

Phil put on his glasses. He bowed his head: *Of course.*

Terry's lips formed a pained smile. "I'd like to start by meting out some justice. I can't believe I wasted all my bullets."

"Hey," Hutch said. He marched to the berm. "I told you before, Ter, you saved my life. I don't think one or two bullets would have scared those guys off. If you had stopped firing, they would have pulled out their machine guns and blown us away."

"Or redirected that thing," Phil said. "Whatever it was got David. Did you see, the guy in the truck was holding something when it happened?"

"I saw it before," Hutch agreed. "When they first came after me."

"You knew they had that weapon," said Phil, "and didn't tell us?"

"I didn't think you'd believe me, and it didn't matter. We had to leave the campsite, we had to find David, and neither of those objectives would have changed if you realized we were up against more than just hillbillies with popguns."

"So what *are* we up against?"

Hutch shook his head.

"What I do know," said Terry, "is they're going to come back. We chased away a monster by throwing rocks at it, but monsters always come back—usually severely ticked off."

"So what do we do?" Phil asked.

Hutch rose to his feet, putting him at eye level with Terry and Phil, who were sitting on the low berm. "We can try hiding until the helicopter comes back for us."

"That's *nine more days!*" Phil threw up his hands. "Don't you think people with weapons like that have ways of tracking down targets? Come on!"

Hutch was silent. Phil was right but he didn't want to say it.

Terry said, "That town is what, five miles from here?"

"Fiddler Falls," Hutch agreed.

"Do they have cops?" Terry asked.

"I would think so."

"And phones?"

"Satellite phones."

"Wait a minute," Phil said. "Where did these guys come from?"

They looked at each other for a few moments.

"Maybe . . ." Hutch said. "Maybe some ritzy hunting lodge in the area. They *were* driving a Hummer."

"Or maybe Fiddler Falls," Phil said.

"What?" said Terry. "Like they're just living in this rinky-dink backwoods town, and they happen to have a cannon or whatever it is—some weapon half the armies of the world would kill for? Does that mean the town's in on it, covering for them? No, I got it. They developed this crazy weapon worth a billion bucks on the open market, but they'd rather rent it out to fat cats who come up here and hunt humans for a thousand bucks a head. Something like that?"

"Look," Hutch said. "There's a lot we don't know. But we have to do something. I say we go look at the town, and if it looks cool, we go in."

21

The spot of the world that hosted the town of Fiddler Falls, Saskatchewan, had rolled into darkness by the time the three men reached its outskirts. A partial moon threw a bluish glow into the avenues and front yards. Hutch remembered finding last night's moon tranquil and as complementary to the landscape as an art lamp was to a Renaissance masterpiece. This one made everything appear sinister: the shadows were deeper and normal objects somehow seemed unreal, as though they were painted props. In fact, much of what the three of them encountered reminded Hutch of a *Twilight Zone* episode.

Intuition got Hutch off the road to walk over yards, close to the trees and eventually the houses. Terry and Phil joined him without comment. The first house they passed, a rustic A-frame, was dark, without even the blue flicker of a television set in its windows.

"We should knock," Terry said.

"What if the townspeople are in on it?" Phil replied.

"I just can't see that."

"Until today, could you see your friend blowing up without apparent cause?"

"Let's move on," Hutch said.

As they drew nearer to the town, houses appeared more frequently, and it became clear that something was rotten in Fiddler Falls. By Hutch's count, only two rooms burned with light out of the eight houses they passed.

"Have you noticed all the garage doors are open?" Terry said.

"Why close them in a town so small that everyone knows each other?" Phil said. "Till snowfall, anyway."

"Hold on a sec." Terry jogged into one of the dark garages. He returned a minute later, looking glum. "That truck in there, its hood is up. I couldn't see anything, but I reached in and felt a mass of wires. They'd been cut."

Hutch glanced up the dirt road toward what he believed was the town center. Now he noticed that each of the three vehicles in view, either on the road or in a driveway, had a raised hood.

"You still think the town's in on it?" Hutch asked.

"What town? This is a ghost town," Phil said. "I do think we should see if anyone's home. Maybe some people are hiding from whatever caused this."

"If they are," Hutch said, "they're not going to answer for us. They might even shoot through the door."

"I would," Phil agreed.

"And if they are home and do answer," continued Hutch, "I wouldn't trust them any farther than I could throw you."

"Hey."

"No, seriously. If this whole town got evacuated or kidnapped or killed, how could you trust anyone *not* evacuated or kidnapped or killed?"

"Okay," said Terry. "How about we break in, see what we can find?"

"Same problem as knocking," said Hutch. "What if you enter the wrong house and get blown away by some poor soul who thinks you're one of them? Let's keep looking."

"For what?" asked Phil.

"People, a phone, a radio . . ."

"Guns, ammo," added Terry.

"Speaking of that," said Phil, "shouldn't you get that ready?" He was looking at the bow rising up from Hutch's back.

"And do what with it?" asked Hutch, but he slung it into his hands. He gazed at it the way Terry might have at his bulletless gun— a lot of potential but of little practical use.

"Shoot the bad guys," said Phil; he could have added, *Duh*?

"I'm thinking we're a little outgunned," Hutch said.

"Anything's better than nothing," said Phil. "Who would have thought a real estate agent with a six-shooter could have saved your butt, when the guy with the invisible grenade wanted to blow it off?"

"At this point I'll take a sharp pencil," said Terry.

"That's the spirit, Terry," Hutch said. "Survivors keep their heads. They don't get panicky. Some people keep flipping through a sort of mental photo album to remember what they have waiting for them back home; others count or do puzzles in their heads. But the number one thing survivors do, that guy said, is they keep their sense of humor. They joke about things you wouldn't think are funny—how they'll give a bear indigestion or how their corpse will be found with its skeletal middle finger raised to the belated rescuers."

It was Terry's way to say things in a slightly twisted manner, but

Hutch knew he really meant that he'd take a pencil. Had Terry not had the gun, Hutch believed he would have been throwing rocks at Declan until all four friends were nothing but little bits of the circle of life in the Canadian wilderness.

As if to prove the point, Terry said, "I'm more afraid of the guy with the invisible grenades than I am of some old lady with a gun. I'll kick the doors in and take my chances." He started for a home.

Hutch grabbed his arm. "Whoa, the noise will just draw attention to us. And besides, don't you think the people who went to the trouble of disabling every vehicle would have cleared the houses of anything that could hinder their plans?"

Terry thought about that. "Okay," he said reluctantly. "So we hit Main Street and see what's what."

Without a word they continued farther into town. After a few minutes, Phil stopped. He peered up at the sky. Hutch and Terry joined him. Curtains of colors rippled across the sky: David's *Revontulet*. They continued on. The houses gave way to the first public building: a school. It was dark and deserted, as it probably should have been at this hour anyway. The school was on their left. It faced the street that intersected the one they were on, but instead of dirt, it was paved and about twice the width.

"Provincial Street, Terry," Phil said, reading a sign.

"So?"

"You called it Main Street. This is obviously their main boulevard." He gestured toward the businesses along the street.

"Okay, listen," Hutch said. "We came down from the north, a little west of town. Fiddler Falls sits on the northern bank of the Fond du Lac. That means the river is south, that way." He pointed right. "Whatever commerce they have, whatever services, will be that way."

In that direction, across the dirt road from the school, was a large

Victorian house. On the front lawn beside the walkway was a metal sign hung between two wrought iron posts capped by horses' heads. The sign read KRAMER'S ROOM AND BOARD, INQUIRE WITHIN.

"A boardinghouse," Terry said. "I'll bet the door is unlocked, at least into the common areas, the living room, kitchen."

"I don't like it," Hutch said, hoping they wouldn't have this debate at every house they passed. "What if Declan's gang are outsiders, and this is where they're staying? Are you ready to confront them?"

Terry shook his head. "Not enough intel yet." He was tenacious but not rash.

In the distance a dog barked. It was answered by another, deeper bark. Then another.

"Hear that?" Hutch asked.

"The dogs?" Terry shook his head. *So what?* he thought.

"Where are they?"

Terry listened. "Up in the hills."

"Not in town," Hutch confirmed. "Places like this, they have dogs galore. But they're all out of town."

"Like something scared them," Phil said.

They started up Provincial. The moon had risen high enough to cast its glow into the town's shallow valley of buildings. The men remained close to the buildings, where the shadows were darkest. They passed a tackle store. The only light inside emanated from an illuminated clock advertising fishing line. Across the street was a church, St. Bartholomew's. Its stones and mortar made it a hulking, solid part of the landscape, more like the hills than anything Fiddler Falls had to offer. They passed another Victorian house. A sign identified it as the office of Dr. Anson Jeffrey. Directly across Provincial, a less impressive house proclaimed itself the MOOSE MOUTH RESTAURANT.

"Say that three times," Terry whispered.

Hutch thought that even on a Tuesday evening, this of all places would be hopping. No lights shone through any of the windows. The next building they passed was a windowless box, marked as the LODGE FOR THE BENEVOLENT AND PROTECTIVE ORDER OF ELKS OF CANADA.

Terry leaned close to Hutch. "Get real! Have you ever seen an empty Elks Lodge?"

"I think we know by now," Hutch said. "Something's happened to this town."

"Something awful," Phil said, pointing up the street.

Hutch saw what was there all along for him to see had he not been so preoccupied with the inhabitancy of each building. A block away on the right side, a burned-out car seemed crushed into the asphalt. In fact, the street directly in front of them had been damaged, seemingly by something incredibly heavy falling onto it. A circle, four or five feet in diameter, was recessed into the pavement. Fissures radiated from the circle like capillaries in bloodshot eyes. Just outside this circle, closest to their position, lay a single boot. Hutch's stomach cramped, and he walked closer.

"Hutch," Terry cautioned.

He held his hand up, hoping for silence and a moment to confirm his suspicion. The boot, what he used to call a "clodhopper," lay sideways on the street, the tread visible. As he neared, he saw that a sock extended from the boot, an ankle joint clearly visible beneath. The sock disappeared into a pant leg, which extended six inches and ended right at the lip of the depression. Not wanting to see but wanting to know, he walked around the perimeter of the depression until the other side of the pant leg was visible. Even having prepared himself, his stomach cramped and his mind reeled. Inside the pant leg was a human leg, severed midcalf. Flesh, muscle, bone—all of it as well defined as an anatomical cutaway in a medical school.

144

The deserted town, already menacing, took on another level of foreboding. Suddenly, Hutch felt watched. The air seemed to thicken. Bad things had happened here, and he sensed they were happening still. He returned to Terry and Phil under the shadowy eve of the Elks Lodge.

"It's a foot," he said. "Part of a leg."

"What?" Phil's voice had risen in pitch. Not yet panicky, but close.

"No blood. Not even on the pant where the leg was cut."

"Like they dressed it after it was cut off?" Phil asked.

Terry slapped his arm with the back of his hand. "No. Like it was instantly cauterized." He looked at Hutch. "Right?"

Hutch pointed at Terry, lost in thought. "Yeah . . . like that."

"I've been thinking about this," Terry said. "The man in the truck, Declan, he's got this controller or communicator that's somehow connected to the explosions, but we don't see anybody shooting or throwing a bomb. What's that mean?"

Hutch and Phil shook their heads.

"Something's coming from the sky," he continued. "Maybe a mortar, shot off somewhere far away. But that doesn't explain not seeing it before it goes off. Or a plane, way overhead, out of sight. This Declan guy tells it where to shoot, and down comes some kind of missile or rocket or something."

Hutch nodded. It sounded right.

Terry held up a finger. He wasn't done. "Or something a little more far-out. I read about these things, these big uranium rods. They're called . . ." He searched his memory. "Um, long-rod penetrators. These things orbit the earth and can be directed to a certain place at a certain time. Then they're essentially turned off, which causes them to fall. They're going so fast that when they hit, it's like an explosion. You can take out tanks and bunkers. Maybe that's what this is."

Hutch shook his head. "That depression in the street, it's flat. These rods would go right into the ground, wouldn't they?"

"Yeah. I think."

"And it sounds like they would take some time to fall. Maybe they'd work for stationary objects. Like you said, a bunker. But Declan chased me with this."

"What about a satellite?" Phil said. "Something that can be aimed from way up there, a missile or a laser?"

"A laser?" Hutch said. "Can they do that?"

"I think so," said Terry. "It's essentially what the Space Defense Initiative is: Star Wars. Lasers on satellites that take down missiles before they reach U.S. airspace."

"I thought that got killed in Congress. No budget for it," Hutch said.

"No budget doesn't mean it can't be done or that somebody hasn't done it. The technology must be there if they were trying to get money for it."

Hutch wondered what else was going to come at him from out of the blue before this trip was over. Physically, emotionally, intellectually: he felt bombarded on all fronts. He was already totally creeped out by this town, and now Terry and Phil were suggesting there were not only eyes in the sky, but death rays as well. Maybe they should have gone to Puerto Vallarta.

Just then, the sound of an engine reached them.

Hutch darted for a breezeway between the lodge and Dr. Jeffrey's office. He entered it and crouched beside the Elks building. Terry and Phil skirted him and did the same. Hutch peered around the corner to see the Hummer appear on the cross street that had been right in front of them. It thumped up onto Provincial and turned toward the river, in the direction they had been walking. Its tires chirped and its engine roared to get the heavy truck moving faster than this tiny town had probably ever witnessed. It flew past the crushed car, crossed another intersection, and screamed to a stop midway into the next block. Hutch stood and leaned farther out. Both the driver's and passenger doors swung open.

"It's the black guy and the kid, the really young one," Hutch reported.

The two from the Hummer jogged toward the same side of the street as Hutch, Terry, and Phil. A row of businesses shielded them from Hutch's view; he heard a heavy door slam. He turned to Terry and Phil. "Something's up. They were in a big hurry."

"The Hummer guys?" Phil asked.

Hutch nodded.

Phil shook his head. "This town is theirs. They probably killed everybody in it. Now they're traipsing around their own private Idaho."

"We need to know more," Hutch said.

"Meaning what?" Phil said, his voice rising. "We go see what they're up to?"

Hutch thought about it, then said simply, "Yeah."

"No," Phil countered. "Whatever these guys have—weapons, guts, I don't know. Well, I do know something, that monster cannon-grenade thing—a satellite weapon if Ter's right! But if that's it or just the beginning of what they have . . . What I'm saying is, they took over this town. *This whole town.* Cops and all. We're no match for that."

Terry gripped his arm. "Phil, this is where I slap you and say, 'Pull yourself together, man.'"

"That's not funny. And I don't care what Hutch says about joking with death and all that. David being dead is not funny. *None* of this is funny."

Hutch said, "I didn't mean—"

Phil held up his hand. He tightened his face. "I *know* what you meant. Why aren't we running the other direction? Why aren't we heading out of this godforsaken town? Why aren't we finding a town that *hasn't* been taken over?"

"Because the nearest town is days away. The nights are freezing cold. We don't have any equipment. We can't light a fire. And these people who want to kill us are scary-good at finding what they're looking for. You want to be out there under those conditions?"

"Better than being here. I mean it. We are in a town that nobody else is in, except the people who got rid of everybody else. There has to be a way to get help. Can we head downriver along the bank until we find a boat or something? There has to be a boat."

"And if there isn't?"

"We make one."

"If you stay outside too long at night, you'll freeze to death. If you fall in the water and can't get out for ten minutes, you'll freeze to death. If you're outside day or night too long, I think these guys will find you."

"So we hole up. Find a place in town they've already searched and stay there till they leave."

Hutch thought about that. Not bad.

Terry chimed in. "Until they start using their weapon to blow up buildings. You don't think they're leaving this place intact, do you? These guys are scorched-earth warriors all the way. You can tell."

Hutch couldn't tell anything, but Terry did have a point. He thought of another one: "What if they're holding the townspeople somewhere? If we run or lie low and find out later we could have saved people who ended up dying, I couldn't live with myself."

"But you'd be alive," Phil said, his voice nearly a whine. "And what if we find out they *do* have hostages? What can we do about it? Nothing!"

"Phil, I hear what you're saying. I do," Hutch assured him. "But I can't just run. I think learning more about what we're up against is our best bet. I don't know that for sure, but I have to go with it."

Phil knew when he was beaten. He nodded.

Hutch studied his eyes a moment longer, then glanced at Terry. Without another word, he stepped around the corner and headed for the Hummer.

22

Laura pressed her ear to the door. Someone was sitting at the desk
in the office on the other side. It was the town manager's office, but
she hadn't seen or heard Buck since this all began. Whoever it was
spent a lot of time clicking away on a keyboard. Every now and then,
someone would enter and start a conversation. Often Declan was one
of the talkers. The words were indistinct. Just syllabic beats. Some
inflection—anger, emphasis. But she had recognized the cadence of
his speech: slow and casual, as though his only audience were himself.
Whenever she heard that speech rhythm, ice chilled her heart and
raced through her body. Instead of pushing it aside or letting it darken
her thoughts, she used it. She drew energy from it.

They'd received several deliveries of food—sandwiches, lukewarm
pizza. When Laura knocked, someone would come to take them to the

bathroom. They were never allowed to go together, and the small bathroom had been stripped of the toilet tank lid and mirror. At least their captors waited outside the door, letting her relieve herself in private.

During these restroom trips, Laura would be taken to one of the auditorium doors. Her escort would unlock and unchain it, then hold it open so she could see inside and the people inside could see her. Until recently, this area had served as gymnasium, meeting hall, community theater, and concert venue—local talent only; no one of any importance would ever venture to Fiddler Falls for the hundred or so people who'd turn out.

Now it was a jail. At least two hundred people milled about and slept on sleeping bags, cots, the floor. They were her friends, neighbors, people she had known for years, the children and the parents of the children she had taught or was currently teaching. As a whole, the community was normally vibrant and jovial. When she stood at the door with her captors, the eyes pointed at her were sad. Conflicting emotions rippled over their faces. They drew hope from her continued existence. At the same time, her presence reminded them of Tom and how bad things had gotten.

Three times now, Lizzie Emery had stood and called out to her. "Laura? Laura, have you seen Roland? He's not here, my Roland."

Her expression broke Laura's heart. She would simply shake her head, and her captors would slam the door.

"Mom?" Dillon was sitting against one of the shelving's upright brackets. His knees were raised in front of him, his hands clasped around them. His eyes shone in the weak light, big and scared. "What are we going to do?" he asked.

It was only a matter of time before Declan would return for another pep talk. She did not think for a moment that he would leave her or Dillon alone. Sooner or later, the same instinct that drove him to kill Tom would send him back to them. She could not bear the thought of the same man who took Tom from them having the opportunity to kill them as well . . . or worse.

She crawled to Dillon. The glass from the broken lightbulb crunched under her hands and knees. It didn't bother her. Just a reminder of the conditions to which they were subjected. She completed the trek to her son. She sat next to him, pulling him close.

"We're doing it, honey," she said reassuringly. "It just takes time." She rubbed the tips of her fingers and thumb together. They were sticky with blood. And sore.

"Are they gonna hurt us?" Dillon asked.

"No, we're gonna hurt them."

"Dad said it's not good to hurt people."

"That's true. But when you hurt somebody who is trying to hurt you, that's not wrong. Dillon, we're all made to love ourselves. That's why we try to eat right and clothe ourselves and not do things that will hurt us. When you stop someone from hurting you, it's just like that. It's something you're supposed to do."

"Can you hurt somebody who is trying to hurt somebody else?"

"If you're protecting somebody weaker, yes."

"Was Daddy protecting people when he went out to see what that explosion was?"

When Tom had left yesterday morning, she had explained to Dillon that he was leaving to do his job. It was his job to protect and serve, and he was proud to do it.

"Yes, he went because a lot of people wouldn't."

"Why wouldn't they?"

"Well . . . it's not their jobs."

He nodded.

She looked into his eyes, still red though he had not cried for hours.

He reached over and picked up her hand. He touched her fingertips, which were raw and bleeding. "Do you want me to work on it now?" he said.

"I almost got it." She kissed his forehead and stood.

She reached under a metal shelf and felt the nut and bolt that secured it to the brace, against which Dillon leaned. The pressure of his body prevented the metal from rattling and screeching on the floor. She had already removed the bolts from three of the four shelves. It was an arduous process. The bolts were rusty, but she found that if she applied steady pressure to the nut, it would eventually turn. After a few rotations, the bolt wanted to turn with the nut. She had tried holding the head of the bolt, but the smooth, round surface would slip through her fingers. Even pressing her thumb and fingernails into the bolt's slotted head would do nothing but snap off her nails. Then she discovered that if she pulled on the nut, she could hold the bolt in place while she slowly, slowly unscrewed it.

Her thumb, index, and middle fingers of both hands throbbed in pain, as though she had touched their tips to a griddle. Still, she had worked the nuts off three bolts. Only three quarters of an inch long, they were insufficient weapons, but the brace was an L-shaped, six-foot-long metal spear. Or club . . . She would decide how to use it at the time of their escape.

As she worked—feeling the bolt turn with the nut more times than not—she looked down at the top of her son's head. Her love for him, her grief for Tom, her hatred for Declan: it was a volatile mix, the way hydrogen peroxide, acetone, and sulfuric acid combined to make the binary liquid explosive that could blow an airplane out of the sky.

"Mom," Dillon said.

She was pushing her left palm into the head of the bolt and pulling the nut on the other side of the upright with all the force she could muster into the thumb and index finger of her right hand.

"Mom," he said more sharply. "They're coming."

She heard the lock snap, and she turned to the door just as it opened.

The teenage boy stepped in. He had told them his name was Kyrill one time when he had brought them sandwiches and she had asked. He had a sweet face and spoke to them gently, but he was too much under Declan's influence, and she would never forget that he had held her son when Declan cut his face.

Declan entered next. The fluorescent light behind him was bright, illuminating the front half of the room while the rear remained in shadow. He studied her, then dropped his eyes to the boy sitting at her feet. He seemed to be puzzling over the activity that would put them in that position.

She held her hands in fists, hiding her bloody fingers and thumbs. Hoping it looked to Declan like she was merely angry.

"You all right?" He said.

"What do you think?"

His eyes roamed down her body, and she felt an icy spider scamper up her spine. She crossed her arms over her chest.

"I think you're very all right," he said.

Don't go there, she thought. *I'm not ready yet, but I'll fight you to the death.* "What do you want?" she said.

He stepped closer. "A favor."

"Yeah?"

He tilted his head back toward the door. "We have a videographer here. He's shooting sort of a documentary, some footage we're going to use in a video game. He was wondering if you'd consent to an interview. You and your son." He looked down at the boy. "What's your name again?"

Dillon answered, almost inaudibly.

"Dillon," Declan repeated. "That's right." He looked up at Laura expectantly.

"You've got to be kidding," she said. When he remained silent, she continued. "Why would I do something like that?"

He took a step closer. "I thought . . . in the interest of reconciliation."

"Reconciliation?"

He smiled. "We didn't make out so well the last time we spoke. I thought you'd like to do something that showed there were no hard feelings."

She couldn't help it: she stepped over Dillon's legs and swung her hand at Declan's face.

He grabbed her wrist before she made contact. Glaring at her, he pulled her hand away. His eyes lowered to her bloody fingers. A scowl broke his icy countenance. Without releasing one wrist, he grabbed the other and twisted it. "Show me."

She loosened her fist to reveal the bloody digits on this hand as well.

He looked at Dillon, who blinked up at him, innocent and unknowing. He scanned the room, squinting into corners, at the objects on the shelves. "What have you—" he started. The handle of the open door behind him banged loudly into the wall as someone crashed into it.

"Declan!" the girl, Cortland, called.

He glared into Laura's eyes, his own moving, searching, as though reading her thoughts.

"Declan!" Cortland repeated.

"What?"

"We found them. They're in town."

His hands tightened on her wrists, pneumatic vises. Then he released his grip, spun, and headed out the door. "Where?" he snapped, passing the girl.

She hurried to follow him. "Coming into town—they're by the Elks Lodge."

Kyrill rushed out the door and slammed it, throwing Laura and Dillon back into a pool of darkness.

Declan left the supply room and headed for the hall.

"Where's the Slacker?" he said to Cortland, who was on his heels.

"Pru's room," she said.

Behind him, Declan heard the storeroom door slam shut and the lock engage. He had more crucial things on his mind, but not hearing the door shut and lock would have nagged at him. Eventually, he would have interrupted the bigger task to discover why he hadn't heard it. It was a slightly obsessive-compulsive thing that he trusted to keep loose ends from entangling his many endeavors. If, in a movie, a character opened a cabinet and walked away, it would bug him to no end that the cabinet door was never shut. But he wouldn't throw a fit and refuse to watch the rest of the movie; the compulsion wasn't disabling that way. He saw it as a skill. Sort of an extra sense—

his Spidey sense, though it wasn't as cool or powerful as Peter Parker's ability.

Just as the absence of a slamming door would have nagged at him, he would not forget to follow up on why the woman's fingers were bloody. This freed him to move on to more important matters. So while OCD tended to inhibit its sufferers, making a mess of priorities, his version of it helped him do the right thing at the right time. It was a mental notepad and security system that he hoped to develop over time.

He breezed into what the folks of Fiddler Falls had apparently used as a meeting room. It had been commandeered by his boys and turned into a bedroom and a getaway from the sound of the cattle mewing through the auditorium doors. Pruitt was sitting on the floor with his back against the far wall, the device in his hands. His ever-present camera lay on the floor beside him, a dog always at its master's side.

"When did you spot them?" Declan asked.

"Just a minute ago. Looked like moving shadows, maybe an animal. Then they crossed the street by the school, and I zoomed in."

Declan snapped his fingers and held out his hand. Simultaneously, he pointed at Cortland. "Get Bad and Julie back here now."

She pulled a gray walkie-talkie off her belt.

Pru gave the device to Declan. Known as SLCR—or Slacker—it was shaped like a horizontally oriented Palm Pilot. Buttons and thumb controls cluttered the left and right sides of its flat face. In the center, a four-inch LCD screen showed an image of the street outside. The camera was situated high above the town, so buildings were represented by their rooftops, cars looked like Matchbox toys, people were mostly heads and shoulders.

Though the screen was color, the video signal received from the satellite was black-and-white. Actually, sixty-four shades of gray, Declan thought. This allowed the lens to zoom in and focus on a newspaper headline from 280 miles in the sky. The drawback was that dark grays became black, and objects that were white or in bright areas tended to bleach out beyond recognition. Nighttime imaging was worse. Optics was not the system's strong suit.

Declan had to admit that what it was designed to do, it did well. It was like programming a video game—trial and error and one bug-fix at a time.

"Where?" he said.

"I was tracking them, heading this way. Nudge it down a bit."

Declan's thumb twitched over a knob, and the image blurred. It quickly resolved itself into a different section of Provincial.

"I don't—" But suddenly, he did see them. First one, then two, then three bodies emerging from shadow. Sticking close to one another. One broke off and stepped into the street. Declan recognized the point of interest and smiled: *Ol' Tom's mortal remains. Not much to look at, a tattered boot and piece of leg.*

After traversing the circular depression that marked the end of Tom's career as a cop, the figure paused. It moved back to the others. A moment later, they all turned to look at something, then darted back into the shadows. Declan tapped the thumb control. He watched the Hummer take the nearest corner—so fast, it appeared to nearly tip.

"Bad's back," he said. "Get your camera ready. You're going out."

Pruitt hoisted himself off the floor, yanking the camera up with him.

A door banged. Moments later, Bad rushed into the room. Julian appeared behind him.

"What, you got them?" Bad said.

Squinting at the screen, Declan said, "Just up the street, heading this way."

They were *right there*. Three little heads, swaying arms, jerky feet.

It had taken a while to get used to watching objects from directly overhead. They crossed the street a block and a half away from the community center. They were now near the site where Declan had gotten the ball rolling by blasting away that trapper and his crappy Subaru. He moved his thumb to bump away a clear plastic cover over another thumb control. He pushed down on the control, causing red crosshairs to appear. He moved the targeting optics over one of the figures. When he let go, the crosshairs disappeared.

"Ah!" he snapped in frustration. If the target had been in range, the crosshairs would have remained active. As a safety precaution, and because of a lot of technical nonsense Declan didn't understand, the designers had built into this prototype what they called PTL—proximity targeting limiter. It required the Slacker to be within two hundred yards of the intended target—sometimes closer, depending on the satellite's precise location. First thing back home, he would insist on conducting another field test without PTL—it had inhibited his desires too many times.

"We gotta get out there," he said. "Julie, you stay. Kyrill, Bad, get your—"

They held up their weapons.

"Cort, your choice."

She thought a moment. "Stay. I wanna get some food for—"

"All right," Declan said, brushing past her. As he strode along a corridor and into the vestibule, he watched the screen. At the front door, he stopped. He turned to face his crew, resting his butt on the push bar that would open the door.

"All I have to do is get close. This should take three minutes, tops."

He heaved backward, rolling off the swinging door and into the night.

24

Hutch paused in front of a used-book store to consider the car in the street. It was crushed and burned. Of course he knew what had happened to it, but he would have liked a closer look; perhaps it would offer more clues to what they were up against. Keeping him from the inspection was the Hummer. It sat in the street only a block away. Doing anything other than reconnoitering the killer's whereabouts would be akin to having a picnic within sight of a lion's den.

Terry nudged him. He gestured at something: a dog in the gutter, nearly torn in half.

They moved in single file, as close to the storefronts as window ledges, mailboxes, and various other protrusions would allow. They reached a glass door that had spiderwebbed. Clinging to the cracked pane, like an Easter decal on a broken egg, were the words

161

SASKATCHEWAN ENVIRONMENTAL RESOURCE MANAGEMENT. A picture window next to the door had lost its glass completely. Shards as long as swords lay on the sidewalk and just inside the interior.

Hutch could not see a way to avoid the glass, which he knew would crunch and snap under their feet. He turned to Terry directly behind him. "We need to move out into the street."

"It's too open," Terry whispered.

"It's that or—" He leaned sideways from his waist so that Terry could see the glass.

"I'd rather be heard than seen," Terry said. "If they're in the building on the next block, they might be watching, and anything in the street this close will be seen. We may not know it until a bullet hits one of us in the head or the cannon takes us all out."

Hutch agreed. "I can't help but feel that smashed car right there and that depression we passed in the road are the tracks of some monster, and it's close."

Phil leaned past Terry. "More like the bones of an ogre's victims scattered in front of its lair."

The image hit home.

Terry said, "I don't want to be seen *or* heard. Let's go back and around. There has to be another way to get to the next block."

"Phil?" Hutch said and gestured for Phil to turn around and lead the way back to the corner. Three steps toward it, Hutch heard the sound of a heavy commercial door opening behind him.

"Go!" he whispered. "Hurry!" Running on tiptoes, they reached the corner and turned one by one. Hutch stopped.

"Right there," he heard someone say. He felt a hand squeezing his guts. They'd been seen.

The voice continued. "I lost them in the shadows, but they were right there, right there."

Feet pounded on the pavement, growing louder.

"Wait!" demanded the same voice. "Back off."

A chime sounded, the faint tinkle of a musical tone.

Then the *whoosh-crack* explosion erupted on the street. The sidewalk under Hutch shook. He heard bricks and wood, stone and glass ripped from the storefronts and hurled in all directions. He ran toward the back of the building around which Terry and Phil had disappeared. On the main street debris rained down, forming a teetering melody.

Hutch swung around the corner and nearly crashed into Terry and Phil.

Phil's eyes were huge. He said, "Holy—"

Another explosion. The building itself vibrated. Something fell off the roof. The destruction of this one blast seemed to extend much longer than the strike itself. Like a scream of agony after a gunshot. All three of them crouched low and covered their heads with their hands. Terry slapped Hutch on the shoulder and said, "That house . . ."

Across a small dirt parking lot and grassless yard was a dark-windowed residence. Terry started for it, but Hutch grabbed his arm.

"Stick to the shadows," he said in a harsh whisper. He rose to lean over Terry and bat at Phil's head. "Stick to the shadows," he repeated. "I heard someone say he lost us in the shadows. I don't think they can see us if we stay under the eaves."

Terry said, "What do you mean, they can't see us? They're blasting at us."

"A shot in the dark," Hutch said. "Literally, a shot in the dark. I think they saw us in front of the stores and thought we were still there. Turning around saved our lives."

Terry shook his head. "Pure luck. What's going to save us next time?"

Phil chimed in. "We can't stay here. What if they blast this whole block?"

Hutch said, "I think they want to see us. They're having fun."

"Except," Terry said, "they know we're armed. They know you have a bow, and they think I have a gun. That might make them a little more trigger happy."

Hutch looked around, thinking. He didn't like staying stationary, either—on the same block, their backs pressed against the same building that the killers were bombarding. But he was convinced they couldn't see them as long as they remained in the shadows. So it was either stay there or run and expose themselves. If the men hunting them truly believed they had their prey pinned down, they would investigate, looking into the stores and eventually circling the building. The only thing slowing them down now was either their intention to continue bombing or, as Terry pointed out, their fear of getting shot.

Hutch slipped past his friends and, waddling in a low crouch, started moving along the length of the building. He let his left knee bump against the brick, assuring that he remained in the shadow of the eaves while his mind explored their options.

"Hey," Phil whipered, coming after him. "What are you doing?"

Hutch slipped his bow off his back and extracted an arrow. He stopped to nock it. "Bringing the fight to them."

Blood seeped from Laura's fingertips. She pulled on the nut and turned, pulled and turned. Declan had seen her fingers, and it would not take him long to return and find out the cause. At minimum, she would lose her potential weapon. He would either refasten the shelves to the upright, making sure they were impossibly tight, or move them altogether. It was possible, however, that he would also punish her. And what was Declan's idea of punishment? He might try to act on his crude ogling of her body. Or worse, get at her by hurting Dillon.

After his senseless slicing of her son's cheek, that seemed the more likely of Declan's choices. She would not let that happen. He would not hurt her son again. Ever. Her fingers tingled with pain, occasionally feeling like needles were sliding under her nails, but she pulled and turned. The palm of her other hand was also raw and bleeding as she pushed it into the head of the bolt, trying to stop it from turning.

"Hey," Dillon said, looking up. He was touching the top of his head. He looked at his fingers and smelled them.

"Blood." She could barely see a trickle of blood coming out of her palm to bead on her wrist. She still needed the pressure of Dillon's body against the crossbeam to prevent it from wiggling: more now than ever, since she was down to the last bolt and it was wiggling freely. She said, "Sorry, honey. Just a little longer."

He covered his head with his hands, as though expecting a brick to fall next.

Pull and turn.

25

Declan stood in the intersection of State and Fife watching smoke pour from the destroyed facades of the bookstore and conservation office. Rafters were on fire, and he believed the entire building would be gutted before too long. He thought they had taken refuge in one of the two stores on the north end of the building or one of the two government offices on the south end. The RCMP substation was the southernmost office, closest to him. If so, either they were already dead, would be soon, or were bolting out a back door. He eyed the monitor and saw no movement behind the building. A strip of shadow along the back edge bothered him. He moved the crosshairs to it and debated where along that band of shadow to let loose. If *he* were hiding, he would be in the corner far from the explosions and on the opposite side of the building from the man with guns.

Bad appeared at his side. He pointed the G11 at the ruined store-fronts. He was shifting from one foot to another, his head bobbing to music only he could hear. The man was itching to get it on. Waiting like this was worse than the delay of a game console loading the next level of play. "Whatcha think?"

"I'm gonna shake up the back of the building. You and Kyrill might want to get where you can see back there."

Bad grinned. "You ever see them burn trash at the dump?"

Declan gave him a sideways glance. "No, and neither have you."

"Well, I . . . I heard about it. As the rats run from the fire, the garbage dudes pick them off with .22s."

Declan caught his eyes. "Fire in the hole," he said.

Bad's grin grew impossibly wide, all teeth. He screamed, high pitched and loud, a siren announcing a level of agony he had never known. Declan saw an arrow jutting from the man's right thigh. A circle of blood already the size of a hand fanned out from the point of entry.

Bad, bellowing like an idiot now, dropped to his knees. The machine gun clattered to the ground. Bad fell on his left side. He was holding his leg up and squeezing his thigh, but not right at the wound.

Declan was fascinated to see a small geyser of blood spray up in the ninety-degree angle between arrow and leg.

From the first moment of Bad's scream to that moment, no more than five seconds had passed. In that time, Declan had startled at Bad's sudden misfortune, watched him fall, marveled at the blood flow, and finally realized that he had better take cover. He leaped over Bad on his way to where the Hummer was parked in the street. He depressed the device's button.

Whoosh-crack.

The far back corner of the building exploded.

Laura's blood-soaked fingers slipped off the nut. She lifted her head, listening.

They were at it again, blowing up things. She hoped those things were not humans. Most likely, they were.

She pressed her palm into the bolt. She gripped the nut, turned it . . . turned it . . . It came off the bolt, slipped from her fingers, then clattered onto the metal shelf. Excited, she pushed on the bolt. Its threads caught the edge of the hole through which it passed. She wiggled it, but it would not budge. She realized that because it was the last bolt holding the brace to the shelves, she didn't have to push it through this way.

"Dillon!" she said excitedly. "I got it, honey. Scoot away."

When he did, she took a half step back and yanked on the brace. It popped free of the shelves, and the last bolt fell to the floor.

She felt Dillon's hand on her calf. "You did it, Mommy."

She smiled. "We did it! We really did."

She hefted the metal, pleased to find it weighed more than she had expected. It was sturdy. As tall as she was, it was the weapon she needed. Her fingers and palms did not ache at all now. Like a gold-medal winner, she found that the thrill of the trophy surpassed the pain endured to get it.

Dillon stood. "Can I hold it?" he asked. She handed it to him. He angled it to inspect it in the dim light coming under the door. He seemed as impressed by it as she was. The light stuttered, dimmed. Someone was at the door.

"Here, here," she whispered, taking the upright from Dillon. She tugged at him as she backed to the wall beside the door. She pushed him toward the corner and raised the upright like a bat.

The lock rattled and clicked. The door swung open. Light flooded in, blinding her—she had not thought of that! She blinked and squinted, catching movement at the door. She swung, aiming high for the head. Two-thirds around she realized that the head coming through the door was lower than she had expected. She adjusted in midswing. The upright made contact with a forehead and continued striking the doorjamb. The vibrating energy that shot up the metal to Laura's hands shocked them, and she released her grip. As the upright came down, so did a tray with plastic cups and paper plates of food. They landed on the midsection of the body that had collapsed in the doorway. Brown liquid from the cups jumped out, spraying the wall, pooling on the floor, spotting the blue jeans of the downed person like blood.

Something flesh-colored plopped onto the floor. A severed hand or piece of head, Laura thought with a suddenly lurching stomach. Then she recognized the thing as a burrito. Another one hit the person's leg and rolled off. Laura scooped up the upright and pulled back to swing at the next person, but no one came. No one shouted. She waited a few moments. The sounds of the blow, dropping body, and spilled dinner had seemed as loud as a gong to her. When no one else appeared, she stepped away from the wall and looked at her victim.

It was the young boy. Julian. Despite herself, she felt a pang of sorrow. The boy had been nice to them. He had smiled and talked for a few minutes to Dillon. She listened for approaching footsteps or voices, then bent to one knee beside the boy. A welt the size and shape of her thumb had already blossomed on his forehead. It was turning blue, and at its crest was a laceration. Blood poured over one temple. She pushed her fingers to his neck and felt a strong pulse in his carotid artery. She leaned closer to examine the wound, and he moaned.

She looked up at Dillon, standing at the boy's feet. "He'll be okay," she said.

She scanned the office and faced the open doorway to the rest of the building. She realized her posture and thought there was something Amazonian about it: on one knee, shoulders square, brace/spear held vertically in one fist. That seemed right. Strong. Fierce. Ready for battle. She took a deep breath, came off her knee, and strode to the door.

Dillon appeared to have noticed something different about her as well. He gazed at her, lips slightly parted, eyes big and amazed. He smiled.

"Ready?" she said.

He nodded, walked carefully past the boy, and joined his mother.

"Stay with me," she said. "But if anything happens, I'll meet you at the cabin."

They moved into the corridor and then through an archway into the building's vestibule. Double doors that opened into the gymnasium where the townsfolk were imprisoned were chained and padlocked. Several loops of chain wound from the push bar of one door through the push bar of the adjoining one. A heavy padlock connected the ends of the chain. She moved quickly to the doors. She slipped the steel beam between the loops of chain and levered it sideways, twisting the chain tightly against the handles. When the beam was nearly horizontal, it stopped. She thought that putting her weight on one end to force the farther rotation of the chain would either break the chain or pry the push bars loose.

"Mom!" Dillon screamed, just as the thunderous roar of a firearm echoed in the vestibule. A fist-sized hole appeared in the wall above the doors. She spun to see the girl in the archway on the other side of the vestibule. A big pistol in her hand.

"Now wait—" Laura started.

The girl squeezed her eyes shut and fired again. The bullet ripped into the linoleum tile ten feet in front of Laura.

"Wait!" Laura screamed.

Opening her eyes to assess the damage she'd caused, the girl appeared surprised that Laura was still standing. She adjusted her aim and squeezed her eyes closed again.

Laura grabbed Dillon's hand and returned to the corridor that led back to Buck's office, the storage room/prison cell, and the unconscious boy. Past a break room, the corridor terminated at a steel fire door. Visitors to the building often left this way to reach the rear parking lot, despite a warning on the door that opening it would set off an alarm. It never did. And even if it did this time, Laura could not care less. Half an ear listened for the squeaking footfalls of the girl's sneakers behind them. Somehow she was certain the long shooting range-like corridor would make a sharpshooter out of the girl. If she got off a shot, they would die, plain and simple.

She hit the fire door with all her strength. It arced out of her way. One foot hit a small concrete stoop, and she tumbled into the dirt beyond. Dillon crashed down with her. She rolled and rose, stopping only when the barrel of a gun pressed into her head.

26

The moment Declan turned away from his fallen comrade, Hutch rose from his position and sprinted across a dirt road toward a big brick building. He was pretty sure that it was from here Declan and his gang had emerged. He angled away from Provincial Street toward the rear of the building. An explosion ripped at the world behind him, not near enough to be a strike on the position he had just left. Either Declan had aimed at a place from which he *thought* Hutch had shot or had aimed randomly, hoping to get lucky. Hutch took this to mean Declan had not seen him bolt for the other building. He figured he had only seconds to take cover in the shadows before Declan felt safe enough to search for him again.

He still didn't know what Declan was using to find his prey and shoot at it, but he was pretty sure Terry's suspicions were close: something was in the sky. The slapping feet of Terry and Phil pursued him. He hit the corner of the building, spun, and slammed his back against the rear wall. Terry tumbled into the dirt, scrambled into the shadow at the edge of the building, and stood. Hutch waited for Phil . . . and waited.

"Where's Phil?"

"I thought he was right behind me."

Hutch peered around the corner, back toward where he had been. The explosion he had heard had taken out the opposite rear corner; Declan had guessed wrong. He could barely make out Phil standing out of the moonlight behind the building.

"He's back at the other building," Hutch informed Terry.

"What's he doing there?"

"Just standing in the shadow. I think he hesitated to run until it was too late."

"It is," Terry agreed. "We've used all the time your distraction bought us."

Terry leaned around the corner and patted the air in front of him, hoping Phil understood to stay. He thought he saw the man nod his head.

"So, one down?" he asked.

"Not really. I got him in the leg."

"All that screaming for a leg shot?" They could still hear Bad moaning in the street.

Hutch pulled an arrow from the quiver, held the broadhead up to Terry. Unlike the simple aluminum-tipped arrows kids shoot at day camp, this thing was like four triangles of razors designed to come together a half inch from a chiseled tip. Hutch indicated the smaller two of the triangular razors.

"These are called bleeders," he said. "The more he moves, the more they're slicing. By the length of the shaft sticking out of his leg, I'd say it didn't go all the way through, and the only thing that would have stopped it was his bone. The power of the arrow probably snapped his femur. If an artery is cut, he could bleed out."

"Let's hope for small favors," Terry said.

"There's at least one other gunman," Hutch said, "but I didn't see him."

"Should we keep our eyes on the guy writhing in the street? Get his buddies when they come for him?"

"I don't think anybody's coming for him. At least not until we're gone."

Terry scowled. "What do you mean, gone?"

Hutch shrugged. "Dead, caught, out of the area."

Bad yelled in agony. It might have been a word.

"Why wouldn't they rescue him?" Terry asked. "He might bleed out."

"These guys don't strike me as all that altruistic. And I'm guessing that extends to one another." He thought a moment. "Except maybe the young boy I told you about."

Hutch looked along the rear of the building. Two bare bulbs under metal shades, set about nine feet high, cast weak yellow light on concrete pads below them. Because of the acute angle of Hutch's inspection, he could not see what he suspected: these lamps marked rear exits. They were situated near the ends of the long building, one only thirty feet from Hutch and Terry.

"Let's try to get inside."

" 'Bout time. But why this building?"

"I think this is where they're holed up. This is their headquarters. If we're going to find anything to help us, it'll be here."

He stepped around Terry, then jogged into the anemic light. He jabbed his bow at the bulb and shattered it. The door was metal, dinged and scuffed—and utterly devoid of entry hardware. No handle, no deadbolt housing. He noted an illuminated doorbell on the wall beside it, and a peephole at a low eye level in the center of the door. If the administrators desired visitors through this door, they'd have to respond to the chime and let them in. Or, he thought, remembering the rec center in Morrison, Colorado, the small town of his childhood, they'd leave the door propped open during events, maybe as a matter of habit during the day, just to save people the trouble of walking around and to get a cross breeze. To satisfy himself, he tried to open the door with the tips of his fingers. No go. He trotted to the next pad, broke the light. Same security door. The killers had chosen well.

Terry came up beside him. "What now?" he asked.

"Gotta be a window somewhere," Hutch said, but he knew there didn't "gotta be" anything. From what he saw on his short visit to the town's main street, the river was a few blocks from here. That meant this building was centrally located. It was also set farther back from the street than the businesses. Hutch hadn't been able to view its facade from the sidewalk or even the street, when he checked out the booted foot and leg. He'd bet that in the space between building and street, there'd be a flagpole or two, perhaps a bike rack, and a flight of wide steps leading to the front doors. He'd seen enough town halls to believe this was the one for Fiddler Falls, and since the community was too small to warrant this much floor space—even if it hosted the administrative offices, fire station, police station, and jail—it was mostly likely their rec center as well. Designers of multi-use buildings like this often avoided limiting potential uses by making them big boxes without windows—or at most, with windows high up near the ceilings.

Checking for accessible windows meant only peering around the corner, so that's the direction they headed. Gunfire rang out, and they ducked. It had been muffled, maybe far off. They heard it again and realized it was coming from inside the building. Terry reached behind him and pulled out his pistol.

"What are you going to do with that?" Hutch asked.

"Better than pointing my finger at someone."

Hutch said, "That's not—"

The fire door beside them burst open, and two people spilled out. They tripped off the pad and into the dirt. A woman and child. Terry darted out, holding the pistol in two hands. As the woman clambered to rise, he pressed the barrel into the side of her head.

"Hold it," he said.

The fire door banged violently against the outside wall and swung shut, too fast for Hutch to grab it.

Keeping his eyes on the woman, Terry asked Hutch, "Is this the girl you said?"

"No. I don't—"

The moonlight made the whites of her eyes seem radiant. They were wild eyes, rolling to take in everything at once—take it in and measure it against options, possibilities, actions. She had worked fear and panic into a rope of determination, but it was fraying.

Panting like a swimmer saved from certain drowning, the woman said, "Don't shoot. I'm sorry. I'm sorry. The boy's okay. Please . . ."

"Please," the child echoed.

Terry gazed at Hutch, confused. Hutch swept forward and picked up the boy.

The boy let out a scared, frustrated whine.

"Shhh," Hutch soothed. He stepped back into the shadows.

"No . . . please . . ." the woman said, reaching out for the child.

"Get her out of the moonlight," Hutch said. "Hurry." To the boy, he whispered, "It's okay. My name's Hutch. What's yours?"

The child searched Hutch's eyes, then said meekly, "Dillon."

"Nice to meet you, Dillon. Is that your mom?"

Dillon nodded.

Terry had shoved the gun into the back of his pants and was helping the woman to her feet.

As he did, Hutch said, "Ma'am, we're not going to hurt you. We're here to help."

Her open expression of hope, of not wanting to hope in vain, plucked a chord of sympathy in him.

"Are there people here trying to hurt you?"

She nodded. Her hair hung in dirty strings over her face. She pushed it back, hooking it behind her ear. "They kept us in a storage room. They killed . . ." Her eyes found her son. She changed direction. "I thought they were going to . . . they have others . . . the whole town . . ."

Terry guided her into the strip of shadows.

Two more shots rang out, louder than the ones before. Holes appeared in the exit door.

"They're after us," she said to Hutch's shocked expression. "A girl. They held us hostage. We got out. I . . . I hit a boy. Knocked him cold. I think they're the only ones left in there."

A girl. Hutch could not know if she was the one he had seen in the Hummer. In fact, the group that had pursued him could be only a small contingent of a much larger force. Why hadn't he considered that before? Wouldn't it take more than the half dozen people he'd encountered to take over a town? No, he rationalized, not with the cannon-thing they had at their disposal.

Hutch assessed the situation. Someone with a gun was about to burst through a door they were standing beside. There was no way to block it. They couldn't run across the parking lot because doing so would expose them to Declan and his weapon. The only thing he could think of . . .

"Around the corner," he said. "Go!"

But before anyone moved, the door banged open. The Hummer girl leaped through the opening. She landed in a crouch. The pistol in her hand seemed bigger than her head, both of which—the pistol and her head—were pointing toward the second rear exit, away from Hutch and the others. Pivoting at the hips, she swung her outstretched arm and the pistol in an arc that would eventually reach them.

The woman—Dillon's mother—rushed past Hutch. He reached for her, but she was gone. She hit the girl in a full-body tackle that knocked them both off the concrete pad and into the dirt. The pistol pinwheeled into the parking lot, its nickel plating sparkling in the moonlight.

Hutch reached out and grabbed the door before it could swing shut again. He glanced in, down a long corridor. Empty . . . for now. He closed the door until it was opened only enough to accommodate his fingers.

The two women rolled toward the gun. Terry shot out, scooped it up. He backpedaled away from the tumbling fighters. He pointed the pistol, trying to keep it aimed at the girl.

"Terry!" Hutch called. Hutch shook his head no. It would be too easy for Terry to shoot the wrong person, and even if he could hit the girl, Hutch wasn't so sure they wanted to. She was with killers, a part of them; she had been shooting at the woman and her son. No doubt she was troubled and possibly evil. But she was so young. He could not fathom killing a person that age and ever being able to look at his own reflection again. If he had seen her kill, then maybe. But he hadn't. Not yet.

Something rolled out of the girl's hand: a grenade!

"Terry!" Hutch yelled. Then he recognized the object as a gray walkie-talkie. His heart came out of his throat—but only a little. The communication device could prove as devastating as a grenade. Had she used it before exiting the building? Were the men even now converging on their location? Was Declan positioning his cannon on them at that moment?

The girl's small, tight fists hammered at the woman. They pounded against her face, her neck, her ribs. The woman gave it right back. She swung wide, roundhouse punches at the girl's head. Her knee rammed into the teen's hip and upper thigh. Again and again.

27

Dillon did not need to see his mother fighting this girl. Hutch turned the boy in his arms away from the sight.

"Terry," he said. He inclined his head at the combatants. "Do something."

Terry approached them as hesitantly as he would have a stick of sweating dynamite.

Hutch backed into the corridor. He saw a wedge of wood on the floor—the doorstop he suspected they used to keep the place from getting stuffy and to allow entry from the back parking lot.

"You okay to walk?" he asked Dillon. He set him down and glanced out at the ongoing fight. Then he slipped the wedge between the door and the jamb as the door closed on it. He guided Dillon along the corridor. The woman had said she thought the girl and the

180

boy she'd knocked unconscious were the only ones left in the building, but he didn't want to find out the hard way she was wrong. He whispered, "What's up this way, do you know?"

"An office . . . the room we were locked in . . ."

All the doors along the corridor were set into the right-hand wall. Hutch assumed the other wall separated the corridor from the big gymnasium-type room he believed was this building's *raison d'être*. He walked with Dillon to the first door and peered in. It was a break room with kitchen counters and cabinets, a refrigerator, microwave, sink, and one long table surrounded by plastic chairs. Hutch hoped to find where the killers had stashed the items confiscated from the townsfolk—satellite phones, weapons. Evidently, that place was somewhere else. He wondered if they would have time to check each room before Declan's gang returned.

"The next room is where they kept us," Dillon said.

"Let's get the others before we go on."

They took a step toward the rear door when an explosion knocked them off their feet. Hutch was momentarily disoriented. A chorus of voices came to him—an indistinct mumble punctuated by screams. He got to his hands and knees and shook the echoing blast out of his head. The voices were coming through the wall: Hutch suddenly realized why this building was Declan's headquarters and where all the townsfolk had gone.

The boy was sitting flat on his rump, legs splayed out in front of him. He was wiping dust out of his eyes.

"You okay?" Hutch asked.

Dillon nodded, blinking. His eyes found a stunning sight that dropped his jaw.

Hutch followed his gaze toward the back door. Through smoke and dust that hung in the air like sediment in a pond, he could see the steel door had been punched inward and knocked out of alignment with its frame. The walls around it were cracked and bulged. The floor directly in front of the door had risen four inches like a tectonic plate. Linoleum squares had been jarred loose and sat askew. Several tiles had been blown twenty feet into the corridor.

Declan had evidently bombed the area just outside the door, where Terry had been attempting to break up the fight between the girl and Dillon's mother.

"Mom!" Dillon screamed. He scrambled to get up, already starting to cry. "Mommy!"

Hutch grabbed him and forced him back down. Locking eyes with him, he said, "Stay here."

He rose and ran to the door. Dillon came up right behind him. He pushed on the door. It didn't budge. Finding a gap, he gripped the door and pulled. It had been wedged in place, pushed back by the explosion. It was as solid as the brick wall defining the building's perimeter. Where the door bulged, a gap of about eight inches allowed Hutch to look out on the destruction. A giant bite had been taken out of the concrete slab's outside edge. The rest of it had crumbled into gravel. The epicenter of the crater lay just beyond the pad. Hutch could not see the bottom of it—either because it was too deep or because the swirling witch's brew of smoke obscured it.

"Terry!" he yelled through the gap. His voice cracked on the second syllable. "Ter—" he tried again, but it came out a quiet plea. When he and Dillon had entered the building less than a minute ago, he—they—had been *right there*. He could not see how anyone could have survived.

Terry's voice reached him. "Hutch!"

"Terry."

Terry appeared from out of the darkness. The moonlight had seemed so bright when they were keeping clear of it; but now that his eyes had grown accustomed to the glare of fluorescents, everything outside looked dark, with no difference between shadow and moonlit night.

Hutch laughed. "How—"

"The girl . . . her walkie-talkie squawked something. I didn't hear what. She broke away from the woman and ran. We were chasing her when . . . this happened." He held his hands open to the crater.

Dillon's mother appeared beside Terry. Her cheek was bruised; an open laceration on her forehead glistened.

Hutch laughed, despite everything.

"Wait, wait." He backed away from the gap and pushed Dillon up to it.

"Mommy," the boy called, elation making both syllables sound like musical notes.

She called his name, and a moment later her face and fingers appeared in the gap. He leaned close, letting her touch his cheek.

"Baby, are you okay?" she asked.

He nodded enthusiastically. Her fingers tightened on the edge of the door, becoming white. Hutch could tell she was trying to move it.

"It's wedged in there tight," he said.

She looked past Dillon to Hutch. "Go around to the other rear door. It's like a big horseshoe. On the other side of the auditorium, through the vestibule."

Hutch grabbed Dillon's arm.

Dillon gripped the edge of the door with one hand and reached out to his mother with the other.

"Mom," he said quietly, sadly.

"Do it, honey. I'll be right here."

Hutch called past them. "Terry! Stay with—" He found the woman's eyes. "I don't know your name," he said.

"Laura."

"I'm Hutch."

"Take care of my boy, Hutch."

"Absolutely. Terry!"

"Yeah?" Just a voice beyond the door.

"Stay with Laura. If we don't meet you at the other back door in a few minutes, find Phil."

"Got it!"

"And get back in the shadows!"

Hutch pulled Dillon back a step.

"Mom—"

"I love you."

She disappeared from the gap, and Hutch gave her credit for that, for temporarily breaking away from her son in hopes of a permanent reunion. He wasn't sure under similar circumstances whether he'd be able to take his eyes off his children even for a few moments.

"Come on. Let's go see her." They began to half run toward the front of the building. There they would cross through the vestibule, then down the opposite corridor.

Noises issued from the front of the building. Hutch and Dillon stopped. Voices, angry, excited.

A female voice—the girl: "You couldn't have known I was clear!"

"I saw you run. I warned you."

"Yeah, 'Fire in the hole'!"

The voices were getting louder, clearer. They were headed for the corridor. Hutch pushed Dillon into the break room. He looked around, moved to the cabinets under the countertop. He opened doors: cans of coffee, coffee filters, glassware, silverware, napkins, paper plates, plastic cups. In a large double-doored cabinet he found two huge coffee urns. The cabinet contained no shelves because of the size of the urns stored within. He hefted them out and lined them against the wall. He hoped no one noticed. He held his finger to his lips, then helped Dillon climb in.

"Let me have that thing and see how you like it!" In the hall now, echoing, loud. "Look what you did to the door!"

Hutch had no time to consider the practicality of his joining the boy in the cabinet. He leaned in to set his bow against its back wall. Dillon held it in place. Hutch bent low, swung in his left leg so it was on the far side of the kid. He pushed his rump into the cabinet. He ducked his head, got it inside, then positioned his right leg on the other side of Dillon. He reached out to shut the doors.

His back was against the right-hand side of the cabinet. Dillon's back was against the left side. They faced each other, though Dillon could sit somewhat normally, and Hutch had to slouch and press his face into his shoulder.

The binoculars, held by harness to his chest, pushed painfully on his chin. He unclipped them and set them near the bow.

A thread of light defined the cabinet doors: a big rectangle and a vertical line right up the center. Hutch tried to remember if he had turned the light on when he first inspected the break room. The memory was gone now. Didn't matter. He thought these punks would not subscribe to a system of either energy conservation or headquarter security so meticulous that they would know or care about such things.

The voices grew louder, not because they were drawing nearer, but in excitement.

"Hey! Hey!" Declan said, genuine anger in his voice.

"I told you."

By the thin threads of light, Dillon must have read Hutch's expression; he whispered in the smallest of voices, "They found the boy. Mom knocked him out."

Hutch nodded awkwardly, his head nearly horizontal. Feet came down the corridor quickly and into the break room. A cupboard door opened and closed, fast. Then another, closer to their position. Another, closer.

Hutch braced himself to jump out. Dillon would probably suffer a good kick in the process, but he didn't see any way to prevent it. He believed the person in the break room was searching for something, but not for them. When the door opened, the person would be bent to look into the cabinet. His or her face would be close. Hutch imagined swinging his arm out of the opening and then immediately up for as solid of a head shot as he could summon. He would then propel himself out of the cupboard, pushing with his foot off the back wall. He would go for the knees, grabbing both and bringing the person down. In a perfect universe he would cup his hand over the mouth before it cried out. He'd swing for a KO in the first round. But in a perfect universe, he wouldn't have had to.

Another cupboard door: open, shut. Very close now.

The rustling of plastic packaging, and instantly Hutch got an image of the napkins he had seen. That's what they'd been after. More steps, right past their hiding place, and a faucet turned on, then off. The steps went toward the door, paused, returned. More doors opened and closed, but this time the sounds emanated from higher up—the overcounter cabinets. The clatter of dishes, metal pans. The water came on again, filling a basin. The feet left the room more slowly. Hutch knew the person was carrying a pot or bowl of water and a handful of napkins. He remembered Laura saying, *The boy's okay.*

He dared to whisper, "Was he bleeding, the boy?"

Dillon nodded and drew a line with his finger across his forehead.

Had to be Julian, he decided. The only one of the bunch who had not exhibited outright hostile behavior, at least toward him.

Dillon said, "He was nice to me."

Yeah, Hutch thought, *Julian*. Wouldn't you know. He had always told his kids, "Gotta watch who you hang with." Julian should have watched. He didn't seem like the kind of boy who had set out to find trouble, but trouble certainly had found him. They were taking care of him in the other room. He hoped they did a good job.

He smiled at Dillon. The boy had sad eyes. Hutch couldn't tell whether it was because they were big and almond shaped or because they had ample reason to be sad. Blue sparkles came from them as Dillon watched the man charged with his care. Hutch ached for what the boy should have been doing at that moment instead—tossing a ball to his dog, wrestling with his dad, *taking a bath*, for crying out loud. Anything but hiding from people intent on killing him. A cut ran from just under his right eye to near the corner of his mouth. Fresh, not yet scabbed over. Its edges were red, sore.

Dillon returned a thin-lipped smile. Hutch could tell the boy's mouth *wanted* to bend upward, probably from habit. It must have been a balm to his parents' spirits on tough days.

Julian had been nice to him. Their age difference did not seem so great that Hutch couldn't imagine the two playing together, instead of being kidnapper and victim. It was as though hell had vented nauseous fumes, skewing the way things ought to be and creating human-demons like Declan and his gang.

Despite recently chiding himself for assuming that the six people he had first seen in the Hummer were all he had to worry about, he now believed that was an accurate assessment. He had seen Declan, Bad, and Kyrill out front. Oh, and that camera guy—Pruitt, he remembered. The girl had been inside and had chased Laura and Dillon. Julian, he now knew, had been unconscious. When he first entered the building with Dillon, he had believed it to be empty of bad guys. There had been no voices, nobody running around—and considering the excitement of Declan's attack on them, including an explosion that had rocked this building, he believed there would have been.

Loud moans came from way outside the break room. They were too deep to come from Julian. The same voice said, "Oh! Oh! Oh!"

Someone else said, "Stop wiggling around, you baby."

A third voice added, "Just faint already. *I'm* about to, looking at it."

Satisfaction pushed Hutch's lips into a different kind of smile from the one had offered Dillon. They had finally gotten around to bringing in Bad. *The gang's all here,* he thought. And that meant they weren't still out there, chasing Terry, Phil, and Laura. A phrase his father used to say came to mind, but it wasn't quite right, so he changed it and thought, *Thank God for really, really big favors.*

He rolled his head to rest it on the other shoulder. He already felt a cramp in his neck. He hoped he would be able to move when he finally departed the cabinet.

He didn't know what they would do with Bad and didn't care. As long as they didn't stretch him out on the break room table and use this room as a makeshift hospital.

He smiled at Dillon. He wanted to give the boy a pleasant expression or a kind word. Then he realized he was asleep. He himself was beat, having awoken this morning at four to hunt. He envied the child's ability to sleep in the midst of chaos.

Before long, he, too, was fast asleep.

28

When the other rear door had not opened after twenty minutes, Laura's panic felt as explosive and destructive as Declan's weapon.

"Hutch would never let anything happen to him," Terry said.

"I'm sure he wouldn't, if he could help it. Neither would Dillon's father, and he's gone. Dead." The top of her chest grew tight and cold, as though her heart were pumping Freon instead of blood. She cupped her hands over her face, but not to hide tears she would not yet let loose. She stared into the darkness of her hands and thought of her husband. She pushed the thought away. She remembered the hours she and Dillon had spent in the storage room, the fear and desperation. She pushed it away. She thought of her son. His smile, his eyes that always appeared trusting and loving. She recalled his voice: "tiny," Tom had called it. To her, it sounded like sunshine in a cloudless sky. Even his slight lisp was perfect, like rounding the edges of a fresh-cut plank. His tongue just got in the way, and she found it adorable.

This image she held on to. She locked it down tight, because it was the only thing that mattered.

They were standing against the wall beside the door, deep in shadow. She lowered her hands, looked to the door, then at Terry.

"We have to go get him. And your friend."

"We will. I promise." He held up the gun the girl had dropped. "But there are only two unspent rounds in here, and I don't think that'll do it."

"It has to."

He narrowed his eyes at her. "I want to make sure Hutch is safe, and I would do the same for Dillon, even if Hutch weren't with him, but we've got to do it right. Going in guns blazing would just get us killed, especially since our guns don't have enough bullets to blaze. Then who's going to make sure Hutch and Dillon are safe?"

She knew he was right, but she couldn't stand the thought of Dillon back with those creeps. Her not being with him made it so much worse.

"What do you suggest?" she asked.

"We have a friend hiding in the next block. Let's get him and put our heads together."

She nodded. What else could she do?

Terry moved to the corner and peered around. "Okay," he said, "let's go."

She followed him across the street to a building that was ablaze. She knew it well. Tom's RCMP office was one of that building's five tenants. That was as much as she thought about Tom at that moment. She had pushed him aside. She had to. If she gave in to even a single memory, there would be a flood and she would drown. She would be no good to herself. No good to Dillon.

"Where's your friend?" she said.

Terry surveyed the area. "I don't know. Phil!" he whispered harshly. "Phil!" He turned to her. "You know the area. Where might he have gone to hide, but still see us when we came for him?"

She shook her head. "Could be anywhere. Why did he stay here when you and Hutch came over to the back of the community center?"

Terry frowned. "I think he just got scared. Didn't follow us when we ran."

She thought about it. "If he was afraid, he could have gone any-where, done anything. You know? I'm angry and worried sick about Dillon, and a minute ago I was ready to walk into the bad guys' camp to get him. A part of me still wants to. That's not rational. Fear does that to people too. It's hard to predict what scared people will do." She paused. "Terry, don't count on finding him. He'll have to find us."

"He mentioned wanting to get to another town. He thought it was crazy to go up against people with a weapon like what Declan has, against people able to make an entire town disappear."

She shook her head. "If he headed out for Fond-du-Lac or Black Lake, he's not going to make it. They're too far. This time of year, the only way is by boat. I heard Declan say they had the waterway cov-ered. Is your friend good in the wild? Can he survive cold nights?"

"No," Terry said heavily, as if hearing Phil was already dead. "That's not Phil."

"Well . . . I hope he realizes that about himself." She took in the shadows around them. "Maybe he's here somewhere. Could be wait-ing for you at a safer place."

Her eyes settled on a house just beyond the parking lot that served the now-burning building. It was the Jorgensens' home. She had taught their two children in the third, fourth, and fifth grades. Kyle was now an eighth grader, becoming strong and already talking about nailing down a hockey scholarship to the University of Saskatchewan in Saskatoon. Heather was in the sixth grade under the tutelage of Mrs. Johnson. Even so, she had invited Laura to her twelfth birthday party less than a month ago. It had been in the backyard of that house. Festooned with streamers and balloons and a SpongeBob piñata.

Heather had laughed, saying the piñata was perfect not because she liked the cartoon sea sponge, but because she absolutely did not. She delighted at the idea of beating it with a broom handle until poor Bob broke open and everybody ate his candy guts. Dillon, who thought SpongeBob was the Second Coming, stormed off and refused to participate in the savagery. But all of them had enjoyed the cake, which was, of course, in the shape of a caribou. The kids giggled and laughed, yelled and screamed for hours.

Laura remembered thinking that twelve had been a good year for her, and Heather was kicking hers off in style. Now the house was dark. Though abandoned only two days, to Laura it felt ancient and dilapidated and full of ghosts.

She had seen Heather, Kyle, and their parents, Hans and Mari, in the gymnasium with the other captives. They had been in a far corner. Mari had sat on a cot, her son and husband on each side. They'd seemed to be consoling her. She'd had her face in her hands, a crumpled tissue sticking out one side. Heather had stood a few paces away, looking miserable and confused. When she had spotted Laura, her face hadn't changed, but she'd given her a little wave.

Declan had captured more than people—he had taken their pride and their spirit. He had demonstrated to children that their parents could not protect them. He had shown the adults that their nightmares were pleasant dreams compared to the real world. Each person in that gymnasium would never be the same. If they were anything like Laura, they would never again believe that the hearth's fire would always keep out the cold; that a mother's care made all things better; that the arms around you could not be torn away because love conquered all.

Terry touched her shoulder and she realized he had said something. "Sorry . . . ?"

Terry leaned closer. "Are you okay?"

She blinked, shook off the reverie. "I was just thinking . . ."

"I mean . . ." He pointed at her face. "You have a nasty bruise, and your lip's bleeding."

She touched her lip, and it stung. But her fingertips felt worse. She looked at them and remembered the hours of working the shelving brace loose. She turned her hand over. Her knuckles also glistened with congealing blood.

"Are all the women up here so tough?" Terry said with a sideways smile.

"You mean the fight? That was fun. Really. I can't tell you how much I enjoyed pounding on that little girl."

Terry actually laughed out loud. He covered his mouth and looked around. "I can't say that I would've got the same thrill, not with her. But those other guys . . ." His face hardened and he shook his head. After a moment he said, "We have to find a place for the night. Do you know where we can go?"

"As long as you don't mind keeping off the lights."

"I just need to catch some shut-eye."

"I don't think I can."

"Tomorrow we'll find Dillon, Hutch, and Phil," Terry said.

"Yeah." She glanced back toward the community center. "Tomorrow."

Phil's shoulder hit a tree, spinning him. He fell to his knees on the moss- and needle-covered ground. Momentum pushed him onto his side, and he rolled down a short incline, crushing dead twigs and jarring his ribs against a rock. He felt his glasses slip away. He lifted himself up on all fours and stopped. He pulled in a deep breath, heaved it out . . . again . . . and again. He was leaking from his eyes and nose and mouth, just letting the stuff drop from his face to the earth.

He was deep in the woods, where only a handful of bright spots like scattered coins proved the moon's presence somewhere above the trees. His eyes were open to the blackness, but superimposed over everything was the image of a flash of rippling green light slicing down from the sky. It was burned not into his retinas, but into his soul. Hutch and Terry had darted across the dirt road to the rear of the big building Hutch had called a recreational center. It had taken Phil a few minutes to free himself from the panic that had seized him. He'd just stepped from the shadows when the light flashed, cracking the air like a bullwhip. A geyser of dirt and debris had risen over the roofline of the rec center.

And he had run. God help him, he had turned and run . . . back past the rear of the burning retail building, behind the Elks Lodge and the town physician's house, all the way to the school. There he had angled left and stumbled and loped past the dead houses, dark as tombs. He had not stopped, not until now, well beyond the town, into the province of trees with branches like hands and animals he had only seen in zoos.

They had to be dead, Hutch and Terry. The *power* of that thing, that weapon . . . That Declan guy, the one who controlled it, somehow he had known where to aim it, had known where they were.

Fifty paces into his retreat, Phil had thought, *What if they're not dead? What if they're injured and need help?* But he could not bear to see his friends mangled. His fear of seeing them like that had been greater than his desire to help. No, that wasn't right: his fear had been greater than his belief that they could have survived.

His respiration slowed. He leaned back to sit on his heels. He ran a sleeve across the lower half of his face, then squeegeed the tears away from his eyes with his finger. A cursory glance around failed to locate his glasses. In the distance a wolf howled, followed by a chorus of scattered dogs, closer. Beyond a few nearby trees, he could not make out the black trunks, branches, needles from the spaces between them. Dark: the night, his heart.

He knew where he was. Sort of. He had gone west out of town, toward the First Nation village of Fond-du-Lac. Black Lake lay in the opposite direction, east. The Fond du Lac River was south. To the north were nothing but the hills, rivers, and forests where they had camped. Hutch had insisted neither neighboring town was accessible on foot. But what choice did he have? He had to try to get to one of them, and since he was already heading in that direction, he supposed it would be Fond-du-Lac.

He returned to his hands and knees, patting the ground for his glasses.

One foot in front of the other, he thought. *One step at a time. How bad could it be?* Survival would drive him on. That and the fire kindled inside him, hot for revenge. What were the cold and the terrain and the miles next to a man's will to live and to avenge his friends? He could do it. He *would* do it.

But first he had to find his glasses.

29

Hutch woke to the gentle chiming of his watch. He started, and his head smacked against something. His neck was twisted at an awkward angle. Then he remembered where he was. Frantically he reached for his watch to turn off the alarm. He listened for voices, for footsteps. Nothing but the slow, deep breathing of Dillon, facing him in the cabinet. The air was humid with the odor of stale breath. It was four in the morning. Yesterday at this time he had crawled over Phil and pushed out of the tent to begin the hunt, which had turned into a hunt for *him*.

Who said, "What a difference a day makes"? David would have challenged him to know. He smiled, thinking of Terry's quip the evening they had arrived: "The ability to quote is a serviceable substitute for wit." And suddenly he remembered who'd said that: W. Somerset Maugham. David would have been proud.

His watch was set to chime at the same hour every day unless he manually changed that function. He had not intended for it to go off this morning; only a fool would hide in the den of his enemies and set an alarm clock. But he was glad it had awakened him (and no others), for now was the ideal time to make his escape.

The freaks had left the break room fluorescents on again, which was fine by him. No crashing over chairs or risking turning on a light to get out of here. He believed Declan's gang would all be asleep. Bad would have required care well into the night, and maybe Julian, depending on how seriously Laura had brained him. These guys were punks more used to partying till dawn than rising at that hour. He couldn't imagine Declan setting up a twenty-four-hour watch or one of his stooges actually staying awake if he did.

Dillon had slipped lower in his sleep. Scrunched now, with his chin on his chest, his legs had stretched out toward Hutch. One crossed Hutch's lap, and the other foot was propped against Hutch's chest. Hutch would have climbed out and stretched before waking Dillon, but now the boy would have to get out first. Gently, he removed Dillon's foot from his chest and leaned forward. His head was still bent sideways, and he wasn't looking forward to straightening it against the cramp that had surely set in. He reached out to tap Dillon on the chest but thought better of it. He would wake this child the way he had often woken his own son, Logan. As a father would. Dillon deserved at least that much.

Softly, he brushed the bangs off the boy's forehead. He ran his big hand over his head and down the side of his face. Dillon stirred. He had escaped this place once already and would have to do it again. Hutch felt for him. He brushed the boy's head again, then his face. Dillon's eyes fluttered. He licked his lips, swallowed. His eyes opened and found Hutch. Instant fear. Bafflement.

"Good morning, Dillon," Hutch said quietly. "It's me, Hutch, from last night. Remember?"

Dillon scowled but nodded. "Where's my mom?"

"We're going to go to her. Are you ready?"

"I'm hungry." He pushed his lips together, looked embarrassed. "I have to go to the bathroom."

Hutch smiled. "I do too, and I'm starving. After we get out of here, we'll find some food and a bathroom. Can you wait that long?"

Dillon nodded.

"Remember, the bad guys are really close. Let's not wake them up. It'll be dark for another two hours, so it's a good time to skedaddle, huh?" He raised his eyebrows, and the boy nodded again.

Hutch pushed open the cabinet doors; they both squinted against the brightness. After a moment, Hutch said, "You first."

He helped Dillon maneuver his legs out and covered Dillon's head as he stooped through the opening, the way a cop would guide a prisoner under the threshold of cruiser's back door. Dillon stood, wincing at the aches in his body.

Hutch was about four times older and figured his aches would be at least that many times worse. As Dillon had done, he swung his legs out first, then slid out of the cabinet much less gracefully. He rolled over onto his hands and knees and slowly, painfully stood. He required assistance from the counter, and Dillon stepped up to hold him. He arched backward and stretched each leg in turn. He rotated his shoulders and only then realized his head was still cocked sideways. It refused to obey his command to straighten. He seized it in both hands and forced it up, hearing tendons pop as he did. That he had to remain silent during this entire process seemed to make the cramped muscles and stiff joints more cramped and stiff.

He resisted the compulsion to leave that very second, to slip from the dragon's lair with nothing but his and Dillon's lives. His right leg tingled, not fully asleep but definitely dozing. He felt that blood had been pressed out of major muscle groups by the confines of the cabinet. While he could walk and move, his mobility felt inhibited, as though he had been wrapped in tight bandages from head to toe. Mummified, he could not do his best. If ever he had to be limber and fast, it would be now, in escaping from Declan's vile presence. Dillon too. The young are naturally resilient, and his small body had not needed to contort as dramatically as had Hutch's in the cabinet, but his muscles must surely ache for the flatness and softness of a mattress.

"Stretch out," he whispered to Dillon. "Shake out your arms and legs, stretch your muscles."

Unsure, Dillon followed Hutch's lead, shaking each hand as though eliminating water from it, then doing the same with their legs. Inexplicably, Dillon smiled. A big grin that showed his Chiclet front teeth and just-cutting-the-gums incisors. It did more to revitalize Hutch than all the stretching and bending.

"What?" Hutch whispered.

Dillon shook his head.

"No, really—what?"

Dillon glanced toward the open door, then stepped closer to Hutch, who leaned down. Quietly Dillon sang, "You put your right foot in, you put your right foot out, you put your right foot in and you shake it all about."

Hutch almost laughed out loud. He gave Dillon's shoulder a squeeze and nodded. "Kinda silly, huh?"

Dillon was too polite to respond.

Hutch said, "Ready to go?"

Dillon made his eyes big and nodded as if to say, *Boy, I thought you'd never ask.*

Hutch retrieved his bow from the cabinet. He gave Dillon a thumbs-up, and Dillon returned it. In certain occupations and sports that required silent communication, such as SWAT operations, scuba diving, and hunting, hand signals were always acknowledged. Hutch had found that people who didn't participate in these activities generally smiled or nodded in reply.

"Do you hunt?" he asked.

"A little."

Hutch wasn't sure precisely how this information would help, but he thought it would. He might expect more of the boy in terms of stealth or spotting than he otherwise would have, which in turn would affect the decisions he made as they escaped—and, if it came to it, ran for their lives.

Working with someone whose strengths and weaknesses were unknown to you was always a disadvantage. He'd spoken to cops with new partners. They said that when facing a life-or-death situation, they would bear the brunt of the responsibility of their own safety, their partner's safety, and the outcome of the operation. By doing so, they might even compromise all of those objectives, since no one could do everything. Whereas if they could count on skills they knew their partner possessed, they could focus on their own strengths, and synergistically the two together performed immeasurably better than the two apart.

Dillon was only a child, and regardless of how well he knew the boy, Hutch would take responsibility for his safety and do everything he could to carry their collective weight. But imagine if he discovered that Dillon was a tae kwon do master or a marksman or could walk through walls. That might change things a bit. As it was, he had been concerned about Dillon's ability to move quietly. If his mother or father had taken him hunting, even once, Dillon would have learned the value of silence and patience and choosing a route that accommo-dated stealth over speed. Unfounded or not, it made him feel better about sneaking out of this place without waking the sleeping ogres.

"One more thing," Hutch whispered. Lowering himself to sit on the floor, he gestured for Dillon to do the same. Hutch unlaced his right boot and tugged it off; his sock followed. He gestured toward the child's feet, and Dillon yanked off his sneaker then his sock. Hutch replaced his boot over his bare skin and then began stretching his sock over his boot.

Dillon pushed his foot into his sneaker and began sheathing it with his sock. His face expressed his confusion.

Hutch bent toward him. "Inside," he whispered, "it will dampen our footsteps, and we don't have to carry our shoes. Outside, it will help mask our footprints, and we won't have to worry about stepping on something sharp."

Dillon smiled in understanding.

What he didn't tell Dillon was that if they had to make a break for it while still in the building, their socks were probably the worst pos-sible things to have on their feet. They would slip and slide and run in place like characters in nightmares he'd had as a kid: running and running without moving as some hideous beast with a mouth exactly the size of Hutch approached. But they were going to get out quietly with no special need for traction.

Dillon finished first and stood. He slid his feet over the tiles and pretty much figured out what Hutch had not told him. Hutch tucked his pant legs into his socks, which would not win him any fashion awards but would keep his feet warm and prevent his cuffs from snag-ging on low-lying obstacles. He stood, slinging his bow over his shoul-der. He reconsidered and pulled it off again. Holding it in his left hand, he nocked an arrow and, as he had done in the tree, held the shaft in place with one finger. He moved to the open door and peered into the corridor.

They would turn right out of the break room to head toward the front of the building. They would pass the office, off of which was the storage room where Dillon and Laura had been held. He didn't know the layout beyond that except that logically there would be more offices on the right and the corridor would open up to the vestibule on the left. At the terminus of the corridor, in that direction, was a restroom. The door was partially open, and though the light was out, he could see a white porcelain sink. He reversed his gaze to see the fire door at the other end of the hall, still buckled and jammed into the walls.

He turned to signal Dillon. The boy was closer than he realized, and his elbow struck Dillon in the head. Dillon lost his balance and fell against the break room door. The door handle banged loudly against the cabinets. Hutch grabbed Dillon, stabilized him, and lifted him off the door. They listened.

From the next room, the office with the storage room, came the groan of somebody waking up. The screech of a chair on tile told Hutch someone was coming.

Dillon blocked his way back into the break room. There was no time to quietly maneuver out of sight. Hutch already had one foot in the corridor. He swung out his other foot and stood facing the break room portal. He stretched his left hand, gripping the bow, toward the office door. With three fingers of his right hand, he hooked the bow-string. In two seconds he could pluck the string and send the arrow flying. His lips pantomimed a *shhh* sound to Dillon.

A man stepped into the hall.

It was the hefty one, Pruitt. Cecil B. DeMille.

He had not glanced in Hutch's direction but came shuffling out of the office and headed directly for the bathroom. His slight weaving-and-plodding gait indicated he was still mostly asleep. Hutch held a bead on a spot just below the man's left scapula. Precisely where his heart was. He wouldn't scream the way Bad had. He would be dead before he hit the floor. In fact, the most noise this kill would make would probably be the *tink* of the metal broadhead—protruding from his chest—striking the floor as he fell facedown.

No! Leave without bloodshed.

His molars crunched against each other. He wasn't a killer. Still, the images of David exploding, of the severed foot in the street, of Dillon sad and afraid—each was a dry log thrown onto the fire of his fury.

This kill would make one down, he thought, reprising the conversation he'd had with himself while hiding in the tree. One less adversary to worry about. But why stop there? There were five more within these walls. Only three deserved his arrow; he did not think he could or would even need to shoot Julian or the girl. But Declan, Kyrill, and Bad—he could do that.

Could I? What am I thinking?

End it here. Shoot them as they sleep. One after the other. David would be avenged. The townsfolk held hostage in the other room would be free.

Hutch's arm began to shake at the proposition of killing a man. No, that wasn't it. He could kill . . . just not this way. Not by shooting his enemy in the back or slaughtering them in their sleep.

Pruitt reached the bathroom and stepped in. The *clink* of a toilet seat rising to strike the tank. Then a waterfall.

Hutch realized he had pulled back on the bowstring a couple inches. Slowly, he relaxed the tension. He closed his eyes. He had been so close to doing it, he felt almost as though he had. It was like *not quite* touching your skin, but feeling the heat, the static electricity, the pressure on the air between fingers and flesh. *That close.*

He stepped into the break room.

Immediately he wondered if he'd made the right decision. Something primal deep down warred with his humanity. After all, these punks were killers. Their deaths would save lives—his own, Dillon's, Laura's, Terry's, Phil's. How could they leave anyone alive? The entire town had witnessed their crimes.

Wait, wait, wait. What about only Declan?

The head of the snake. Cut it off, and the rest is harmless. He could do that. He could kill Declan, here and now. He fantasized about it: finding the man sleeping, standing over him, arrow drawn.

He'd clear his throat, and when Declan's eyes sprang open, when he recognized Hutch and realized he had been beaten, Hutch would let the arrow fly into his chest. It would penetrate through and through to bury its tip in the floor. No one would blame him. He would never see the inside of a courtroom, not after the media and the district attorney discovered that Hutch had not killed a man, but a beast.

Dillon touched his arm, and he jumped. The boy's face showed an eagerness for reassurance. Hutch smiled and realized he could not go after Declan or anyone else in Dillon's presence. If something went wrong, if Declan got the upper hand, if the others came to his rescue or to avenge him, Hutch would not be able to hold them off. He would be responsible for Dillon's death. That was unacceptable.

The man stopped peeing and padded down the corridor toward them. Hutch expected him to return to the office. But in case he did not, he stepped back and held his fingers to the bowstring once more. He stood like that, pointing the arrow at the open doorway until he heard the sound of the chair scraping the floor . . . followed by silence.

Again he relaxed. And waited. He and Dillon stared at each other, the boy anxious, afraid, but quiet.

After a few minutes Hutch moved into the hall, Dillon right behind him. His first few steps were slow, methodical examinations of the tiles' stability, of the quietness of his own tread, of the way the corridor's illumination cast his shadow. He walked in the center of the corridor to avoid bumping a wall. After each step he stopped, listened. Dillon's following footstep would softly sound . . . then silence. On the other side of the wall to his left, where two-hundred-some-odd townsfolk slumbered in captivity, someone coughed. It was a muffled, quiet sound that their captors had probably grown accustomed to. As Hutch approached the first door on his right, he heard the rhythmic breathing of sleepers. He looked in.

By the light from the corridor and an illuminated banker's lamp on a desk, he saw two cots. Julian was sleeping on his back. A folded hand towel that had evidently covered his injury was now crumpled by his ear. His forehead was swollen and the color of a Saskatchewan sunset. A crusty ridge ran its length. Someone had put six or eight stitches into it. Beside Julian, on top of a blanket, was Hutch's arrow, the one the boy had retrieved from the field. His hand rested over the shaft. It seemed to have become a keepsake, a lucky charm. The broadhead pointed toward the foot of the cot, about even with Julian's knee. Still, it could slice him a good one if he rolled onto it or moved it in his sleep. Hutch hoped that wouldn't happen.

Bad lay in the second cot. To observers he would appear to be just a guy catching some Z's, until they noticed the hand-sized circle of red over his leg and a matching splatter glistening on the floor directly beneath. Pruitt sat in a chair, his arms and head on the desk. The steady rise and fall of his back said he'd returned to the dreams his bladder had interrupted.

Hutch turned away, took a step, and stopped. He gazed back into the room, to the objects on the desk.

You've got to be kidding, he thought.

On the desk were scattered papers, soda cans, food wrappers, and a laptop computer tethered by cable to Pruitt's camera. What interested Hutch was something else. There, by Pruitt's hand, was a key ring connecting two objects: a key and a fat metal *H*. Hummer. Hutch stood there. He could think of no reason to pass up this chance. He considered the logistics of reaching that key and realized his knowledge of Dillon's hunting experience was already bearing fruit. Dillon would be able to maneuver between the closely spaced cots better than he could, if he could at all. Also, Hutch could provide cover, whereas Dillon could not.

He signaled for the boy to back up several paces, then he leaned to his ear and told him the plan. Without hesitation, Dillon nodded. Hutch moved into the doorway, yielding just enough space for Dillon to slip in. The men and boy slept heavily, deep breaths in and stuttering exhalations. They did not appear ready to end their slumber, unless something startled them. The air was stale with body odor and bad breath.

Hutch aimed the arrow at Bad. Of the three, Hutch considered him most dangerous, despite his injury.

Dillon positioned himself at the foot of the cots and sidestepped his way between them, faster than Hutch would have thought possible. He reached the desk and reached for the key. Before he grabbed it, he looked back to confirm this is what the man wanted.

Hutch nodded. And thought of something: If Dillon picked up the key by its ring, when he lifted it off the desk, the key and the metal Hummer logo would slide down and clink against each other. That close to Pruitt, it would sound like a rattling chain or, more accurately, an alarm clock. He wanted to warn Dillon but could say nothing.

Dillon plucked up the key chain. He grabbed it by the Hummer logo so the key flipped down to bounce silently against his thumb. He grinned at Hutch, but all Hutch could think about was the fist that was pounding on the inside of his chest. It was at this moment that Pruitt would seize the boy's hair in his left hand while revealing a pistol in his right. He would say, "Aha!"

But that didn't happen. Dillon sidestepped back between the cots. His right foot cleared them; his left foot kicked Bad's cot.

The fist pounded more insistently, thumping against Hutch's sternum and ribs. Every muscle tightened as he prepared to pull back on the bowstring, straighten his fingers, and release the arrow.

Bad moaned. His head rotated on a thin pillow. His arm flopped off his chest and bridged the gap between his cot and Julian's.

Hutch realized that had Dillon bumped the head of the cot instead of the foot, resulting in the same movement of Bad's arm, Dillon would have been imprisoned by two cots, a desk, and Bad's arm. This time, though, luck was on their side. Dillon had frozen when his foot struck the cot; now he moved again. He passed in front of Hutch, under his taut arrow. When Dillon reached the hall, Hutch eased the tension on the bowstring and returned it to a ready-but-not-firing position. He backed into the hall. Boy and man found each other's eyes. They communicated more in that glance than they could have in an hour of talking. Hutch took the lead once again.

They reached a spot in the corridor where the left wall opened up in a wide arch. The vestibule was as large as a theater's. Its front wall contained two sets of double doors, which Hutch was sure opened to the outside, to the town's main street. Directly opposite was a wall that separated the vestibule from the building's main room, probably a combination gymnasium-theater-meeting hall. Two more sets of double doors allowed access to this area. Both sets were heavily chained and padlocked. The archway leading into the vestibule was on Hutch's left; on the right was a closed door. Another office, guessed Hutch. Another resting place for Declan's gang. Probably Declan himself.

Knowing he shouldn't, unable to resist, he reached for the door handle. If he witnessed Declan sleeping in there, would he, could he do it? He did not know, but the stakes were too high not to find out. To be this close to ending this evil episode . . . He had to know if he had the chance and whether he would take it.

The handle felt cold on his palm. He tightened his fingers around it, trying not to rattle the hardware. He turned it and envisioned Declan on the other side watching it turn. Then it turned no more. The door was locked. He did not know for certain that Declan occupied the room on the other side; even if he did know, he would not have kicked the door open, not with Dillon here. He turned the door handle back into position and released it. He had his answer: the opportunity was not his to take. Not yet anyway. He moved into the vestibule, cocking his head to catch Dillon in his peripheral vision.

The chained doors opposite the front entrance seemed hideous to him, like the gangplank of a slave ship or the holding pens of Rome's ancient coliseum. At that moment, he gladly would have traded the Hummer key for one that fit those locks. But that was not the hand dealt him. The best he could hope for was to fight for these people another day. The same frustration and hope etched lines in Dillon's young face. Hutch set his jaw and offered the boy a firm nod. He would come back. If God allowed him to, he would come back.

They padded to the closest set of double-entry doors. Push bars opened them. Wanting to take more care than he could have with one hand, and refusing to give up the readiness of his bow, he whispered to Dillon, "Go ahead. Very gently."

Dillon seized the push bar with both hands and slowly pushed it down and in. The latch clicked out of its receptacle. The door angled open into the predawn blackness. A cold breeze blew in.

That's when the alarm bells sounded.

31

Declan vaulted out of his cot fully alert. He had expected something like this: a breach. He assumed the townsfolk had found a way to open an auditorium door. Declan's intel had informed him that the auditorium itself had been wired into the building's alarm system to attract antique, art, and gun shows to the town. It was one of the reasons they had chosen this building, though its size alone made it the most logical venue. If not an auditorium door, then an external door had opened. Considering the hunters' bold approach and assault on Bad the night before, it would not have surprised him to find that they were the source of his disrupted sleep.

He unlocked and opened his room's door. Another door clanked shut; he recognized it as one of the front entrances. Kyrill came out of his room to Declan's right, Pruitt to his left.

"Julie," Declan called. "Get out here. You too, Bad. Don't pretend you can't walk."

He quickly scanned the vestibule. No immediate threat. He rushed to an entry door and pushed through. The Hummer squealed away from the curb and banked left onto the first side street. He turned around to face his crew. Kyrill and Pruitt at the door, Cort just coming out. Behind them, Julian shuffled slowly, his hand on his head, looking pale, tired, and in dire need of a couple of Percocet.

Declan showed them his palms. "Who had the car keys?"

No one fessed up. He pushed through them and headed for his room.

"All I have to say," he called, "is it's a good thing *one of us* had the foresight to keep a couple town vehicles for our own use." At the archway to the corridor, he turned. "Someone turn that alarm off!"

Bad hobbled toward a wall-mounted keypad.

"All right," Declan said, checking his watch. "We'll be online pretty soon. We can use the cameras to find them." His dead eyes panned the group. In a tone of perfect boredom, he said, "Let's go get them." Then he called over his shoulder. "Bad, you better be in the car when I get there, or you're going to walk home."

Laura woke to the alarm clock's *waa-waa-waa*. She came out of a dream as a pearl diver rises from the pressure and darkness of deep water to finally break surface. Groggy, she tried to distinguish her waking life from sleep. Grief returned to her, and she remembered that Tom's loss had not been imagined. Then an urgency washed over the grief, and she remembered Dillon. She sat up in bed, and everything came back.

She hadn't set a clock, and it wasn't a clock that woke her. She threw back the covers and leaped over Terry on the floor. He was starting to stir.

At the window she pushed back a drape. Directly across the street was the community center. The sound emanated from that building. The front doors were shut and nothing appeared amiss, as long as you ignored the smoking building next to it and didn't know that an entire town's population was being held against its will inside.

Movement snagged her attention. A figure ran around the rear of the Hummer, which had been parked in the street in front of the center. She recognized Hutch, the man who had been with her son. She slapped her palm repeatedly against the pane.

"Hey! Hey! Wait!"

He climbed into the driver's seat and shut the door. Frantically she looked around for something to shatter the glass. She grabbed a lamp from a dresser and yanked its cord out of the wall. She reeled back to hurl it through the window when she saw the door across the street open. Declan stepped out, and the Hummer squealed away. She dropped the lamp.

"What's going on?" Terry said, peering over the bed.

She kept her eyes on Declan as he turned to face a gathering crowd in the doorway. She was four feet from the window in a dark room. No way anyone over there could see her.

"What?" Terry repeated.

"Just a sec."

Declan reentered the building. His flunkies followed. The door swung shut.

Laura turned. "Your friend just drove off in the Hummer."

"Who?"

"Hutch!"

"In the Hummer?"

Laura sighed. She dropped into an overstuffed chair. These rooms above the town's florist and art gallery had been set up for use as a hotel, though they caught only the overflow from the two bed-and-breakfasts. The owner lived in an apartment behind the florist. Most likely he was now among the town's captive masses.

"You sure it was him?" Terry asked.

"Yes." She did not know whether to be elated or depressed.

"Was Dillon with him?"

"That's just it, I don't know. I didn't see him, but Hutch ran around from the passenger side, as if he'd helped someone in. That's why I didn't see him at first."

"Where did he go?"

"Up the street. I think he turned on Shatu' T'ine Way."

Terry kicked his blankets off and used the bed to push himself up. "Was anyone after him?"

"Declan watched him leave."

Terry's face skewed. "Like waving good-bye?"

"Like he didn't know he was leaving until he did, and by that time it was too late for Declan to do anything about it."

Terry looked out the window. "Whose are those other cars?" he said. "Looks like a Jeep Cherokee and an old Bronco."

Laura lowered her head into her hands. "They belong to some people in town, but I think Declan's using them."

Terry sat on the arm of the chair. He put his hand on her shoulder. "Hutch would never, ever leave Dillon. I know that about him. He would die first. So we have to assume they're together."

She looked up at him. Nothing but resolve on his face. He believed what he'd said.

"So now what?" he said.

She tried to make sense of the chaos in her head. "Hutch might try to make it to Fond-du-Lac or Black Lake, but Dillon knows that's slow going this time of year."

"But still, another town."

Laura shook her head. "I don't mean slow like a traffic jam. I mean slow like you can walk faster. And that's assuming you don't break an axle or completely slide or rattle right off the road."

"How do you get supplies?"

"Everyone stocks up in the winter. Winter roads are smooth as concrete. Supply trucks drive right across the river. Floatplanes bring campers and fishermen once a week in the summer, twice a month this time of year, if that."

"What if somebody gets injured or sick?"

"Dr. Jeffrey—"

"But he can't do everything. He doesn't have all the things a hospital emergency room would have."

"He's better equipped than most small-town docs because of the isolation. Besides, Black Lake has a hospital."

"That's Black Lake. You just said it may as well be the moon."

She stood up. "Let's go get your friend and my son."

"But where? If Dillon talks Hutch out of heading to one of the neighboring towns, where will they end up?"

"Dillon, Tom, and I—we have a cabin. It was my father's. Dillon will try to convince Hutch to take him there."

"I don't know if Hutch . . ."

Laura smiled. "Dillon can be very persuasive."

"We need to head north." Dillon was standing on the floor in front of the passenger seat. He swayed like a drunken sailor as the Hummer bumped over deep potholes and boulders, invisible in the darkness. Hutch was starting to think they'd make better time pushing the vehicle.

The heater howled with hot breath, but it was losing its battle with the chilly wind that came through the glassless window in the door behind Dillon.

Bracing himself, Dillon leaned over the wide center console. He looked Hutch square in the face. "We *need* to turn."

"What we need to do," Hutch said, trying to avoid Dillon's big, pleading eyes, quivering bottom lip, and about-to-cry whine, "is get help, and that means getting to another town."

"My dad says you can't get to Black Lake now. In a month or two the mud will freeze over, and then you can."

"With all respect to your dad, Dillon, we don't really have a couple of months."

Dillon's face dropped. He sat in the passenger seat, which just about swallowed him.

Hutch glanced over. "I'm trying to help us," he explained.

"My dad's dead," Dillon said.

"I'm sorry. When?"

"Two days ago."

Hutch braked to a stop, which wasn't much slower than they'd been moving anyway. He put the transmission in park and turned in his seat to face Dillon. "What?" he said.

Dillon stared down into the footwell. "Two days ago. Those men killed him. There was like . . . thunder . . . an explosion."

Hutch felt as though someone had punched him in the gut, again and again. He ached. The revelations of grief and pain just never stopped. He had thought it was really something that Dillon's mother had survived the explosion outside the back door of the rec center, and he had thought it was really something that he and Dillon had escaped the heart of Declan's lair. But Dillon had already suffered a catastrophic tragedy. It wasn't that those other things didn't count now, but it was like feeling elated at rescuing a man lost at sea, only to find that his legs had been bitten off by sharks.

"Dillon." He reached over and touched his hair. "I am so sorry. I am not going to let those people hurt you anymore. You or your mom. If I can, I'll see that they pay for what they did to your dad." He wondered what he would have done if he had had this information when he had his arrow pointed at Pruitt and then at Bad. He thought it would be a different world now, without Pruitt, without Bad, without Declan—or without him and without Dillon.

Hutch peered through the windshield. They had been driving with the headlamps off in an effort to keep Declan's eye in the sky from spotting the Hummer.

He didn't know what kind of technology was involved, whether whatever was up there had night-vision optics or infrared; all he could do were the things that made sense to him given his admittedly limited knowledge of what they were up against. As much as it seemed that Declan's resources made him omniscient and omnipotent, that really wasn't the case. If it were, he and Dillon would not be alive. Terry and Laura would not have survived Declan's last blast.

Hutch had escaped from them in the woods and again when David was murdered, thanks only to Terry's relatively insignificant pistol. True to what Hutch knew about life, Declan's powers seemed wildly inconsistent. Here was a man who could take over a town and imprison more than two hundred people, but in the course of pursuing four men, he'd succeeded in getting only one of them. One was enough, but it said something about the limits of his power.

Beside him, Dillon sniffed, and he realized the boy was crying. He had lost his father, which meant another success to Declan. He was sure there were others he didn't know about. He could not help but believe there was something about Phil, Terry, and himself that somehow neutralized Declan's power.

What was it? What had they done differently from David and Dillon's father? He had been there when David died. Had almost died himself. To find a common denominator, he needed to know more about how Dillon's dad had died. Regardless of how potentially crucial the details could be, he would never ask them of Dillon. He needed to find Laura. He could not return to town, and he had no way of knowing where she might be. She was with Terry and, he hoped, Phil, but now, after this much time, he didn't know where any of them were. Then it dawned on him.

"Dillon?"

The boy barely glanced at him. His eyes were red and leaking. He did not seem ashamed, as though his grief supplanted every other feeling in the spectrum of human emotion.

"Dillon, why do you want us to head north?"

In a small voice Dillon said, "There's a cabin."

"A cabin? What about it?"

"Mom said to go there."

"Then that's where we'll go."

Dillon looked at him, really looked at him.

"If that's what you want, Dillon, that's what we'll do. Your mom is a smart lady, setting up something like that way before she could have known that you would ever need it. You want to go there?"

Dillon nodded.

"Do you know how to get to this cabin?"

Dillon nodded.

"Without . . . wait a minute . . . I have a map." Hutch retrieved the vinyl topo map from his inside pocket. "Will this help?"

Dillon shook his head. "Don't need it. It's by the fire."

"The fire?"

"Last year's fire. It burned miles of forest, but Dad and I went back to the cabin and it wasn't burned. The fire came really close, but it turned away. Dad said that proved the cabin was special."

Hutch remembered flying over the burned land. How many miles from the campsite had their pilot said it was? He couldn't remember, but it wasn't too terribly far. Fiddler Falls and Black Lake had been evacuated, the pilot had said.

"Is it walking distance from your house?"

Dillon shook his head. "Dad takes a Jeep."

"How long a drive is it?"

Dillon shrugged. "Couple hours."

"Are the trails really bad? Like this one?" Hutch didn't want to go to a cabin to meet Laura if it would have been just as easy to get to Black Lake. But at the rate they were going, Black Lake was considerably farther than a couple of hours. Ten, twelve maybe.

Dillon raised his eyebrows. "Not *this* bad."

Hutch used his thumb to wipe a tear from Dillon's face. An intimate gesture he hoped Dillon would recognize as a sign of caring. He wanted the boy to trust him and to know he wasn't alone. He said, "I can't get there without you. You need to be my navigator. Can you do that?"

Dillon smiled and nodded.

Hutch held out his hand. "Partners?"

Dillon took it in his own. His grip was surprisingly firm. They shook.

Hutch looked out the windshield. In the dark, the road did not appear nearly as rugged as it was. "So where to, Mr. Navigator?"

"There's a trail a little ways back. It leads into the hills above town. We go that way."

"How far back?" In an effort to throw pursuers off their tail, he had started toward Fond-du-Lac to the west before circling back to head for Black Lake, due east. He could not be sure the trick had worked or that Declan hadn't spotted them after they'd changed course. He dreaded the possibility of running headlong into them.

"Just there!" He turned in his seat and pointed.

Hutch saluted. He popped the vehicle into reverse and backed off the road. He threw it in drive and pulled onto the road, heading back the way they'd come. He prayed he was making the right decision.

Julian appeared in the doorway of the office Declan had appropriated for his headquarters and bedroom. Hunched over a briefcase full of electronic equipment, Declan glanced up briefly, then again to hold on Julian. The boy held the arrow he had found in the field in one hand, tapping it against his leg. He had brushed his long dark hair down over his forehead, as was his style. The bruise and gash were not evident. Still, he looked as miserable as a death-row prisoner after his last meal.

"What?" Declan asked impatiently.

Julian shuffled in. "Dec . . ." He paused, searching for words. "I don't know about this."

"What's *this*?"

"All of this, everything we're doing up here."

Declan straightened. "What's the problem, Julie?"

The boy shrugged, seemed to study the tile floor. "Pru's video . . . I mean, who kills people and puts the footage in a video game? Isn't that like saying, 'Look what we did'?"

Declan laughed. "You gotta trust me, kid. First, everything we do up here's going to get scrubbed clean. You don't think Dad would leave us exposed, do you?"

"I don't think he—"

"*Whatever* happens here, Julian. He'll take care of it, okay? He always does. Besides, Kyrill's going to tweak the images, change the look of the people, the town, the landscape. We might run it all through a filter to make it look computer generated. The important thing is, we'll get the physics right—the explosions, the crashes, the facial expressions. It's going to take gaming to the next level, wait and see."

Julian nodded, the movement seeming to take all his strength. He turned to leave.

"Julie." Declan approached him. "You've got to get over this, dude." He wrapped an arm around Julian's neck. "If every bump and bruise puts you out of the game, you might as well not play at all."

"I didn't ask to come."

"You like hanging with me. Dad wanted you to."

"I didn't know . . . never mind."

"I won't. But you gotta grow a spine, okay?"

"The doctor said I got a *concussion*, Dec."

"He gave you meds, didn't he?"

"Yeah, and I don't know if the way I feel is from the knock on the head or all the pills. I'm sick and dizzy. I feel like I'm moving underwater."

Declan slapped Julian's forehead, hard.

The boy cried out and tried to jerk away, but Declan's arm held him firm. He waited until Julian stopped struggling, then said flatly, "Get over it." He released him, went to the case on the cot, shut the lid, and latched it. "Bring this out to the Jeep," he said.

Julian was touching his forehead and examining his fingers. Declan saw the blood. The kid really did have to toughen up. Reared in a world of chauffeured cars, tutored education, and nannies to towel you off after every shower, it was easy to be soft.

Poverty and rough streets often drove people like their father to inhuman levels of work and determination, innovation and manipulation. So it was more than ironic and sad that the children of self-made men were pampered to the point of weakness and dependency. If these kids accepted only the comforts and did not go out of their way to find the challenges that would make them strong, they would be nothing more than possessions to be placed where they looked pretty, displayed as evidence of their parents' humanity.

Declan and Julian's father had sired five children, each from a different wife. Declan's slightly younger sister was institutionalized somewhere in Europe. A younger brother, older than Julian, had killed himself five years ago. Then there was the baby, two-year-old Clarissa, from Dad's current wife, who was three years younger than Declan. So two Page siblings were already lost, either dead or as good as. Declan was determined to avoid their fate.

He had offered to help Julian as well, but his little brother didn't seem interested in being his own man. Money bought lots of things—freedom to live and travel in opulence, to experience the entire banquet of life's possibilities; power and control over people. But it did not make you strong. Only struggle did that. Adversity. Poets said it: "When it is dark enough, you can see the stars"—Ralph Waldo Emerson. Buddhist philosophers believed it: "We must embrace pain and burn it as fuel for our journey"—Kenji Miyazawa. The Christian Bible confirmed it: "See, I have refined you, though not as silver; I have tested you in the furnace of affliction."

So what were people born into wealth to do? How were you supposed to grow strong when there was no weight, no friction to challenge your muscles, your mind, your will? Unless you were satisfied being nothing more than a consumer, a spender of inherited fortune, you needed to create the challenge, the struggle, the friction. You needed to cut a tree down and catch it. To set your house on fire and leap through the flames. To kill and not be caught, or be caught and beat the rap.

Grudgingly, Julie snatched up the case. He stopped at the door. He said, "I want to go home."

"I know." Declan thought a moment. "Come here."

Julian didn't move.

"Come here," Declan repeated.

Julian turned and walked back.

Declan untied a bracelet from his right wrist. Gestured for Julian to lift his arm.

"I don't want that," the boy said.

"Yes, you do. It's peyote root from the Apaches. It'll make you brave."

Julian shifted the arrow to the hand that also held the case. He raised his wrist.

Declan indicated the arrow. "What's that for?"

Julian shrugged. "I like it. It's cool."

Declan tied the bracelet to him. "There," he said. "Your first amulet. Wait'll you see what that does."

Julian looked at it. He rotated his wrist.

"Yeah?" Declan said.

Julian nodded. He shuffled out.

Declan called, "Cort! Cortland!"

She breezed in, considerably perkier than Julian.

"I want you to stay here," he said.

"Dec—" she started.

"Keep your eye on the place. Lock the doors after we leave. Don't unchain the auditorium doors. Where's your gun?"

She lowered her head.

"Cort?"

"I think it got destroyed in the explosion out back."

"Or those guys out there got it?" he said, realizing but not caring that his tone was like kicking the already shaky scaffolding of her self-confidence.

While the doctor was tending to Bad and Julian, he, Kyrill, and Pruitt had gone out to examine the destruction. Shockingly, there had been no bodies, no body parts. He did not know how that last strike had missed. At least two—and he had thought four—people were in the kill zone when he fired.

Too many glitches in the system. He supposed weeding them out was in part what he was there for in the first place. He only hoped that the deficiencies lay in one of the other divisions' workmanship and not in the control pad Declan's own company had designed. This was an ideal opportunity to show his father that video gaming was no longer about distraction and entertainment, but touched all aspects of life, especially when it came to the industry of war.

Unfortunately, the glitches he was discovering extended beyond technology. The people around him were as defective as miscoded programs.

Julie was being a wuss, not at all the stand-up guy Declan thought would emerge on this trip. Certainly he was not as savvy about the way things were as Declan had been at his age.

Bad, his most effective soldier, had allowed himself to get shot—by an *arrow* at that! He wasn't down for the count yet; Declan intended on pushing him as hard as ever, on showing him that winners didn't run home crying at the first sight of blood.

And now Cort. Declan and the guys had spent countless hours disabling vehicles, collecting keys, searching for communication devices, and locking up as many guns as they could find, either on their own or by coercing their locations from townsfolk. It took only one rogue individual to muck everything up. He'd seen it before: Die Hard, Lethal Weapon, even The Lord of the Rings—and *that* little troublemaker was a hobbit! And here Cortland goes and gives a weapon to these interlopers, his own real-life Bruce Willises. One of them already had a gun, as the shattered window of the Hummer attested. But either the people who came into town last night did not include the gunslinger, or something had happened to his weapon. Otherwise why resort to a weapon as primitive as a bow and arrow? As every shooting game proved, the more technology invested in a weapon, the better it was. Spears beat knives, pistols beat spears, automatic rifles beat pistols, bombs beat rifles, and Declan controlled the weapon that beat them all.

But despite his belief in the value of escalating technology, he knew that one man with one bullet could change the course of history. *"For want of a nail" and all that*, he thought.

He turned away from Cortland to retrieve his Jean Dunand wristwatch from the desk, but primarily to emphasize his displeasure. He said, "When Julie comes back from the car, tell him to get you a gun from the stash we locked up." He fiddled with the clasp on his watch until he heard her footsteps heading for the door.

He glanced over his shoulder. "And, Cort? You won't lose this one, right?"

She nodded and left.

The Slacker was in a metal case the size of a hefty paperback book. He plucked it up from the cot and followed her out of the room, stopping in the corridor.

"Pru!" he called.

Pruitt stepped into the corridor from the next room. He held the camera in his hands. An LCD monitor jutted out from the camera body. Declan could see flashes of moving color on the screen. A cord dropped down from a plug in the camera, then looped up to Pruitt's ear. "Yeah?"

"Have you reviewed the footage so far?"

"Good stuff, Dec."

"What do we still need?"

Pruitt pursed his lips in thought. He looked down at the camera, as though gazing at his own memory bank.

"Uh . . . we could use a couple more human targets, maybe some animals, definitely some vehicles . . ." He closed his eyes. "Burning trees, buildings, some misses would be nice." His eyes snapped open. "Those night shots turned out fantastic! And the river yesterday, with that guy? Couldn't ask for more."

"Great. We'll see what we can do about those other things. Got everything? Ready?"

Pruitt gestured with his head. "Let me grab an extra battery and a different lens. I'll be right there."

"Bad! I don't see you!"

"I'm coming, Dec, man! My leg hurts like—"

"I don't want to hear it!"

The same well from which Bad drew his competitive spirit—his ability to see everything as a game to be won or lost—also produced buckets of fierce independence. That his father was a multimillionaire didn't help matters. But it was Declan's father who had made Bad's family rich. So it was to Declan that Bad owed his allegiance, even if it meant suppressing a natural desire to guide his own ship.

"Let's go, people!" Declan bellowed. To Julian, who was heading toward the far corridor with Cortland, he said, "Hurry, Julie. We don't have time for your shuffling around."

Kyrill jogged up to him, .50-cal rifle in hand. "Ready, boss," he said.

Declan punched his arm. "Good man, Kyrill. You drive the Jeep."

The teen's face lit up. "Yeah?"

"Yeah. Pru! You and Bad take the Bronco. Now! We're leaving!"

He crossed the vestibule and pushed out the door.

"What's going on?" Laura said. She sat on the bed in the hotel room across from the community center. By the dim moonlight coming through the windows, she peeled away bandages on her fingers and knuckles, replacing them with fresh ones from Terry's first aid kit.

"They're leaving," Terry said. He had spent the past ten minutes watching for additional activity. "Declan . . . one, two rifles . . . that camera guy . . ."

"Going after Hutch and Dillon," Laura said, certain.

He turned from the window. "Any suggestions?"

She scrunched her face, shook her head. "What you said, about the vehicles you saw coming into town being all disabled. I heard them talking about it, getting all the keys, cutting wires. Cars, boats, ATVs. Sounded like they were pretty thorough."

"They couldn't have gotten *every* mode of transportation in the whole town." It sounded more like a question than a statement.

"Not every family in town owns a car," she said. "Everything we need is here or in walking distance. Some families pool their money and buy a beater. Lots of off-road toys, though: four-wheelers, three-wheelers, dirt bikes. Snowmobiles, but that won't help now."

Headlamps from outside suddenly glowed against Terry's face, catching worry lines as well as stern determination. The illumination rolled off his face. Engines rose in pitch, then faded as the trucks drove away. Terry came over and sat on the bed next to her.

"Let me do that," he said.

"I got it." Then she realized not only that it would be nice to have someone caring for her, even a stranger with this small thing, but that it would help him as well to feel he was doing something. She handed him the package and showed him her knuckles.

"We should put something on that." He rooted around in the first aid bag and found a tube of antibiotic ointment. He applied it to the bandage, then laid it on her wound. "This cabin you say Dillon will go to—can we walk?"

"No, it's pretty far. If Declan's gang searches methodically for Hutch and Dillon, they'll find it way before we get there by foot."

"Do we have options?"

"I say we start searching houses for something—anything—we can use to get there."

"I'd like to find a gun or two, or at least ammo for the ones we have. And there's no chance of getting word out, as far as you know?"

"I'm sure they got all the satellite phones. They're expensive and a big deal up here. Nobody would own one without the whole town knowing. Shortwave doesn't work too well up here. Nobody within talking distance. I'd say light a building on fire and get the attention of the other towns that way, but Declan doesn't seem too worried about drawing that kind of attention. They must have already informed the other towns that Fiddler Falls would be conducting some controlled burns or something like that. Otherwise, somebody would have already come."

"I'm just amazed that there are still places in this world that are so isolated."

"You said that's what you guys were looking for, right?"

"Yeah."

"Well, you're not the only ones."

Terry finished with the bandages.

Laura looked at them, impressed by how tight and professional they appeared. She flexed her hand, feeling the tape. "Okay," she said. "I got a kid waiting for me to pick him up."

Hutch and Dillon felt like stowaways on a crashing plane. The Hummer jostled them so severely, Hutch had hit his head on the high ceiling and Dillon had vibrated right out of the passenger seat, onto the floor. Now they both wore seat belts, and if they were no longer in a crashing plane, they had hitched a ride on a mechanical paint shaker. They went through fields of rocks and fallen timber and along paths designed for animals treading in single file. One side of the truck or the other seemed to be constantly canting down into a ravine.

"The road to Black Lake is worse than this?" Hutch asked.

"That's what Dad says . . . said." Dillon turned his face toward the window.

He was pushing back some serious hurt. *When this is over, the kid is going to have a meltdown,* Hutch thought.

230

The sky had lightened to reveal dark gray clouds rolling in from the north. Even the red-yellow-orange sunrise could not penetrate them. That beautiful light seemed far away, as remote as the towns they could not reach. Chilly wind howled through the glassless window behind Dillon.

"Are you sure we're heading in the right direction?"

Dillon nodded.

Hutch scanned the instruments and LCD screens arrayed on the dash and center console. One large monitor had glowed white since leaving town. Every once in a while a serpentine blue line would appear, making him believe it was a GPS unit without the benefit of local maps. Other dials and gauges were as foreign to him as an Arabic recipe for *samboosak*. Hutch did not want to stop until they reached their destination, so he had made a mental note to ask Dillon to search the interior for anything useful as soon as they came to a patch of flat land. He was beginning to wonder if this region contained any smooth topography at all. The lightening day finally outshone the headlamps, which had seemed to shake independently of the passenger compartment, compounding an already disorienting and nauseating ride.

They rolled over a grassy knoll, and Dillon yelled, "Look!"

Hutch followed his finger to see two vehicles bouncing and leaping toward them. They were the SUVs that had been parked in front of the community center: a dark green Jeep Cherokee and a red Ford Bronco. They were descending the opposite incline of a shallow valley separating Hutch and Dillon.

"Oh no. How—"

If the Hummer continued its current trajectory, the Jeep and Bronco would intercept them at a ninety-degree angle in about five minutes. Instead, Hutch cranked the wheel right. They were now on the same compass bearing as Declan; instead of intercepting the

Hummer, the freak would have to outrun it. They rose over a grassy hill and down into an adjoining valley. At the wide, gentle arc of the valley floor, he stopped. Somehow Declan had found them. He suspected the culprit was whatever contraption he had overhead that had also tracked Hutch to the campsite and spotted him, Terry, and Phil in town. That or some kind of tracking device on the Hummer itself.

He pulled out his topo map, studied it. He had started the sport of hunting well before the advent of GPS location systems and preferred printed maps to devices whose software he didn't completely trust and whose batteries could fail at the worst possible times. Consequently, he could read the thread-thin lines of a topo as easily as a Grisham novel. Having a decent sense of their route since leaving town, and now scanning for topographical markers most other people would have overlooked, he identified their position. His eyes moved in each direction until he found what he was looking for.

"Okay," he said, unsnapping his seat belt. He instructed Dillon to do the same. He rubbed his shoulder, sore from the constant chafing of the shoulder strap. "This is going to be scary, but you gotta trust me. Can you do that, partner?"

"Yes," Dillon said firmly. The *s* sound revealed a slight lisp.

Hutch smiled at that.

He got the Hummer moving and turned to travel the length of the valley floor. It pitched and rolled like a roller coaster. Forward visibility was no more than three or four hundred yards, but he knew from the map that it sloped steadily and nearly without bend or yaw all the way to the Fond du Lac River, intersecting it a half mile west of Fiddler Falls.

The Hummer banked sharply and disappeared over the next rise.

"They're onto us," Kyrill said.

"What gave you that idea?" Declan intoned. He checked the cell phone-like device in his hand. It showed his position in relation to the Hummer. Until the Hummer turned again, there was no way for them to angle for an interception as they had done this time. As long as all three vehicles traveled in essentially the same direction, it was nothing more than a race, and the Hummer, which was the superior off-road vehicle, would win every time. He had a feeling the driver of the Hummer knew this as well. He checked his watch. He pushed the GPS tracker between his legs and pulled the silver case from the footwell onto his lap. He opened it and withdrew the controller. The controller that had been both a joy and a pain on this adventure. He pushed the case off his lap and flicked on the controller. The monitor showed static, and he checked his watch again. Very soon.

"Just get me within a hundred yards," he told Kyrill. They reached the nadir of the valley and began climbing the other side.

"Dec," Julian said from the rear seat. "I can't take this shaking. I feel like my head's going to split in two."

Declan turned in the passenger seat. "You're kidding me, right? Do you see what we're doing here? We almost got the guys who stole the Hummer." He raised his eyebrows. "If your head splits in two, Julie, I'm sure Dad's got a doctor on the payroll who'll glue it together for you. Okay?"

Julian looked out the window. The Bronco bounded and rattled beside them.

Declan could see Pruitt's determined countenance behind the wheel. Bad sat in the rear seat looking worse than Julian. Declan smiled thinking about Bad's leg bouncing up and down in the seat. If that didn't make him mean enough to tear heads off, nothing would.

He remembered attending a training session for one guard dog of his father's. The trainer had donned a ski mask and poked and prodded the rottweiler mercilessly. The trainer had explained that he would continue agitating the animal using several different disguises, the kind kidnappers used, such as Halloween masks and stockings over their faces. Eventually, the dog would attack to kill anyone on the property in such a disguise. Declan had wondered what would happen if he could convince one of his school friends to put on a mask and run outside.

That was one of the few curiosities he had not satisfied. But the reason the memory came to him now was not regret for opportunities not taken, but confirmation of how he was handling Bad's injury. Pushing him would make him more determined to exact revenge, and that would return him to the warrior state he had been in prior to finding himself shish kebabed. So instead of being weakened by the experience, Bad would be strengthened.

Declan smiled. He was a leader in every sense of the word, always encouraging people to reach heights that even they had not imagined possible. He wasn't monitoring the GPS, so it came as a surprise when they crested the hill to see the Hummer so close. It had reached the next valley floor and turned onto it to head toward the river way below. It disappeared over a low rise.

"Go, go!" Declan instructed, anticipating victory. He plucked a walkie-talkie from his jacket's breast pocket and keyed the transmit button. He looked over his right shoulder to see Pruitt behind the Bronco's wheel, lifting in his seat to retrieve his walkie-talkie from a back pocket or belt clip. He raised it to his mouth. His voice came through, tinny and staticky.

"Hello," he said. "This is Pruitt."

Declan rolled his eyes. He keyed the button and said, "Can Pruitt come out and play?" Through the windows of the vehicles, Declan witnessed Pru's utter confusion.

"Pardon?" came his voice.

"Nothing," Declan said. "Just get ready to film."

"Now?"

"Think you can do it and drive at the same time?"

"What? No . . . I . . . well . . ."

Declan regretted his decision to let Pruitt drive. Julian would have been a better candidate; he was still years from getting a license, but he'd learned to drive on their father's vast properties. If Julie had been driving, Pruitt could have filmed from the passenger seat. Then again, Julian, being Julian, probably would not have kept up, and there would be no chance to photograph the upcoming fireworks.

"How about Bad? Can he film?" said Declan into the walkie-talkie. He saw Bad shaking his head and forming his lips into a big *no*.

"He says no. And he can't move around too much. I don't think he'd get it."

"All right. Never mind. As soon as the thing goes up, get your butt out there and get what you can."

"Affirmative," Pruitt said. "Ten-four."

Declan dropped the walkie-talkie back into his pocket. They reached the apex of the next hill just as the Hummer dropped out of view over the following hummock. It was still a good sixty seconds ahead.

"Step on it! Come on!"

Woods swung into view from the right, narrowing the drivable width of the valley floor. Kyrill edged left to keep from being anywhere near the trees. Declan glanced back, pleased to see that there was still enough room for the vehicles to drive somewhat side by side. He didn't want Pruitt and his camera or Bad and his gun to fall too far behind. They flew over the rise, an elevator's lurch in Declan's stomach.

They had gained on the Hummer—by a lot. It was angling away from the trees, and Declan wondered if they had nearly crashed, the driver having to brake and adjust.

"Almost," he said. He checked the device and saw that the monitor was online. A few clicks and both the Jeep and the Hummer came into view. He centered the Hummer in the monitor and expertly followed it using the thumb controls. He flipped open the targeting control; red crosshairs appeared on the screen. He positioned it just ahead of the Hummer. When he removed his thumb, the crosshairs blinked out.

"We need to get closer—step on it."

Kyrill said, "We're already—"

"Just do it."

The Hummer banked up the left-hand valley wall, which was no more than a steep grassy hill. It came back into the valley and shot toward the trees before it arced back onto the valley floor. It seemed to be following the natural contours of the land, but Declan suspected the driver was trying to be evasive.

Not today, friend, he thought.

The Hummer's zigzagging allowed Kyrill to narrow the gap. They were traveling fast now, and Declan felt a surge of excitement bordering on giddiness. The people in the Hummer must realize what was coming, what Declan was capable of doing to them. He checked the targeting mechanism again. This time when he released his thumb, the crosshairs remained.

The Hummer was in range.

Keeping the camera on the Hummer and the crosshairs directly in front of it with one practiced thumb, Declan retrieved the walkie-talkie again and said, "Okay, get ready."

He pushed the trigger control with his right index finger. Slacker confirmed the order with a quick three-note chime. The tone was too quiet for targets to hear, unless they were close and the air was free of ambient noise. But if they did, it would be the last thing they heard, a death knell played fast because that's the way they were about to die.

"Stop stop stop!" Declan told Kyrill.

They braked, sliding on the grass. The familiar visible rippling of air currents, which seemed to cocoon a green rod of radiant light, appeared instantly before them, its descent too fast for human eyes. In less than a nanosecond the Hummer stopped, pushed into the ground, and instantly superheated. It came apart. Metal that was not fused by the strike flew up with dirt and gravel and grass, appearing to explode, but without explosives. Then its gas tank ruptured and it did explode, spewing burning fuel over the hillside. The front right wheel continued on, bouncing and rolling and disappearing right over the next hill.

The Jeep slid sideways to a complete stop. Declan hopped out and trotted toward the destroyed Hummer until a hot wind pushed him back a step. He turned to wave Pruitt forward.

"Come on, come on."

Pruitt had the camera resting on his shoulder, the eyepiece in place, adjusting the focusing wheel as he approached.

Kyrill stepped up beside Declan. He said, "Wanna put a chase like that in the game?"

Declan thought about it. "Yeah," he said finally. "That was pretty cool. But let's throw in some more evasive maneuvers." He waggled his hand in front of him. "We could put in an algorithm that makes targeting more difficult but slows them down. Kind of like what happened here, you know? And let's bring trees in on the other side too. That'll make it more challenging, like a slalom."

Kyrill looked around, scratching his head. "We could put a river right here, maybe a waterfall."

"Let's not get carried away. Pru!" he called. "Pru! Get the river valley and the sunrise. That's beautiful." He turned to Kyrill again. "Don't you think that's beautiful?"

Every time Laura felt bad about violating the privacy of her neigh-bors, she reminded herself that Tom was dead and Dillon was in jeop-ardy. There was nothing she could do now for her husband. It was Dillon who drove her on and absolved her guilt. She and Terry had spontaneously developed an effective method for searching for the things they needed. They would check garages first. If there were no vehicles, or the ones they found had been disabled, they would take a quick glance for a gun rack or something that looked like a safe place to store firearms. Then they would move on. They had realized they could not search every home and felt that firearms kept inside would be too well hidden. So far they'd inspected six garages, finding three four-wheel drives, a dirt bike, and a four-wheeler. All of them had been rendered useless. In the seventh garage they found a rifle rack mounted to the bare studs, but no weapons. The hood of the old truck there was down, giving them hope.

"This is Emmett Cooper's. He's a fishing guide. He's always using this thing. I know it runs."

Terry told her, "Pop the latch."

She did and came around to the front as he lifted the hood. The spark plug wires had been sliced, the distributor cap cracked and broken.

Laura felt her heart sink. In the hotel room she had bought in to Terry's conviction that every vehicle could not possibly have been disabled. Now she was starting to believe that it was possible, that they would not get to the cabin. What would happen to Dillon then? Would Hutch stay with him? Would he feel come back for his friends? Would Declan and his gang find them? She had not given any of these questions much thought, choosing instead to believe that she would get there and be with him.

Terry lowered the hood.

He said with a half smile, "Would've liked to slam it."

She shared his frustration. She felt like pounding her fists against the hood, kicking the sheet metal until the truck looked like it had rolled end over end from the hunting cabins in the hills above town. But they did not know who of their assailants remained in town, within hearing distance. So they searched quietly. Most garage doors had been raised and left open. When Terry or Laura had to open one, they pulled slowly, though in their hearts they wanted to slam the things up, noise be damned.

In one garage—it was Bonnie Tithly's, the sixth-, seventh-, and eighth-grade teacher—they found a Jeep CJ7 thoroughly disabled. Beside it was a four-wheel ATV. Laura remembered Bonnie arriving at school on it. It appeared to have been overlooked by the vandals, but there were no keys. They looked for them in the garage, perhaps hanging on a nail or inside a cabinet, but found nothing. Terry checked the interior garage door. It was unlocked and opened into a kitchen. Next to the door was a key rack in the shape of a wiener dog, little brass hooks in a row—all void of keys.

Laura had allowed hope into her heart. As they searched kitchen drawers, coat pockets, closets, and countertops, the diminishing of that hope ached like a sore tooth.

"Can't you hot-wire it?" she asked, more desperation in her voice than she had intended.

He shook his head. "Not much use for that skill in real estate."

She wondered if she could do it. Movies made it look so simple. Yank a couple wires, touch them together. But she knew that wasn't the way it really worked. If it were that simple, there would be no point to keys in the first place. She felt it would take forever just to find out she couldn't reach any wires, let alone which two, if only two, combined to ignite the ATV's engine.

Disappointed, increasingly frustrated and depressed, they moved to the next house.

Flat on his stomach, in the long grass, Hutch watched. First the green Cherokee, then the red Bronco roared past. He wished he still had his camouflage makeup, but he thought the woodland foliage provided ample cover, especially with their pursuers so intent on catching the Hummer. Lying beside him, Dillon raised his head. His hair was roughly the same color as the brown grass. Every little bit helped.

As they had traveled over the valley floor, Hutch had removed his belt. He'd looped it through the steering wheel and let it hang. Dillon had retrieved Hutch's bow from the backseat, selected an arrow from the quiver, and handed it to him. After the woods had appeared on their right—as Hutch knew they would from the topo map—he watched for just the right place to pull over. He had adjusted the speed of the Hummer to make his lead ideal in terms of the amount of time they would be out of sight. They crested a hill just as the Jeep crested the one behind them so that the two vehicles would be near the bottom of the following dips simultaneously as well.

Hutch's plan had worked perfectly.

When he pulled to a stop near the trees, Dillon immediately hopped out with Hutch's bow and slammed the door. He ran into the trees and dropped straight down.

Hutch disengaged the transmission and wedged the arrow between the accelerator pedal and the front panel of the driver's seat. The engine raced. He slid out and shut the door, then jumped up to rest his stomach on the open windowsill and tied the belt to a handhold on the door, keeping some slack in it. That would limit its movement in both directions without forcing it into a robotically straight inclination.

Finally he slammed the transmission shifter into drive and shoved himself out of the window and away. The vehicle had spun its tires, found traction, and accelerated away. The preparations had allowed him to accomplish this feat in less than ten seconds.

He then kicked grass over the two marks made by the Hummer's spinning tires and was in the grass with Dillon twenty seconds before Declan's vehicles came over the rise.

The Hummer breached the next hill and disappeared, followed closely by the Jeep and the Bronco.

Hutch hoped the Hummer would travel all the way to the Fond du Lac and plunge in. That would move their enemies a good distance from them; if Declan thought he had witnessed a suicide or a crazy, inscrutable escape attempt, he might not bother to come looking for them again.

After watching the vehicles disappear over the hill, Hutch and Dillon shared a smile. Dirt clung to the boy's face, grass made his hair look wild, but in the short time Hutch had known him, he'd never looked so healthy, so happy . . . so *good*. It was the first time they were not hiding or running. At this moment, they were free. That knowledge transformed Dillon into the sort of child you'd see in a Disneyland commercial: carefree and boyish. His father's death seemed to have temporarily fallen away from his consciousness, a brief reprieve from a burden Hutch knew the boy would bear his entire life.

"The cabin?" he asked, giving Dillon a role to play in this adventure.

Dillon seemed to understand Hutch's intentions—he pretended to think about it. Then he said, "Yeah, I think the cabin should be our next stop."

Hutch reached for his binoculars, but found only their lightweight harness on his chest. He'd removed the binocs in the cabinet and had forgotten them there. He hoped he wouldn't need them. He crawled backward on his hands and knees until the trees and the shadows grew thicker, then he stood. Dillon followed. Hutch had the boy's face squarely in his vision when an explosion reached them from the near distance. Dillon jumped a bit. His hair rose, if not actually standing on end, as his scalp tightened in surprise. His eyes flashed wide, then his eyebrows came together in a scowl. His mouth offered a silent scream. The expression may have been comical had Hutch not realized that his own face had contorted similarly, and the emotion behind it was anything but funny.

Another explosion, much smaller.

Hutch thought he understood what had happened. Declan had fired upon the Hummer. He had not heard the *whoosh-crack* this time, because at that distance, the sounds of whatever it was coming down and the resulting explosion all blurred together. The second smaller explosion must have been the gas tank or some kind of munitions that had been stored in the Hummer.

It shocked him to realize how very close he and Dillon had been to death. Again.

He wondered what this sudden end to the chase meant to them. Did Declan have enough experience blowing up occupied vehicles to recognize the absence of bodies? Would he even check? Did it mean the pursuit was over or that it was about to start fresh?

Hutch had gleaned enough from his previous encounters with Declan's weapon to know that whatever provided the firepower also enabled Declan to peer down from the sky. He was convinced this was the reason Declan's aim had been so far off when he had gone after Hutch in the woods, and why Hutch had been able to hide in the tree limbs, then flee back to camp. Several times during that trek he had crossed open fields; Declan must have spotted him at least once when he had done so.

He had noticed something else about Declan's weapon—and if it were true, it would give Declan's targets an advantage. No, not an advantage, but a *chance*. Even if only a small one. What he had noticed was this: Declan's attacks came in spurts. A brief, furious, almost staccato pounding followed by long periods of cease-fire. Cease-fire at least from the cannon. It was primarily during these times that Declan's men armed themselves to continue the pursuit.

These respites from the cannon attacks were fact; what bothered him was not having an explanation for them. Were they self-imposed for some reason, or were they forced upon Declan by the limits of technology? Probably the latter, since Hutch did not believe Declan exercised self-control.

With his topo map, Hutch carried a grease pencil to mark animal sightings, possible campsites, and other points of interest. Now he withdrew both and recorded the time on the blank back of the map. He returned the pen and map to his jacket pocket.

The boy from the television commercial was gone. Fear had returned. Dillon's eyes brimmed with unshed tears. Whether they flowed from terror, from the realization of the close call, or from the reminder of his father, Hutch could not tell. He dropped to his knees, took the boy in his arms, and hugged him. Dillon squeezed tightly around his neck, weeping quietly, his small chest heaving against Hutch.

But in giving comfort it was impossible not to receive it, and Hutch realized he had hugged Dillon not only for the boy's sake but for his own as well. Each of them needed to know the comfort of another human. To know he was not alone in his fright.

Despite an urgency to put ground between them and Declan's gang, Hutch held Dillon until the child's tears stopped. Even then, Hutch refused to relinquish his hug. When the boy lifted his head from Hutch's shoulder and eased his hold, Hutch unwrapped his arms and leaned back. His patience was rewarded with a sad smile, but a smile nonetheless.

"We gotta go," Hutch said.

"I know."

Hutch had expected no more than the nod Dillon had offered so many times before. He thought these words marked a deepening of their relationship, or at least of Dillon's trust in him—and that was good enough.

Turning his thoughts toward the journey ahead, Hutch retrieved the map again and spread it out on the ground. He lay down before it and asked Dillon to join him.

"If I explain the terrain to you, on this map, do you think you could show me where the cabin is?"

Dillon scanned the map—all of its thread-thin contour lines, tiny elevation numbers, color-coded ecosystem indicators. Finally he shrugged.

Hutch said, "We'll do it this way . . ." He pointed into the woods, in the direction they were heading, away from the place, where the

Hummer was most certainly a smoldering wreck. "Over this wooded rise is another long, shallow valley, lots of trees. From the top of this hill we should see two mountains. One to our left would have trees coming around both sides, but not joining in front, like it's wearing a shawl or cape . . ."

Dillon listened, nodding. His eyes stared into the woods, but he was seeing Hutch's landscape.

38

Laura sat on the rear bumper of an anonymous four-wheel-drive pickup truck, yet another vehicle disabled by Declan's gang. She had lost count of how many garages they had entered, how many cars and trucks and motorcycles and ATVs they had checked. At last count the population of Fiddler Falls was 242. The number of households was roughly eighty-five, which included half a dozen at the Kramer boardinghouse and at least two dozen small cabins and mobile homes fanning out well beyond what Laura considered the town proper. That left approximately fifty residences in town. She knew not everyone owned a vehicle, but it seemed to her they had checked at least that many in the last ninety minutes or so. Terry leaned against the frame of the garage opening.

"So I was wrong," he said. "It seems they did reach every vehicle in town."

Laura frowned. "I heard they recruited some townsfolk to help them, threatened them if they didn't. I suppose, with eight or ten people, it wouldn't be too difficult to find everything with wheels and disable them."

Terry shrugged. "Look how many we got to. It's not like they had to start them or spend any time with them. They just had to make them immobile." They had found a few cars with broken driver's side windows. Terry had speculated that they had been locked and broken into so the vandals could access the hood latches.

"They collected keys as well," Laura said. "They got mine, and I heard them demanding them from others. Kyrill and Bad, with their rifles."

"Doesn't look like they needed to. They were thorough enough destroying the cars."

Laura thought about it, then said, "Except they kept a couple for themselves."

"The ones they used to follow the Hummer," Terry agreed.

"It makes sense. Why have all this going on and rely on only one truck? They would want a backup and maybe a couple if they had to go in different directions, run different errands, or whatever it is they do."

"Are you thinking they kept a few more for themselves, not just the ones they're driving now?"

Laura nodded, lost in thought.

Terry continued. "I didn't see any other vehicles in front of the community center."

"Maybe they're keeping them somewhere else. In some parking lot or garage we haven't got to. That makes sense too: that they would have a backup, but hidden away, out of sight."

"So what do we do about it?"

"They're gone, aren't they? Off chasing Dillon and Hutch?"

"I don't know if all of them—"

Thunder cracked the silence. But it wasn't thunder. They had both heard it before. Laura bounded off the bumper as though it had struck her at a good clip. She ran the length of the crush-rocked driveway and into the dirt road. She looked up to the hills, scanning. Terry reached her and saw it first.

"There!"

She saw where he was pointing, to a ribbon of smoke high in the hills. The point of origin was masked by distance and a nearer hill. It was in one of the clear areas, one of the low valleys that had been formed by a glacier eons ago.

Laura pulled in a sharp breath and covered her mouth.

"No. No. No," she thought, then realized she had spoken aloud when Terry rushed to say, "No, it's okay. We don't know what that is. It could be anything."

"Anything? It's them. It's Declan. And Declan was after Dillon." Panic hit her brain like raw alcohol. She felt light-headed. Shadows crowded the edges of her vision. She reached out and grabbed Terry's arm.

"Laura . . . ?"

He stepped behind her to put a hand under her arm, but she didn't need it. The dizziness passed, followed by the cloudy vision. She spun to face him. "Where's the gun? The one we got from the girl?"

"I have it, but—"

"Give it to me!"

"Laura . . ."

"Terry, let me have it."

He read something in her eyes, and his confusion softened to concern. Resignedly he reached behind his back and pulled out a pistol.

She glanced at it and repeated, "The one we took from the girl. The one with bullets."

Terry shook his head, returning the gun to his waistband and reaching around with the other hand. "I thought that was it. I didn't realize . . ." He let the thought trail off and handed her the other pistol.

She opened the breach, dumped the contents into her hand: two unused bullets, four empty shells. She pushed the bullets to her palm with her thumb and turned her hand over; the empty shells fell to the dirt. She put bullets back in the cylinder and shut it, making sure the chamber that would come around when she pulled the trigger contained a bullet.

To Terry's slightly amazed expression, she said, "Wife of a cop." Gripping the revolver in her right hand, she started to run.

On her heels, between breaths, Terry asked, "Where are we . . . going?"

"To find out . . . where they're keeping . . . the spare cars."

Dillon had seemed sure of the cabin's location when he pointed at the map. Based on the topographical references it provided, Hutch had described the terrain in detail. Like an air-traffic radar, his descriptions had panned back and forth over the map until Dillon recognized the landmarks. It had been a slow process, but one that Hutch felt would pay off in fewer false starts as they trekked toward the cabin. After pointing out the location of the cabin, Dillon had, on his own, described nearby hills that the map confirmed.

He had not seen or heard Declan's vehicles reapproach the area. He was as certain as he could be that the man had accepted the sacrificial offering of the Hummer as evidence of their deaths. More than likely, the Jeep and the Bronco had continued down the hill, back to town. Still lying on the ground, Hutch folded the map.

"Good job," he told Dillon. He pushed up and rolled back onto his butt. He tugged at one of the socks he had stretched over his boots back in the rec center. "We can put our socks on now."

Dillon sat, crossed his legs, and corrected his footwear.

When they had finished, Hutch said, "How 'bout we go find this cabin of yours?"

"Yeah." Dillon grinned, pleased to have helped and to be heading toward the place his mother had promised to meet him.

It started to rain.

The first drops struck Laura's forehead and nose as she slowed down, approaching the corner of Shatu' T'ine Way and Provincial. She stopped and pressed her back against the side wall of the Fiddler Diner. The rain quickly escalated to a torrent.

Terry stopped beside her, panting hard. "I've never felt such cold rain," he said.

"That time of year. Their trucks aren't back yet."

The community center was directly across the street. By looking diagonally through the diner's side window and then through its front window, Laura could see most of the building's facade.

"Think we can get in?" Terry asked.

"One way or another."

"What if someone's there?"

"There better be. Else who's going to give us the keys and tell us what we want to know?"

"They're just gonna tell us?"

She held up the pistol. "Yes."

She tucked the gun inside her coat, keeping her hand on it. The rain had already drenched her hair and clothes. Only a swath down the center of her back remained dry, thanks to the building she leaned against. Without another word she rounded the corner and headed directly toward the center's front doors. She lowered her head to let the rain strike her hair and pour off; its iciness and velocity would have stung her eyes and blinded her. She was glad they had reached the town's one paved street before the rain got heavy. Navigating the muddy side streets on foot was treacherous business. Head down, she kept only the pavement in front of her in view. She trusted that no one would open the center's doors until she summoned them. Terry's sloshing gait stayed right behind her.

She crossed the main portion of the street and entered the drop-off-and-pickup semicircle directly in front of the building. She had rarely used this convenience, since their home was three blocks up Provincial and two down Camsel. But she had stood out here often, either as a parent or a teacher. During community or school events held here, townsfolk enjoyed catching up as they arrived or departed. Of course, none of them ever would have imagined the building as their prison, and she never would have guessed that someday she would cross this area, gun in hand, with every intention of using it.

She tried not to retain the memory of the thundering explosion or the ripple of smoke on the hillside, but it wouldn't let her go. Her certainty of their meaning was a knife in her guts—and also the steel in her back. It was this that would drive her to do what must be done. She reached one of the doors and cautiously, quietly tried the latch.

She moved to the next door: also locked. She signaled for Terry to step near. She put her lips close to his ear so he could hear her above the pounding rain.

"Knock. Hard. Like you're one of them. Whoever comes to the door, don't do anything threatening. Take a step back, put your hands up. If there's only one person, clear your throat."

He blinked at her, water flicking off his eyelids. She wasn't sure he completely understood, but he nodded once and stepped up to the door. She pressed her back against the wall.

Using his fist, Terry beat on the door. He didn't stop but carried on with a continuous pounding, even after a voice from the other side asked who was there. Something rattled inside, and a latch clicked. The door opened partway. Terry took a step back and raised his hands. He cleared his throat.

"I . . . I . . ."

A pistol emerged from behind the door, pointed at his face. It moved toward him. Then a hand and arm.

Laura seized the wrist with her left hand, raising it as she would a branch she was passing under. She stepped forward, between Terry and the gunman. Her own pistol swung around until it touched the nose of the young girl with whom she had fought the night before.

The girl said, "*You.*"

"Drop it," Laura commanded.

Terry stepped up behind her and wrenched the pistol from the girl's hand. "Don't yell out. Who else is here?"

The girl's dark eyes darted back and forth, thinking, conniving. "Everybody. You'll die if you do this."

Terry spoke over Laura's shoulder. "We saw them leave."

"They came back," she said too quickly. "They parked out back."

"You're lying, Cortland," Laura said.

The girl scrunched her brows.

"I'm a teacher and a mother. You can't lie to me. Now move." With the barrel of the gun, she pushed Cortland's nose flat, forcing her to take a step backward. They walked like that until the door behind them clicked shut. The roar of the rain became a purr. Water poured off Laura and Terry, striking and pooling on the tile floor.

Terry stepped out from behind Laura. He shook his head and said, "You're just a kid."

"I'm older than I look."

"Right," Laura said. She punctuated her next words with little jabs at the girl's nose. "We want a vehicle."

"Well, I want a mansion in Beverly Hills." Said with a contemptuousness only a teenage girl could achieve.

"A car, ATV, motorcycle. I know they have something stashed."

Cortland blinked. "If they do, they haven't told me."

"You're lying again."

"Whatever."

"Cortland, maybe your mother didn't love you and that's why you're here. I don't care what made you this way. But I love my son, and a car will help me get him the hell away from you people." She wanted to give this girl as little information as possible. "Now if you don't want your fellow freaks to come back and find your brains splattered all over the wall, then you'll tell me what I want to know."

Genuine fear crept into the girl's eyes. Her lips moved to say something, then stopped. Finally she said, "If I knew I would tell you, but it doesn't matter because they would find you anyway. You have no idea what you're up against."

"Then tell me." Laura jabbed again, harder.

Cortland flinched and her eyes grew moist. Not from fear or even an insincere attempt at sympathy, Laura knew, but because Laura had shoved the barrel that hard.

The girl said nothing; she blinked, spilling one tear.

"Hey!" Terry called. He had wandered to the corridor on the right, the one opposite where Laura and Dillon had been held. "Come here. You've gotta see this."

Cortland rolled her eyes. Laura kept the barrel pressed to the girl's nose but bent her elbow in order to grab her by the shirt. She tugged her back toward Terry.

"If you try to get away," Laura said, "I'll shoot you. And if I don't, *he* will."

"You bet," Terry confirmed.

Laura arrived at the corridor and followed Terry's gaze down to the end where the undamaged fire door stood closed. Positioned in front of the door, as though in preparation for a quick getaway, was a dirt bike.

Laura smiled. "Keys?"

Terry jogged the length of the corridor, leaned over the bike, and called out, "They're in the ignition! Can we use this in this weather?"

Laura said, "Terry, I'd find a way to use a skateboard."

Terry squeezed past the bike and pushed the bar that opened the door. Rain fell outside. No alarm. He said, "We're good to go."

"Wait a second," Laura said. "Terry, come here." She pushed Cortland back into the vestibule, never releasing her grip or changing her aim. When Terry stepped in, she said, "Can you get those open?" She jerked her head toward the chained auditorium doors.

He walked toward them. "We should see what else we can get from this place. What about the satellite phones?"

Cortland closed her eyes and kept them shut.

Terry squatted in front of the padlock. "I can shoot this off."

Car engines revved outside. Brakes squealed.

The girl's eyes flashed open. "Hah!" she said.

Terry darted for the front door, stopped. "This won't work," he said. "We can't shoot it out with these guys. Not with that weapon they have."

Laura said, "We got Declan's girlfriend."

"I don't think that matters."

"It doesn't," Cortland said flatly.

Laura looked into the girl's eyes and believed she was telling the truth this time. She pulled her gun away from Cortland's face and swung it, hard, into the side of her head. The girl collapsed.

"Let's go," she told Terry, who was staring down at the girl, stunned. "Terry!"

She ran down the corridor toward the bike. Before she was half-way there, she heard Terry fall in behind her.

40

Kyrill pulled the Jeep Cherokee into the circular pull-off in front
of the community center. Behind it, the headlights of the Bronco cut
through the grey haze, ignited the rainwater on the Jeep's back window into a bright medallion, and winked out. When he reached for the
key, Declan stopped him.

"Keep it running," Declan said. "I'm going to the B&B for a shower."

"Sounds good to me."

"Not you. Me."

Kyrill frowned, resignedly. He opened the door, gazed into the
downpour, then back at Declan. He reached between the seatbacks
and pulled his rifle through. He seemed ready to plead his case for a
shower, thought better of it, and slipped off the seat. The long barrel
clanked against the doorframe, and the door slammed shut.

Declan lifted his left leg over the center console, followed by his butt, then his right leg. Settled into the driver's seat, he hitched an arm to get a better look at Julian in the back. He gestured with his head. "You too. Out."

"Dec . . ." he started. He stopped when Declan raised his right eyebrow. He climbed out and jogged around the front of the Jeep, the rain and headlamps momentarily turning him spectral and otherworldly.

Declan pulled away, glad to be separating himself from the others for a while. Their constant neediness was sapping him. *An hour alone,* he thought. *Half of that in a hot shower.* Just the thought of it made him feel stronger, ready for more.

Kyrill splashed up to one of the community center's heavy wooden doors. He banged his fist against it, waited, then pounded harder.

"Come on!" he yelled at the door.

The others moved up behind him, their heads lowered against the downpour.

Pruitt had it the worst. He had removed his jacket to cover the camera. Even in the gray light of the overcast day, his skin had taken on a bluish hue. His bottom lip, arms, and shoulders quivered, as though he were a bed in a cheap motel and someone had fed him a quarter. "Cortland!" he yelled.

"Cort! Sometime today!" Kyrill called and continued pounding on the door.

"Maybe she's in the bathroom," Julian offered. He was squeezing his collar tight and raising his shoulders to keep the water from finding his jacket's neck hole.

Kyrill squinted at him. "She should hear us even in there." He looked at the door as though expecting an answer from it.

Bad pushed him. "Go around," he said. "Check the back door."

"Why me?" Kyrill complained.

"Just do it. And keep the barrel down so water doesn't get in."

Kyrill lowered his head and adjusted his weapon. He jumped off the concrete landing onto the grass. A few fast steps revealed how slippery the ground had become. He slowed to a walk and cursed Cortland all the way to the corner.

As soon as the Kawasaki 250's rear tire cleared the back door, Terry climbed on.

"Wait! Wait!" Laura called to him. She pushed the door tight, leaning close to hear the click of the latch. She moved to Terry's side. "Don't start it yet. Let's get it over to a side street and up a ways first."

"But I thought . . . With those guys showing up . . ."

"That's why I cracked the girl on the head. To give us time. If you start it now, they'll be on our tail in thirty seconds."

Terry climbed off the bike. He leaned over it so Laura could hear through the rain. "If they're locked out, they'll come around to these doors." He pushed the bike through the muddy parking lot. She tried to help him, but her pushing and tugging made moving the bike more awkward. She let go and concentrated on watching for Declan's gang.

They were still approaching the first house behind the parking lot when someone came around the front of the community center. She could not tell who it was through the rain, but the rifle in his hands was unmistakable.

Neither of them moved. As the figure approached the back of the building, she recognized the teen boy, Kyrill. He held the rifle diagonally across his torso. His head was lowered against the downpour. He had not seen them yet. He rounded the corner and walked carefully to the first rear door, from which she and Terry had exited with the bike. He tried the handle, started banging on the steel door.

Terry back-stepped toward the corner of the house, pulling the motorbike with him. Laura followed. When it appeared that Kyrill was about to look their way, they stopped. He was once again nothing more than a misty silhouette in the rain. Had she not known of his presence, he would be all but invisible. She reasoned that he would have as hard a time spotting them.

He was darting for the damaged second rear door when they wheeled the bike past the corner of the house, and the community center disappeared.

Getting from one place to another had never been so difficult, so exhausting.

Hutch was convinced the clouds above were as impenetrable as trees to Declan's eye in the sky, so he and Dillon beelined it for the cabin, straight through the wide-open span of fields and meadows. The drencher hammered mercilessly on their heads and shoulders and backs. The ground became slick with mud and grasses; even the slightest inclination sent his and Dillon's feet out from under them. No matter which part of their bodies hit the ground first, they would wind up twisting and turning and rolling in the slop before regaining their feet.

The terrain had become nearly impassible faster than Hutch would have thought possible. It was as though the entire countryside was made out of soap. Something about the soil, the foliaged ground-cover, maybe the cold, cold temperature of the water, combined to knock bipeds low. He knew caribou possessed uniquely scooped and sharp-edged hooves that allowed them to maneuver on steep and icy slopes; he now realized it was also for this type of terrain in this type of weather.

He slipped again, and Dillon smacked down beside him. They rolled on their sides, facing each other. Dillon's hair was plastered against his skull. Mud painted one side of his face. It washed away in quick, heavy rivulets as the rain continued to hammer, hammer. Somewhere in the struggle with the weather and the impossibly slick terrain, the wound on his face had opened up. Blood oozed out and was instantly washed away. It was difficult for Hutch to gauge the amount of blood or the severity of the laceration. Since it had been scabbed over when he had met the boy, he believed that it wasn't as bad as it appeared. He touched Dillon's face and said, "Does it hurt?"

Dillon looked puzzled.

"The cut," he explained.

Dillon's eyes opened wide, remembering. He shook his head.

Hutch surveyed the sky. Gray clouds formed a low ceiling from horizon to horizon.

"We need to get out of this," he said, shouting over the water's incessant pounding against the earth. "As soon as we get back into the trees, I'll make a lean-to out of cut branches. It won't be perfect, but it will be better than this."

"I don't mind," Dillon said.

Hutch smiled. The kid's resilience impressed him. Then he noticed Dillon's expression; he had missed something. He leaned closer and said, "What?"

Dillon drew closer still. Their noses were almost touching when he repeated, "How about a mine?"

Hutch drew back. "Mine?"

"An old uranium mine. Pretty close."

"Abandoned?"

Dillon nodded.

"Where?"

Dillon pointed, only a few degrees off their intended direction. "Over that hill."

Hutch had not seen a mine on the map, but many man-made changes to the terrain took longer to appear on topos. If the mine had operated for only a few years, the cartographers may have overlooked it or deemed it unimportant.

"Dillon," he said, "you are a brilliant guide and navigator. Let's go."

41

Declan's skin was pink from long minutes of hot water. He was patting his shoulder with a thick towel when he heard the door downstairs bang open.

"Dec! Declan!" It was Pruitt. He sounded excited or panicked or something Pruittish.

Declan lifted his foot to the cushion of a settee. He began drying his leg. Below, doors banged and Pru continued calling out to him. Declan shifted the towel to the other leg. He stood, tossed one end of the towel over his shoulder, grabbed it near his opposite hip, and buffed his back. Pru's heavy footsteps stamped up the stairs.

"Declan!" The knob on a door down the hall slammed into a wall. A few moments later another door crashed open.

Declan had not bothered to shut either the master bedroom door or the door to the adjoining bathroom; when Pru appeared, it was with considerably less banging but no less drama. His shoulder hit the bathroom doorjamb.

"There you are."

"Here I am." Declan brusquely moved the towel over his hair. "Did you see the dryer downstairs? Did you notice if my clothes are dry?"

"Uh . . . I didn't notice. Sorry." In a rush Pru said, "We couldn't get in the community center. Cort didn't answer."

Declan's hands stopped. The towel draped over his head like a boxer's hooded robe. "That was twenty-five minutes ago, dude. Why are you just now—"

Pru held up his hand. "We kept knocking. Tried all the doors. She finally opened up. Somebody broke in and *knocked her out.* Two people, they had guns. That woman with the kid, Laura, and some other guy. She thinks it was the one who shot at us after that fisherman—"

"Did they release the cattle?"

"No. They took the bike, the motorbike. You know the one we had—"

"That's it?" He looked up at the ceiling, thinking it through. "They break in. Knock out the only person we have there. And all they do is take the dirt bike?"

"Yeah, but that's not all . . . I mean that's not it . . . I mean . . ."

Declan pulled the towel off his head. "What?"

Pruitt stepped fully into the bathroom. He lifted his camera, angling it to show Declan the monitor. The crushed and burning Hummer was frozen to the screen. "While we were waiting for Cort, I went back to the car to review this new footage. Look."

He pushed a button. The flames and smoke on the monitor sprang to life. The focus was on the interior, seen through six-inch-high gaps that used to be the side windows. Pruitt had circled the car. A short-

ened, accordioned windshield pillar blurred past, and they were view-
ing the interior through the now-glassless windshield opening.

"So?" said Declan, losing patience.

Pru's eyes widened. "So . . . what's missing? What's not there that
should be?"

Declan raised his head away from the monitor. "I know what the
word *missing* means. Are you going to tell me, or do you just like sharing the bathroom with my naked self?"

"Declan, there are no bodies. Nobody's in there. The Hummer
was empty."

Declan squinted at the monitor. "That can't be. We followed them
the whole way."

"Did you see their heads before targeting them?"

Declan didn't look up from the monitor. "The windows were too
dark. You know that."

"And look here." Pruitt pointed at the screen.

The camera had moved around to the passenger side window.
Through flames that had engulfed the seats and center console,
Declan could tell the steering wheel had been crushed.

Pruitt pushed a button, and the image froze. He pointed. "On the
steering wheel," he said. "I think that's a belt. See? Here's the strap
. . . and doesn't this look like a buckle?"

"Could be . . . anything."

"Declan, *look*—"

Declan backed a step away from the camera. He ran the towel under
his arm. "Could be a belt. Could be anything. That's one messed-up
Hummer." When his mouth closed, his lips were tight. This did not sit
well with him. Not at all. He wasn't so worried about people reaching
the next town. That wasn't going to happen. And he didn't think anyone possessed the means to communicate Fiddler Falls' distress. If they

did, it would have happened already. It sort of bothered him that these loose cannons were rolling all over the countryside and in town. One of them might hit him. What truly bothered him, however, was that there were people out there convinced they had fooled him. Wherever they were, they were probably laughing it up, tickled pink that they had used Declan's own vehicle and weapon to pull one over on him.

He brought his tight countenance to bear on Pruitt. "These people Cort says broke in, they can't be the same people."

"I don't know."

"They couldn't have turned the Hummer loose, rushed all the way back down here, and done that. Not without a vehicle. And if they had a vehicle, what would they want with a dirt bike?"

Pru cocked his head. "So there's two sets of people running around causing trouble?"

Declan lowered the toilet seat lid and sat on it. He draped the towel over his legs. He held up one finger. "We know about the hunters."

"But I thought you got them last night, behind the community center."

Declan shook his head slowly. "There's a glitch in the control, in the imaging. If I got them, there would have been something left. An arm, a leg, something. So we have to assume they're out there." He held up a second finger. "Then the woman and the kid. Cort said one of the *hunters* was with her, not the kid?"

"She didn't mention him."

"Weird," Declan said simply.

After a minute Pruitt said, "So what are we gonna do?"

"Our two teams of insurgents know each other. One team just lost their wheels; the other gained a set. I think they're going to get together. And we're going to be there."

The mining had started in a natural basin formed by several hills. The walls of this basin had been carved away, creating a gradual spiraling ramp from the top to the bottom. It appeared to Hutch that the ramp had been used to drive heavy equipment to the bottom of the basin. About halfway down there appeared to be an opening in the carved wall—an adit boring into the hill. That was the shelter Hutch wanted.

The rain continued to drench man and boy in an apparent effort to outperform the deluge that had forced Noah to build an ark. Curtains of water flowed down the walls of the basin. The ramp looked muddy and slick, but Hutch saw no other way to reach the adit. They needed to traverse the ramp for a full spiral and a half around the basin wall. He turned to Dillon, standing at his side on the edge of the big bowl.

"You did it," he said. "Thirty minutes and we'll be out of this dishwasher."

Dillon smiled.

Hutch stepped toward the beginning of the ramp. His feet slid out from under him, and he plunged over the edge. He slipped down a steep sloping wall to the ramp one full spiral below the lip of the basin. He dug his fingers into the gravelly mud to stop his momentum from taking him over another edge and down to the next level of ramp. If he fell below the level of the adit, the slipperiness of the mud would prevent him from climbing or even crawling back up to it until the rain stopped and the earth dried. He heard a scream and saw Dillon coming over the edge and down the wall toward him. He seemed to be riding a wave of water and mud.

The boy splashed down beside him. Hutch seized the collar of his coat, preventing him from plunging farther. They were both covered, head to toe, in thin coffee-colored mud. They could have been the works-in-progress of an ambitious clay sculptor. The adit was now directly across the basin from them and a little lower. Their plummet had saved them a full circumnavigation of the basin's top level.

"Correction," Hutch said. "Our new ETA is five minutes."

They walked, slipped, and slid single file, far away from the outside edge of the ramp. They attempted to stabilize themselves by running their right hands along the ascending wall that marked its inside edge. Following Dillon, Hutch narrowed his field of vision to the boy and the mud directly in front of them. *Step . . . make it stick . . . step.*

He almost ran into Dillon. The boy had stopped at the mine's entrance. Hutch stepped around him and entered the dark, cavernous tunnel. He immediately felt relief from the pounding rain, mentally and physically. He felt like a swimmer pulled from the water, three strokes from complete exhaustion.

Dillon stepped out of the rain. He instantly collapsed. Hutch knelt over him.

"Hey! You okay?"

Dillon didn't move. His eyes remained closed. He said, "So . . . tired . . ."

"I hear you, kid."

He lifted the boy and propped him against the tunnel wall. The rain had sluiced the mud from his hair and face and most of his clothes, a testament to his increasing ability to stay on his feet. The hair and skin at his right temple was matted and muddy, but otherwise he was a thoroughly laundered boy.

Blood—diluted by rainwater as soon as it left the wound—still oozed from Dillon's cheek. Hutch leaned close. He pushed on the skin next to the cut. A fat drop spilled out, but it didn't look bad. He kept a couple butterfly bandages in one of the pouches on his utility belt; lacerations, for which butterfly strips were designed, were the primary injury suffered by hunters. Arrow blades, branches, gutting knives all contributed to the disproportionate profits attributed to hunters by the Band-Aid company. He pulled one out and wiped away a spot of the water, mud, and blood. He applied the strip. It immediately came loose and fell away. His face was simply too wet. He'd try again later.

Hutch cocked his head toward the opening of the mine. "The rain, does it come down like this a lot?"

"Sometimes. About this time of year. Mom says it comes when people have been really bad. It's supposed to wash everything clean again."

Hutch nodded. He looked out at the downpour. Probably the worst he'd ever seen, which made what Dillon's mother told him seem as true as a knight's honor.

42

The shower had been just what Declan needed. He felt scrubbed and fresh and ready to go. Even the icy rain that caught him between the B&B and the Jeep and then again between the Jeep and the community center could not dampen his spirits. The thought of people laughing at his inability to find them, despite his superior resources, did what the rain could not. If he had been cold and waterlogged—like a wet dog—when the news of the empty Hummer had come, his chi would have been knocked completely out of alignment. Clean and warm, he had felt the news only darken his aura from blue to purple.

Stepping into the community center's vestibule, he witnessed the sorry soul he could have been. Julian shuffled in from the corridor, shoulders sloped. His hair clung to his head like spilled paint. His eyes were red, canted on the outsides, reflecting misery. His skin had paled to a shade only several degrees from his teeth. He had not changed out of his wet things, despite having brought extra clothes. His brother was either trying to elicit sympathy from him or was wallowing in self-pity.

He'd better discover it was the latter, because Declan would not tolerate efforts to manipulate him. The person who did would find not a cache of concern and care, but indifference tinged with anger.

"Did Pru find you?" Julian asked.

When the boy spoke, Declan recognized that he had allowed defeat to sap the vitality from his physicality.

Declan didn't want to keep Julian in his vision. Just the sight of such weakness could infect him like a cold germ. He may not experience symptoms for a while, but it would be there, waiting for a moment of vulnerability. Declan was inoculated against such feelings of utter despair, but like a powerful athlete, he recognized that peak performance was achieved not only through the building of strength but also through the avoidance of anything that did not build strength.

Seconds before he had been lamenting where he would be had he not taken the time to shower; then he saw Julian and recognized himself without the care he invested to prevent looking and feeling like that. He wasn't stupid. He may be strong and cognizant of the needs of his mind and body, but he knew how easy it was to slip from champion gladiator to lion chow. Indeed, the difference was not a lifetime of conditioning but one . . . little . . . slip. It was thrusting a sword when you should have parried; it was watching a TV show when you should have gone to bed; it was remaining in cold, wet clothes when you could have tossed them in a dryer and taken a hot shower.

"Dec, did Pru find you?" Julian repeated.

"He did. Why haven't you changed out of those clothes?"

From the corridor, Kyrill peered out at him. Though slightly more

273

bright-eyed, he could have been taking lessons from Julian in depressive behavior. He had not run a comb through his hair since the deluge had plastered it, and he, too, had not found dry clothes. For just a moment, Declan wondered if this lack of self-care was a product of the teen years as opposed to a deficiency in attitude. Then he remembered his own passage through that age, when he had discovered the benefits of vitamins, yoga, earth-centric gemstones, the wisdom of the ages, regardless of the world's efforts to minimize it by labeling it this or that religion. No, it wasn't years on Earth; it was personality. It was who you were: you had it or you didn't.

He swung his attention back to Julian, flitting over him, not dwelling.

Julian looked down at his clothes as if noticing for the first time their condition. He shrugged. "Just didn't."

"Where's Pru?" Kyrill asked. "Didn't he come back with you?"

"He's walking. Julie, if you take care of yourself better, you'll *be* better."

"I wanted to take a shower too. You told me to stay here."

Declan turned the full force of his apathetic eyes to Julian. "That's just it. You have to earn it. If you were the kind of person who changed out of cold, wet clothes when he could, then I'd have figured you would truly benefit from a long, hot shower on a day like this. Medieval kingdoms didn't armor their jesters. The ones who got the equipment were the fighters who could do the job."

He put his arm around Julian's shoulders. "Show me that you care about yourself, that you want to be stronger and smarter and more in tune with the cosmos. Stop putting dead animals in your body. Start meditating. *Then* you'll get what you want from me."

Hesitantly, Julian asked, "What do I want from you?"

Declan laughed. "You want me to teach you how to be like me, right? Isn't that what you've always wanted? Little man looking up to his big brother? Dad's never around, and all *he* can be is a money-making machine. You were just a little squirt when you recognized that I was figuring it out, how to use money and people to live life more fully than most humans could even imagine. One in a million, one in a billion. That's what I am. That's what you could be."

Julian shook his head. "I don't think I want to be like you, Dec. I mean—"

"I got it. I got it." Declan's arm rose up Julian's shoulder until it encircled the boy's neck. It tightened.

Julian coughed, cleared his throat. He touched Declan's arm. "Dec?"

"I was like that, too, at your age," Declan said, infusing his voice with good-natured enthusiasm. "I wanted to be more than I was, but also my own person. See? To be more like me, you don't have to necessarily be less like yourself. You just have to bring out the *me* that's already inside you."

Julian was silent. After a moment he said, "Yeah. Sure. I get it."

Declan released him. He leaned his face close to Julian's. His eyes flicked around and he whispered conspiratorially, "You and I aren't like these others. We're not idiots. We have everything going for us: money, brains, good looks." He winked. "But you've got to work it, Julie. They're all like muscles. They can grow strong, or they can atrophy, get flabby. What we're doing here is important for your future. It could put you at the top of the food chain."

He gripped Julian's shoulder. The boy flinched. He studied his brother's eyes—green-blue, not his own ebony, which helped keep people out of his head. "Or not. It's your call, little man."

Julian nodded.

Declan stretched his back, glanced around. "Where's Bad?"

"Back on the cot. He—"

275

"Bad! Get your butt out here!"

Julian sauntered away, toward the corridor.

"Julie, I want you with me. We're heading out."

Julian looked toward the doors. Rain was still battering them. A million tiny elves knocking to get in. "Now? With the rain?"

"You do what you have to do."

Julian continued toward the corridor.

"Julie."

"Just let me hit the head, Declan. I'll be right back."

Cortland came out of the office/bedroom. Spotting Declan, she maneuvered around Julian and moped up to her man, head down, bottom lip puffed out.

"You too?" Declan said. "What?"

Cort reached him and wrapped her arms around his neck. She leaned back so he could see the full tragedy of her face. "She hit me, Dec. I was out cold."

Declan scanned for damage, but didn't see any.

Cort disengaged one arm to rub her head just above her ear. "Right here. I got a big bump. It was bleeding. Like Julian's, but right here."

Declan poked at the spot.

Cort pulled away. "Owwww!"

"How'd they get the jump on you, baby? I thought you were smarter than that."

"They surprised me at the door. I thought it was you. She had a gun."

"Did they take yours?"

"They had their own. They . . ." Her voice trailed off.

Declan said what she had realized. "They had the gun you gave them last night. Didn't they?"

She nodded demurely.

"And they took the new one Julian gave you, didn't they?"

"Dec, they—"

"No, no, no. That's okay. I understand. But if I give you another gun, will you *please* not hand it to the enemy?"

She smiled, pleased by his forgiveness. "I'll shoot them first."

"There you go."

Bad entered, dragging his leg behind him. His machine gun was slung over one shoulder.

Cort rolled to Declan's side, her arm around his back, hooked on his waist.

He draped an arm over her shoulder and said, "Did you hear the news?"

"About what?" Bad said.

"Well, first, that Bad's lost his funk. Where's the Bad I know and love?"

"His funk juice leaked out when that arrow cut him. Looked like blood, but it was funk juice." He said this with all the solemnity he would have used to say that his mama had died. But then a little smile played on his lips.

"What do I see? What do I see?" Declan teased.

Bad grinned. He shook his head. "Dec, I'm gonna shoot you with an arrow one of these days. See how it feels."

"I know it hurts. I do. But don't let pain change who you are, dawg. You gotta be that happy, dancing fool you are. Just do it with pain."

Bad continued shaking his glistening bald head. His grin grew wider, all teeth. "You are one crazy dude."

Declan pointed at him. "But you know I'm right. You're hurting like a dog got run over in the street, but you're not going to let it get you. You're going to be Bad. Smiling Bad. Dancin' Bad. You're gonna find them that tried to lay you low, and you're gonna get 'em. You're gonna make them pay for what they did to you. Pay bad, 'cuz that's who you are. And you're gonna do it with a smile. Then you'll dance on their graves."

Bad was nodding. Grinning and nodding. "Yeah . . . I can do that."

"If your leg tries to bring you down, pop some Percs. Not too many. We need you sharp and quick, right?"

"I hear you."

"Okay. Pru says the guys we thought we got in the Hummer weren't in the Hummer. They're out there somewhere, and that ticks me off. We're gonna go finish the job."

Bad's head bobbed up and down. A lot of his old self had returned.

Declan continued. "So go get your G11 and whatever else you need, and let's get back up into those hills."

Bad bopped off toward his room, all but his injured leg having found the rhythm again.

43

Man, I'm good.

Declan wished he had his fingers on *Julian's* strings as he did on Bad's, but Julian had Page blood in him. Of course he would be less prone to manipulation. Carrara marble was difficult to chisel, but once it was, it made beautiful and lasting works of art. Declan held out hope for his little brother. He would continue to tap that chisel into him. Julian would either emerge as a fine prodigy or, like the blocks of marble that contained weak veins, he would shatter. Declan was acutely interested in discovering which would be Julian's fate.

The door behind him opened. Pru entered, appearing to have swum from the B&B. His coat protected the camera.

"You don't have a case for that?" Declan asked.

Pru shrugged. "What for? I'm always using it. Would've been nice to get a ride."

"Walking's good for you. Now that you're here, go fetch Kyrill and unlock the auditorium."

Pru pulled the door shut and sloshed toward the corridor.

Cort leaned her head against his chest and said, "You're too hard on them sometimes."

"Baby, I'm only as hard as I have to be. You know what they say: iron sharpens iron."

"Who said that?"

"I don't know. I think maybe Ben Franklin."

Kyrill entered the vestibule from the back rooms. He was holding a key, his rifle on his back. Declan nodded toward the auditorium. He said, "Open it up."

Pruitt entered, sans camera. He sloshed and squished as though he were still trekking through puddles of mud.

Kyrill unraveled the heavy chain that braced two doors together. He dropped it on the floor and pushed the door open. The stuffy odor of perspiration wafted out.

Declan extracted himself from Cort. "Wait here," he said and walked into the auditorium. He leaned back to whisper to Pruitt, who had stepped in behind him, and Kyrill, who was holding the door. "Pru, you get the door. Kyrill, unsling that rifle and make a show of having it ready."

They nodded. Declan stepped further in. The gun rattled in Kyrill's hands behind him. All the faces in the room—those not pressed into a makeshift pillow or the crook of an arm—turned to him like monkeys in a zoo or, as he had thought before, like livestock hoping for a bit of grub or a salt lick or whatever it was that tripped a cow's trigger.

A couple dozen people backed away from him. Most, however,

looked dazed, sitting on the floor or in the bleachers. It appeared that the men had relinquished their rights to the few cots Declan's boys had found and tossed in. Wasn't that sweet? It amazed Declan that almost a quarter of a thousand people would allow themselves to be locked up by a half dozen. Didn't they realize their sheer numbers made them capable of overpowering their captors? So a handful would take rounds from Kyrill's rifle—where was their sense of duty, their sense of community? Their understanding that the interest of many outweighed the interest of a few?

As if Declan really believed that.

The phenomenon he was witnessing was further proof that the mind was greater than the body. Here, six minds—though really one in him—had subdued two hundred and forty bodies. End of lesson.

He spread his hands wide. "I need a volunteer. Someone who knows the hills to the north above town for several miles."

No one moved.

"I know, I know. We invited some of your friends out before and they haven't come back. This is different. I'll let whoever helps stop by a store or his home to pick up something and bring it back here." He thought for a moment. "Not a gun, though." He smiled. The cattle didn't.

Somebody cleared his throat. A large man with a heavy, scraggly beard hoisted himself off the floor. At the same time, a hand went up toward the back of the auditorium. A skinny man in his sixties slowly rose to his feet.

Declan pointed at him. "You know the hills up there?"

"What'd you do with them ones you took?"

"They're okay. We got them doing some work for us." What was he going to say? *We blew them up?* Now *that* might upside the balance of things. "So you a backwoods guy or what?"

"Been going up there my whole life."

Declan looked around the room. He called out, "That true?"

Heads nodded.

"Okay . . ."

He pointed to the younger one. "How about you?"

"Yep." His voice was deep and rumbling, a GTO to the old guy's Fiat.

Again Declan asked the room, "That true?"

About the same number of heads nodded.

Kyrill stepped toward the big guy. He said, "Step forward, buddy."

Declan knew Kyrill's mind: *Anyone is better than some old geezer.* Declan wasn't so sure. He raised his hand. "Hold up, Grizzly Adams. Take a seat, man. Go back into hibernation or whatever you were doing." He pointed to the old man. "You. Come on."

He turned to face Kyrill and whispered, "I'm sure none of these people are too pleased with us, right? Might try to escape, get one over on us. If you gotta tango, go with the skinny guy."

He walked to the doorway. To Pruitt he said, "This might be something you should be filming. Kinda interesting."

Pruitt answered, "You want me to get what's gonna happen in the hills, right? Even with the rain and stuff?"

"Oh, you bet. I think we're just getting started."

44

Not far inside the adit, hidden at first by shadows, Hutch and Dillon found two metal doors. Each was in the shape of a quarter circle. Closed, they formed a half circle that perfectly conformed with the entrance tunnel.

Hutch pushed on one of the closed doors, expecting to find it as firm as a wall. It creaked open. He stepped through. The tunnel continued some distance. It was dark, but not as musty as he thought it should be . . . and warm. The wind and rain blowing into the first thirty feet, before the doors, turned the area—which Hutch now thought of as an alcove or courtyard—frigid. It had effectively shielded them from the downpour, but it had been anything but cozy.

From a nylon holster on his utility belt, he produced a penlight. He twisted it on and stepped further into the area beyond the doors. Beer and soda cans, snack bags, and cigarette butts littered the concrete floor. People had been using the shelter as a hunting cabin. The penlight's illumination was murky and seemed to be dimming quickly. He did not remember changing the battery prior to the trip as he normally did. The last time he had used the light, he had restrung his bow in the shadows of heavy woods. It wasn't something he typically needed for a daytime hunting excursion.

Of course, he thought. *When you really need something is when you can't find it, it breaks, or you forgot to change the batteries.*

The gray light coming through the door shifted, and he turned to see Dillon standing there. "I'm gonna check it out," he said. "Do you want to wait here or come with me?"

Before he had finished the question, Dillon was at his side.

They moved deeper into the tunnel. The detritus of its visitors diminished and disappeared, as though intruders had never ventured very far from the door. The gloom emphasized the weakness of Hutch's light. He shook it, which resulted in a brief flaring that dimmed to a level of illumination worse than before. They reached a T in the tunnel. The new passageway was narrower with a lower ceiling than the entrance tunnel, but otherwise it was similar: it was a half circle in shape, with a flat floor of poured concrete.

For no other reason than he was on the right side of the tunnel, Hutch turned right. The darkness here seemed as black and heavy as a monk's robe. The penlight pushed little of it away, and seemingly a little less with each step they took. They passed another tunnel on their left, which Hutch thought would take them deeper into the hill, away from the crater. Another two dozen steps brought them to what at first appeared to be the mouth of a much smaller tunnel on the right. Peering in, Hutch saw that it was a room about thirty feet square.

When he turned from the doorway, Dillon said, "Wait. I saw something."

They stepped in, and Dillon pointed. In a near corner was a body. Hutch jumped and moved his arm in front of Dillon. He squinted at the canvas-covered bundle and took a step closer to shed more light on it.

"Stay back," he instructed. He moved closer and realized his mistake. Unless it was that of a child or small woman, whatever lay under the canvas was too small to be a body. He reached it and carefully lifted off the covering. Supplies. Sleeping bag, blankets, a large Ziploc bag containing cigarettes, some kind of jerky, and—*oh, let it be*—a camper's lantern. Hutch picked up this last item. It was heavy—battery-powered, not propane or gas. He found the on-off switch and flipped it. Bright white light blinded him. He blinked against it and turned to grin at Dillon.

"Merry Christmas," he chimed. "I think we can stay here awhile, maybe until rescue people come and find us." But he didn't really believe his own words. Their ride out of the wilderness wasn't due for another eight days. And it wouldn't take Declan *that* long to find the mine, not with his resources. And who's to say Franklin or anyone else coming in the area wouldn't wind up like David? There were so many hurdles . . .

"What about food?" Dillon asked.

There ya go, Hutch thought glumly. "You're right. That's a problem. There's some jerky here. I don't know if it's good. I have a few more energy bars, but if we don't find a stash of eats in here somewhere, we'll have to go looking outside. I can arrow a small animal or make a snare. We'd have to start a fire, and that might be a problem, but let's not worry about it until we have to. Hey, look." He held up a piece of metal that looked something like a tuning fork with an open round end.

"What is it?"

"A mouth harp. I know a few hunters who pack either one of these or a harmonica wherever they go. It's an easy way to make music on lonely nights."

"Can you play it?"

Hutch rolled his eyes. "Not me. The piano a bit, but I hurt my back once lugging it on a hiking trip, so I leave it at home now."

Dillon smiled.

Hutch dropped the mouth harp back on top of the supplies.

They returned to the entrance doors. Five feet behind the right-hand door Hutch found a hole that someone had chiseled into the concrete floor. Near it was a length of timber. It appeared to be a crossbeam or railroad tie. Acting on his suspicions, he set the lantern down and shut the door. A horizontal metal brace ran at chest height across both doors. It was heavy, maybe three inches thick. Just below this brace, near the edge of the door, was a square area that had been rubbed free of rust.

Okay.

He picked up the heavy beam, angled one end into the hole, and rested the other against the door. The beam fit perfectly into the rubbed-off area. The other door had been fitted, evidently when the mine was new, with bolts that slid into the floor and ceiling. The door he had used was latchless, probably locked with some device the former tenants had taken when they left. Whoever was using the mine for shelter apparently suffered from security issues. They wanted to enjoy their rest without fear of interruption, so they had created this brace for the door. That it perfectly suited Hutch and Dillon's needs was just another sign, along with the lantern and blankets, that Someone was watching out for them.

With the door shut, the ambient temperature started to rise. Still, a brisk breeze slipped in under the doors. Hutch looked around at the trash. Everything seemed to encourage their staking out a different place to spend time. Aside from the draft and the trash, Hutch did not want the lantern light to reveal their presence from outside the door. He explained his rationale to Dillon, and they agreed to make camp deeper within the tunnel system. When they returned for the sleeping bag, blankets, and beef jerky, Hutch suggested calling the room theirs. Dillon did not look pleased.

"What's the matter? You don't like it?"

Dillon shook his head slowly. "It's okay, but . . ."

"We don't have to stay here. It's a big place."

"It's just . . . it's kinda like the storage room where they kept us."

"I understand. Let's go somewhere else."

They found several other rooms, all empty, but decided to bed down in the tunnel itself. It seemed less musty than the rooms, and Hutch liked being able to hear if someone attempted to enter through the metal doors. He unrolled the sleeping bag for Dillon and gave him a blanket to use as a pillow. For himself, he spread out another of the rough army blankets to dampen the chilliness of the concrete floor. That left two blankets to cover him when it was time to sleep.

He sat on his floor blanket, leaning against the wall. Dillon faced him against the other wall. The camper's lantern burned as brightly, though infinitely less warmly, as a campfire. After twenty-five feet in each direction, the darkness of the tunnels reclaimed its domain.

Dillon peered one way, then the other. "Creepy," he said.

"Yeah, but I'd rather be in here than out there." He leaned beyond the blanket to where his bow stood against the wall and his utility belt lay on the ground. From a pouch he retrieved the last of his butterfly bandages. He walked on his knees to Dillon. The boy's face appeared clean and dry, but the wound still glistened, not ready to mend.

"These will help," Hutch said. He applied the bandages, gently pinching the edges of the cut together.

Dillon grimaced but said nothing.

Returning to his blanket, Hutch said, "How'd it happen?"

"That man . . ."

"Declan?"

Dillon nodded. "He . . ."

"That's all you need to say, Dillon. Not a nice guy, is he?" Immediately he regretted the words. Calling the man who'd killed a child's father "not a nice guy" was like saying hell was a tad warm.

Dillon pulled his lips in and let his eyelids lower almost imperceptibly. The effect was an expression of both sadness and resignation. Hutch didn't know what to say, so he said nothing. The boy settled into the silence he seemed to prefer. Hutch wondered if this was his natural disposition or one forced upon him by the circumstances.

Finally Hutch asked, "Want a PowerBar?"

Dillon nodded.

He held up two PowerBars. "Chocolate or cookies and cream?"

Dillon shrugged.

Hutch raised his eyebrows. "Cookies and cream?"

Dillon held out his hand, and Hutch tossed both energy bars into it.

"One for later." Hutch took the last one in the pouch for himself.

As he tore open the packaging, Dillon said, "Thank you."

Hutch bit into the gooey wafer. "You're welcome."

Dillon was staring at him; he was holding the energy bars in his lap.

Hutch said, "Wanna try the jerky instead?"

"I meant thank you for everything."

Hutch smiled. "You're welcome for everything. I'm only sorry we couldn't have met in . . . happier times."

Dillon opened an energy bar and took a bite. He chewed slowly, watching Hutch, and said, "Do you have a family?"

"A son and daughter."

"What about your wife?"

Hutch skewed his face in one direction. "Not anymore," he said.

"Why?"

Hutch shrugged. "She decided she didn't . . . I guess, love me anymore. She didn't want to live with me anymore."

"Did you want to live with her?"

"Oh yeah."

"You still love her?"

"She's been really mean lately, you know? Not a nice person to be around. She . . . uh . . ."

"But you still love her." Not a question.

Hutch thought about it. "Yeah, I guess I do. Not a lot I can do about it though."

Dillon took another bite. "What about your children?"

Painful territory, but to Hutch there was nothing prying or out of line about Dillon's curiosity. For some reason it felt right. Among all this craziness, in the chaos of death and the struggle for survival, this topic mattered. He didn't know why—maybe it anchored him or contextualized Declan's evil. Hutch's life, back in Colorado, crappy as it was, was nevertheless his to live. To change, if he could; accept it, if he couldn't. Being so far from home, geographically, emotionally, being in such an alien environment, made David's death and all the rest of it surreal, but it *wasn't* surreal. It wasn't a fantasy or a nightmare or merely the events of future headlines. It was real and it mattered. Dillon's questions brought that home.

His *children*. Hutch smiled despite everything. Half of the energy bar was still in the wrapper. He pulled at the packaging, making it straight, twisted it, watching how the foil caught the light. Not really watching—fiddling, occupying his hands while his mind opened a scrapbook.

"Macie is seven," he said, seemingly to the energy bar. "Cute as any kid I've seen on TV, but of course I'm going to say that, right?" He smiled, glanced up at Dillon, continued fiddling with the wrapper. "Really, she is. Blonde hair, green eyes, freckles, no front teeth." He ran the tip of his index finger along his own teeth. "I always figured if I had a daughter, she'd be a tomboy. I'd get her out there playing catch, camping, being as rough as I was as a kid. But that's not Macie." He shook his head. "She likes frilly pink dresses and tea parties and putting on makeup when her mother lets her. I don't know if she's that way despite me, or if I let her go with her girliness because I got my masculinity quota met through my son."

The wrapper started to rip and he let it, slowly peeling it away from the sticky bar.

"What's his name?" Dillon said.

"Logan." He smiled up at Dillon, crunched his eyebrows. "He's older than you, eleven. You're what, nine?"

Dillon nodded.

"You remind me of him. He's handsome . . . and a lot smarter than I am."

Dillon blushed.

"He has blue eyes, like yours. Really dark hair, longer than I'd like it to be. He says he wants to be a writer—I think because that's what I am. We used to spend a lot of time together. We like the same kind of movies. I used to read to him every night, and last year he started reading to me. I miss that."

"Why doesn't he read to you anymore?"

Hutch shrugged. "He lives with his mother. He gets to come over only once a week."

"Why?"

"I guess his mother loves him as much as I do. She doesn't want to share him."

"What does he want?"

"He wants his mother and father back together. He doesn't want to choose."

"Could he see you more if he wanted to?"

Hutch shook his head. "He wants to. His mother kind of . . . made it so he can't. And it doesn't matter what I want either."

After a moment, Dillon said, "You're right."

"About what?"

"Your wife *is* mean." He looked pained. "Sorry."

"Well . . . she's just trying to find happiness, I guess."

"My dad says if getting what you want hurts other people, you don't deserve it."

"I think I'd have liked your dad."

They fell into silence again, Hutch thinking about how lives can unravel at the whim of other people, Dillon undoubtedly missing his father. Whatever pain Dillon felt inside, he kept it there this time. He seemed to find his sneakers fascinating. He blinked at them and frowned. Hutch felt selfish and petty. He had considered the previous nine months the worst of his life. And perhaps they were. But next to what Dillon had suffered in the last two days, and what he would experience in the days and months and years to come, Hutch's problems were nothing. A splinter next to amputation.

Some people had no problem saving themselves. Their sense of self-preservation was adequate to get them moving. Others performed better as rescuers. That survivalist he had interviewed told him about a man lost alone in the wilderness. This guy had imagined—actually *pretended*—that he was saving a beautiful woman, getting her out alive.

He would talk to her, reassure her. A week after he'd been given up for dead, a hunter found him alive.

"It has to do with personality, not heroism," the survivalist had said. "Some people can simply do for others what they wouldn't do for themselves."

Hutch wondered if that was what was going on here. He was rescuing Dillon, and in doing so saving himself. Did that mean he was using Dillon? As quickly as the thought had entered his head, he dismissed it. If it got them both out alive, so be it.

He watched the boy's eyes grow heavy and close. Before long, his chest rose and fell steadily. His mouth drooped open. Hutch went to him and laid him on top of the sleeping bag. Getting him inside would wake him, so he unfolded one of his own blankets and draped it over him, tucking it in around his legs and arms.

He switched off the lantern.

45

Terry leaned over the handlebars. Laura knew he had to be squinting and blinking to see past the water constantly rushing into his face. She had shared this torture until she realized that such a sacrifice from her was unnecessary. He had wanted to drive; she was a mere passenger, sitting behind him, her arms wrapped tightly around his waist. She had lowered her head against his back, which kept the spray on her face to a minimum.

The dirt bike whined over ruts and rocks. It admirably found traction even in the slickest mud. Terry drove like an expert motocross rider. He would pull back on the handlebars to assist the bike's climb over a particularly steep hill or to maneuver out of a dirt bike–eating crevasse. What impressed Laura most was his counterintuitive ability to apply more gas when the bike felt as though it wanted to flip backward. Early in their marriage, she and Tom tore up these hills on twin 240s. While she had ridden her whole life, Tom had learned only after moving to Fiddler Falls. He had dumped the bike at least a couple dozen times before her instruction stuck: more gas meant more power, and with more power the bike could climb almost anything.

Terry had obviously ridden before.

Between the driving rain and the gray light, they traveled half-blind. She had told Terry the general direction of the cabin. He was getting them there, though with no regard for the niceties of smooth terrain. Sometimes the front wheel would plummet straight into a ditch or hole, and he would expertly pull it out. Other times it felt as though he would ride head-on into a sheer cliff face or some other impassible obstacle. He would rear back and maneuver around the problem. More than once the rear wheel found a steep upward slope that it wanted to fully experience, only to have Terry pull it back onto the arbitrary route he treated like a well-planned itinerary.

With each yard, mud climbed their legs. By the time they had hit the grassier hills well above town, earth caked Laura's clothes up to her armpits and the back of her head. When they stopped, the rain would wash some of it away, but more than likely, this coating was hers until her next opportunity to change her clothes and shower.

To the east, the gray mass of clouds had broken away from the horizon, like an ice shelf in the Arctic. Over there, yellow beams dropped in glorious splendor; she was certain a choir of voices ushered in that far-off sunlight, but here, now, the soundtrack was stuck on the deafening static of rain.

How wonderful it would be for a golden sky to illuminate her reunion with Dillon. A dark thought scampered into her consciousness before she could slam it out: there would be no reunion because the smoke she had seen on the hill had been his last wave good-bye. If the day brought her to that truth, she would run with this weather forever, always drenched, never to behold the sun again. She knew God would somehow let her do this, to be a phantom of the storm, because He understood grand gestures and deep sorrow. Her mental protector finally gave that scampering beast the boot, and she imagined, once again, the reunion of mother and child.

She felt Terry's back lift under her chin, and she realized that they had stopped. The rain and the memory of the bike's jarring ride made her feel, even now, as though they were still in motion.

Terry yelled back over his shoulder. "Are we getting close?"

"Not even."

"Feels like we've been riding all day."

"Rough stuff, but we'll get there."

Terry gunned the engine. "Okay! Hold on!"

The sky cleared as quickly as it had filled with clouds. Declan watched the last fat drops strike the windshield of the Jeep Cherokee. Kyrill turned off the wipers as they crested the hill immediately before the burned wreck of the Hummer. He coasted toward it.

"What happened to your car?" the old man said. He was leaning forward in the backseat, peering between Kyrill and Declan.

"Don't worry about it," Declan said. "What's your name, anyway?"

"Evan J. MacElroy."

"Evan? You don't look like an Evan."

Kyrill laughed. "What does he look like?"

Declan sized him up. "Jasper . . . no . . . Elmer. He's an Elmer. Julie, what do you think?" He glanced over his shoulder at Julian directly behind him.

"I don't know," he said. "Yeah, Elmer."

Declan gave a single firm nod, as though a major debate had been settled. The vehicle slowed and stopped twenty yards from the Hummer. Declan, Kyrill, and Julian climbed out. The Bronco pulled beside them. Declan had made the executive decision to bring the entire crew. The auditorium was secure enough to hold the timid cattle inside, and Cort had proved that guarding it sounded good but didn't mean spit.

Pru exited the Bronco and slipped into cinematographer mode. His head swiveled for a scene-establishing pan. The passenger door opened, and Bad pulled himself out, leaning heavily on the door. Cort had offered him the backseat, but he had said, "Nah, I'm not gonna let a little thing like this change my funk."

Cort hopped out of the rear door and hurried to hover around Declan. The old man remained seated until Declan opened his door.

"Come on out here," Declan instructed. When the man obeyed, his sneaker-shod feet slipped on the grass, and only Declan's quick moves prevented him from going down hard.

Declan said, "You sure you spent your life up here, old man?"

"My parents brought me up here to picnic when I was a baby."

"Must've been on a glacier," Kyrill quipped.

Holding the man's arm, Declan walked him to the front of the Jeep. "Here's the deal. Some people hopped out of this thing before it exploded. We didn't see where they went, but now we want to find them." He paused.

The old man missed his cue, so Declan said, "What do you think?"

"About what?"

"Shoulda brought the big guy," Kyrill said.

Declan slapped the old man on the side of the head, hard enough that Julian, who had wandered to the edge of the trees, turned to look.

To his credit, the old man kept his tongue. He dropped his head and raised his hand to it, but nothing more.

"Listen up, Elmer," Declan said. "We've been real nice to you and all, but we're not up here for a picnic with Mommy and Daddy. We have a job to do, and either you can help us do it . . . or you can't." He gripped the back of the old man's neck and squeezed. "Now, I'll ask you again. What do you think?" He released his grip.

The man rubbed his neck and tried not to let his eyes roll over Declan. He looked up into the hills and at the woods. "How many j'say?"

"Don't know. One to four."

"Men? Women?"

"Men. I think."

"Children?"

Declan shook his head, thinking.

"Maybe," Bad said.

"Yeah, maybe," Declan said. "Might be a boy, ten or eleven."

"Nine." Julian spoke up. "Dillon's nine."

The old man perked up. "Dillon? Dillon Fuller?"

Declan said, "Don't even go there. Don't make this personal. There may have been a kid. Leave it at that."

The old man continued to rub his neck, but it seemed to Declan that it was more to help him think than to caress out a kink Declan might have put there. Evan/Elmer seemed to plug the facts they had given him into some run-for-your-lives-in-the-hills-above-Fiddler-Falls algorithm. Finally he pointed left, west, and said, "I'da gone that way. There's a ranger station couple miles."

"I don't think so," Declan said. With the woods right there, he was sure that was the side of the valley they'd started from. Even if they'd forgotten his weapon—which wasn't likely—the explosion soon after their disembarkation from the Hummer would have reminded them. If they had enough brains to pull off this bit of misdirection, they would have figured out by now that the weapon was aerial, if not space-based. And if it could target, then it could see. He didn't think they would venture into the open, especially right behind where Declan had passed. They would have stayed in the trees as long as possible. He pointed east. "What about that way, or possibly further north through the woods or south toward town, as long as they could stay in the trees?"

"Oh, well . . ." The old man didn't like that idea. Going against his first inclination threw him off the scent. He behaved as though he were on the run and they'd just told him that he couldn't take the route that he knew was best.

Good, Declan thought. *He's taking it seriously. Amazing what a solid bop on the head will accomplish.*

"Okay," the old man said slowly, thinking. "Then . . ." His hand came off his neck, and the other one came up to absently rub the place where Declan had made contact. "I'da followed the woods back to town."

"No breaks in the trees?"

"Couple, but mostly woods."

Declan thought about it. The town didn't sound right. They had tracked the Hummer to this area, well away from Fiddler Falls. It may have been a ruse, an elaborate goose chase, but it seemed over the top. Why wouldn't they have done their little evasive thing and then shot for one of the houses, where they could park in a closed garage? No, they were out this way for a reason—whether to retrieve supplies, weapons, or communication devices, or simply to hide until the trouble in town blew over. To Elmer he said, "Nothing east? No place to hide?"

"Well . . ." His fingers slid down his jawline to rub the gray stubble on his chin. "Couple cabins that way. Caves all through them hills. An old mine."

"What's closest?"

"The mine." He pointed. "Over them hills. Closed. Coupla years ago."

"Can you check it out from here, Dec?" Bad asked. He was leaning against the Bronco's grille, poking at his bloody pant leg. Each poke elicited a flinch of pain.

Declan checked his watch. "Not for almost an hour."

"Then let's drive over there," Kyrill said.

Declan took in his crew. Bad, poking at his wound; Pru, pointing the camera at him from thirty yards away; Kyrill, itching to drive; Julian, still miserable, the kid who wants to go home from camp after two days but isn't allowed to make the call; Cort, willing to do anything as long as it was with Declan. All of them were bees waiting for Declan to tell them how to buzz.

He clapped his hands together. "Let's do it."

Phil had made it through the cold night by burrowing under the groundcover, a trick Hutch had once mentioned in passing. He wished more of Hutch's wilderness trivia would surface, but this tidbit had been enough when he needed it. His blanket of needles and moss was sufficiently woven to hold in his body heat. He had tried not to think of the creepy crawlies sharing his earthen bed. Now he was famished, but he didn't trust himself to know which plants or bugs were safe to eat. All the more reason to get to Fond-du-Lac quickly. But *quick* was a word he'd lost along with his glasses. Since then, he'd tumbled down hills, plunged into marshes, and walked into enough branches to build a fortress out of them. His clothes were as grungy and tattered as his spirit. His joints and muscles ached. His flesh was bruised and torn. He had half a mind to sit and . . . *just sit.* Let the weather get him, or the animals. Who cared? His friends were gone. His life back home didn't amount to much. No job. No girlfriend. If luck were money, he wouldn't have enough to buy a cup of coffee.

But the other half of his mind said, *Do it for them, for David, Terry, and Hutch.* He wanted to survive to point a finger at their killers. If he died, the bad guys won, free and clear. He couldn't let that happen.

So he pushed on, sloshing through muskeg, clawing his way up hills, stepping or rolling over boulders and the decaying trunks of toppled trees.

One step at a time.

He tried not to dwell on his injuries, on his hunger, on his pathetically slow progress, on the distance remaining, on the loss of his friends, on the possibility of Declan knowing about him and coming after him, on the slim chances of actually making it to the next town.

He stumbled through an area where the trees thinned out and the uneven ground almost caught his foot and tossed him over. He had ventured a few steps back into thick forest when he realized that he'd passed a road. Well, a trail of some sort, at least. Two parallel ruts whose distance apart approximated the width of a four-wheel drive. He turned back to it, fell on the grassy center hump. His eyes followed it until it disappeared around a bend. He laughed, causing the birds to stop chirping for a few seconds. This had to be the way to Fond-du-Lac. Following it would be infinitely easier than blazing his own path through the trees. And it would take him directly to the First Nation town, he was sure of it. He'd lose the protection of the trees overhead, but he thought that was a small price to pay for avoiding the tortures of woodland travel. He wondered if the town would have Pop-Tarts. He could really use a Pop-Tart about now.

He'd been on the trail for an hour when he heard a helicopter. Its throaty flutter rose and faded, then grew strong again, louder. He scanned the sky, afraid to miss it, afraid to be missed. The sound faded into silence.

"Hey!" he yelled, his voice strained and broken. "I'm here!"

Birds, their incessant chirping. The surflike wind through the trees. Eerily creaking wood. Nothing more.

He dropped to his knees and hung his head. His eyes closed. He must have dozed off, for when he heard the pounding blades again, the helicopter was directly over him.

46

Forty minutes later, Declan sat on the hood of the Cherokee. His legs were draped over the grille, his feet on the bumper. Cortland's head rested against his lower back. Her feet were propped on the windshield. She was singing softly to him, some song Declan didn't understand. It seemed to be about two lovers who spent four verses trying to reunite. Someone had punched the repeat button on Cort's brain, and she kept singing these same verses over and over.

The SUVs were parked on a large man-made plateau, which had been the mine's parking lot and the location of the mobile homes that served as administrative offices. It was now grassed over and would have made a nice place to picnic or park with your girl had it not been so far from town. The spiraling crater of the mine lay over a small berm.

Kyrill, Pru, and Bad had taken the old man to scout out the spiraling ramp, especially the opening, set into an upper level of the crater.

Julian had stayed behind, saying he thought it was stupid chasing people all through the wilderness. That had suited Declan, who wanted an armed guard staying with him on the plateau. He had supposed it was a slim possibility that the mine was a decoy and their prey were waiting to ambush them; but these interlopers had proven themselves to be cunning and persistent, so he wouldn't put an ambush past them. He had asked Julian to roam the plateau and make sure no one was sneaking up the slopes. The boy had navigated the perimeter once and was heading back toward the cars.

The walkie-talkie in Declan's lap squawked. Kyrill's voice came through: "We're at the mouth of the tunnel now."

Declan pictured Kyrill standing there, rifle in one hand, walkie-talkie in the other. The old man would be back a little, not believing he was complicit in the hunting of humans. Pruitt would be even farther away, maybe on the other side of the mine opening to catch Kyrill's reaction should a surprise spring out of the darkness. Bad would be sitting right where he had slipped and fallen, within ten feet of the start of the spiral ramp. He had taken a closer look at the slick mud and decided not to go any further. He was in a position to see the mine opening. Had Declan scoped out the geography beforehand, he would have suggested Bad position himself there anyway. If something went wrong at the mouth of the mine, Bad would not be caught up in it, could communicate the situation, and could fire across the crater at the threat.

Declan keyed the talk button. "And . . ."

Kyrill: "Hold on."

Bad: "He's peering 'round the corner. He's going in."

Kyrill: "Some paper on the floor. Gum wrappers . . . no, wait . . .

Band-Aid wrappers. They're clean. Haven't been here long. Wait a minute."

Julian appeared at the front of the Jeep. He leaned on the hood to listen.

Kyrill: "Footprints. I can't tell how many. Hold on."

Bad: "The old man's going in."

A moment later, Kyrill: "Elmer says he's done some tracking. He thinks it's one adult and one child or a woman."

"Dillon," Julian said.

"Or his *mom*," Cort said, her words hard as bones.

"Nah," Declan said. "She was punching your ticket when the ones up here got away. It's the kid."

Julian stood straight. "What are you going to do?"

"We'll see."

Kyrill: "There's a metal door about thirty feet in. Won't budge. But the footprints lead right up to it. Half of one, the heel comes right out from under the door."

Into the walkie-talkie, Declan said, "You can't get in? Can you shoot a lock out?"

Kyrill: "No. Whatever's holding it is on the inside."

"Ask the old man what's up."

Declan waited. He and Julian exchanged a glance.

"Sounds like they found themselves a fortress," Cort said.

Kyrill: "He says all the mines are like this. I guess they're modern . . . not like the old gold-digging mines. Not like . . ." Long pause. "What was that old Bogie one?"

Declan keyed the walkie-talkie. "*Treasure of the Sierra Madre.*"

Kyrill: "Yeah. Not like that. It's got concrete tunnels and stuff."

Declan lowered the walkie-talkie, thinking.

Julian elbowed his knee. "Just leave 'em alone. What are they gonna do? By the time they come out, we'll be long gone."

Declan thumped Julian's head, directly on his injury.

Julian jumped back. "Hey . . . !" he whined. He touched his forehead, looked at his fingers.

"Think, little man. They've seen us, and we're not exactly part of the anonymous masses."

Julian scowled at him, considering it. "But, Declan—"

Kyrill: "Dec? What do you want to do?"

Smiling at Julian with tight, thin lips, he held the walkie-talkie in front of him for a few moments. Finally he keyed the button and said, "Pull back. Return to the trucks." He checked his watch.

"Declan," Julian said. "The whole town has seen us."

Declan held his gaze. "I know."

47

In his dream, Hutch was happy.

He was happier than he had been in ages, but he could not remember why this sort of joy had eluded him. He was lying on a blanket outside. His head was propped up on his arm, and he was watching his children play. Logan was an attentive older brother. Eleven years old, he easily carried his seven-year-old sister on his back. He was running toward Hutch, a big smile pushing his cheeks into rosy globes. Macie peered over her brother's shoulder at Hutch. She laughed and laughed. As Logan approached, he circled around his father. Hutch craned his head to follow until Logan and Macie were completely behind him and he had to turn his head to gaze over his other shoulder to see them.

When he did, they were adults. Logan was tall and handsome.

306

Same blue eyes, dark brown hair. The woman standing beside him had his little girl's sparkling green eyes and dishwater-blonde hair, pulled back from her face and tied in a ponytail. That this man and woman were his son and daughter, all grown up, Hutch had no doubt.

Logan sat at his father's feet. Macie crouched next to him.

"Where were you?" Logan said. His voice was simultaneously that of a man and of the boy he was the last time Hutch had spoken to him. It was as though Hutch's ears heard the man's timbre, but somewhere between ear and brain the voice traveled back twenty years.

"I didn't go anywhere," Hutch pleaded. He realized he had gone away, even if it was vague knowledge, not supported by memory.

"You did!" Macie said sharply.

His heart felt squeezed, as though suffering the gravity of a world spinning, spinning ten times faster than the earth. And that made sense. Faster. Time out of control. He tried to explain. "I didn't . . . you have to know . . ."

"What?" she said. "I have to know what? That you didn't love us?"

"No!" He knew everything would be all right if he could only explain, if he could only convince them that it wasn't his fault.

She responded as though reading his mind. "It was your fault!" She stood up. "You stopped loving us!"

With each word she became younger, smaller, until she was the seven-year-old Macie he remembered. She turned and ran across the meadow toward trees that cast shadows darker than they should have been.

"Macie!"

He felt his son's hand on his leg. He was still a man, but his eyes were young and innocent. "She's always blamed you. I tried to explain . . ."

"Logan." He reached out to him, hope welling in his chest.

Logan continued. "I tried to explain that people can't choose how they feel. They just feel it. And you stopped feeling love for us."

"No."

"There you are!"

They both looked to see Hutch's wife walking toward them through the field. By the time she reached the blanket, Logan was a boy again. Eleven . . . and nine . . . seven . . . five . . .

Janet reached down and picked Logan up by the scruff of the neck. Somehow she was able to lift him completely off the ground without raising her arm too high. His feet kicked; she turned and walked away. With each step she grew bigger and bigger. Logan appeared to shrink in relation to the hand clasping him. As Janet grew, her steps shook the ground with greater and greater force.

Hutch felt the earth below him shake. He opened his eyes. Cement dust filtered down through the air like fine snowflakes.

He sat up. He was in the mine tunnel. He reached out, found the camping lantern, and switched it on.

Dillon lay curled on the opposite side of the tunnel floor. The boy breathed steadily, deeply. He was asleep.

Hutch knew where he was, how he had gotten there. He remembered the conversation he had shared with Dillon. But he felt disoriented. The dream had felt so real, but he was certain the shaking that had awakened him had not been a remnant of that dream. The silt drifting down. It was gone now, but it proved he had not imagined the disturbance.

The tunnel shook. A crack appeared directly over his head; concrete dust and dirt spilled down. There was a deep rumble, like the growl of a barrel-chested dog. He was not sure whether he had heard it or felt it.

Dillon woke. He blinked and lifted his head. His face expressed confusion, and Hutch knew for certain this was not a dream.

Hutch's bow, propped against the wall, fell over.

Hutch and Dillon watched each other, anticipation thick between them, waiting. Something in Hutch's chest pulled tighter and tighter, like a bowstring waiting for release. Past full draw, it continued pulling taut.

Then release: the tunnel shook. The crack above them widened. A thin sheet of dirt sifted down like a veil. It made a straight line of dirt an inch high across the tunnel floor, nearly linking Hutch to Dillon. The proverbial dog growled again, deep in the bowels of the mine. Something farther up the tunnel, in the darkness, cracked and snapped.

Slowly, terror transformed Dillon's face. The sleepy boy aged with fear. Big eyes, twisted lips. It occurred to Hutch that in his short acquaintance with Dillon, the child had swung from extreme tension to relief and back again, countless times. An image came to mind of a heart made not of muscle, but of rubber. How many times could Dillon's heart stretch and snap back before it became inflexible and useless?

Dillon's eyes flicked around—to Hutch, to the crack in the ceiling, to the dirt on the floor, to the dark tunnels on each side of them. Fear battered the boy far beyond a face laceration and bruised ribs.

Hutch did not know how to respond, either to the pounding threat or to Dillon's anxiety. Perhaps his own fear was debilitating him, or sleep was slow to release its grasp, or the unfamiliarity of the situation was sludge in the engine of his mind. But for Dillon's sake he forced a smile and held open his arms.

Dillon pushed back a blanket and scampered across the floor. He settled onto Hutch's lap, squeezing him tight and pushing his head into his chest.

The tunnel shook more severely. Another crack developed; this one running from the apex of the tunnel to the floor in lightning-like branches and fissures. They appeared on the tunnel wall in an instant. The sound that accompanied it was not dissimilar to the crack of thunder. Behind that sound, and stretching longer, was the growling rumble.

For just a moment Hutch desired nothing more than to hold the boy, to once again give comfort and to be comforted. He remembered the dream. His heart ached for Logan and Macie. In so many ways, Dillon was like Logan. He did not believe it was a coincidence that this boy, so close in age and even personality and physical appearance to his own son, was now looking to him for survival. In the dream, Logan had grown up blaming him for not being a part of his life. Without Hutch there was a very good chance that Dillon would not grow up at all. He had been forced out of his own son's life. Nothing could make him abandon Dillon.

He rubbed the boy's back and said, "It will be okay." And he believed it. It would be okay. Somehow, it would.

"What is it?" Dillon asked, his voice small.

Hutch looked up at the ceiling, as though seeing beyond the cracks, cement, and earth to the sky above—to something in that sky that gave Declan an awesome and awful power. "The people who want to hurt us are not finished trying."

The tunnel shook. A chunk of concrete the size of a mailbox fell from the ceiling. Dirt followed it like a comet's tail. It shattered on the floor five feet from Dillon and Hutch. A rumbling, crunching sound, like rocks in a clothes dryer, communicated the tunnel's distress and destruction.

Dillon squeezed tighter. He seemed intent on pushing himself inside Hutch's protective arms. A cocoon, safe from what the world had become.

"Dillon, we have to go. We need to find a way out."

Dillon shook his head against Hutch's chest. He moaned a word. Hutch thought it was *no*.

"I know I said we'd be safe here, but Declan found us. We got away from him before. We'll do it again." When the boy didn't move, he continued. "But only if we take action. Only if we don't sit here and let Declan do what he wants to us."

He hated himself for doing it, but he gripped Dillon and tried to push him away. The boy clung to him.

Another rumble. The tunnel to their left, beyond the reach of the camper's light, roared out as it apparently collapsed. A plume of dust and dirt pushed into the light and blew past Hutch and Dillon. Granules of sand settled over them. As sand wafted across the surface of the lantern, shadows rose on the walls and shifted like beasts awakened from slumber.

48

The rain had stopped almost an hour ago, but the ground was still muddy where it was dirt and slick where it was grass. Laura tapped Terry's shoulder. He let off on the gas and leaned his head back toward her.

"Let's stop for a few," she yelled. They had been giving themselves breaks whenever one of them felt ready to rattle into madness.

He immediately brought the dirt bike to a halt. He killed the engine and waited for her to climb off.

She swung her leg over the back of the seat and the rear fender, shakily taking the ground. She hobbled away, groaning. She stretched her back and her legs, pinwheeled her arms, swung her head in a full circle one way, then the other.

Terry performed the same ritual, though more vocally. He said, "I feel shaken *and* stirred."

"Shaken the way a dog shakes a chew toy," she agreed. "An insane dog who goes for two hours straight." She found a boulder protruding from the field and sat on it. "I want to get to Dillon as fast as possible, but I'm not going to be any good to him rattled like this."

Terry sat cross-legged in the grass. The ground was soaked, but no more so than they were.

They wore more mud than clothing. *About twenty pounds of it,* Laura thought.

He leaned back on his arms. "Tell me we're close."

She squinted at the terrain, at familiar landmarks. "Maybe an hour. The rain and then residual mud and wet grass . . ." She shook her head. "We just haven't made good time."

Terry closed his eyes, leaned his head back. He craned it right, then left, touched his chin to his chest.

She watched him, then said, "Why are you doing this, Terry?"

"Doing what?"

"Helping me. You could find some safe place and ride this whole thing out if you wanted to."

"I don't think I could."

"Why not?"

"Wouldn't be me," he said. He pondered something. "I never really thought about helping or not helping. Hutch, Phil . . ." He paused. "Hutch, Phil, David, and I, we kind of did for one another, you know? Four musketeers."

She smiled. "All for one and one for all."

"Like that. So when it comes to going after Hutch, that's a no-brainer. And when you have people watching your back, when people care about you, it's a lot easier to care for other people. Strangers. We all do something, me and the guys. Thanksgiving, we help out at the downtown mission." He shrugged. "Stuff like that. I told you Hutch would never leave Dillon. That's Hutch. I also said I'd get Dillon to safety even if Hutch weren't with him. It's just who we are."

"Pretty special."

He shrugged. "Shouldn't everyone be like that?"

"Places like Fiddler, everyone's family. We know who's sick, who's having money problems, whose marriages are strained. Gets on your nerves sometimes, but I don't think anyone would choose more privacy over the bowls of soup that automatically come when they get a bug, the free hand with plumbing, or car problems when times are tight." She narrowed her eyes at him. "You and your friends would surprise my dad. He lives in Black Lake. His brothers took off as soon as they could. Vancouver and Calgary. Dad's always wondering who's got their back. He says folks *out there* don't care about each other, not the way we do."

"Lot of people feel alone," Terry agreed. "All the indifference forces you to either put up a wall or band together. Most people put up walls."

She looked around. "Up here life gives back what you put in. You can see it. The town council decides to make literacy a priority, and within months kids are reading everywhere. They declare that young people are important, and suddenly teens are getting scholarships or starting businesses. One person convinces her neighbors we need to improve the water, and within a year you can taste it. Where else can you see your efforts pay off so clearly, so quickly?"

He picked at the drying mud on his forearm, thinking. He said, "What the rest of us do is create little towns out of our social networks. We don't see our tax dollars working directly for us, so we pass our own entertainment bill and buy a big-screen TV. The lucky ones find a handful of friends who care about them the way people in small towns do."

"How did you—"

Thunder boomed in the sky some distance away.

Laura jumped up. Her eyes swept over the distant hills. She locked in on an area from where the sound seemed to have emanated.

Terry joined her, and as they watched, a streak of green light, perfectly straight, perfectly vertical, flashed from heaven to earth. In less time than it took for the image to travel from eye to brain, it was gone. Then the crack of thunder reached them. A thick snake of white smoke began rising, as if the light were returning to the skies, not nearly the spectacular being it was on the way down.

Laura ran for the bike. She yelled over her shoulder, "Terry! We gotta go! Let's go!"

Hutch stopped trying to force Dillon away from him. Instead he stood, accepting the burden of the boy the way he would an injured companion. Dillon's legs encircled his waist. He was firmly attached. Hutch picked up his bow and slung it over his shoulder. Next he picked up his utility belt, buckled it, and draped it over the same shoulder. He picked up the camper's lantern and considered taking one of the blankets. His left arm was crooked under Dillon's rump and not good for anything else. He could barely carry what he had, so he opted against the blanket.

Another strike. The vibrations came through the floor and ran up his legs. His ankles and knees took the shock, but still he nearly fell. He imagined Declan's weapon pounding into the hill above them. He checked his watch. He knew that Declan's cannon became operational in cycles of time. He believed that Declan had access to the weapon every eighty to one hundred minutes. But how long could he use it each time? As Hutch moved toward the mine's entrance, he thought about the pattern of firepower he had witnessed. Insane as Declan was, he did not simply release unaimed volleys of explosions as soon as and for as long as he was able. Targeting was part of his game. A guy like Declan, a control freak if Hutch read him right, he wanted not only to call down the power of lightning but to direct it, to be precise in his destruction.

Consequently, Hutch could not count on having heard a perfect start and finish to the operating time of the weapon. From when the caribou blew up to the end of that first cannon attack on him seemed like ten or fifteen minutes, but he couldn't be sure. First, he'd been running for his life, scared out of his mind. If he discovered that his estimation was off by double, it would not completely surprise him. And second, he had no way of knowing if the strike on the caribou marked the beginning of the weapon's functionality for that circuit or whether Declan had been using it for a while before he attacked the caribou.

The attack in town also seemed to last ten or fifteen minutes. After the explosion at the back door, Terry and Laura had remained exposed in the moonlight for several minutes. Why hadn't Declan attacked again? The most logical answer was that his window of opportunity had passed.

Okay . . . so if the weapon's periodic functionality was ten or fifteen minutes, could Declan bring the entire mountain down on him and Dillon? Probably. But if they could manage to stay alive, the pounding would eventually stop—and pretty soon too. Then they'd be free of it for about an hour and a half. Enough time to make an escape.

Another explosion shook the tunnel, pitching Hutch into its concaved wall. At the last moment he bent and twisted to prevent Dillon's head from connecting with the concrete. Rubble fell and rolled out of sight. He reached an intersecting passageway and turned left. The entrance should lie roughly forty yards ahead. He did not expect to see daylight at this point because of the shut door. Then the illumination of the lamp revealed fine fissures that expanded into gaping cracks, which in turn gave way to the complete destruction of the concrete and the collapse of the tunnel. Rock and dirt and bits of concrete tunnel, like huge eggshells, sloped from the floor to the ceiling, blocking the passage.

A strike of Declan's weapon rattled him to his knees. He managed to keep hold of Dillon and the light. More of the tunnel's ceiling and walls in front of him not only sloughed in, but also exploded into the passage. Hutch backpedaled away from falling dirt and concrete. It seemed that Declan was targeting the hill above the adit, either assuming they would have remained near it or with the intention of sealing them in.

He turned and quick-stepped back to the intersecting tunnel, where they had talked and slept. He didn't know much of what lay beyond. More tunnels, the few rooms he had seen the night before. He knew only that they had to get away from the tunnels near the adit.

He remembered the way Declan's weapon had stripped the branches and leaves from directly above its striking point in the woods. A well-defined circular pattern. Declan was jabbing a finger at them, a big, invisible, infinitely strong finger.

Jab: the crushed car on Provincial Street.

Jab: the depression in the asphalt, beside which lay some poor soul's foot.

Jab: the destruction of the rec center's back door.

Jab: David.

We're nothing more than ants to him, Hutch thought. He'd never bitten his lip in anxiety, but he did now, drawing blood, tasting it.

A finger jabbing into the hill above them. Jabbing into the mine. He imagined a finger-shaped hole opening up, rising like a chimney to the surface, exposing the network of tunnels. Declan's gang would fan out from its edge into the passageways, shooting any survivors.

The tunnel shook, and this time it felt like the entire hillside shifted.

Survivors? At this rate there would be none. Hutch moved quickly through the tunnels, ignoring some cross-passageways, turning into others. Though there were no markers identifying specific tunnels or distances, Hutch felt they were moving deeper into the hill, farther from the adit.

He hoped to find . . . he did not know what he hoped to find. Something that would save them from the jabbing finger: a place to wait it out, another exit. He was thankful for the camper's lantern.

The mine most likely had been wired with battery-powered lamps that illuminated automatically with the disruption of AC current. Along with everything else, emergency equipment had left with the previous tenants. If they only had his small penlight, which was now juiceless, they'd be stumbling around in the dark. Any chance of finding either a safe haven or an exit would have been reduced to sheer luck.

And Hutch did not believe in luck.

49

Hutch ran, stopping only to brace himself when the tunnel shook.

He felt Dillon's weight, his tightly gripping arms and legs. Survival meant more to him than his own life—it meant the life of this boy. For the first time he really understood what it meant to care more for another person than himself. It was a sentiment he had felt for Janet and Logan and Macie, but in the comfort of his home in a country not racked by war. Would he have died for his wife and children? He believed he would have. But the luxuries and relative safety of his life had never forced him to take the question seriously.

Here he was with a child he had known for less than a day, but he knew the answer. He would die for Dillon.

A terrible thought occurred to him. The damaged street, the severed foot: could that have been Dillon's dad? Dillon had said his father

319

had died the other day with the strike of Declan's weapon. He had no way of knowing this, but Hutch believed Dillon's father had given his life trying to protect the town, his family. Why else would he have been targeted? Most of the townsfolk had been corralled into the auditorium. Something Dillon's father had done provoked Declan. What would have irritated Declan was someone standing up to him.

A portal opened on the right, different from the intersecting tunnels. Hutch paused to peer in, holding the lantern up. It was a room devoid of furniture. Paper posters remained taped to the concrete walls. Several corners had come loose to dog-ear over the message. Enough of the posters showed for Hutch to understand their purpose: safety messages, both general ("Report all injuries at once to management") and mine-specific ("Never descend without your partner"). As he turned to leave, a notice by the door caught his attention. The size of a sheet of copy paper, it was mounted behind a sheet of scratched and murky Plexiglas. His heart raced as he held the lantern closer.

It was a map of the tunnel system showing routes for emergency evacuation. From an X, which Hutch took to indicate this room, a series of heavy red arrows turned left and right through a diagram of the tunnels ending at the main entrance. A series of orange squiggles like tildes followed a serpentine path in the opposite direction. A legend at the bottom of the map identified the red arrows as the "primary emergency evacuation route" and the orange squiggles as the "secondary emergency evacuation route."

"Dillon, I think I found a way out. I need to set you down for a minute."

Dillon leaned his head back to look Hutch in the face. "I'm okay now. I can walk."

Hutch bent forward to set the boy on his feet. "Can you hold this for me?" he said, handing the lantern to Dillon. Dillon took it and held it high. Hutch pulled at the Plexiglas, but it was solidly affixed to the wall by a screw in each corner. Time had not loosened any of them even enough for him to wedge his fingertips between the wall and the Plexiglas. Hutch had nothing on him to unscrew the mounts or pop the covering free.

The room shook. Nearby, a wall cracked. In the tunnel rubble tumbled and fell.

"Come with me," he told Dillon. He stepped into the hall. His shadow grew long and swung like a time-lapsed movie of a sundial as Dillon brought the lantern up behind him. He did not have to step far into the tunnel to find what he was looking for. He bent and hefted a chunk of concrete.

"Okay. Back into the room."

With Dillon holding the lantern a few feet from the map, Hutch said, "Turn your head away." He smashed the concrete into the map's clear covering, creating a small white bruise in the Plexiglas. He hit it again and again. Either the concrete was not as hard as it should have been, or the Plexiglas was tougher than it needed to be; whichever, the combination wasn't working. He dropped the concrete and stared at the map. The volume of tunnels, coupled by the number of turns required to reach the first secondary exit, defeated his thought of memorizing the route or even accurately copying it to the back of the topo map.

Another strike. The floor canted and leaned. Dillon staggered back.

"I have an idea," Hutch said. "Set the lantern on the floor and go into the hall for a sec."

Unsure, Dillon relinquished the lantern, walked to the portal, and stopped. Hutch removed his utility belt from his shoulder and snapped it around his waist. He unslung his bow, removed an arrow, and nodded at Dillon. "Just around the corner."

Dillon stepped into the tunnel and stopped.

"I know it's dark, Dillon. But it'll be okay, and I need only ten seconds." Slowly Dillon edged around the corner.

Hutch backed to the center of the room, nocked the arrow onto the bowstring, and pulled back. The broadhead struck the Plexiglas at 240 feet per second and ricocheted back into the room. It clattered against a wall before settling on the floor.

"Okay, Dillon," Hutch said.

The boy hopped into the room as though he'd heard something whispering to him in the dark.

"See?" Hutch pointed toward the map.

The arrow had struck the Plexiglas two inches below its top edge and horizontally dead center. It had caused a shard of Plexiglas to break off and a crack to run in a jagged line down to the bottom edge. Hutch pried at the break with his fingers. It lifted, allowing him to get a grip. He pulled hard and half of the cover snapped away. He did the same with the other half. Hutch suddenly worried that the map had been plastered to the wall and would not come free intact. But when he picked at a corner, the entire page fluttered loose. Dehydrated squares of rolled tape remained on the wall.

Hutch smiled at Dillon. "And they say men don't ask for directions."

The room shook more violently than ever. It may have been his imagination, but Hutch would have sworn the dog-growl had become a full-throated snarl, as though they were no longer hearing the cannon strikes, the finger jabs, through tons of earth and concrete; somewhere the tunnels had opened up to the sky. If Declan had continued to pound at the area near the entrance, most likely he would now target the tunnels deeper into the mine, closer to where Hutch and Dillon were. If they didn't move fast, all the maps in the world, all the secondary exits, would be as helpful as a parka in hell.

The room shook again, and the beast's voice bellowed through the tunnels on a current of hot air. The blasts were coming quicker. Inscrutably optimistic, part of Hutch believed that this signaled the approaching end of the weapon's window of opportunity. Declan was racing against a clock.

Dillon had just picked up the lantern when yet another strike came. He staggered sideways, took two steps back, and plopped on his butt to the floor. A second shock wave—or a new blast—rippled the ground, flipping Dillon backward. His leg rose straight up; his arms shot out for balance.

As Hutch watched in horror, the lantern crashed to the concrete and winked out.

50

Declan sat on the ridge of the crater directly opposite the mine's entrance. He held the weapon's control device in two hands, playing it as he would a video game.

That was, after all, the point. For years he had been telling his father that the future of warfare lay in the technology of video games. Not only did hyperrealistic simulations train soldiers and pilots, but since an entire generation of game-heads were reaching fighting age, equipping them with weapons modeled on controllers and games would facilitate their success on the battlefield. Instead of video games mimicking reality, reality would be shaped by the imaginations of video-game programmers. In the gaming community, the learning of new skill sets occurred lightning fast. Each new game required new abilities, new disciplines. Hand a new recruit a traditional assault rifle, and with intense instruction and practice he might master it—that is, use it to kill before being killed—in a month or two. Give a gamer a weapon patterned after one used in a popular first-person shooter, and he'd be down with it in two days.

His father owned several companies that serviced the industrial military complex. They designed weapons, both small and large. One division focused on antipersonnel weapons—such cool little devices as cluster bombs, which explode in the air and hurl shrapnel over a wide radius. Other divisions worked on anti-bunker, -building, and -vehicle devices; large-scale destruction; antimissile technology; and satellite weaponry.

These companies worked closely with DARPA, the Defense Advanced Research Project Agency, the Pentagon's division responsible for thinking up crazy, sci-fi technology and getting it into soldiers' hands. DARPA was credited with developing stealth jets, night-vision optics, the M16 rifle, and the computer mouse. Countless weapons and devices still on DARPA's drawing boards had already found their way into the video games Declan's company created. These cutting-edge, seemingly fanciful tools of warfare made his business one of the fastest growing and most successful game producers in the world.

Not that Declan was satisfied. He was convinced that entertainment was only the tip of the gaming iceberg. The ergonomic, time-sensitive nature of video games made their technology ideal for many other aspects of a busy, frantic world. For instance, smart homes, controlled by remotes modeled on handheld gaming devices, could save hours a day in a homemaker's life. Are the kids doing their homework? Check the controller. Did you forget to shut the garage door? The controller will check and shut it if necessary. Ready to start dinner? You get the idea.

Declan believed the best opportunity for synergy, growth, and profit was the incorporation of gaming culture into the art of war. Not only could weaponry and training bring warfare into a new age, but gamers were hungry for military scenarios. Money would flow in both directions. And money was Daddy's language.

Declan's father had finally consented to bring Declan into the loop on a top-secret new weapon. Everything about this weapon demanded the skills found in top gamers: hand-eye coordination, quick thinking, digital dexterity, the ability to scan a series of numbers and icons and instantly know what they meant in all their various combinations, and the ability to manipulate a dozen different buttons and combinations of buttons in response, all in three seconds. The weapon his father's company had created was a satellite laser cannon—SLC. Current satellite weapons were relatively weak because their chemical oxygen iodine lasers tended to be solar powered, which didn't give them enough "oomph" (a word his dad's scientists had frowned at, but ultimately agreed was accurate). Couple that with atmospheric turbulence, which dissipates laser beams, and by the time they reached the earth's surface, they couldn't light a birthday candle. His father's company had developed a laser powered by a nuclear reactor. The reactor amped up the laser to a degree that made it an effective weapon against earthbound targets. In addition, the nuclear power allowed the laser to recharge in seconds rather than the minutes or even hours of previous laser-weapon technology.

Trouble was, the Outer Space Treaty of 1967 prohibited nuclear weapons in space. It was his father's belief that demonstrating the effectiveness of this weapon to the powers at the Pentagon would convince them to find a way around the treaty. One loophole his father's attorneys found was large enough to sail a satellite through: the nuclear reactor they needed was not itself the weapon; it only powered the weapon. It should be classified not as a nuclear weapon, but as a nuclear power source.

But theories carried little weight with the people who controlled armies and big checks. What mattered to them were results. Laws and treaties championed by politicians who knew little about the way the world really worked created a catch-22 for companies like Declan's father's. They could not build the weapons the military needed because the government required proof of viability. Only prototypes produced proof. Few companies were willing to risk the hundreds of millions of dollars new weapon systems required without the contracts and funding the government would not provide. His father had become obscenely wealthy by taking the path less traveled and investing in hunches.

Declan loved that about the old man.

The part of the SLC program for which his father's designers turned to Declan was the control unit, named Slacker for Satellite Laser Cannon Remote (SLCR). Testing the Slacker now, Declan was *almost* impressed. Response time was quick, but the targeting controls needed some work. Despite borrowing the code for the crosshair graphics and firing command from one of his company's popular apocalyptic games, in the context of SLC it didn't work to Declan's satisfaction. That was one of maybe three dozen notes he had scribbled into his BlackBerry.

Still, watching the cannon bore into the hillside, drilling its way into the mine tunnels, he had to admit it was pretty cool. Slacker allowed intensity adjustments. If your target was a man, you wouldn't want to create a huge gaping hole below him, especially if he were standing on a bridge or a building you might still need. Then again, if somebody holed up in a bunker—which, essentially, was the case here—you could crank the intensity level and be relatively sure that a few well-placed events would burrow him out.

Declan had not only punched a hole through the top of the tunnels; he also had begun to stitch a crater through the hill, exposing the labyrinth within. Slacker's screen flashed red, and the device beeped.

"Oh, oh, oh . . . I'm losing her."

"Has it been eighteen minutes already?" Cortland said from behind him, where she kneaded the muscles of his shoulders and neck.

Declan grunted. One of the big problems he'd found was the limited time he had to use the SLC in each ninety-five-minute period. To keep her in the air without a great expenditure of energy, the satellite had been placed into orbit 280 miles above the earth. Orbiting Earth seven degrees off the polar axis brought her overhead roughly every hour and a half for eighteen minutes at a time. He was one minute away from losing his toy for that long.

He looked around. Kyrill and Bad were watching from the same berm, not far away. Their legs draped over the edge. Pru and his camera were halfway around the crater, trying to catch the destruction from various angles. Julian had said he didn't want to participate and stayed at the truck. Declan lifted a walkie-talkie and keyed it. "Julie? Julie!"

Julian's voice crackled back: "What?"

"Put Elmer on."

Julian: *"What?"*

"The old man, put him on."

Cortland said, "What do you want with him?"

"I don't have much time . . ."

Elmer: "Yeah?"

"Where would you go if you were in that mine and you couldn't walk out the front door?"

Elmer: "What do you mean, where would I go?"

Declan sighed in exasperation. He triggered a laser strike, watched the flash of green and the billowing volcanic explosion. Then for fun he did it again, right away. He keyed the mike. "You're in the mine and somebody's just blown up the front door—what do you do?"

Elmer: "Well, unless I got bonked on the head or I was stupid or—"

"Elmer!"

Elmer: "I'd go out the back door!"

"There's a back door? Where?" Declan looked up, could not see anything beyond the crater, beyond the smoke. He was sure if there was a way out, it would be one of the hills sloping away from the mined crater. He wouldn't be able to see it even without the smoke. "Elmer!"

Elmer: "Emergency escape route! Follow straight back from the front door, on the rump side of the hill."

Moving his thumbs quickly, Declan maneuvered the satellite to focus on the far side of the crater, on the hill that sloped down beyond it. He was about to lose access to the weapon, and the optical system, the camera, would go with it. He moved his thumb, scanning, scanning, looking for anything that appeared man-made or like a cave. He really didn't know what he was looking for. Then he saw it: a perfect circle, like a manhole cover. He aligned the crosshairs on it, lifted his thumb to push the button, and the crosshairs disappeared; he was too far. He jumped up and began running around the berm, continually checking the crosshairs. As he bent around the crater, the image flickered and went to static.

51

A darkness blacker than night engulfed them.

Hutch saw Dillon fall and heard a sharp *thunk!* Dillon's head or the lantern striking the floor.

The boy moaned.

"Dillon!" He dropped to all fours and crawled toward the last place he had seen him. He heard movement, reached out, and found Dillon on his knees.

"I broke the light," Dillon said, anguished.

"Are *you* okay?"

"I broke the light!" He started to cry.

"Dillon, no. It's okay." Hutch rose to his knees, shuffled closer, and put an arm around Dillon.

Quietly, between sobs, Dillon repeated, "I broke the light."

"What are you, a moth? We don't need it, okay?" But Hutch knew they did need it. Without it the map was useless, and he didn't think they could find the emergency exit without both a map and a light.

Dillon leaned out of his embrace, then rose back into it. Hutch reached out with his other hand and confirmed that Dillon had picked up the lantern. He heard its switch *click, click, click*. Dillon shook it, releasing the tinkle of broken glass. He moaned again.

Hutch tightened his grasp. "Dillon, it's all right. And listen."

After a few moments Dillon said, "I don't hear anything."

"The explosions have stopped."

"They'll just start up again." His voice could have put the entire troupe of Cirque du Soleil on Prozac.

"I don't think so. Not for a while, anyway."

"What are we supposed to do? How can we get around in the dark?"

Hutch thought about it. "Well . . . fortunately we're stuck in a network of tunnels. It's easy to feel our way along the walls."

Dillon gasped.

"What? Dillon?"

"*Feel* . . . Our school toured the Cluff Lake Mine. It had bumps in the floor, near the edge." He paused, remembering.

"What about the bumps?" But Hutch was starting to understand.

"They were put there to help people get out in an emergency. The bumps led straight to the exit."

Hutch remembered seeing a raised line in the floor of the tunnel, two in fact. His mind had passed over them, chocking them up as seams or flaws. It made sense for an operation like this to provide a way for its personnel to escape in the event of an emergency. Battery-powered lights could not always be counted on, especially in the event of a partial collapse. The two raised ridges he had seen in the floor were side by side. He hadn't noticed before, but he was sure one was straight. It represented the route that would lead to the main entrance, which they knew was now buried in rubble. The other line was tilde-shaped, leading to the emergency exit.

"Dilllon, you're a genius. You've just saved our lives." He explained what he had learned from the legend on the emergency route map and what he believed it meant. He snapped open a pouch on his utility belt and found a coil of spare bowstring. He always kept two because nothing ruined a day like tracking an animal for eight hours just to have your bowstring snap. He uncoiled the string and, slipping one end into the manufactured loop at the other, he formed a lasso. He slipped the lasso over his foot and tugged it tight at his ankle.

"I'm gonna tie this string to your wrist," he told Dillon. "I'll crawl ahead of you and follow the ridges to the exit. If something should happen, like the explosions start up again, yell for me if the string breaks or comes loose. I don't want to lose you."

He couldn't see it in the dark, but he knew Dillon nodded.

52

"Bad, Kyrill! Come here, quick."

Declan could have stomped on them for moving so slowly. Seeing his agitation, they began jogging toward him on the top of the mining crater's berm.

"Sometime—" Declan started.

Julian's voice came over the walkie-talkie. "Elmer's gone! A car's coming!"

Declan sighed. It was always something. He pointed toward the plateau and yelled at Bad and Kyrill. "Elmer's taking off. Julie says some car's coming."

The two gunmen veered off the berm, making double time to the plateau. Declan followed. He glanced back to see Cort plop down. She was wearing out. Behind her, Pru continued filming.

As Bad and Kyrill approached Julian, the boy gestured toward the valley and the big meadow beyond the plateau. "There's a car heading this way. Elmer said it was somebody Red Bear, a conservation officer or something. He just started running."

Both Bad and Kyrill unslung their weapons in midstride.

Julian waved frantically at them. "No, no! Just go get him. Don't shoot him!"

Ignoring him, they jogged to the edge of the plateau.

Declan stopped twenty yards away, at a spot where he could take in all the action: Elmer barreling down the hill from the plateau, a Jeep CJ7 moving fast across the valley toward the old man, his boys taking aim.

Julian grabbed at Bad. "No!"

Bad knocked him down. He sprang up, grabbed at Bad again. Bad elbowed him in the chest, the side of the head.

Julian crumpled.

Bad aimed, fired. Three rounds so fast it sounded like one. Another three, finding his bearing. Dirt and grass kicked up to Elmer's left.

Elmer slowed, tried to stop, finally did. He raised his hands over his head. "What?" he yelled. "I didn't do nothing!"

Bad fired again. The slugs tore the ground at Elmer's feet.

The old man turned and ran. His legs moved faster than Declan had ever seen legs move.

Might be a cool video game effect, he thought. He hollered, "Check it out, Kyrill! His legs!"

Kyrill nodded. He was busy unfolding the bipod in front of the trigger mechanism of his rifle. That finished, he flipped down the unipod on the telescoping stock. He lowered the weapon to the ground and lay down behind it.

Still a good half mile distant, the CJ7 continued bouncing over the rough terrain.

Bad let loose with two more three-round bursts. The last one found Elmer's back, sending his body tumbling.

Bad raised the barrel toward the 4x4. He fired, then again.

"Too far for me," he said.

Kyrill's rifle cracked. A hole the size of a donut appeared in the windshield directly in front of the driver. The vehicle swerved and slowed. It traveled four hundred feet before coming to a complete stop.

"Dude!" Bad said.

Kyrill stood, smiling.

Bad said, "Props to you, bro!"

They touched fists.

Julian had recovered. He lay on the ground, pressing a palm to his cheek. He surveyed the destruction below. He stood and walked to Declan.

Before Julian could speak, Declan said, "I don't want to hear it, Julie. You thought we'd go chasing poor Elmer and forget about the guys in the mine, didn't you?"

Julian stared at him, eyes moist.

"Don't try to outsmart me, kid brother. You're not up to it."

Declan swiveled around and strode back toward the mine. In a singsong voice, he called, "Bad . . . Kyrill . . . I *neeeeeed* you!"

The concrete floor was dusty. Occasionally drifts of dirt obscured the bumps Hutch followed. He crawled on his hands and knees, his right-hand fingers tracing the path to the secondary emergency exit. An arrowhead capped one end of each line, indicating the proper direction. The air smelled of concrete, dirt, and smoke.

At first, every time he brought his right leg forward he felt the resistance of Dillon's hand, tethered by the bowstring. About the time he was ready to stop, to find a way to stay together without constantly tugging at the child's arm, Dillon resolved the problem himself. He stayed closer to Hutch and moved his arm in sync with Hutch's leg. Hutch reached another spot where the bumps in the floor angled ninety degrees—this time to the left. He stopped. The ninety-degree turn indicated that they were at the intersection of another tunnel. He

336

had learned to trust that the bumps would not lead him into a wall, though he found it strange and disorienting not only that he was completely blind to his environment, but also that nothing else—a light breeze, perhaps—signaled new passageways.

"Doin' okay?" he asked.

"Yep."

"Another turn."

"Gotcha."

Hutch checked his watch and turned into the new tunnel, following the bumps. They had been crawling like that for twenty-five minutes. Twenty-five minutes as well since the explosions stopped. If his calculations were correct, they had about another hour before Declan would have use of that particular weapon again. He wanted to be well away from the area by that time. He wished he knew how much farther, how much longer to the exit.

For the last fifteen minutes or so he had felt that bowstring tautness in his chest again. Pulling it tight was the anticipation of hearing Declan's gang getting into the tunnel system through the opening made by the explosions. Considering their cockiness and their larger-than-life weapons, he did not think they would be quiet about rooting him out. Yet he had heard nothing, no pounding of footsteps, no automatic gunfire. He didn't know whether the silence should relieve him or worry him. Every now and then a breeze would blow past, not from a cross tunnel but along the current one. Sometimes it came from behind, sometimes from ahead, billowing dust into his mouth and eyes. Always, it was a chilly wind. Hutch thought it came from the rent Declan had torn into the mine.

A minute or so along this new tunnel, Dillon cleared his throat. "Hutch?"

"Yeah?"

"What's going to happen with your children?"

Hutch tried to discern Dillon's meaning. When he couldn't, he asked, "Happen?"

"I mean with you and them. You and Logan."

"I don't know, Dillon." The boy had slept on this, thought about it.

"But you want to spend more time with him, and he wants to spend more time with you, right?"

"Yeah."

"When did you stop living with him?"

"Nine months ago."

"Do you see him more now than you did right after you moved out?"

"No." The next word was painful. "Less."

Silence. Dillon thinking. He finally asked, "Then in nine more months you'll probably see him even less, right?"

Hutch stopped. He rose and leaned back so he was kneeling, his rump resting on his heels. Dillon bumped into him.

"Why would you say that?" Hutch asked.

"If something is going one direction, it will continue going in that direction unless something . . ."

Hutch could almost hear the wheels turning in the boy's head.

Dillon continued: "Unless something *acts* on it."

"Did your parents teach you that?"

"Yeah. They said if I want something to happen, I have to make it happen. Otherwise, it will keep going the way it's always gone. Like when I made a slingshot, the rubber bands kept breaking. My dad said, 'What are you going to do to stop them from breaking?' I said, 'Not pull back so hard.' He said, 'Doesn't that mean you won't be able to shoot as far or as fast?' I said, 'Yeah,' and he said, 'Why don't you think about it some more?'" He paused.

Hutch said, "And did you?"

"Yeah."

"What did you come up with?"

"I went to Mr. Nelson at Kelsie's and asked for thicker rubber bands. He didn't sell them, but he had some in his office. They're used to hold bundles of books together."

"What did your dad say?"

"He took me for a banana split."

Quietly, wanting to hear it from Dillon, Hutch said, "What did you learn from that?"

"If you want to make something better, you have to do something to make it better."

Funny, Hutch thought, how wisdom was often so simple, something you always knew but had to be reminded of at the right time.

Dillon had pondered Hutch's problem. That said something about Dillon. Hutch thought he owed him a response and honesty. He said, "Dillon, I really don't know what to do."

"But you love your son, right?"

"Very much."

He expected Dillon to continue, but the boy was finished with what he had to say.

The silence left Hutch as shaken as Declan's attack. He found Dillon's head and mussed his hair.

"Let's go," Hutch said.

Ten minutes and another turn later, the bumps in the floor ceased. He patted the floor beyond their point of termination but could not find where they picked up again. He felt the walls on both sides of the tunnel. No door, no cross passageway. Could the tactile guide be incomplete? Didn't make sense. Could the bumps have been sheered off by the passage of some heavy equipment? He had not felt any change in the texture of the floor indicating where the bumps had been.

Hutch stood and again felt the walls. Nothing. He raised his hands and repeated the procedure; his left hand struck metal. Feeling, he realized that it was a ladder. It rattled under his inspection. He found a latch and, holding a rung, flipped it. The rung and ladder it was attached to suddenly grew heavier in his hand. He lowered his arm, letting gravity bring the ladder down. It stopped three feet from the floor. He sat and removed the bowstring from Dillon's wrist and then from his own ankle.

He told Dillon, "I'm gonna go up, see what's there. You stay here. If I'm not back in five minutes, go back along the ridges in the floor and hide."

Dillon started to complain.

"I'll be back. Don't worry. I just want to check it out." He found Dillon's shoulder and squeezed it. He stood, made sure his bow was securely slung around his shoulder, and started up the ladder. He climbed forty or fifty rungs. His hand touched metal at the top. He tugged on a latch and it snapped back. He pushed, and the round panel above him lifted an inch. Daylight sliced in. He closed his eyes and held himself in that position for ten, fifteen seconds. Slowly, he opened his eyes again. He lifted the panel higher; it was hinged on one side. He rose another rung and peered out. A hill slanted down, trees heavy to his right. He pushed the door fully open. It swung over and slammed down on the other side. Squinting in the light, he climbed up.

Footsteps crunched behind him. Fast, running. Hands grabbed him, pulled him out of the shaft.

Kyrill and Pruitt.

"No!" he yelled.

Kyrill batted him with the barrel of his big rifle, knocking him to the ground.

He felt his bow yanked off his shoulder. Someone brushed past them and climbed up onto the concrete housing of the shaft. It was Bad. He looked down through the open door of the shaft and fired his machine gun.

54

Declan's voice, hazy with static, said, "What's that? Talk to me."

Bad was peering down into the shaft. Smoke curled from the muzzle of his rifle. He stared another few seconds, then pulled a walkie-talkie out of a breast pocket. "Hold on," he said. "Clearing this position."

Pruitt was holding Hutch's bow. Awkwardly, he slipped an arm through the bow so it would rest on his shoulder. Under the opposite arm, his camera hung from a thick strap. He pulled it up to his face, turned from Hutch, and leaned his thighs against the concrete shaft which protruded from the sloping ground two and a half, three feet. He bent to point the lens down into the shaft.

Bad tapped Pruitt's head with the toe of his boot. "Get out of here, man."

Kyrill poked Hutch in the ribs with the barrel of his gun. "Give me that."

"What?"

"Your belt, man. Take it off, now. Slowly."

Hutch unsnapped his utility belt and held it up.

Kyrill took it, resnapped it, then slung it over his head like a bandolier. He jabbed at Hutch again. "Who else is down there?"

"Didn't see nobody," Bad said.

"The footprints at the front door," Kyrill reminded him. "Somebody went in with him."

"The kid," Hutch said, angrily. "He's dead, all right? Don't you think he'd be with me if he were alive? Those *explosions* . . . your . . . your . . ." He hitched in a choppy breath, turned his head away.

"Go see," Kyrill said.

"I can't get down there with my leg. You go."

Declan's voice came through the walkie-talkie. "What's up, guys?"

Bad responded. "We got 'im."

"Who?"

"The guy with the arrows."

Standing above Hutch, on the top of the shaft, Bad looked powerful, ready to mete out a death sentence. He keyed the walkie-talkie. "Says you got the kid when you blasted the mine. He's dead."

Declan: "No sign of him?"

Bad gazed into the hole. He looked up at Kyrill, who shrugged.

Hutch said venomously, "You want to gawk at a dead nine-year-old, I'll take you to his corpse."

"Shut up!" Bad snapped. Into the walkie-talkie he said, "This dude's alone, Dec. Want Kyrill to go down, check it out?"

Silence, then Declan squawked back. "Nah, get your butts up here."

Kyrill's barrel bit Hutch's scalp again. "You heard the man."

Before rising, he watched Bad assess the short jump to the ground from the rim of the shaft. Someone had dressed his wound by wrapping white gauze around his thigh, over his pants. The entire front portion shimmered with fresh blood. Bad saw him watching, so Hutch gave him a tight smile.

Bad's facial muscles tightened, and he jumped to the ground in front of Hutch. He gave no indication that he was in pain. He stared into Hutch's eyes and said, "Get moving, punk." He lifted his boot and brought it down on Hutch's left hand.

Hutch hissed and hurried to get up before one of his captors considered the advantage of having him on the ground. His hand throbbed but wasn't as damaged as it would have been had the rain not softened the ground. Pruitt, his camera in one hand, Hutch's bow over his shoulder, led the way up a hill.

"Go on," Kyrill said. Hutch fell in behind Pruitt. Kyrill and Bad followed.

Hutch believed that Dillon was safe below. If one of Bad's bullets had struck the boy, surely they would have heard something. With Hutch captured, Declan would have no reason to continue attacking the mine. If Hutch could not return to Dillon, the boy would be safe, at least for a while. If he could hold out down there, until the police or a rescue team found him, he'd be okay. Hunger or thirst might drive him out early, however. Hutch hoped that he could return to Dillon before then. That, or when Dillon did emerge, Declan would be off on some new distraction.

As they climbed, Pruitt slipped the bow off his shoulder. He turned it in his hand, examining it. "This is pretty cool," he said. "Kyrill, think you can fit one of these in the game?"

Kyrill answered, "We got a satellite laser, dude. What do we want with something like that?"

"And it ain't cool," Bad called out. "Hold up!"

Pruitt stopped to look back. Hutch and Kyrill did too. Bad was having some difficulty maneuvering the hill with his leg. He was using his good leg to climb, dragging the injured leg behind. When he reached Kyrill, Pruitt turned to continue up the hill, but Bad snapped, "I said hold up, man."

He climbed past Kyrill. When he passed Hutch, he jabbed the stock of his machine gun into Hutch's ribs. Reaching Pruitt, he slung his weapon over one shoulder and said, "Gimme that thing."

Pruitt handed him the bow.

Bad eyed it up and down, looked at Hutch. "This ain't cool at all," Bad told him. "If I knew how to shoot, I'd put every one of these arrows into you."

He sidestepped a couple paces to the nearest tree. He swung the bow around, hitting the trunk hard. The laminated wood cracked. Another swing into the tree. The quiver broke off and the arrows sprang out, bounding and flipping in all directions. Bad pulled back and swung again. One of the limbs of the bow snapped off. It fell and wanted to spin down the hill, but the bowstring snapped it back like a retractable leash. Bad held the bow high, drawing the broken limb close to his foot. He stepped on it and yanked until the bowstring snapped loose. Then he hurled the bow over Hutch and Kyrill's heads. It went into the trees, and Hutch thought it got tangled in the top of one of them.

Bad smiled at him triumphantly. "Robin Hood ain't nothin' without his bow, huh?"

Hutch shrugged.

Infuriated, Bad scooped up an arrow. He appeared ready to dismember him with it. He took a step forward and jabbed it at Hutch, striking his shoulder. The broadhead sliced through Hutch's jacket and shirt, skin and muscle. Hutch fell back and the arrow came out, still in Bad's hand. Hutch fell against Kyrill, who pushed him away. He rolled, fell on his knees, then onto his face. He started to slide over the slick grass. Kyrill stomped on his ankle, stopping his descent and sending a bolt of pain up his leg.

Hutch didn't know whether to grab his shoulder or his ankle. Since it was nearest and it worried him the most, he touched his fingers to the shoulder wound. It was bleeding but not profusely. In fact, painful as it was, he believed it was only slightly more than a flesh wound.

"Get up," Kyrill commanded.

He turned like the hands of a clock until his feet were downslope. Then he rose, standing gingerly on the ankle that now felt tight in his boot, already swollen.

Without the bow, Pruitt had once again become the cameraman. Where his face was supposed to be, a lens caught the light and glinted. He panned from Hutch to Bad, as though expecting a brawl then and there.

Bad noticed and slapped the camera hard. "Get that out of my face," he said. He turned and began dragging his leg up the slope.

Kyrill jerked his head toward Hutch. "Let's go."

55

They climbed. Hutch's ankle protested every step. His shoulder became tacky with blood. His shirt stuck and pulled away, stuck and pulled away. He was glad Dillon wasn't there.

Bad reached the top of the slope, stood, and glared down. His legs apart, his arms coming away from his body as though muscles prevented them from hanging by his sides, he looked gladiatorial. Pruitt stepped up next to him, and the difference in physique would have been comical in a different situation.

Hutch rose up beside Bad. He half expected the man to shove him back over the edge. Instead Bad reached out, grabbed the front of Hutch's coat, and began pulling him. They were on a large, grassy plateau. On their right, a berm rose another three feet. It arced around, and Hutch recognized the lip of the mine crater.

At the far side of the plateau were the two trucks Declan and his gang had used to pursue the Hummer. One of the SUVs started up. It pulled forward and sped directly for them.

Bad halted.

The Cherokee must have reached sixty miles an hour when Hutch recognized Declan in the passenger seat. His girlfriend was behind the wheel, seeming too small to drive a car. From what Hutch knew of her, he would not be surprised if she plowed into him and Bad and then Kyrill and Pruitt before continuing right over the edge. Of course, he didn't expect any of them to join him on his journey to his final destination, so there would be nobody there to chastise for giving Cort the keys.

Bad released Hutch and leaped out of the way just as the Cherokee locked its brakes. Its front end dipped, and it slid on the grass. Hutch leaped in the opposite direction from Bad. The SUV stopped where he had been standing. As he hit the ground and rolled, fifteen scenarios, all involving his running and escaping, flashed through his mind in three seconds. Getting his feet under him, hunching low, he glanced over to take a bearing on the Jeep. A big-barreled pistol was pointed directly at him. Declan extended the Glock from the open window. His impassive face told Hutch that pulling the trigger or refraining from pulling the trigger made no difference to him. Hutch froze.

Beside Declan, Cortland said, "Wheee! That was fun."

On the far side of the car, Bad yelled, "Cortland! Look at my leg. It's *pouring* blood. You think that was funny?"

The young boy, Julian, stared at Hutch from the rear passenger window.

Declan opened the door and stepped out. He called, "Kyrill, you got this monkey?"

"'Course." He stood between the bumper and the edge of the plateau, pointing the big rifle at Hutch.

Declan tucked his pistol into the waistband at the small of his back. He tugged at his smoke-colored Under Armour shirt, smoothing its wrinkles, showing off his sinewy torso. "Stay down," he commanded.

Hutch sat and leaned back on one arm.

Declan approached him. "You're the caribou hunter," he said. "You gave us a run for our money."

"Wasn't difficult," Hutch replied.

Declan fingered one his necklaces. It appeared to be a string of teeth. He let one eyebrow rise infinitesimally.

Hutch took that as an invitation to continue. "I mean, come on. I've never seen so many idiots in one place."

Declan looked up at his crew, a thin smile rising on one side. He shook his head. "Why are you provoking me?" He looked into the sky. "I think you're trying to distract me." He glanced toward the edge of the plateau, toward the hill that Hutch, Pruitt, Bad, and Kyrill had ascended. "That boy you said was dead. Is he really?"

Hutch's mouth went dry. He said, "I just don't like games. Whatever you're gonna do, just do it."

"You don't like games?" Declan's smile became big and broad, teeth showing.

Kyrill laughed. Even Bad, who had come to stand in front of the Jeep, leaning one hip against its grille, grinned. Pruitt came around the back of the car, his camera-face pointed at Hutch.

"All we do is play games," Declan pronounced. "I mean, really, that's *all* we do." He pointed at Pruitt. "Why do you think this man is here? Why do you think any of us are here? If, by some grand miracle, you're around next Christmas, you can buy our game, and you know what you'll see? A big bad satellite laser cannon blowing people away. One of the victims will look suspiciously like that fisherman friend of yours. And I'm thinking right now another one is gonna look an awful lot like you. Which means, of course, you won't be buying the game."

Declan rolled his head, thinking. "Do me a favor. When you think we got you, look straight up. It's a great effect, looking up before the laser nails you. You'll see a twinkle of light . . . then nothing." Something occurred to him, and he called out to Kyrill. "Maybe we should have the targets see the actual laser coming at them. That would be cool." He turned back to Hutch. "In reality, the light you'll see isn't the laser . . . at least not *that* laser. It's a beam of light, part of the adaptive optical system, that analyzes the atmospheric conditions. Then a computer intentionally distorts the real laser in the exact opposite way the atmosphere would have distorted it. So then the atmosphere actually tightens and focuses the laser. They call it reciprocity. Incredible stuff."

What could Hutch say? *You're mad! You won't get away with it!* Any declaration just seemed pathetic.

Declan's eyes drifted away. He retreated a few steps, then came back. "You got away from us once."

"Three times," Hutch corrected.

"Think you can do it again?"

Hutch felt his heart pick up its pace, beating to the rhythm of hope. Unless Declan pulled the trigger at the precise moment he released him, Hutch would indeed do it again.

Declan raised a finger. "But first," he said, turning away again, "I think Bad has his own score to settle. Don't you, Bad?"

"Wait a minute," Hutch said as Bad approached. "Are you saying your big bad weapon can't get me unless I'm beat up?"

"Not at all," Declan said. "I simply don't want to deprive Bad of the opportunity to share his feelings with you."

"How's it gonna look in your game when the satellite weapon takes out some guy who's already bleeding and broken? That's not sportsmanship."

"You really don't play games, do you?" Declan asked. "It's a lot of fun whopping muscular army dudes, but no gamer's gonna pass up an opportunity to rain hell down on *anyone*, injured or not."

Bad circled around, then closed in on Hutch. Apparently finding support in his injured leg, Bad swung his good leg back. It kicked forward, and Hutch grabbed his foot in both hands. The toe shook two inches from his face. Hutch glared into Bad's eyes.

His head exploded in pain. It snapped back on his neck. He released Bad's foot. Kyrill stood over him, lowering his foot from the roundhouse he had just delivered to Hutch's temple.

Bad shifted on his feet, again lifted the foot of his uninjured leg, and stomped down on Hutch's bleeding shoulder. White-hot bolts of lightning flared through his chest. They found his vision, blurring Bad into an indistinct monolith, towering over him.

A strike to his ribs, his kidneys . . . another. A kick to his arm, his leg, his stomach. He wanted to fight, to at least swing his leg around and knock his attackers down. But with the furious pounding coming as fast and steady as a train's steady clicking over the rails, all he could do was curl up to protect the most vital parts of his body. He saw the flash of a boot; under it his biceps compressed with the force of Barry Bonds's bat. He reached out to grab a pant leg or ankle, only to feel the bat-strike in his ribs under his arm. Insanely, a phrase used in medical forensics came to mind, but one he learned from television, so he wasn't sure of its verisimilitude or nuances: *blunt force trauma.* When they autopsied his body, that term would come up with nauseating frequency, and it would again—now!—as a boot came down on his knee. If he survived the beating and Declan had his way, he would leave no body to autopsy. One big blunt force trauma would vanquish Hutch's material being from earth. Some pathologists would be spared the trouble of cataloging all his wounds.

He must have passed out, but only for a second or two; suddenly Bad was standing over him, his left hand holding Hutch in place by the collar of his coat, the other pistoning up and down into Hutch's face, punctuating whatever it was he was yelling.

"Tough guy now, huh?" *Punch.* "No bow, no guts!" *Punch.* "What are you gonna do now, huh?" *Punch.*

It was a curious thing, being beaten senseless. He began hearing sounds that were disconnected from the actions that made them, as though a sound track had jumped out of sync by a few seconds. Or his sense of hearing got jarred and started taking the long way to his brain, causing sounds to reach it seconds after they should have. He heard *thump-thump-thump* and Bad would punch.

Thump-thump-thump-thump

Punch.

Thump-thump

Punch.

Maybe it was his heart he was hearing. At least it was steady. *Thump-thump-thump.*

Bad released him, rose to his full height, straddling Hutch. He looked up. Beyond Bad's head—

Thump-thump-thump

In the sky—

Thump-thump-thump

A helicopter came into view. Hovering. Slowly turning left and right as though taking in the scene.

Thump-thump-thump

It was black and sleek, long and glistening. Infinitely fancier, more expensive than the one he, Terry, Phil, and David had ridden into this defining chapter of their lives.

While he watched, landing gear folded out of the smooth under-carriage.

Shocked into immobility, Bad stood over Hutch, watching the heli-copter. Certainly the man would bolt any second now. He would rec-ognize his need to run, to get in a vehicle and drive away. To flee from the authorities, come to take him away. Hallelujah.

Hutch did not want to lose this opportunity. Ignoring his aches and pains, the stiffness and screams of protest from his muscles and bones, with all of his might he brought his fist up into Bad's crotch. The bellowing roar, which for at least a few moments drowned out even the helicopter's *thump-thump-thump*, was immensely satisfying. Bad folded over and fell away.

56

The helicopter loomed larger, descending. Hutch lifted his head to watch it come down on the plateau forty yards from where the group had gathered to mete out Hutch's punishment.

Declan watched, then glanced over at Hutch as a child would look at a shattered lamp upon his parents' return home.

Yeah, how you gonna explain this? Hutch thought. *And I'm just the start of it. The smoke from the mine got their attention, but wait till I show them what you did in town, what you did to Dillon's father and to David.*

Declan leaned into the window of the Cherokee. Hutch wanted to call out, *He's got a gun!* but Bad's machine gun was right there on the hood and Kyrill was still holding his gun in plain view. Surely the people in the helicopter saw them. They must be even more powerfully armed.

Declan put a black canvas bag on the hood, rummaged through it, then tossed something to Kyrill. The teen slung the rifle over his shoulder and stepped over to Hutch. He slammed Hutch's ankles together and bound them with a long zip-tie.

"Wait a minute," Hutch said, confused. Then it dawned on him. The people in the helicopter were not rescuers, but accomplices. Declan's gang did not have to run or worry about evidence. In fact, they may take these new arrivals on the tour Hutch thought he would lead—to point out not atrocities, but accomplishments.

Kyrill kicked him onto his side, grabbed his shoulders, and dragged him toward the edge of the plateau. He hoisted Hutch into a sitting position, pushed his back into a tree, wrenched his arms around it, and zip-tied his wrists together. The agony of his shoulders and arms threatened to cloud his ability to reason, to figure a way out of this mess. If there were words convincing enough to negotiate his release, the dizzying distraction of pain rendered them inaccessible to Hutch's consciousness.

Kyrill sauntered back to the Cherokee, haltingly, as though not sure where he should be.

Julian opened the rear door of the SUV and stood to watch the helicopter set down on the grass. The propellers washed a cold wind over them. Leaves, needles, and the little dirt that had dried since the deluge had ended whipped into the air and blew away. The whine of the helicopter's jet engine died. The blades slowed.

Hutch's current view of the helicopter in profile supported his first impression: it was a sleek machine that would have seemed more at home on a racetrack than in the sky. Glossy black, with black tinted windows, it bore no markings except a white tail number.

It was alien and insectile. If a black whiplike tongue shot out to ensnarl Cortland and pull her into its gaping maw, Hutch would have been shocked but later would have thought, *Yeah, I saw that one coming*.

Nothing moved as the blades slowed to a stop. Even Declan and Julian seemed to be holding their breath. Then a rear door opened and a big man with a little machine gun draped around his neck hopped out.

The ultimate bling, Hutch thought.

He was bald, but unlike Bad, rolls of fat rippled from the back of his head into his shirt collar. Coupled with a beefy double chin, the effect was that the man either wore a neck brace of flesh or possessed no neck at all. The black sunglasses shielding his eyes may have been designed as an accessory to the helicopter. His black suit appeared to be a size too small. A white shirt and thin black tie completed the ensemble, evidently purchased from Bodyguards-Я-Us.

He moved away from the helicopter, taking in everyone's position —Declan, closest to the helicopter; Cort, a step behind; Julian, standing at the open door of the Cherokee; Bad and Kyrill, at its grille; Pruitt, filming from the top of the low berm; and Hutch, restrained to a tree. The man did not seem bothered by the sniper's rifle Kyrill held or the machine gun within Bad's reach on the hood of the SUV. He pointed at Pruitt, however, and ran a finger across his neck. Pruitt's shoulders slumped, and the camera came away from his face. He set it on the ground, lens facing backward into the void over the crater.

Another man came through the open helicopter door. He stepped onto the grass and looked around. He was tall and thin with silver hair. Even from a distance, Hutch realized he had intense blue eyes.

Julian ran forward and threw his arms around him. The man returned the hug, leaning his head over Julian's. Julian said something. The man nodded. He lifted Julian's bangs to examine the wound. He patted the boy on the shoulder, and Julian returned to the Jeep.

The man approached Declan, stopping a pace or two away. In a clear, crisp voice—a voice Hutch thought a stage actor would have—he greeted Declan's gang. "Cortland, how are you, honey?"

Hutch did not hear her reply.

The man cocked his head at Kyrill and Bad. "Kyrill. William, how's your father?"

Bad replied, "Fine, sir."

"Pruitt. I trust you're getting all the footage you need for the game?"

"I think so, sir."

"Back in my day we used film, which was measured by the foot. Do you digital guys still say 'footage'?" He chuckled.

"I do, sir."

The man took a step sideways to peer past Declan at Hutch. He studied him awhile, his face unreadable.

Declan took a step forward. The man turned toward him and slapped him across the face, hard. Cortland jumped, took a tentative step back, then another.

Declan did not respond.

The man said, "This is *not* what we agreed to." The light tone he had used to address the others was gone. His words were hard and cold, bones clattering together, blowing across an icy tundra.

Declan brought up a finger. He pointed at the man's chin, seeming ready to scold him. He changed his mind and used the finger to tap his lower lip. Without a word, he turned to Cort.

"Go for a walk," he said. Then to the others: "Take off!"

Cortland hesitated but finally headed for the entrance to the spiraling ramp inside the crater. The others followed.

Except Julian, who exchanged a glance with Declan. He retrieved something from the Cherokee, then shut the door. He meandered around the rear of the SUV and along the other side to its front bumper. Evidently, he did not want to leave the area or to accept orders from Declan. He had an object in his hand, which he tapped impatiently against the metal. It made a light *ting, ting* sound. Hutch realized it was the arrow the boy had recovered from the field where the caribou exploded.

Declan and the newcomer watched the others disappear around the berm and down the ramp. The man said something Hutch didn't catch, and the two headed toward the Jeep. Declan jerked his head sharply at Julian.

The boy backed away. He turned and walked to the edge of the plateau. Turning right, he approached Hutch. He stopped beside him, tapping the tree with the arrow.

The man clattered his briefcase onto the hood and snapped its latches open. Declan lifted one foot to the bumper and leaned to drape his arms over his knee. He acted casual and relaxed and not like someone who had just been slapped.

Julian walked behind Hutch to stand on his other side. He knelt at Hutch's shoulder. He looked into his eyes, then nervously toward Declan and the man. It seemed to Hutch that the boy wanted to be near but not to be seen.

"My Uncle Andrew," Julian whispered, and Hutch detected a tremor in his voice. Julian shrugged. "Not my real uncle. My Dad's best friend. Takes care of family business."

Hutch kept his voice low. "Looks like Declan's up the creek."

Julian took in Hutch's injuries, pained by them. He said, "I'm sorry."

"How did you get pulled into this?"

Julian's eyes pooled with tears. He blinked, spilling one down his face. He didn't have an answer.

"He's your brother, right?"

Julian's lips tightened; his head barely moved up and down.

"You're not like him, Julian. Your life is not his. Nothing good can come out of what he's doing."

The man's raised voice drew their attention. He was pointing at papers and saying, "Do you understand what these spikes are?" Pause. "Declan, every time you fire that thing, a heat signature shows up in the atmosphere. NORAD thought the Canadians were messing with some kind of new nuclear threat or missiles or . . ." In frustration he tossed the sheaf of papers back into his briefcase. "They didn't know what to think. We stepped in to inform them of a test we had going on up here. We had to call in all sorts of favors at DARPA." He pointed down the valley. "Son, we flew over that town. There are buildings destroyed! Cars! Who knows what else! We didn't see any civilians." He swung his pointing finger at Hutch without looking.

Julian crouched lower.

"You've got bleeding men tied to trees. And . . . and . . ." He then turned to the big bald man at the helicopter. He snapped his fingers and beckoned with his fingers.

The man turned to the open door of the helicopter and made the same gesture.

Shadows stirred, and another man came into view, hunched over, blinking. His wrists were handcuffed in front and a cloth gag cut into his mouth.

"Phil!" Hutch called.

57

Standing in the open door of the helicopter, Phil's head shot up. He squinted in Hutch's direction; his glasses were gone. Finally he spotted Hutch. He jumped down and ran toward him. He was favoring his right foot. Between the limp and the handcuffs, his approach resembled a fast waddle more than it did a run. His clothes were torn and filthy. Dried mud and blood smeared his face, hair, hands . . . everything. His eyes were locked on Hutch, and they started glistening as tears filled them.

As he drew closer, Declan lightly skipped out from the Jeep, spun, and planted a flying roundhouse kick to Phil's sternum. Phil went down hard.

"Hey!" Hutch said. He struggled against his bonds.

Phil rolled and craned his neck to put his friend back in his sight, as though Hutch would disappear without that visual connection. He stared at Hutch, tears streaking his face, dripping off of his lids and the tip of his nose.

Hutch smiled and nodded at him, trying to convey assurances no words could provide.

"Declan!" Uncle Andrew shouted.

Declan glared at Phil. He shifted his eyes to Hutch before turning and dropping his head in a posture of contrition. He stepped back to the Jeep.

"This is what I'm talking about," his uncle scolded. "We found this man on the road to Black Lake from Fiddler Falls. I assumed he was one of your loose ends, and I see that was a correct assumption. Did you even realize you had these kinds of problems?"

"Of course," Declan answered. He said something Hutch could not hear.

"Tell me, Declan. Just what *is* going on here?"

Again Declan spoke quietly.

"That's not what we agreed!" The man, Julian and Declan's "uncle," was livid. "You were supposed to do two or three test events, no more. On trees and rocks and . . ." He waved his hands around the area as if searching for a word. Finally he said, "Maybe a *rabbit*! Look at this!" He jabbed a finger into his briefcase. "NORAD's going nuts. Twenty, thirty events in two days. They want to know what's going on, and so do I."

Declan spoke; his hands, his head, his body did not move at all as he did.

Phil glanced around, quick, panicky gestures, then looked back to Hutch. His eyes were red and anguished. Hutch made a *shhh* gesture with his lips. No telling what Declan would do if Phil caught his attention again.

"I'm going home with my uncle," Julian whispered. "I don't . . ." His voice trailed off. He looked at Hutch, his eyes pleading as though Hutch had the power to absolve him of his burdens.

Hutch did not know what crimes Julian may have committed. Or if simply not stopping Declan was enough to make him an accessory. Or if Julian's age and the control his brother had over him would be enough to exonerate him.

"You have to do something, Julian. You have to tell somebody what's going on up here, what Declan is doing. You've got to come clean. You've got to break away from your brother. It's the only way to keep from going where he's going. You understand?"

He nodded. More tears.

"How old are you, son?"

Julian cleared his throat. "Thirteen."

"That's too young to have your life ruined by someone else's self-ishness and madness. Get away. Tell someone."

"Julian!" His uncle was waving him over. Declan started speaking, and the man turned his attention to him.

"I'm sorry," Julian said. He stood. He tapped the arrow against his leg a couple times, then stepped behind the tree. Hutch felt a tug at his wrists, felt the shaft of the arrow in his hand.

Julian walked to his uncle.

Hutch moved his hands apart, feeling the slightest tug of resistance, and then the zip-tie fell away.

The uncle lifted his arm to accept Julian into an embrace. He nodded toward the helicopter. Julian stepped around his brother, threw a glance at Hutch, and headed for his ride home.

Go, kid, go, Hutch thought. Slowly, he brought his left arm from around the tree, his body blocking his movements from Declan and the man. His hand gripped the shaft of the arrow near the vanes so the arrow extended to his ankle. He moved his fist to his lap, and the razor edge of the broadhead rested on the length of zip-tie that restrained his ankles. As gently as a violinist touching his bow to a string, he sawed the broadhead over the plastic restraint. He watched Declan and the man continue their conversation. Declan's shoulder rose in agitation. Julian had easily cut away the zip-tie from his wrists with the broadhead, but he had been able to apply pressure at the tip. Holding the arrow so far back did not give the broadhead enough force to cut the tie. Despite this, Hutch continued his covert sawing.

The man slammed the briefcase shut and snapped its latches. He pulled it off the hood. He walked around Declan and stopped. He gave Hutch a long look. It was neither sad nor disappointed; it was the look of a businessman whose balance sheet would cause him trouble at the next stockholders' meeting. He turned back to Declan. "Clean this up," he said.

"Wait a minute," Hutch said. "You've got to stop this. He's killing people."

Uncle Andrew's attention flitted over Hutch. To Declan he said, "No witnesses."

Declan nodded obediently.

The man marched toward the helicopter.

"Hey! Hey! You can't do this. You can't allow it!" Hutch yelled. He watched the man walk away. He could do it, and he was allowing it. "There are over two hundred and forty people in town. Women and children."

The man stopped halfway between Hutch and the helicopter. He did not turn, he did not say a word. After a few seconds, he continued walking.

Declan checked his watch. He looked at Hutch but didn't see him. He was thinking. "Uncle?" he said.

The man turned.

"May I . . . may I . . . see those heat signatures again?"

"It doesn't matter now, Declan. Just clean this up and come home."

"I have an idea. It's important."

The uncle sighed. He walked back toward Declan.

Phil was still lying where he had fallen. He rolled his head to follow Uncle Andrew, then looked desperately at Hutch.

Hutch jerked his head sideways: *Get over here.*

Phil glanced around. He got to his knees, then to his feet. Apparently believing his captors expected him to follow certain rules of etiquette, he faced the chopper and slowly backed toward Hutch.

Uncle Andrew had reached Declan. He said, "No more big ideas. Just wrap this up."

"I know. I know. Just let me see them again for a minute."

The man put his briefcase on the hood again, popped it open, and handed Declan a sheaf of papers. Declan turned from him to examine the sheets, but Hutch saw that Declan's eyes were lost in the distance beyond the plateau.

Hutch considered that he was witnessing the breakdown of a mind. Perhaps having been found out by his family, and possibly the U.S. military, was enough to shatter his already fragile psyche. He seemed like a man about to come undone. Someone unsure of what to do when no options were palatable. He nervously glanced at his watch, then, without giving the papers the slightest glance, he turned, tossed them into the open briefcase, and said, "Thanks."

The man looked puzzled but dismissed it. He shut the briefcase and once again headed for the helicopter. Declan walked alongside, his hand on the man's back.

At the helicopter, Declan said, "Julian, I need you."

No, no, no, Hutch thought. Julian must have expressed something similar, for Declan said, "Julian! Now! Come on." He gestured with his head for Julian to disembark.

The man said, "Julian's coming home with me."

Declan gripped the man's arm. "I need him. He's a crucial part of this operation. We'll clean all this up and be home by tomorrow."

"I don't want Julian—"

"He won't be part of the cleanup. I promise. I need his technical expertise." He turned to his brother, still in the helicopter. "Julian, really."

"I want to go home!"

"You will, tomorrow."

Declan looked at his uncle. Something passed between them. The man nodded. He said, "Julian, you'd better stay. Just one more day."

Julian appeared in the portal.

"But, Uncle—"

The man said something.

Julian hesitated, then jumped out. Everything about him slumped with defeat.

Uncle Andrew climbed aboard, followed by the big bodyguard. The door shut. The engine whined. The blades spun. Julian and Declan backed up. Their hair whipped wildly in the downdraft. The helicopter lifted.

Phil had backed to within ten paces of Hutch. Now he watched the helicopter without moving.

"Phil!" Hutch said in a loud whisper.

He seemed not to hear.

Declan turned from the helicopter and strode to the Jeep. He leaned in through the open passenger window, then straightened again.

The helicopter rose higher, taking its billowy winds with it. It drifted away from the plateau slowly, giving Uncle Andrew a final look.

Julian waved and turned. Noticing something, he immediately broke into a sprint toward Declan. "What are you doing!"

Hutch now noticed the laser cannon's firing device in Declan's hands. He heard a musical chime. Hutch's eyes flicked up toward the helicopter in time to see a shaft of rippling air and a green flash punch down from the sky and vanish. The helicopter crumpled; it simply buckled in midair. The boom, stretching back to the rear propeller from the cabin, rose like the tail of a happy dog. The cockpit window shattered as the nose torqued up under the pressure of the laser's downward thrust to the center of the cabin and engine assembly. Instead of spinning out of control or even breaking apart, as Hutch had seen in movies, it tucked in on itself and plummeted straight down, like an elevator with a broken cable. It disappeared below the far edge of the plateau.

A moment later a plume of smoke and dirt erupted, rising high. The shriek of crushed and twisted metal, the winding down of a jet engine, the deep *whoop* of an exploding fuel tank, the shattering of glass, the groan of disrupted earth and trees—all became a symphony of destruction and death, an overture to the people on the plateau. It rose from below the hill, as from an orchestra pit.

The visual spectacle of the helicopter's destruction drove Phil back several paces.

Even as the plume of smoke and dust started to rise over the plateau, Hutch slid his hand along the arrow shaft, closer to the broadhead. He sliced through the zip-tie and hopped up. His right knee wanted to give out. His ribs on both sides felt bruised and cracked, playing ping-pong with pain back and forth through his organs. The wound in his shoulder sent a Morse code of agony to his brain.

Despite this, his head felt worse. He could easily believe the arrow had not penetrated his shoulder but had been pushed through his left eye and into the gray matter behind.

In less than a blink he determined to ignore all these sensations. Even if his injuries prevented him from obeying his commands, from sprinting forward or jagging sideways, he would dismiss the trauma and instantly adjust.

A quick glance at Declan and Julian showed them captivated by the helicopter's demise—and, of course, the demise of the pilot and bodyguard and their Uncle Andrew; even Hutch, in these few seconds, felt a distancing of their deaths by virtue of their being out of sight. Were their deaths any less real, any less tragic than they would have been had Declan used a knife to slit their throats? Of course not, but without witnessing the spraying of blood, the shock in their eyes, the gasp of their last breaths, Hutch felt their deaths had become muted, symbolic. Declan's weapon was frightening not only because of its ease of use and destructive power, but because, like the worst weapons man has devised, it allowed impersonal killing.

He stepped forward, gripped the back of Phil's jacket collar and, without looking, backpedaled right over the edge of the plateau.

58

They tumbled down the slope through the trees, kicking up layers of matted and wet needles, moss, and twigs. Phil smacked into a tree and *oophed* through his gag. A second later Hutch did the same. Continuing to use his arm as a tether to Phil, he tried to swing his feet downslope. He dug his heels in and used his other hand to slow their descent. When they stopped, they were halfway down the slope toward one of the narrow valleys Hutch had grown accustomed to in this region. Frantically, he looked through the trees to the edge of the plateau. No one was there. He believed the woods were heavy enough here to prevent Declan from using his satellite to spy them out, but that didn't mean the man would not blindly blast the area as he had when he pursued Hutch after killing the caribou. They had to move fast.

Phil seemed to realize this; he fought against Hutch's iron grip on his collar. He tried to rise and continue downhill. Hutch did not release Phil but yanked him back. His friend's hands were still hand-cuffed in front of him. The white rag tied around his head over his mouth, which silenced him for Uncle Andrew, had probably given them at least a little extra time, and also silenced his screams when Hutch yanked him off the plateau. He pulled Phil's ear to within inches of his mouth and said, "We have to head back up."

Instantly Phil's head shook no. He mumbled against the rag.

"I'll explain later, and I'll get this rag off you, but right now we just have to go. Fast." He moved Phil around to give him a view of his face. He said, "You have to trust me, okay? Do you trust me?"

A second's pause. Phil nodded. Hutch moved diagonally up the hill, praying no one would appear at the plateau's edge for at least another couple minutes.

Julian's wailing screams—"What did you do? Uncle Andrew!"—came from above, and Hutch hoped the boy was also flailing and punching in displeasure with his brother. He thought Declan would want to witness the result of his latest insubordination. By the dimin-ishing volume of his answer to Julian—"I saved your life. Shut up"—it did seem that he was moving away, toward the far end of the plateau, which would overlook the helicopter's wreckage. Evidently he had not yet noticed Hutch and Phil's escape, distracted, no doubt, by Julian and the thrill of the kill; besides, having been tied to a tree, Hutch did not warrant consideration. Right?

About thirty feet from the edge of the plateau and the same dis-ance over from where they had jumped, Hutch found a fallen tree. As its foliated branches deteriorated, what used to be it's crown began sliding down the slope, anchored at the other end by its root system. Eventually the dead tree would have swung around to point perfectly

369

downslope and, over time, the roots would crumble and send it shooting to the valley below. However, the top of this tree's pendulum swing had been frustrated by the trunk of another tree. It now lay nearly horizontal to the edge of the plateau above. Rainwater coming off the plateau and simple gravity had pushed piles of dirt and dead needles onto the top of the blowdown and into the crevice formed where its uphill side met the slope. To an observer above, the timber would appear to be a ledge, followed by a small drop to the continuing slope. Because the trunk was round, and water sluiced under it, washing away earth, a long cavelike depression had formed under it.

Hutch helped Phil position himself in this depression. Then he lay next to him. He pulled overgrowth and dead needles from the forest floor, careful not to take so much that his efforts became obvious. He packed this detritus over them.

He whispered, "Phil, don't say a word and don't move." Hutch worked on slowing his breathing.

On the plateau the others had returned.

"What happened?"

"Was your uncle in there?"

"Who else?"

"Hey! Where's the guy?"

Footsteps. The voices became louder, closer, more distinct.

"He got away." Whiny like Cortland.

"How? Wasn't he tied up?"—Bad.

Declan said, "Julie was over here talking to him."

"Julian? Why would he—"

"Julie being Julie." Evidently calling out to Hutch, Declan yelled, "You just killed yourself! You and your friend!"

Bad: "What friend?"

Declan, calling: "Don't forget to look up!"

Hutch whispered, "Here it comes. Don't move."

That musical tone he'd heard before. *Whoosh-crack.*

A section of woods below them blew up. Trees cracked and fell.

Phil started, but did not make a sound or get panicky. He had already seen the power of the weapon. As terrifying as it was, at least he did not have to contend with the greater fright of experiencing it for the first time.

Twice more: *Whoosh-crack Whoosh-crack.*

Right where they would have been had they continued straight toward the valley.

Two more explosions. Off to the right, deeper into the woods—in case he and Phil had veered off. It was the only other way they would have gone. To the left of the woods was the open slope and the mine's secondary exit. He hoped Declan realized that this exit lay too far from the woods for Hutch to have made a break for it. It would have been stupid to be in the open that long, not knowing when their absence would be noticed.

Several more explosions erupted farther down the hill.

Declan said, "Go check it out."

"What?"

"You and Bad, go check it out. See if you can find them."

"Who's this friend guy?"

"Just somebody Uncle Andrew brought. Doesn't matter. Two guys got away. Either get two guys or find their bodies."

"Send Pru. My leg—"

"Forget your leg. Go." Somebody hit the slope hard, running. No, Hutch realized—tumbling. Declan must have shoved Bad over. Somebody else—Kyrill, most likely—started down at a more controlled pace. Whoever was tumbling stopped and began swearing and yelling.

371

The outburst devolved into incoherent mumbling as Bad slowly continued down.

Declan yelled, "Fire in the hole!"

Bad and Kyrill simultaneously said, "What? Where?"

Whoosh-crack.

An explosion—way to the left, in the open part of the slope.

The two in the woods were not happy: "Don't do that!" "I about peed myself!"

Hutch closed his eyes, suspecting the strike hit the very thing he had hoped Declan would overlook: the mine's secondary exit.

Please let Dillon have obeyed my instructions to go back into the tunnels, away from the escape shaft.

He imagined Dillon at the bottom of the shaft, peering up at the square of sky, at the sunlight not penetrating even half of the shaft. After Hutch had climbed up, he would have heard Bad's machine gun, the ricochets of the bullets on the concrete floor near him. He would have understood that their enemies had taken Hutch captive. He may have expected the bad guys to come down and look for more people or scope out where Hutch had been. After a while, would he have circled back, not knowing what else to do, hoping for Hutch's return? Would he have sat there on the floor below the shaft, waiting? Hutch prayed he did not.

He tried not to think of Dillon down there, crushed by that poking finger or the rubble it would have rained into the tunnels. He tried not to think about the (somehow worse) perspective of Dillon down there—injured, bleeding to death, and scared; Hutch unable to go to him. Death by satellite laser cannon had to be relatively painless, too quick and too definitive to leave a victim in wet, frantic agony. Unless the injuries came from fallout: shrapnel, collapsing structures, super heated air.

His heart had migrated into his throat and now drummed to get out. His stomach rolled and churned out acid. He realized, when Phil touched his head to Hutch's shoulder, that he had started hyperventilating. He stopped breathing. Slowly exhaled. Pulled in a controlled breath.

Feet crunching over twigs and ground cover below. Silence at the plateau. He supposed if Declan had heard him, he would never know. He would experience that relatively painless death. A finger jab too quick to see coming or to feel once it had arrived. He waited. Would he notice *anything*? A blinding flash? A *boom* cut short? Or blackness? Then what? Speculating on his journey to eternity was something he could not do right then. It was beyond his ability to fathom. He could better see himself suddenly becoming a superhero with laser vision, bulletproof skin, and a sword that flew out of his hand to smite his enemies and return.

Okay. Was this the last thought he would have on this earth?

He forced himself to envision the laughing faces of his children: Macie . . . Logan . . . and oddly, considering their short time together, Dillon. Stranger still, the image of his wife came to mind. It was not the harsh countenance of her leaving him, but the comforting face he had known for so many years.

"Go sit in the truck." It was Declan. Apparently concentrating on something other than targeting Hutch and Phil's hiding place.

Cortland whined, and Declan said, "Go." A few moments later Declan called, "Julie, get over here!" It took the boy a minute to obey. Finally Declan asked, "What did you do?"

"Nothing."

A hard sound, and someone scuffling or falling to the ground. Wheezing, trying to catch his breath.

Hutch realized that Declan had punched his brother in the stomach, knocking the wind out of him. It was almost enough to draw him out from under the tree, to drive him screaming to Julian's aid. He had the arrow, but without a bow it was as limited as a knife. Declan would destroy him before he could take five steps. So he seethed. Hutch wanted, more than anything at that moment, to live to see Julian in court testifying against his brother, free from Declan's control.

"If you're going to do nothing, then at least do nothing," said Declan, stern. "That man did not free himself."

Julian spoke in halting gasps. "I don't—know what—"

"Where's the arrow you've been carrying around?"

Hutch grimaced. Julian had enough trouble. As much as Hutch had needed Julian's help, it pained him to know the boy would incur Declan's wrath for giving it.

"I lost it," Julian managed. A hard *thunk*. Julian hissed and groaned slowly.

Hutch hoped Declan had only punched him. He waited anxiously for Julian to say something, to communicate his being okay and not dead or dying. He would not put it past Declan to murder his brother for no other reason than Julian's compassion and desire to do right. Declan had said that he could do anything, good or evil; Hutch believed he had meant at any time to anyone at his whim. Declan liked the idea of being unpredictable. That made him more than dangerous; it made him insane.

Finally Julian spoke up. "You killed Uncle Andrew."

It was accusatory and weepy and full of heartache. The man may not have been their true uncle, but he had obviously meant something to Julian. Hutch had a feeling Uncle Andrew had been more of a father to Julian than his biological father. Yet the man knew Declan was a killer and had left Julian with him. If he had been more caring than his real father, how terrible his real father must be.

"No witnesses," Declan stated flatly. "He said it himself."

"But, Declan, he was leaving."

"To report back to father."

"Who probably already knows. Don't you think they talk?"

Declan was silent for a while. Then he said, "Leave that to me. All you need to worry about is not ticking me off any further. I knew Uncle Andrew my whole life. I loved him. If I were you, I would think long and hard about that."

Something beeped.

"Ahhhh," Declan said, frustrated. "I'm losing the satellite, and I can't throw down any events 'cuz I can't see where Kyrill and Bad went." He yelled, "Kyrill! Bad!" No answer, so he called again.

Finally Kyrill: "What?" Way down there somewhere.

"Move!"

"What?"

"Fire in the hole!"

"What?"

Declan sighed dramatically. "Never mind!" he yelled.

In his normal speaking voice, maybe a little softer: "Come here. No really, come here. I'm trying to look out for you, you know." Pause. "You gotta be tougher than you are. And never, ever go against me. You hear me? *You hear me?*"

Julian said something too quiet for Hutch to make out.

"I love you," Declan said. "You're my brother. That's why I got you off that copter. You got another chance." Silence followed.

"I'll be in the car," Julian said.

"Tell Cort I'll be right there. Tell her to raise these guys on the walkie-talkie. Get their butts back up here."

Declan remained at the edge of the plateau until he—and Hutch—heard the crunching, complaining ascent of Kyrill and Bad. The truck

door slammed and the engine started at about the time the two pursuers were level with Hutch and Phil's hideout. Had they ascended
thirty feet deeper into the woods, they would have walked right into
Hutch. Hutch had been primarily concerned with being spotted from
the plateau. He did not believe his covering would sufficiently hide
them from someone approaching from the other side. Had Kyrill and
Bad been hunters, known the outdoors better, or simply been more
motivated, they would have indeed ascended deeper in the woods or,
at minimum, made a zigzag pattern back up.

"This is crap," Bad said.

"I know," Kyrill said, sounding like he really didn't want to hear
from Bad at all.

"I mean, really. He's got control of that weapon, and he sends *us*
to find these people. If I had control of that thing, I wouldn't need no
hired guns."

"It's still in development, Bad. Give him a break."

"Give him a break? Give me a break." After a pause: "Come here
and I'll give you a break."

"Shut up."

Hutch heard a vehicle pull close to the edge.

Declan's voice: "We're gonna go get some grub. Check on the cattle.
You guys stay here."

"And do what?" Bad whined.

"Keep looking for those guys."

"What?"

"Ten thousand dollars a head. I mean it. Pru's getting some shots
of the mine. Take him with you."

The vehicle sped away.

"Man, I don't need his money," Bad said.

"I do."

"Let's go get Pruitt. I don't want to be out here when the sun goes down."

"Are we still leaving tomorrow?"

"I think we have a few more days here, at least."

Their voices trailed away. The last thing Hutch heard was: "Dec wants to level the town, maybe get some crowd shots of an SLC strike . . ."

59

Hutch pushed off his blanket of moss, dirt, and needles. Quietly he rolled away from Phil, out from under the blowdown. He half expected to hear a shout, someone standing at the edge of the plateau, but no calls rang out. Kneeling on the slope, he leaned close to Phil.

"Hold still," he said. He brought the arrow's broadhead up to the gag and made little slices in the material. It came free. As Phil yanked it out of his mouth, Hutch noticed that the tip of the broadhead had drawn blood. Phil wiped at the cut, a minor annoyance. He stretched his mouth and before he could say anything out loud, Hutch held his finger up to his mouth.

Phil whispered, "I think I was close to a town when that helicopter swung down to pick me up. I thought it was a rescue chopper."

"Tell me later." He squinted at Phil's restraints. The handcuffs were professional, solid shackles connected by a short, thick chain. Hutch had the arrow but not his utility belt. He could think of nothing that would unlock the restraints or break their chain.

"Hutch, I didn't mean to leave you guys like that. I saw that cannon thing blast the back of that big building, and I thought—"

"Wait a minute. You never met up with Terry? I thought he was with you."

"I never saw him. I thought you guys . . . I thought that cannon got you."

"You didn't see a woman either? She was with Terry."

"A woman?"

"We got separated." Hutch looked up to the plateau, then out toward the open area. "The woman's son was with me. I left him around that hill. I've got to go get him. You stay here."

Phil swung his legs out. He tried to sit up, conked his head on the wood. "No way!" he said, too loudly. "Don't leave me here."

"This is the safest place for you. I've got to cross some open space to reach the boy. I'm pretty sure the door to where he is got hit by the laser. I might need to find another way in. You can't be traipsing around this steep slope in the open with your hands bound."

"But if you . . . What laser?"

Hutch had forgotten Phil had shown up after Declan had explained his weapon. "That's what it is. That's what got David and keeps blasting down. It's called a satellite laser cannon."

"Satellite . . . laser . . . cannon." He said it slowly, as though in doing so some secret to its existence and defeat would come to him, but then he simply nodded.

"So stay here, okay? You'll be safe."

Phil shook his head. "No way."

Hutch did not want to waste time arguing with him. He was anxious to find Dillon. And who knew when Kyrill and Bad would decide that, if not for the money then to please Declan, it was worth their efforts to find the escapees?

"All right," he said. "Just be really quiet and don't ask questions. I'm not giving you a guided tour of where I've been or where I'm going. So if you want to tag along, be quiet."

Phil nodded.

"Where are your glasses? Can you see?"

"I'm fine," he said dismissively, but his eyes were squeezed into narrow slits. "They weren't that strong."

Hutch slapped Phil on the arm. "We'll get you out of those hand-cuffs as soon as we can."

They walked parallel to the edge of the plateau and stopped where the trees ended. The open area was grassy and gravelly. It had dried quite a bit, which made the grass less slick but the gravel more eager to slip out from under their feet. Hutch was afraid one of them, espe-cially Phil, would fall and not stop until reaching the valley floor. The noise could very well draw Kyrill or Bad's attention; he could not tell for sure that they were in the car and not heading, at that moment, to the edge of the plateau.

"We'll move downslope through the trees. The ground covering here is quieter, and the trees will keep us steady."

They began descending. After a short time, a glint in the dirt caught Hutch's eye. One of his arrows. He retrieved it and found two more. He felt better. Four arrows instead of one. Never mind his bow was gone. He continued down the slope. When he believed they were even with the secondary exit, Hutch left the forest to walk across the slope, around the bend of the hill.

A smoking hole marked where the exit had been. His insides felt pulled tight, as though a net had caught them. Huge chunks of concrete lay around the gaping hole. Having come around the bend of the hill, he and Phil were no longer visible to someone at the edge of the plateau. If Kyrill, Bad, or Pruitt walked the perimeter of the crater, perhaps to reconnoiter the area from that higher advantage, or if they came down the slope to pick up their search where they had left off, they would spot the two men.

While they were far from home free—far, far from home free—the relief of not being within sight of their pursuers was like shrugging off a crushing coat of chain mail.

Hutch climbed atop a ripped chunk of concrete and peered into the hole below. It was no longer the cement shaft he had ascended, but it was still a shaft. Wider now, lined with earth, but a straight chimney all the same. The laser had not struck the shaft perfectly centered. It had left a semicircular column of concrete and roughly half of the metal ladder, sheared vertically its entire length. It looked like half a spinal column dangling down into the dark. The remaining rungs did not look strong enough to support him, since only one length of the metal side rail remained. In two spots visible to Hutch, the cement beneath the rungs had buckled and broken, causing the ladder to become unmoored. *Unsafe* was not the word. More like *suicidal*.

He did not have a rope, didn't know where to find one, and did not have the time to weave one out of branches. Still, even without the partial rungs, he would have found a way to climb down into the mining tunnels.

He set the arrows down and stepped down onto a shelf in the cement to maneuver his way toward the rungs. He was vaguely aware that his body ached in a dozen places—head, arms, legs, ribs, guts. His desire to get to Dillon pushed the pain away, back into a foggy place where its shadows stirred, but the full extent of its horror was masked and muted.

"Hutch," Phil whispered. "You can't get down there."

Hutch tapped his lip with his finger, reminding Phil of their bargain. He whispered, "I'll be back as soon as I find Dillon. You don't have any matches, do you?"

Phil shook his head.

"I had some . . . not anymore. I know where I can find a few, but I may be able to do without. Find some branches with dead needles and toss them down to me in five minutes. Don't worry about where I am. Don't call down. Just toss them in the hole."

Phil nodded.

Hutch made his way to what was left of the ladder. He tried his weight on one of the rungs. It creaked and bent down. He moved his foot closer to the metal brace to which the rung was welded. He lowered his weight onto it. The rung bent slightly, but held.

The ladder disappeared into the dark below. He lowered himself one rung at a time. His mind kept urging his body to rush. He pushed aside the image of Dillon and focused on reaching the bottom of the shaft alive. At the first bulge in the concrete and ladder, he leaned out over the shaft and tried to stretch his foot back in below the hump. The shift in weight distribution caused an anchor bolt to pop loose. The ladder came away from the wall several inches, jarring Hutch sharply. That movement, in turn, caused the next bolt up to snap out of the concrete. The metal ladder jerked out further from the wall. The next bolt popped out.

"Hutch!" Phil called, as quietly as his concern allowed him.

Hutch swung over the empty space below him. With each lost bolt, he had levered farther and farther from the wall. A fourth bolt snapped out of the concrete. Hutch released his left hand from a rung, grabbed the one below it, did the same with his right hand. Using only his arm muscles, he shimmied hand over hand past the bulge. When the ladder was straight again, he stood on a rung, breathing hard. He rested like that for twenty seconds, then continued on.

At the next bulge, he immediately stepped off the ladder and lowered himself by hand. No bolts gave way. As the dark shadows of the shaft swallowed him, a thought formed in his brain: *I'm descending through the throat and into the stomach of a great beast.*

The fragrance of rich soil and ozone hung heavily in the air. Something like the smell of faulty brake pads also tinged his senses; he thought it was probably burnt concrete. God help him, he sniffed for that pungent, charbroiled-meat odor he remembered from when David had died. When he did not detect it, a surge of hope hit his heart like adrenaline.

After the circle of light above had become a distant disc, the ladder became whole again. He moved down more quickly. He stopped once to gauge his progress and thought he was near the bottom.

"Hello?" he called.

An echo. No answer. A sound—like pant legs rubbing together.

"Dil—"

A tree branch struck his head. It continued on, its needles brushing against the wall of the shaft. He looked up to see another branch sailing down. He ducked out of its way. The branches landed just under him.

He found the end of the ladder and hopped down. A large boulder immediately met his feet, he slipped on it, fell. His head struck more debris from the widened shaft. He felt around and realized most of the concrete that had come out of the shaft had pulverized into powder. The larger blocks evidently broke off after the laser strike; they had not been directly in its path. He found what he was expecting to—a length of metal rebar and, after some searching, a particularly stony fist-sized wedge of concrete. With these items and the branches, Hutch moved deeper into the tunnel.

"Dillon," he called. And again. "It's me, Hutch!"

He laid the branches in the center of the tunnel, speared the rebar through the bundle of needles, and started striking it with the concrete. After a few strikes he found the sweet spot, and sparks flew. The needles did not ignite, and after twenty strikes he worried that the rain had drenched them too thoroughly.

He kept striking and striking. With each blow he called into the tunnel: "Dillon! . . . Dillon! . . . Dillon! . . . Dillon!"

His voice grew hoarse. He stared into the darkness, which seemed to shift, black on black. Every time it did, he expected to see the boy. A flicker caught his attention. He looked down to see flames. They were indistinct and blurry. He realized his eyes had teared up.

Teared up? He had wept in frustration and worry.

None of that now, he thought, wiping his eyes with the back of his hand. That was no good. Useless. Pointless. Weird.

He tossed the rebar and the cement chunk aside and blew gently at the flames. The fire grew larger. He had made a torch. Smoke curled from the dry needles, stinging his eyes, making him cough. He picked up the branches, holding them together. He went back to the open shaft, slowly arcing the torch across the area. There were large chunks of fallen concrete, a lot of powder, but no Dillon. He felt relief wash over him. Now it was a matter of finding the boy, not burying him. He noticed something in the dust and bent to retrieve it. It was his bowstring, the one he had used to tether himself to Dillon. He would need it. He looped it into a tight coil and slipped it into his coat pocket.

He considered briefly which way to head. He had told Dillon to go back into the tunnels. He believed the boy would head back to the beds they had made and wait for Hutch there. With the fire flickering, spreading yellow light five or ten feet into the tunnel ahead of him, and smoke pooling like gravity-deprived liquid on the roof of the tunnel, he headed toward the mine's main entrance, calling Dillon's name.

Laura clung to Terry, trusting his navigation. The smoke, rising from where the green light had flashed down, had become almost invisible against the white-blue sky. The ferocity of that green light, coupled with its thundering peal, had made her think that the smoke would go on forever, but it hadn't. By the time they realized they could not use it as a marker, they were already near enough that they didn't need it.

Twice more she thought she heard the same crack of thunder that was not thunder. Each time Terry had stopped and killed the engine. They'd listened, heard nothing, and started up again.

Terry had tried to keep their route as straight to the smoke as possible. He was now traversing a swath of woods, slaloming around trees, crashing through brambles and tangled clumps of dead branches.

As his confidence increased, so did his speed. Laura gritted her teeth and held on tightly. She wanted to reach the spot of that strike from the sky as fast as she could, but it would be nice to arrive alive. Several times Terry had zoomed so close to a tree that Laura felt her knee and thigh scrape it. She was happy to recognize the end of the woods not far off.

She did not know why she believed that Declan had used his sky cannon to shoot at Dillon and Hutch. She just could not imagine that other people were out here, or that he would be doing anything but pursuing her son and his protector. Terry came out of the trees and slid to a stop. A shallow hill sloped down to a long wide valley and up again, becoming woods and more hills upon which the smoke emanated. Now she saw a second column of smoke, darker than the first. Coming from some place lower than the first, it dissipated and vanished lower in the sky.

Almost directly in front of them, heading for town, was a green Cherokee. It was coming from the direction of the smoke.

"Maybe they haven't seen us," Terry said.

"I don't care if they do," she said, not really meaning it. "Just get to those hills, okay?"

He nodded.

Then the truck turned directly toward them.

People were always amazing Declan. He needed to work that fact into his video games. Most often, programmers were immersed in a corporate environment, despite believing themselves to be independent and artistic souls. Their monsters were deadlines, bosses, and the never-ending competition for employee of the month. The games they created often involved characters battling invading armies or creatures from hell or from another planet, or a biological experiment gone haywire. Always, they were pitted against things that wanted to tear them apart, to destroy them; the stakes were as high as they could possibly be. The Harley-riding, tattooed MIT graduates who fancied themselves both tough enough and smart enough to design video games always created characters who earned stamina and strength by surviving increasingly difficult challenges. To programmers it was a logical progression: lift a hundred pounds today, a hundred and ten tomorrow; kick little Tommy's butt today, his big brother's tomorrow.

Made sense to Declan as well—until this trip. What he'd witnessed up here was not so much a progression of strength and skill. After all, in a condensed timeline, people grew tired, tempering their physical and mental abilities. No, what he learned was that people developed stamina and ingenuity in proportion to their level of attachment to whatever it was they stood to lose—a loved one, their life—or the anger of having been attacked. Call it the adrenaline factor. *That's* what he wanted to work into future games.

And it would look like this: The woman he'd kept in the storage room—Laura—whose husband he had killed, whose son he had cut. Finding a weapon in a room full of paper. Knocking out her captor. Escaping. Joining forces with—

Declan squinted through the windshield.

"Is that the guy who shot at us? The hunter?"

Cort leaned forward in the passenger seat. "I think maybe . . ."

Okay. Joining forces with another rogue element of the adventure. Great stuff. *The adrenaline factor.* He liked that.

If Laura had been a character in a video game, by this time she would be either dead or holed up somewhere, waiting for rescue. Or, on the other end of the spectrum, she'd have acquisitioned a bulletproof flying suit, acquired martial arts skills, and found a gun to rival Declan's to vanquish her enemies. The vanquishing part Laura seemed to have got. That she would attempt it without a special suit, skills, or weapon was something nobody in the world Declan came from would understand.

Chaos theory. The unpredictability of life. Programmers talked about these things, but they didn't get it. Not really. The hunter who had taken shots at them; the man with the bow; jacking their Hummer; Laura and her kid escaping from the community center. The archer had said Dillon was dead. Declan had suspected otherwise. The blast to the mine's emergency hatch had been meant to kill anyone hiding in the shaft, or at least turn the tunnels into an inescapable tomb. But now, here was the kid's mom, looking to wreak some serious havoc. Declan was learning what chaos theory meant in the real world. This knowledge was so invaluable he would not have believed it without experiencing it. Excellent.

"Get your gun, Cort."

"I don't have one, remember?"

"Julie, give her your gun."

Without a word, he did.

Cortland held the pistol in both hands. She bounced up on the seat, tucking her legs under her. "What are we gonna do?"

"We're gonna go get 'em." Declan's answer made the question sound stupid.

He accelerated toward the motorcycle. Instead of peeling away in another direction, to his astonishment it came straight for them. No, *not* to his astonishment. Not anymore: Chaos. Unpredictability. Adrenaline.

The Jeep bounded through the open field. In the rearview mirror, Declan glimpsed Julian pulling the seat belt over his shoulder. He laughed.

"Shoot them," he instructed.

"Now?" Cortland asked. The motorcycle was still at least a hundred yards distant.

"Plug away, baby."

She rose onto her knees. "Like Bonnie and Clyde," she said, a big grin splitting her face.

"I was thinking more *True Grit.*"

She skewed her face: *Whatever.* Then she popped her head and shoulders out the window.

The speedometer edged up to fifty. The ruts and rocks of the field shook them like dice in a backgammon cup. The motorcycle—sixty yards away, closing fast.

Cort's body was shaking wildly, responding to the Jeep's dance over the terrain. Her head smacked the window frame hard enough for Declan to hear it. She might not be able to hit a hill under these conditions, but . . . who knew? That would be something they'd talk about for years, her blasting someone off a motorcycle. Forget *Bonnie and Clyde* and *True Grit.* They were in *Easy Rider* territory. Very cool.

When no shots rang out, Declan's smile faltered. "Shoot 'em, baby. Shoot 'em!"

Cort returned her upper half to the cab. She was holding the top of her head with both hands. A pained grimace contorted her features.

"Where's the gun?" Declan asked.

"I banged my head, hard. I think I'm bleeding." But when she looked at her hands, no blood.

"What are you saying? You've got to be kidding."

"I hit my head, Dec! I mean really hard."

"You lost *another* gun? Another gun?"

They were right on top of the motorcycle. Declan cranked the wheel to collide with it.

Laura leaned around Terry to watch the Jeep as the dirt bike tore for the smoking hills. She strained to see Dillon in the vehicle. If she did not see him, their best hope was to get to the location of Declan's last attack. As they drew closer she recognized Declan. He was driving. How badly she wanted to rip those tight, smug lips off his face. She considered drawing one of the two pistols they had put in Terry's pack to keep them safe from all the rattling and shaking on the bike. She calculated that the two vehicles would pass before she could retrieve a gun, and she knew without question that the effort would result in wasted ammo.

Apparently someone thought differently. The girl, Cortland, rose up from the passenger window. Something was in her hand, and you didn't have to be Einstein to know what it was. Her head bounced up and down, seeming to make several jarring points of contact with the doorframe. Then the something in her hand flew away. Holding her head, the girl slid back into the vehicle.

They were almost on top of it, ready to pass it. She heard Terry let up on the accelerator a second before he swerved sharply left. As he did, the Jeep's right front corner lunged at them like an attacking dog. It missed Laura's leg and the rear wheel by inches. Had Terry not anticipated Declan's move, they would be performing bone-shattering cartwheels through the field right now.

Terry corrected their direction and continued heading toward the hills marked by columns of fading smoke. Laura craned her head around to see the Jeep making a tight circle, turning around.

"They're coming back," she informed Terry.

"We can outpace them . . . on the bike," Terry called back to her between jostles up and down. "But we're still not gonna have . . . much time . . . to find out what . . . he was shooting at!"

"I have to *know*," she said. The shoulder of a hill encroached onto the valley floor. It created a steep slope that Laura assumed was matched on the other side.

Instead of going around it, Terry hit it head-on. They rose up and up, both Terry and Laura leaning forward to prevent the bike from tumbling backward. It was the sort of hill off-roaders loved to tackle, though they were not always victorious.

Declan might attempt to follow them; he had the personality required to attempt it, but considering his desire to get them, he might not risk it. At the top, the shoulder crested in a jumplike ridge; the bike sailed over it. Terry and Laura stood on the pegs to better position the bike when it came down and to use their legs as shock absorbers. When they landed, their rear wheel wanted to slide out from under them. Terry expertly steered into the slide and kept the bike up. The long wide valley continued for another half mile before becoming the hills of their destination.

Laura looked back. The Jeep had not yet appeared at the crest of the shoulder, and she believed now that Declan would go around. The maneuver bought them probably an extra three or four minutes. At the pace they were going, there was a good chance they'd have seven or eight minutes on Declan by the time they reached the source of the smoke. The valley slowly arced up toward the hills. She could now see an old road cutting across the hill at a shallow incline and then turning to the opposite direction to complete its climb to the top. The right half of the hill appeared to have been shaved off to form a plateau lower than the left half. The road came from around a bend, but Terry had the bike pointed directly at the hill. They would meet the road halfway up.

She turned in the seat to see the Jeep coming around the shoulder, bouncing and leaping over the rough terrain.

They passed another vehicle she had not noticed before. It was a different model Jeep. It sat unmoving in the meadow. She looked back. The windshield was spiderwebbed from a hole in front of the steering wheel. She did not see anyone inside.

Something *popped!* In a split second, a catalog of possibilities unfolded in her mind: The bike had backfired from low gas or no gas. A piston or lifter had snapped—but they were not decelerating, as they would in that case. A tire had blown—but wouldn't they be eating dirt about now? They had been shot at—but the Jeep seemed too far away.

More pops, louder—

Pop-pop-pop-pop-pop.

Terry swerved away from the hill, angling right this time. She saw that two men . . . now three . . . stood at the top of the hill on the plateau. From one of them came flashing starbursts of light.

Pop-pop-pop-pop-pop.

"No go on your plan!" Terry yelled.

"We'll figure something else out! Just go!" She slapped him on the shoulder blade.

She saw now this was a place of carnage: A body lay sprawled on the hill. The second column of smoke rose from a downed helicopter.

Pop-pop-pop-pop-pop.

Puffs of dust kicked up in a line twenty feet to their left. At the two o'clock position, the Jeep grew as it closed the distance. Evidently Declan realized that Terry and Laura were trying to slip out between the two factions of his gang like a fly avoiding the clap of two hands. He angled right so he was heading not directly at them, but at a point ahead of them where he believed they would intersect. Now that they were moving with the valley's length instead of against it, the jostling mellowed and Terry was able to give the bike more gas.

The Jeep picked up speed as well, but Laura thought the bike could escape its intended collision.

It was more than a thought. It was a prayer.

61

Dillon was not in the mine tunnels.

Couldn't be.

While Hutch knew he had not covered every tunnel, every room, where he had not been physically his voice had certainly reached. The possibility of the boy having been seriously injured in Declan's strike on the secondary exit had not escaped him. In fact it haunted him. As he pushed the burning branches ahead of him, squinting to see farther than the light would allow, he studied the floor closely. He told himself that he was watching for Dillon's tracks in the dust, but he equally expected a trail of blood.

How could it be that Dillon was alive and well and not calling out to him? Did Dillon believe that their pursuers would hear him?

Wouldn't he follow Hutch's lead and return his yells? Since he and Dillon had been locked in the rec center with Declan's gang, Hutch was convinced that only the six people he knew about were participating in Declan's weapon-testing/video-producing scheme. Hutch had seen all six of them on the plateau, so he did not believe Dillon had run into any others; no one was holding the boy captive, in the tunnels or elsewhere.

When Hutch reached the place where he and Dillon had taken a short nap, everything seemed the way they had left it. Hutch tore the blankets into strips. He tied the first strip to the branches while the bunches of needles still burned. The additional strips would allow him to look for Dillon longer than he otherwise could. He went into the room where they had found the blankets to collect a few more supplies, including a half-used book of matches. He had missed them before, in the excitement of finding the lantern.

He went as close to the front entrance as the collapsed mine allowed. Where the tunnel ceiling had collapsed, the sky showed through. Deep ravines had been blasted into the hill above this section. Hutch found other tunnels that had become impassible as a result of what seemed like random strikes from Declan's laser weapon. Had Hutch not paid such careful attention to the strikes Declan had meted out during the satellite's last window of functionality—when Declan had killed his uncle and when Hutch and Phil had escaped—he would be frantically searching for Dillon under the rubble. There had been, however, only one strike on the mine during that last volley.

Hutch now returned to that damaged part of the tunnel. Realizing he had ignored the section of tunnel that led in the other direction from the ladder, Hutch's stomach clutched as tightly as a fist. It was the only area he had not searched where Dillon might have fled if he had been injured.

Hutch did not think he would find Dillon here. He *knew* he would

He stepped around the blocks of broken concrete, past the damaged ladder. And stopped.

On the strip of concrete remaining in the shaft just below the bottom of the ladder were two capital letters: *CA*. If there were ever more letters—and Hutch knew there had been—the laser cannon had obliterated them with the rest of the shaft. He hadn't seen the letters earlier because he had descended the ladder in darkness. Had he possessed a flashlight or lighted the torch topside, he would have immediately seen Dillon's message. It had been scrawled using the pasty chocolate energy bar he had left with the boy. He imagined Dillon making the substance gooier with his mouth, wanting to be sure it left a discernable image. Dillon would not have been certain it did. The light from above penetrated only partially down the shaft.

Writing blind, he had done well. The *C* was big and bold. The *A* too close to it, the first slanting arm running into the bottom arc of the *C*. A hint of the next letter was visible, too high on the wall.

Had Dillon's smiling face appeared at the top of the shaft and given him a perky *Hiya, Hutch!* he would not have felt more relief than he did at that moment. Well . . . that wasn't true. He would rather have the boy in his sights than merely know where to find him.

Not willing to wait to reach the surface, Hutch wedged his torch into the metal workings of the ladder. By its flickering light, Hutch removed the vinyl topo map from the inside pocket of his jacket. He unfolded it and found the location of the abandoned mine, though the map omitted it. He ran his finger southeast to a small square he had placed there with his black grease pencil: the cabin.

He and Dillon had talked about it at length. They had invested a solid ten or fifteen minutes transferring its location from Dillon's memory to the map. It was where his mother had told him to meet her, and where he and Hutch had been heading when the storm had driven them into the mine. He had told Dillon to wait for him in the mine in case something happened and they became separated. He understood, however, the anxiety and impatience that would have impelled Dillon up the ladder and to the cabin.

His great relief would not let him ponder the what-if scenarios of Dillon being at the bottom of the shaft or climbing the ladder or exiting the door above at the time of Declan's strike. He believed, with all his heart, that Dillon had already been making his way to the cabin. Never mind that two minutes earlier Hutch had been equally certain that he would find Dillon's body in the tunnel on the other side of the shaft.

He assessed the map one last time and judged the cabin to be roughly two hours away by foot. Even as an adult and with his experience in the outdoors, Hutch had no real advantage over Dillon in reaching the cabin faster. Dillon was an outdoorsy kid, and the shortfall of his weaker muscles and smaller lungs was still better than Hutch's bruised and battered body.

He replaced the map, removed the torch from the ladder, and dropped it to the floor.

He hoisted himself up and climbed. The ladder was shakier than before, but relief for Dillon made it easier to climb up than it had been to climb down. He thought he would be able to climb the buckled areas hand over hand without the use of his legs, but he found that his bruised arms and shoulders did not support his weight as they would have uninjured. Several bolts popped out of the concrete, making the ladder shake and cant over the shaft, but he did not stop to consider more careful movements. Twenty feet from the surface he heard Phil's hushed voice.

"Hutch? That you, Hutch?"

"Almost there."

"Did you hear the gunfire?"

That made Hutch stop. "What do you mean?"

"Gunfire. Machine-gun fire. Lots of it."

"When? Where?" He prayed it had not emanated from the hills or valleys to the southeast, but there was no guarantee that the shots had not been directed at Dillon, regardless of the direction from which they came.

"Fifteen, twenty minutes ago. I can't believe you didn't hear it. Up on the plateau. I thought they were shooting at me. I almost had a coronary. Then I thought they were shooting at you, but I couldn't figure out how you would've got up there. Or why you would want to."

Hutch continued to climb.

"I think they were shooting at a motorcycle," Phil said.

"Motorcycle?"

"Yeah, I heard a motorcycle engine. High-pitched, unmuffled, like those dirt bikes we tried a couple years ago."

Hutch reached the top and swung himself out. Phil was crouched between a boulder and a man-sized chunk of concrete. Patches of red had surfaced on his cheeks and forehead, accompanied by beads of perspiration.

"Still cuffed?" Hutch asked.

Phil lifted his arms. His wrists were raw, bleeding, and bruised. "I tried to squeeze out." He made an exasperated sound. "Then I tried to pry them apart. I heard it was possible."

"If you're Arnold Schwarzenegger. People have pulled out their biceps doing that."

"I didn't go that far."

"Give me a chance to catch my breath. I'll see what I can do."

Hutch pushed away from the edge and fell back into the dirt. His heart was pounding, pounding. The breaths he pulled in felt like cold water on a parched tongue. He suspected his discomfort wasn't entirely from the climb or even from the beating he'd taken; anxiety had amplified the effects of his physical exertion the way sea salt brings out the flavor of meat.

He said, "Tell me again what you heard."

Phil considered for a moment. "First, there was this buzzing. Coulda been an engine, but it was like an echo in the hills, you know? Then it got louder, and I thought maybe a dirt bike. A few seconds later, ten or fifteen, the shooting started. Seemed to go on for about a minute."

"You said up on the plateau?"

"The shooting. Not the motorcycle. I couldn't tell where the motorcycle was."

"Are our friends still up there, or did they chase after whatever they were shooting at?"

"I don't know." Something dawned on Phil. He rose and leaned toward the hole. "Where's the kid?"

Hutch took in the sky. You'd never know that just a few hours before, a swirling cauldron of iron clouds had filled it from horizon to horizon. The air was chilly on his skin, but nothing like the open-freezer draft that had accompanied the downpour. He closed his eyes and felt his pulse and respiration slow. He said, "He went on ahead of me. He'll meet us at the cabin."

"What cabin?"

"It's where we were heading before we stopped here."

"Why were you going there?"

Hutch thought about it. "Good question. It seems so long ago. I guess it was only this morning, before dawn. We wouldn't have made it to the next town, and Dillon thought the cabin would be a safe place to wait all this out. It's where his mother said she'd meet him."

"Dillon's the kid?"

"Yeah."

"You're going there because the kid wanted to go there?"

Hutch sat up. He looked over the concrete block at Phil. "You did better? Where were you?"

"I told you. Halfway to the next town, I think, when Uncle Creepo showed up in that helicopter."

Hutch moved around the block and knelt in front of Phil. He pulled the jaw harp from his breast pocket. "Well, Creepo's dead, and you're not," he said. "Now let me see those cuffs."

"Must be doing something right, huh?" He held his hands in front of Hutch, as though in prayer.

Hutch examined the keyhole and said, "To jimmy or jar your way out of handcuffs means releasing yourself without fiddling with the keyhole. Sometimes you can slip a piece of hard wire in and disengage the pawl from the ratchet, but that's actually more difficult than going into the keyhole, which is called *picking*."

"Let me guess. You interviewed a magician."

"Better than that," Hutch said, working the metal tongue of the harp into the keyhole. "I profiled a shoplifter who kept escaping from the security offices and twice from the cops after they picked him up."

"How did he represent the 'spirit of Colorado'?"

"He had a great story. Teacher. Lost his job. Down on his luck. Family to feed. Don't you read my columns?"

"Sometimes."

"Well, having all this time on his hands, and being sort of a research nerd, he planned exactly what he was going to steal. You know, what things would be easy to pocket and pawn and yield the highest risk-to-reward ratio."

"*Man.*"

"He also researched how not to get caught—what kind of stores had the best security, stuff like that. As part of all that—"

The steel cuff on Phil's right wrist opened and fell off.

"Hey!" Phil said.

Hutch smiled coyly. "As part of that, he learned how to pick hand-cuffs." He set to work on the left cuff.

"And he showed you?"

"I always try to learn at least one thing from my subjects, and I didn't have any interest in shoplifting."

"But getting out of handcuffs . . ."

"I figured it'd be a cool thing to dazzle the kids. I never got around to buying a set of cuffs, though."

The second cuff opened. The set dropped into Phil's lap.

Hutch stood.

"So what now?"

"Go to the cabin."

Phil looked around, sighed. "How far is that?"

"Couple hours, maybe, but I gotta do something first."

Hutch rose. His legs felt unstable, and he took a step back. The grassy slope almost sent him tumbling. He gripped the concrete to steady himself. He surveyed the area, turning a complete circle, and pointed northeast to where the woods picked up again. It was in the opposite direction of the cabin. However, it was only a couple hundred yards out of the way and would allow him to reach the valley below without staying in the open. Besides the cover the woods provided, it would also supply his greatest need.

"Got those arrows?" he asked Phil.

"Right here." Phil stood, groaning at the effort. He handed Hutch four arrows, the one Julian had returned and three he had found in the dirt.

Hutch started for the woods, cutting diagonally down and across the slope.

Twenty minutes later Hutch had found what he wanted: a seven-foot-tall birch sapling, roughly three inches wide at its base. He bent it, then stomped down on it until it snapped. He used a broadhead to sever the remaining strands. The wood was soft. Perfect.

"That for your knee and your ankle?" Phil asked. "To take the pressure off?"

"Not off of my leg."

"Then what?"

Hutch knelt on the cushy loam of the woods floor. He laid down his arrows and sapling and withdrew the map. Staying in the woods meant continuing northeast for over a mile before arcing back toward the cabin. He looked at his watch. He believed they had twenty minutes before Declan's satellite would once again become available to him. If they hurried, that was enough time to cross the open valley floor to the forest beyond, saving them probably forty-five minutes. In their situation those extra minutes could mean the difference between living and dying, and right now he was thinking about Dillon's safety. He wanted to get to the boy as quickly as he could. The cabin was merely a destination, not necessarily the safe haven Dillon or Laura presumed it was. With Declan roaming the area—with eyes in the sky to boot—no place was safe.

He held up three arrows to Phil. "Carry these for me?"

Phil accepted them, pointed at one more still on the ground. "That one?"

Hutch stashed the map and stood, branch in one hand, arrow in the other. "This one I need," he said. "I'll work on the way."

"Work on what?"

"You'll see. Let's go."

They headed for the open valley floor. Despite his injuries, Hutch began to jog. "Hurry. We have to be back under the trees before Declan's satellite sees us."

62

eclan had lost the motorbike.

The old Jeep just could not keep up on such heavy terrain. The summer maybe, but no sense whining about that now. The bike had stayed in the valley, heading toward the Fond du Lac River, miles to the south. He had expected them to turn into the woods, along which they had traveled a long way; but they had not. Their decision had worked for them, since it had allowed them to travel faster than Declan dared push the Jeep.

He slowed the vehicle and stopped. They were facing south. Before them, the land sloped for miles to the river. On the other side of the water it began to rise again in a series of rolling, ever-rising hills.

"They got away," Cortland said stupidly. "What are we gonna do?"

"We'll find 'em." He looked at his watch. "In fact, any minute now we'll know exactly where they are. Whether we can get close enough to stop them in their tracks is another matter."

From the backseat Julian said, "I'm hungry, Dec. I thought we were going into town to get some food."

Declan turned in his seat to look back at his brother. "You think too much about your stomach . . . and not enough about what we talked about." He raised his eyebrows.

Julian looked away, out the window and into the woods.

The Slacker's notification of the satellite's availability chimed: the first three bars of Beethoven's Fifth Symphony.

"There we go," Declan said. He leaned over to retrieve the satellite control from the glove compartment. He fiddled with it, watching the screen intently. He spun a control wheel, and the satellite's cameras pulled back to reveal square miles of territory instead of square yards. He said, "Oh yeah. They think they're pretty smart."

"Where are they? What'd they do?" Cortland rose on her knees and leaned toward him, trying to catch a glimpse of the monitor.

"They circled back around. About a mile, mile and a half up another valley meets this one on the left, angling northeast. This forest we're next to is a big pie shape. They're on the other side, not quite equal to us." He pointed into the woods as though they were right there within reach.

"All right." He started to set the Slacker device in his lap and stopped. "What's this?"

"What? What?"

He squinted at the screen. "Those two guys. Those two hunters who got away when Uncle Andrew checked out. They're right there. Heading into the woods." He smiled at Cortland. "Can you believe this thing? Two guys get away an hour ago and I find 'em." He snapped his fingers. "Two more get away fifteen minutes ago, and I find 'em

He snapped his fingers again. "If those idiots hadn't activated the proximity targeting limiter, I'd have them now. Can you imagine this thing fully functioning?"

He watched the screen. "And you know something . . ." His thumbs moved over the controls. "Those two and these two are heading in the same direction. Follow one and then the other." His thumbs moved. "And you find . . . a cabin." He smiled at Cort again and turned in his seat to show Julian his pleasure.

He produced a walkie-talkie. Keyed it. "Bad? Bad, pick up."

"He's taking a leak, Dec. What's up?" It was Kyrill.

"Okay, listen. Those two guys? The ones you were looking for?"

"Yeah? The hunters."

"They're heading for a cabin due east by southeast." Declan looked at Cort. "That's how you say it, isn't it?"

She shrugged. Of course.

Kyrill: "Okay . . . ?"

"Listen . . ." Declan panned over the area, giving Kyrill landmarks by which to navigate: a jutting ridge, a large grove of yellowing birches, the convergence of two streams. At last he said, "You got all that?"

Kyrill: "East by southeast?"

Declan rolled his eyes. "Will you just *go*?"

Kyrill: "Which way is that?"

Dec made an unsure face at Cortland. "You know where the town from where you are?"

Kyrill: "Yeah. I can almost see it."

"That's twelve o'clock. Head toward ten o'clock."

Kyrill: "Got it. How far?"

"Five miles."

Kyrill: "Gotcha."

"We'll see you soon. But, Kyrill?"

Kyrill: "Yeah."

"Don't wait for me. Get over there and take care of everybody, you understand?"

"Wipe 'em out," Kyrill said matter-of-factly.

"Declan!" Julian said from the backseat.

"Exactly," Declan said into the walkie-talkie. "Everybody you see. We can draw from the herd as we need later. These guys are more trouble than they're worth. Just take care of them."

Kyrill: "Dec? Did you get the food?"

"What's with you guys? We'll eat later." He dropped the walkie-talkie into his pocket. "*Teenagers!*"

"Hey!" Cortland protested.

He looked at the monitor, then pushed the device under his leg. He put the transmission into drive and said, "This ought to be fun." He cranked the wheel left and drove into the woods. The Jeep bounded over fallen trees and small bushes, but thanks to the cushion of the constantly falling foliage, it wasn't as bad as Declan had expected. He swerved around trees; branches squealed against the car. Before long they emerged on the other side. He snatched up the device and looked.

"They're heading right for us," he said, "but I'm about to lose the sat." He peered around, thinking. A glance back at Slacker's monitor confirmed the satellite had orbited out of range. He jammed the transmission into reverse and slowly backed into the foliage.

"What's going on?" Julian asked.

"Shhh" was all Declan offered.

Julian turned the window crank a full revolution. The glass lowered and he listened. Wind in the trees, the idling engine, nothing more. "Declan, don't do this. The satellite works, and you got plenty of footage for the game. Let's just go home. Let's—"

"They're coming," Cort whispered.

Like a bee swooping in, the dirt bike's whine reached their ears and quickly rose in volume.

With the transmission in park, Declan gunned the engine. He gripped the shifter and leaned toward the windshield.

Julian bobbed his head around, trying to see past Cort.

The motorcycle, bearing the man and woman, came over the hill. Declan waited . . . waited . . . Then he wrenched the shifter down. There was the grinding sound of a robot clearing its metal throat, and the tranny clunked into gear. The Jeep leaped forward, up and over some ground obstacle. The faces of the bike's riders turned in surprise seconds before the Jeep broadsided them. They rose and went down, tumbling—man and woman in separate directions, away from the bike, which fractured into pieces that spun off in every direction.

Declan braked hard and jumped out of the vehicle.

"Declan!" Julian screamed. He scrambled to open the door, spilled out onto the ground, rose and ran after Declan. "Stop!"

Cortland came around from the other side. The three of them stopped at once. The bodies sprawled in the meadow, bloody humps of clothing and hair.

The downed man recovered first. He pushed himself up, slowly. Hands and feet in the grass, trying to unbend at the hips, trying to stand tall. Finally he did. Blood dripped from his face. He looked dazed. He squinted at the three, reached his hand over his shoulder, fumbled at a backpack. His fingers hooked on the strap over his shoulder, and he slipped it off his arm. Same movements on the other side, and the pack was in his hand. He stumbled back a step, glared again at them. He opened his mouth to say something, but nothing came out. He looked toward the woman, concern carving deep lines into his brow, at the corners of his eyes. She rolled over in the grass, moaned. He returned his eyes to the bag . . . finding the zipper.

"I don't think so," Declan said. He raised his fist, clutching a black pistol.

Julian grabbed it. Declan maneuvered away. The pistol cracked out a sharp report.

The man went down. He dropped to his knees, then forward onto his face—the small part of his face the bullet hadn't ripped away.

A breeze caught the cloud of dust and smoke, blowing it over Declan, Cort, and Julian. Granules of sand washed over the Jeep with the sound of tiny shells in a surf. The smell of ozone and ash gave way to the tangy metallic odor of blood.

The boy wretched.

Cortland clapped her hand over her mouth. She shoved Julian. Through her fingers, she said in a muffled voice, "If you're going to puke again, go over there."

He stumbled toward the trees. He stood bent at the waist, hands on his knees, heaving air in, out, in, out.

"Terry!"

The woman was standing—sort of. She could not quite find her legs or spine. She wavered and staggered. Blood trickled from her scalp, over her forehead, into an eyebrow, and along the bridge of her nose. The effect, Declan thought, was that of a split face, symbolically separating the person she would have been, had he not entered her world from this pathetic, wretched creature before him.

She staggered toward the corpse Declan had just made of this Terry person. Squinting at it, she stopped, swaying, as if her time up here had made her part tree. She wiped at her eyes and appeared unsure of the body before her. Lifting in jittery movements, her eyes found Declan and her mouth moved, emitting noises. At first, nothing intelligible came out, just a wail, like an incantation that would lay him low. In this context, the blood on her face was war paint.

Declan got an image for an advertisement. Black-and-white. A woman screaming in rage, a smoking crater behind her, a severed hand grasping at nothing beside it. Only the blood on her face colored: bright red. *Something rendered by comic book king Frank Miller,* Declan thought. But the woman in the game ad would require more muscles; her clothes needed to be ripped in strategic places to reveal that she was as tough as any man and as sexy as any woman.

Declan made a conscious effort to commit this image to memory —both the stylized Frank Miller drawing and the real woman. Mud or blood—probably both—smeared her right temple and matted her hair on that side. Grass was stuck in it. Her left forearm sported a blue-green-yellow bruise from elbow to wrist. Oh, and a touch he may not have considered on his own: she had lost one shoe. Her foot was bare, muddy, and lacerated; it was a wonderful counterpoint to the casual leather slip-on on the other foot. Of course, in the ad, the woman would have to be less muddy: on this woman, on Laura, the mud caked much of her pants and jacket, obscuring the textures and curves that would make the illustration intriguing.

"You insane . . . madman . . ."

Declan anticipated a display of rage of epic proportions, but it lost power quickly.

Laura fell to her knees. She kept her eyes on Declan. Tears washed away the bloody-muddy stuff, and Declan thought that would never do for the advertisement. Spent, defeated, she said, "Tom . . . Tom . . ."

She waved a hand at the body. "Terry . . . *why?*" She hung her head. Hair on the unmatted side spilled down like a veil. "Why?"

"It always comes to that, doesn't it?" Declan said. "Can't things just happen? Can't we just experience life—the good, the bad—without always questioning the reason?" He shook his head. "You never heard that 'curiosity killed the cat'?"

He raised his pistol. He held his aim on Laura's sternum, then raised it to the top of her bowed head, debating placement of the shot. Too bad Pru wasn't here. He'd have enjoyed a video memento of this.

Julian stepped between him and the woman.

Declan pointed a cautionary finger at him. "Back off, Julie. I don't need this right now." He sidestepped to bring Laura back in view.

Julian moved with him. "Listen," he said, "Listen . . . you can use her. Hold her until you get the rest of them, the people out here. You can use her to . . ." He paused, then said, "Get her son, get . . . Dillon."

"No!" She yelled behind him.

"Julie, I'll shoot right through you if I have to. Get out of the way."

The boy held up both hands in a calming gesture. "Dec, listen. . . ."

"No!" Laura yelled again.

Julian looked at her. Declan could not see his face, but he thought his brother said something. She lowered her head.

Declan said, "Julie, I'll do it. You know I will."

"Dec, just think about it. Maybe the laser, the guns aren't enough, not for everyone. In a . . . um . . ." He was thinking, trying to find the word. "In a *tactical* situation, it might take more. The weapon and . . . and outthinking the enemy. *Bait!* Drawing them out with bait."

"I don't need her. Bad and Kyrill will get the other stragglers."

"We don't know that. Chasing them with the satellite hasn't worked so far. You said whatever works. Like with that . . . that sheriff."

Laura yelled some wordless raging thing.

Julian gestured at her, as though patting the head of a large invisible dog. He whispered something.

Clenching her teeth, she said, "No! You . . ."

Julian whispered something again, emphatic.

She shook her head, closed her eyes.

Declan realized it was, in fact, this woman and her son who had drawn out Sheriff Tom. That fact made the possibility of her doing it again very interesting to him. A professional lure, the mythical siren. That would be her role, her calling. From the people came their fall. Poisoned from within. The idea intrigued him. It was game-worthy. He could not recall it ever being done in quite the same way. Yes, Zelda's objective was to save the princess. But those were straight forward quests, no different from seeking a treasure. Using the woman would be more psychological, more devious. Infinitely trickier to pull off in a video game.

Declan nodded. He gestured with the gun. "Okay. Get her in the car. She's your responsibility, Julie. If this goes bad, it's on you." He glared at the boy, making sure his meaning was clear. "On you," he repeated.

Julian nodded.

Cortland jumped up to kiss Declan on the cheek. She said, "That's sweet, Dec."

Declan said, "Let's get up to that cabin and see what's what." He started to walk around his brother toward Laura.

Julian stopped him. "I got her."

"Knock her out," Declan said, frustrated at having to tell the boy everything.

"Look at her. She won't be any trouble."

Declan raised an eyebrow, cocked his head. "Better not be." He went back to the Jeep and climbed inside.

The boy leaned beside her. He put his hands on her shoulder and back. "Come on," he said gently.

She swung her hand around and under the back of his shirt. She had seen a bulge there and knew he carried a gun. Startled, he simultaneously shoved her away and leaped backward.

Her fingers had brushed the grip and a tease of cold steel. She sat back hard, then got her feet under her, ready to leap at him, to claw for the weapon.

He had the gun in his right hand, pointed away from her. He raised his left hand as if to ward her off.

"Don't do this!" he whispered harshly. He glanced at the Jeep which was angling slightly away from them. Both Declan and the girl had climbed into it. She could see them through the windshield, intent on something Declan held below the level of the dash.

"He'll kill you. He will." His voice was strained. His eyes brimmed with tears.

She noticed the hand he extended toward her was shaking. They were in a terrible situation, far beyond repair, and he knew it. Unlike Declan and the others, he knew what they had done. He was not living in a bubble. More accurately, he recognized that they were not playing a video game. They were destroying lives, whole families, an entire town. The reality of that bore deep into Julian's soul. His eyes were at once haunted and intense. He did not want to be here any more than Laura did. And like her, he did not know what to do about it.

But he had said something, and she had to know—

"You told Declan to use me to get to Dillon."

"I didn't mean it. I was trying to stop him from killing you. That's all."

"But Dillon . . . is he alive? Please."

Julian shook his head. "We haven't seen him." His lips were dehydrated, cracking. He moistened them now with his tongue. "We didn't kill him."

"We can't let him do what you said. Declan wants to get him . . ." Her thoughts tumbled like jigsaw puzzle pieces falling from the sky. She grabbed at them, not knowing how they could fit together into something that would save her and Dillon. Declan had mentioned the cabin. Somehow, he knew about the cabin. No matter what they tried to do, he seemed always to be either one step ahead or so close behind it didn't matter. Grasping, grasping, she said, "Give me your gun."

Julian considered it: she saw it on his face.

He looked at it, then at her. "I can't," he said.

"Then what is this about?" she snapped. "Your good intentions don't mean anything. Your being sorry for what your brother is doing doesn't matter. None of it matters if you don't help now."

His face pleaded with her. He was a child caught in a situation that would crush most adults. He did not know what to do, and his fear of Declan did not leave room to hear her. Anguish made him appear much older than he was. Uncertainty gave him much more youth. The result was not a compromise that approximated his actual age, but an awful coexistence of innocence and guilt. He was a man-child being torn apart.

He sighed deeply, heavily. He inclined his head. "Come on."

"Julian, please. You *know* Dillon. He's going to die if you do this. Do you want that?"

Julian shook his head. "No. Of course I don't."

"Then help me."

The Jeep's horn blared—twice, long.

Julian jumped. He stared at the Jeep in thought. Without looking at her he said, "You have to come. Maybe . . . I don't know . . ."

Quietly, she said his name.

He snapped his gaze at her. "Come on," he said more firmly. "Declan won't like us talking. We have to move. We have to go. Do you need help?"

She studied the ground, shook her head. She rose to her feet and straightened her back, feeling bruises she couldn't see. She walked stiffly to the rear passenger door. Julian fell in behind her, keeping his distance. She opened the door, sat, and slid across the bench seat to the other side. Declan was in the driver's seat in front of her. Julian got in and shut the door.

"I don't think so, honey," Declan said, gazing over his shoulder at her. "Far back for you. Go ahead, climb over the seat."

She did, feeling every bruise and cut on her body.

Declan watched her in the rearview mirror. He said, "I don't know if you can open the back hatch from the inside. Don't. If you do, I'll just turn around and run you over. Then I'll drag your body behind the car."

She glared at his reflected eyes. Her fury meant nothing to him. Her white-hot anger was a spark against an iceberg. She sat back, leaning against the hatch, then shifted so her weight was against a molded spare tire cover. She did not want to risk even accidentally opening the rear hatch.

Declan presented his open palm between the front bucket seats. "Give me the gun, Julie." The boy did, and Declan's hand disappeared with it. His eyes came back to her in the mirror. "You know, I thought for a minute Julie was gonna give you his gun. If he had . . ." He waggled a semiautomatic pistol where she could see it. She recognized it: it had been Tom's.

A chill tickled Laura's arms, lightly, like walking through fog. Her stomach tightened, but not as much as it should have realizing that it was only Julian's defiance of her request that had saved them both. She was growing numb, and that scared her. While fear could paralyze her, make her think irrationally, numbness would make her lethargic and slow to react. If an opportunity to escape presented itself, she wanted to seize it quickly and passionately.

Declan lowered the gun. He sighed, sounding bored. He plucked the walkie-talkie from his breast pocket and keyed the mike. "Kyrill? Bad?"

After a moment, a fuzzy voice came through: "It's Bad. What's up?"

"What are you doing?"

Bad: "We're looking for those guys you said."

"In the woods?"

Bad: "Following the tree line."

Declan said, "You're not going to find them that way. They'll stay out of sight. Go straight through. You can do it."

Bad: "Straight through? Straight through where?"

Declan was silent. He looked out the window and said to Cortland, "It's them I should blow off the face of the earth."

Cortland laughed.

Declan keyed the walkie-talkie: "The woods, Bad. Do you know where you're going?"

Long pause. Then Bad's voice came through: "Okay, we got it."

Declan dropped the walkie-talkie into a cup holder in the center console. He draped an arm over the back of his seat and watched Julian return his gaze. "You ever hear the joke about the farmer and his bride?"

Julian said nothing.

"This farmer was heading back home after marrying some gal in an arranged wedding. They're in this old carriage, getting pulled by a donkey. The donkey stops to eat some grass. The old farmer whips it and whips it until it starts going again. The guy says, 'Donkey, that's one.' After a while, they pass a water trough, and the donkey stops to drink. The man whips it to get it going again and says, 'Donkey, that's two.' After a while, the donkey sees something interesting and stops to check it out. The man says, 'Donkey, that's three.' He gets out of the carriage with a shotgun and shoots the donkey dead. His wife yells, 'How can you do such a thing!' And the man looks up at her and says, 'Woman, that's one.'"

Cortland giggled.

Declan could have been carved from stone.

Julian did not respond.

Declan lifted his hand so that it was positioned between the brothers' faces. He held up one finger. "Your helping that hunter escape on the plateau was one. Your trying to grab the gun from me just now and then sticking up for the woman—I'll count both of those as number two." He held the fingers in place for a long time.

Finally Julian slapped them away.

"You know I'm not joking," Declan said. He sat back in his seat and got the car moving.

Cortland glanced over the seat at Julian. Even she appeared shaken.

64

As they walked, Hutch used the broadhead as he would a knife, slicing and hacking away bits of wood from the sapling. He had asked Phil to keep watch for pursuers.

In tending to his duty, Phil turned and spun and jumped at every sound.

Finally Hutch said, "Listen for the big things, Phil. A car engine, footsteps crunching over the ground, gunfire. Things like that."

"No wind in the trees? No squirrels?"

"Only if the squirrels have machine guns."

He went back to whittling, hoping he wasn't wasting his time. Hoping more than that: if his efforts proved fruitless, it meant more than a waste of time; it meant certain death—no more running, no more chances. It would take at least a few hours to reach the cabin. He hoped that was enough time.

As Hutch's project took shape, the sun dipped closer to the horizon, the shadows grew darker, and the two of them pressed on. On occasion, Hutch stopped to check his compass and the topographical map. He would sometimes glance around, half expecting to see some sign of Dillon's passing—something unintentional, like a broken branch or a sneaker print, or a clear indicator of the boy's hope for a reunion with Hutch, like a piece of cloth tied to a tree or a smiley face written with a gooey energy bar. He realized the chances of their treading the same path were more than slim. Hutch was cutting as straight a line to the cabin as the terrain would allow. Dillon most likely would have followed landmarks he recognized to get him there.

Hutch had no idea what he would find when he reached the cabin. In his mind it had become mythically important to their survival. It was their quest, and no matter how firmly or frequently he warned himself against hoping for a sudden solution to this whole stinking mess, he did think of it that way. What other place would a mother send her child in an emergency? To what other place would a child insist on going even when it meant forgoing the next town, with people and phones and shelter? To Hutch, the cabin had become a fortress, set among towering trees that provided not only seclusion but vantage points from which to guard and protect. The cabin-cum-fortress would be impenetrable and contain not only a well-stocked kitchen but several satellite phones. And an armory.

Yeah. If this was not what Hutch expected, it was what he hoped for. Unrealistic, to be sure, but in the middle of a nightmare couldn't one dream?

At minimum it would be set among trees, as most hunting cabins were. And as he walked, he worked to turn that fact into an advantage.

Phil trudged along, now and then stopping to listen. "I think we're being followed," he said.

Hutch stopped, cocking his head. "I don't hear anything," he whispered.

Phil said, "An engine . . . sometimes. Sometimes, kind of a crunching sound, like you said. Something moving in the woods." It had not yet become twilight, but in the woods it could have been. The distant trees and shadows became indistinct, murky, the way silt could make clear water opaque.

"There's not much we can do about it now," Hutch said and continued walking. But fifteen minutes later he found a heavy bush. He and Phil crouched behind it, low. They stayed there for five minutes, listening, waiting. Hutch heard the engine Phil had mentioned. It seemed far away, but he knew not to trust his ears. The trees' foliage and hills made visual confirmation almost a necessity. The vehicle could be traveling directly outside the woods, its noises severely dampened as they traveled through the trees, or it could be miles away with the hills and open valleys magnifying its sound.

"Definitely a vehicle," he whispered. "But I can't tell if it's near or far, coming or going."

"Creepy," Phil said. "It's like a ghost messing with my mind." He punched a finger at his temple to illustrate the point.

Hutch smiled. "So now we've got ghosts too?"

Phil shrugged. "I don't believe in ghosts, but if I did, David would be watching out for us."

"I think David's the one messing with you. Getting back at you for always calling him Pretty Boy."

They waited a few more minutes. When no other sounds reached them, they continued toward the cabin. He believed they were almost there when he held up the branch. "What do you think?"

"What is it?"

"What is it? It's a bow."

"I thought bows were arced."

"It will be, when I string it." He held a flat length of wood, six feet long and two inches wide. It was thicker in the center than at the ends. He had whittled a groove into each end to hold the bowstring. His recurve had featured an arrow rest at the handle; for this one, he would rest the arrow on his hand. He said, "It's called a longbow. It gets its firing power from its length."

Phil said, "You got string?"

"Yep."

"Put it on, man."

"I have one more thing to do with it. It may not be the smartest thing to do, especially if we're being pursued, but I'm pretty sure it needs it."

"What's that?"

"It needs to be fire-hardened."

"You want to start a fire?"

"It won't take long. I'd like to do it before we reach the cabin. I want to have this thing ready in case they're already there; if they aren't, I don't want the smoke to lead them there."

"Aren't we close?"

"Close isn't there."

Hutch cleared away a patch of loam while Phil gathered twigs.

"The drier the better," Hutch reminded him.

"I know, I know."

Hutch made a fist-sized pile. He asked Phil to keep feeding the fire as necessary. He wanted the flame to be as small as possible. Using the matches he had taken from the mine when he had also retrieved the mouth harp, he lit his open kiln. Several inches at a time, he fed the bow into the fire, turning it slowly. When he thought the wood might ignite, he removed that section, feeding in another. When all the wood had been thoroughly heated, he stomped out the fire.

"We'd better get moving," he said.

They walked, and Hutch withdrew the bowstring from his pocket. He stopped. He slipped a loop into the groove on one end, flipped the bow over, and wedged the stringed end against his boot. He pulled back on the riser—the center of the bow—while pushing down on the other end. He slipped the loose end of the bowstring into the groove. He had a bow.

"Yeah," Phil said.

"We'll see."

He nocked the arrow that he had used to whittle the bow onto the string and rested the shaft on the notch at the center. He drew back, thinking of all the things that could go wrong: one of the string grooves could crack the end of the bow, a bow arm itself could snap, the draw weight could be insufficient to propel an arrow straight or to penetrate a target.

The draw weight felt heavy: sixty, seventy pounds. Keeping his left arm slightly bent, he pulled the string but stopped before its ideal position, where his thumb could fit into the notch of his jaw, below the earlobe. Intuitively, he believed pulling back further would snap the bow. The trick with recurve bows, which did not use cams to counter the draw weights as did compound bows, was to find that fine line between drawing power and bow strength. Hutch would rather fire an arrow at slightly less than maximum power than risk losing the weapon altogether.

Phil pointed at a tree some distance off. "That one right there," he said and described it.

"No . . . see that mushroom near it?"

"Mushroom?"

Hutch let the arrow fly. It struck the ground ten feet before its target and disappeared under a blanket of needles, peat, and moss.

"Not as strong as it felt," Hutch commented, walking toward the mushroom. He retrieved his arrow and returned to Phil.

"Hit a tree," Phil urged.

Nocking the arrow and drawing back on the string, Hutch said, "I don't have enough arrows. A tree might break the broadhead, or the arrow could get wedged in too deep to remove."

This time the arrow sailed inches above the mushroom. On the fourth shot Hutch bagged himself a fungus.

Phil hooted in triumph, then caught himself. "You made yourself a pretty nice bow," he said.

Hutch nodded, appraising the bow with appreciation. "I'm doing some compensating in the shooting, letting the arrow come off the bow a little bit, guessing the right draw length. Means I can't be precise . . . but close."

Phil sounded concerned. "Is close good enough?"

Hutch looked at him. "Gonna have to be." He went for the arrow.

They walked another half hour. When Hutch checked the map, he found that they were about five minutes from the cabin, give or take, considering it was based on Dillon's recollection.

He pushed the bow onto his shoulder. He hoped he wouldn't need it. But he knew he would.

65

Fifteen minutes later they stepped out of the trees into a meadow.

Hutch closed his eyes in despair.

Phil said, "You've gotta be kidding."

Three hundred yards across the grassy meadow sat a rustic log cabin, roughly the size of a single-car garage. One of the narrow sides faced them. There was a window, dead center, and above it, near the apex of the inverted-V roofline, someone had mounted a set of moose antlers. The visible long side must have been the rear wall; it bore no doors or windows. Made sense: it meant the facade faced down the valley meadow, toward Fiddler Falls, the Fond du Lac River, and a picturesque vista of rolling trees and hills.

Beyond the cabin, the land had been scorched bare by fire for as far as Hutch could see. At one time, the cabin had been positioned on the outskirts of what was probably a lush, verdant forest. The fire had burned to within fifty feet of the cabin. The line delineating undamaged soil from a sea of black ash and burned timber formed a scalloped pattern down that far side of the meadow—coming from far north, ebbing around the cabin, and continuing down the valley.

Hadn't Dillon mentioned something about the cabin surviving the fire naturally? That was one reason his family considered it special. Hutch understood the sentiment. It seemed miraculous that this one structure had survived. He wondered if the trees had been cut back around it to form a firebreak or if someone had dumped water on it from a crop duster–type plane. He did not know enough about fires up here or how attached people were to their cabins to guess how they'd behave in such circumstances.

Clearly, the area had been beautiful before the fire. Now, however, the cabin was a lonely building in the center of . . . nothing. Worse than nothing. The blackened landscape and astringent odor of smoke and charred wood made it seem like an outpost on the periphery of hell, where even the flames only passed through occasionally.

The only living trees within sight were the ones from whose shadows Hutch and Phil had just stepped—way, way beyond his effective firing distance. Maybe he could hide on one side of the pitched roof and at the proper moment spring up and fire. Two problems with that: both sides of the roof were visible from the most likely approach to the cabin; and if Declan used the optics available to him from the satellite, Hutch would be in plain view. He had hoped the cabin was set among the trees not only to shield it from Declan, but also to provide plenty of places for him to protect it from outside and out of sight.

Had the cabin been more of what he thought it would be, they would have been able to rest out of the weather and safe from Declan, at least for the night. Now he didn't know. How could they stay there, and how could they venture away? He and Phil were injured and ex-hausted. Darkness was coming on, and with it a numbing cold. Fires were out of the question. He wasn't sure *he* could handle a night in the wilderness; how could Dillon?

Dillon.

The disappointment of the cabin had distracted him from the most important part of it.

"Please, God, let him be here," he said and started for the cabin.

Phil looked overhead. "I don't like the idea of that thing being up there. I can't see it, but it can see me. When you were a kid, you ever fry ants with a magnifying glass?"

"Shhh," Hutch said. "Come on."

A railless porch, made of wooden planks and roughly five feet wide, ran the length of the facade. It creaked and cracked as Hutch stepped onto it. A locking door handle latched a hinged slab of wood to the entry threshold. Right away, he saw that the jamb at the latch had been splintered. Scuff marks—dried mud, the peanut butter color of the earth around the porch—marred the door between the handle and the bottom edge.

He pushed on it. The door moved a half inch and stopped. An unseen object on the inside held it shut. He pushed harder, and something heavy slid against the floor. The door opened two inches. He stuck his face into the opening. He could see the window that faced the meadow, and below it, a picnic table and two bench seats. Just enough litter was scattered on the table to make him think someone had eaten a single meal there.

"Dillon," he called. "It's me, Hutch."

He turned his ear to the crack. Nothing.

"Dillon?"

Hutch wondered if Declan's men could be waiting for him inside

Maybe one of them held his hand over Dillon's mouth . . . or had they done something worse to the boy? He should have looked in the window near the door. Hesitating would not change the situation awaiting him. He hit the door with his shoulder. Whatever was holding it pushed away. He stepped in.

The room was lighted by only the two murky windows. On his left was the dining setup. An old woodburning stove sat in a corner to his right. In the opposite corner, along the back wall, was a bunk bed. The mattresses were bare. Folded blankets, linens, and a pillow were stacked at the foot of each mattress. On the same wall, near the beds and closer to the door, was a floor-to-ceiling bookcase. One shelf was lined with paperback books, their broken, tattered spines evidence of long nights spent in the cabin. A deck of cards, loose poker chips, and a Sorry board game sat on another shelf. Magazines, coffee cups, a half dozen worn shoe boxes—probably the cabin's tools, first aid kit, and other necessities—occupied the remaining shelves. Two over-stuffed chairs draped with heavy woolen blankets faced each other in front of the bookcase.

Someone, probably Laura, had tried to temper the cabin's inher-ent maleness with wilderness-themed decorations: bear salt and pep-per shakers on the table, a metal moose silhouette paper towel holder, a carved wood plaque with evergreens and the words Home Sweet Cabin. On the floor between the chairs lay a round rug with the big, amiable face of a bear woven into it.

The rest of the floor—a tile puzzle of plywood sheets—was thick with dust. Most of it resembled ash. Hutch figured the charred land-scape kicked up in the wind and some of it found its way inside. Guests would be dusting the stuff for years to come; it coated every surface. As though distributed for his benefit, it was proof of Dillon's having been there: handprints on the table, rump-print on the bench seat, tiny sneaker prints all over the floor, facing every which way like a dance-step diagram.

A three-foot-square box of stove-length firewood had been positioned behind the door. He could see where it had been dragged across the floor from its normal spot near the stove.

Evidence of the boy . . . but no boy himself. It made all the signs of his presence seem intentional and cruel.

"Dillon!" Hutch said again. "If you're hiding, it's okay to come out. It's me, Hutch."

His eyes came back to the box of firewood. It had been used to hold the door closed, since the splintered jamb gave the latch nothing to cling to. The only other exits were the windows. The dust on the wood lengths that acted as sills showed only a few finger- and handprints; it did not appear that anyone had left the room through one of them. Dillon had to be inside.

Hutch scanned the room. Few hiding places. The space behind the stove and most of the area under the bed were visible. That left only a cabinet under a countertop, against the wall between the bed and the stove. Set into the right side of the countertop, nearest the stove, was a small, wet bar–style sink. He had seen fixtures like this before. The faucet handle acted as a pump, which brought water from a reservoir in the cabinet. On the left side of the countertop was a free-standing propane griddle. The space under this side of the counter would be large enough for a limber nine-year-old boy.

He knelt and opened the cupboard door. Cans of hash, dried beef, and boxes of military MREs, a staple among hunters and survivalists, were the only items inside. Hutch's heart sank. Was it possible to position the woodbox against the door and leave? He supposed a smart boy could lay a belt on the floor by the door, put the woodbox on it, slip through a partially closed door, then pull the belt under the door, sliding the woodbox against it. But why? Perhaps to trick people into believing someone was inside. He shook his head. That didn't make sense either.

Hutch closed his eyes. All of this felt like overthinking. He was growing panicky about Dillon and grasping at explanations for why he wasn't there. He shut the cabinet and again looked around the room. The ceiling followed the line of the roof. There was no attic or loft. He supposed a crawl space lay between the floor and the ground. As long as it was tall enough, it would make a fine hiding place. If Dillon got into it from inside the cabin, there must be either loose floorboards or an actual hatch in the floor. His eyes swept the floor for anything obvious. He got on all fours to look under the bed. Nothing.

"Hutch," came a whisper, soft as the wind in the trees. His heart accelerated.

"Dillon?"

"Hutch!"

The shadows in the corner under the bed unfolded to reveal a boy. The weakening daylight caught his eyes first. For just a second, Hutch feared this moving lack of light—black and gray, facelessly blinking at him—was the product of his panic. Then the eyes moved closer, and a smiling mouth appeared: it was familiar, with big front teeth. Then the whole boy. He slid out to where the light embraced him.

Hutch reached in, pulled him out by the arms, and did his own embracing.

"I knew you'd come," Dillon said. "I didn't know it was you. All I saw were boots."

"That's okay, Dillon. You did the right thing. You made it here. Have you seen . . ."

He did not finish the thought. Of course Laura had not yet arrived.

Once she found Dillon, she would never again leave him. If she set out to forage food, find help, investigate a noise or some other curiosity, she would absolutely have taken her son. Besides, hadn't Terry been with her? He would be here as well.

Hutch grasped the boy's biceps and held him at arm's length: he wanted to *see*. Dillon's hair was a mess, stringy with clumps of dirt and a powdering of dust. All but one of the butterfly bandages had come off—and this one had turned from flesh tone to black. The cut itself had developed a healthy scab. Hutch remembered thinking at the mine how the rain had made Dillon appear freshly laundered. No more. If the boy informed him that he had traveled through the forest and fields on his hands and knees, occasionally rolling for fun, Hutch would have believed him. The exposed flesh on his face, neck and hands bore new cuts and bruises, but overall he seemed healthy and uninjured.

Dillon let Hutch examine him, as certainly his parents had when he came home late from playing in the woods or generally looking as he did now, if he ever had. Hutch wished he had something to give him. Weren't the movies filled with reunions in which the parent presented a souvenir or candy or *something*? That Hutch was not Dillon's father edged into his consciousness, and he pushed the thought away. He felt parental toward this boy. If that was one of the things that kept them both going to ultimately survive this challenge, then so be it. When this was all said and done, if he could not claim Dillon as his child, he would call him his friend.

Dillon looked anxiously toward the door. "Are they . . . Do we have to go?"

Hutch thought about it. He did not think they had been followed. If Declan was still after them, if killing his uncle hadn't changed his plans, how long would it take for him to find the cabin? Where would

Hutch, Dillon, and Phil go from here? He needed to examine the topo again, to formulate a plan. At the very minimum, they needed to give Laura and Terry time to get there.

"No," he answered. "I think we have some time."

"Are you hungry?" Dillon asked. "There're some boxes of food under the cabinet." He made a face. "Really gross, but Mom and Dad said they last forever. You can eat them and not get sick."

Hutch smiled. "I'm starving. I have a friend outside. Is there enough for all of us?"

Dillon nodded enthusiastically.

Hutch considered asking why he had left the mine, but it would have been just something to say; he knew Dillon's motives. Instead he said, "How long have you been here?"

"Uh . . . a little while. An hour?"

Hutch realized that he and Phil had started out for the cabin no more than a couple hours after Dillon probably had. The total time Dillon had been out of his sight had been only four or five hours. It felt like days.

"I couldn't find the key," Dillon continued. "It's usually on a nail under the porch." He shook his head. "I kicked and kicked. Finally it opened."

"Good job." Hutch took in the cabin's interior. "So this is—"

Clattering footsteps on the front porch. Phil ducked in behind the door, crouching.

"Hutch! They're here!"

Hutch started to rise. Phil held his hand out to stop him. "Stay down. They'll see you through the window." Phil pointed at the panes set in the narrow side of the cabin. "They're coming through the woods not far from where we came out."

"On foot?"

"They got a truck or something."

Hutch nodded. That patch of woods across the meadow stretched south another couple of miles. If Declan's gang was trying to follow them or catch up to them, cutting through the woods made sense—especially if they knew the location of the cabin. They would know cutting through would get them there quicker. In addition, coming up the long open meadow would give anyone in the cabin a healthy heads-up of their approach, whereas popping out of the woods put them only a couple hundred yards away.

Phil duck-walked to the window and peered over the sill, squinting. "They're not quite through the trees," he reported. "I think they're stuck."

So maybe they had five or six minutes. Hutch pictured the surrounding terrain. No trees in three directions for miles. The fire had burned . . . what had their pilot said? Five thousand acres. It had consumed several entire areas of forest, including the one this cabin had abutted. The only trees in sight were the ones across the meadow from which their pursuers were emerging. He knew from looking for Dillon that the cabin offered no place to hide. The crawl space maybe. He thought about it: he did not know how much of a crawl space there was, nor how they would access it. Besides . . . he checked his watch. Declan's satellite would come online any minute now, if it hadn't already. He had no doubt that upon finding the cabin empty Declan would suspect a hidey-hole and blast the whole thing into splinters. If his imagination stopped short of hidey-hole possibilities he would most likely destroy the cabin anyway, just for kicks. No matter how he looked at it, they could not stay here. Yet there was no place to run. Truly, Hutch was clueless.

Dillon seemed to sense Hutch's deliberation, at least part of it. He said, "I hid under the bed. You didn't see me." He glanced at Phil then back at Hutch, his face expressing both hope and doubt. "Maybe we can all fit."

Hutch smiled at the boy's naiveté. It was sweet and . . .

And it gave Hutch an idea.

66

The satellite came online.

Speeding north as fast as the ruts and bumps and boulders would allow, Declan heard the chime and reached for the glove compartment. Without slowing, he held the remote and maneuvered the controls with the same hand. He glanced at the monitor, fiddled with the thumb control, glanced again. He held it closer to his face.

He growled, frustrated. He set the control in his lap and retrieved the walkie-talkie from the center console and keyed it. "Bad! Kyrill! Where are you? I don't see you."

Bad answered. "We're just coming through the woods into meadow. We see the cabin."

"That meadow is part of a valley that stretches almost to town. We're in it, coming up to you. About ten minutes away. Don't wait for

434

ne." He looked down at the monitor in his lap. Into the walkie-talkie
he said, "I see them. Can you hear me? I see them."

Bad: "I don't see anything. I see the cabin, but—"

"They just stepped out onto the front porch. They're keeping close
to the front of the cabin. Okay, I can see you now, your hood. They're
just out of your sight. Drive around to the front and you got 'em."

Bad: "We're almost out of the woods. Kyrill's trying to drive over
some big tree that fell. Idiot."

"Go! Go!"

He caught Laura glaring at him in the rearview.

"One by one," he said. "Just a matter of time."

He checked the monitor. The people were gone. The image
showed the cabin from directly overhead. He had seen three people
on the front porch. Now nothing. The shaking and rattling of the car
did not help. He looked up to make sure he wasn't about to drive into
ravine or over fallen timber or a boulder. He glanced down again.
Either they had gone back into the cabin, or they were standing under
the eaves.

On the left side of the screen, the Bronco broke free of the woods
and shot directly toward the cabin. It slid to a stop at the cabin's south-
ast corner, kicking up a plume of dust. Three doors opened. Kyrill
popped out of the driver's side and ran to the front bumper. Bad got
out more slowly, appearing to steady himself on the door. Pruitt exited
the rear passenger door and immediately lifted the camera into posi-
on. He stood behind the door, filming through the window.

The walkie-talkie spat out static, then Bad's voice came on. "I don't
e 'em."

"Check inside."

On the monitor, Kyrill and Bad—their weapons panning tightly
ack and forth in front of them—moved onto the porch.

Appearing more militaristic than they had in the woods, Kyrill and
Bad flattened themselves against the cabin's facade, beside its door
Bad leaned out, then back again. He turned to Kyrill, held two finger
to his own eyes, then pointed to the front window. Kyrill nodded
He stepped past the closed door. He dropped low to edge up unde
the window.

Declan's voice, tinny and overloud, said, "Right there! They wer
right there. Bad? See 'em? Bad?"

Bad started and brought his hand to a breast pocket. He fumble
with it.

"Maybe under the—" Declan's voice cut off.

Kyrill popped his head over the sill and lowered it again quickly. H
performed this move three times. Someone witnessing his behavic
under different circumstances would have assumed he was imitatin
some exotic bird. He looked at Bad, shook his head.

Bad didn't move, thinking. He held tightly in front of him the plan
of green metal that was his machine gun. He gestured toward the do
with his head.

Kyrill moved out from under the window. He stood erect, his bac
against the wood logs of the cabin's facade. He unclamped one of h
hands from the sniper's rifle to wave impatiently at Bad.

Bad shook his head and indicated his injured leg.

Kyrill nodded. He stepped in front of the door and kicked it in. F
disappeared inside. A single shot rang out. The bullet ripped throu;
the side of the cabin, splinters spraying out. Right where the cabin
was. Bad hobbled in, and the quick maraca shake sounded, echoi
in the tight space. The next sounds they made indicated a viole
search: splintered cabinet doors, broken shelving, tipped-over bu;
beds.

After twenty seconds, Bad emerged. He stayed close to the cak

vall and edged along the front porch toward the only side they had
1ot been able to see when they approached.

Kyrill appeared and moved in the other direction, toward the Jeep.
Ie reached the corner before Bad did and peered around. When Bad
eached his corner, his movements were similar to Kyrill's at the win-
low. He popped his head beyond the edge and back again, fast
nough to absorb the vision of the side of the cabin without analyzing
nything he saw. Two seconds later his brain had caught up with his
yes. He did it again. He checked on Kyrill at the far end of the porch.
`he teenager shook his head.

Bad plucked the walkie-talkie from his pocket and spoke into it.
They're not here," he said in a harsh whisper.

Declan's voice crackled through. "I've been trying to raise you for
1ree minutes. What happened?"

"Uh . . . the walkie-talkie went dead. We cleared the cabin. They're
ot in it."

Declan: "They were just there! I'm looking right at the cabin. They
ave to be there. Did you look under the porch?"

"Hold on."

The walkie-talkie disappeared back into his pocket. To Kyrill, he
1ce more pointed at his eyes, then at the porch. Kyrill stepped off.
ad did the same on his end. Both dropped to their knees and bent
w, pressing their faces into the dirt. They peered into the two- or
ree-inch-high space under the porch. Bad brushed the dirt from his
ce and returned to the porch.

Kyrill snapped his fingers once and indicated his intention to circle
e cabin.

Bad nodded. He gazed out over the meadow, down the valley
ward town, then panned his eyes over the black otherworldly terrain
the burned woods.

He brought the walkie-talkie back to his mouth. "They're not here. I'm telling you, they—"

He stopped. He was gazing out into the ashen wasteland.

Hutch watched Bad's entire body become stone, then the man slowly moved the walkie-talkie to his pocket.

Hutch flicked his eyes to the right, following Bad's gaze. He was looking directly at Dillon, who was four feet to Hutch's left, lying on the ground. Like Hutch, his entire body—clothes, head, hands, face, hair—had been smeared with black soot. He looked like nothing more than another cindered deadfall in a landscape of ash and crumpled timber. Phil, on Hutch's other side, also lay, black and covered, motionless.

Only Hutch stood, imitating one of the stubborn trunks that had lost its limbs, had blackened and died, but had refused to fall. These charred columns studded the barren landscape like memorials to faceless soldiers. Some were mere stumps, others as tall as three men.

Hutch had hoped to be just another one of these dead ghost trees. Soot blackened him completely as he stood facing the cabin, his bow and arrow held out in front of him. As Declan's satellite laser was present but unseen, so in their much more primitive way were they invisible but deadly. The satellite—and now Hutch—were hiding in plain sight. He had watched the Bronco arrive and Kyrill and Bad enter the cabin. With each second he became more convinced that their ruse would work. They would remain unseen and their enemies would simply go away.

Not anymore.

67

ad was eyeing the lump of blackened timber that was Dillon.

Hutch saw why. He had considered positioning both Dillon and Phil on their sides, facing away from the cabin. In the end, and with no time for consideration or discussion, they had lain in a posture that allowed them to watch the events unfold. Despite Hutch's warnings to keep their eyes closed, Dillon's eyes were now open. They blinked. The whites of his eyes alone may not have attracted attention. The blinking, however, would catch a sharp sentry's attention as surely as a strobe. He could not blame the boy. Hearing the movements of your would-be killer would drive open any reasonable person's eyes. He suspected that Phil, too, had peeked. He simply had not been caught.

Hutch himself had squinted the entire time, watching Kyrill and Bad through his eyelashes, blinking only when he was sure they were turned away.

As Hutch watched, Dillon dropped his lids, holding them tightly shut. Hutch realized the boy knew he had been seen.

Bad dropped the walkie-talkie into his pocket as he brought the barrel of his machine gun down. He swiveled it toward Dillon.

With the speed and fluidity he had practiced a thousand times, Hutch drew back on the bowstring and released it, all in one smooth, two-second motion. He held still for another half second to make sure the arrow cleared the bow. Then he dropped his right arm to a second arrow that rose straight up from the ground beside his leg. His bow arm never moved. His head never moved. His eyes never came off of Bad. As the arrow sliced a groove through Bad's skin at the temple, Hutch was already nocking the next arrow.

The arrow that had nicked Bad *thunked* into the cabin's facade behind him. Bad's head flew back, and the machine gun rose toward the sky and barked out three quick shots. He stumbled back, then instantly recovered. He brought his attention back to the blinking eyes, convinced it was their owner who had attacked him. The machine gun came down again.

Hutch adjusted his draw and his sight in accordance with the defective trajectory of his last shot and released the second arrow. Again he waited one-half second before dropping his hand, gripping another arrow, and bringing it up to nock it. His head, shoulders, and body never moved.

The arrow found Bad's sternum. It shattered through it and traveled another eighteen inches. When Bad plopped into a sitting position against the front of the cabin, only five inches of the arrow and all three of its orange feathers protruded from his chest. His eyes were large, his face shocked. Blood spilled over his bottom lip. The machine gun fell from his dead hand to clatter on the porch planks.

Dillon hissed.

In his peripheral vision, Hutch saw the boy move. Movement in the other direction told him Phil had stopped mimicking a log as well. Hutch said sharply, quietly, "Don't move! Don't move! Hold your positions!"

Hutch broke his own command when a clatter from the car made him shift his head to look. Pruitt had dropped the camera and was now running at full speed across the meadow toward the woods. He glanced back, his eyes pointed at Bad. Hutch wondered if the man had seen him at all, or just the demise of his friend. For someone like Pruitt, that was enough.

He put his head back into position as Kyrill ran around from the rear of the cabin.

The teen's eyes swept over the landscape, right past Dillon, Hutch, and Phil. He stopped at the front corner of the cabin. He saw Bad and, to Hutch's surprise, he did not run to him. Instead he dropped straight to the ground. This teenager would have made a great soldier. Hutch reconsidered: he'd have to grow a moral backbone first and learn to distinguish between video games and reality.

Kyrill looked in all directions. More than once he panned past Hutch without seeing any of them. He said, "Bad? Bad?"

"Hey!" Bad replied, making Hutch's blood run cold until he realized it was Declan's voice over the walkie-talkie.

"Hey! What's happening? What are you doing? Kyrill, what happened to Bad?"

Kyrill pushed himself up and crouched at the corner of the cabin. Staying low, he stepped up onto the porch. He swung his sniper's rifle in a semicircle around him. He inched toward Bad.

Declan: "Kyrill, you hear me?"

Kyrill made a hushing sound with his lips. S*hut up already,* Hutch thought for the kid. *I've got things goin' down here.*

He was three feet from Bad when he shifted his gun to his other hand and stretched to reach the walkie-talkie in Bad's breast pocket.

His eyes locked on Hutch's. He squinted.

Hutch did not move.

Kyrill did not move.

Slowly, slowly, the barrel of the big sniper's rifle turned toward Hutch.

Slowly, slowly, Hutch shook his head no.

Kyrill's eyes widened. Had he simply finished aiming the weapon and pulled the trigger, he could have blown a nasty hole through Hutch's chest. Instead he pulled the hand that had been reaching for the walkie-talkie back to steady the rifle. In those seconds, Hutch plucked the bowstring, sending the arrow through Kyrill's right shoulder.

Kyrill screamed. He fell back into the cabin's facade. His rifle clunked to the porch, all but forgotten as he gripped the shaft of the arrow.

Hutch had already nocked his last arrow. He called out. "Don' move, Kyrill."

The teen held his breath long enough to scowl in Hutch's direction. He squinted, still unable to completely make out his foe.

"I have another arrow aimed at your head. Don't make me use it."

Kyrill's face registered pain and confusion. "You shot me, man."

"And I'll do it again if you don't shut up and kick those weapon off the porch."

Kyrill looked around. He pushed his rifle toward the edge of th porch. He bent his leg and kicked it off. Bad's machine gun wa already close to the edge, so he kicked out with his other foot, sending the gun spinning into the dirt.

Hutch took a step forward.

The Jeep's engine roared behind him and to his left. It was in the meadow and had just come over the hill nearest the cabin. He froze. He knew, from the time and from Declan's communication over the walkie-talkie, the satellite was online. He did not know if Declan had seen their positions or just that his men had fallen. If Declan did not know where they were, any movement now would give them away. Declan might decide to blast the entire area, but there were too many possible places for invisible people to hide. He did not believe that Declan's first few shots would be lucky enough to strike them. He would probably take out the cabin first, thinking since he could not see them they must have been shooting through the walls or windows.

He said, "Guys, stay perfectly still and quiet. Let's see how this plays out. Hear me?"

Neither Phil nor Dillon responded. Perfect.

He called out to Kyrill, "Don't say anything. Don't move. If you do, the last arrow I shoot will skewer your head to the wall. Do you understand?"

Kyrill pushed loud, grunting screams through his clenched teeth.

"Good," Hutch said.

Slower than Kyrill had moved the barrel of the gun, slower than Hutch had warned him to stop, he began rotating at the hips toward the oncoming Jeep. His bow arm and shooting hand and shoulders and head remained as firm and unmoving as one of Medusa's failed assailants. His torso pivoted while his legs were locked in place. Declan's attention would be on the cabin. And then on Bad and Kyrill. If Kyrill kept quiet about his position, Hutch thought he would be able to get off a shot.

The Jeep slid to a stop on the dry grass. It was catty-corner to the cabin, ten feet from the Bronco. If it had been night, the Jeep's headlamps would have illuminated the entire front of the cabin.

Bad and Kyrill had been near-perfect twenty-five-yard shots. The Jeep was farther, forty, forty-one yards. With his new bow, Hutch was uncomfortable going for a target at that distance. And he was down to his last arrow. He hoped Declan would move onto the porch, perhaps to examine his fallen men. He doubted it. He thought he would be attempting the forty-yard shot, and he braced himself to make it count.

Through the windshield he saw Cort in the passenger seat. She leaned forward until her chin touched the dash. Her eyes were wide as she took in the bodies on the porch. Her mouth moved, but Hutch could hear nothing but his own heartbeat in his ears.

The driver's side door opened. Declan rose and peered over it at Bad and Kyrill.

Hutch took a bead on his head. His arrow would have to sail over the Jeep's hood and within inches of its windshield and perhaps even skim the doorframe to find its mark. It was an impossible shot, even if Hutch had his old bow. But that bow was no more. And if he shot and missed, then he, Dillon, and Phil would be no more as well. He expected Declan to step at least as far as the front bumper of the Jeep. That was a shot he could take.

Instead of coming around the door, Declan walked to the rear. The hatch came up, and he struggled with something.

He appeared on the passenger side with nothing between him and Hutch but Laura. His arm was around her neck. She bucked and kicked. His arm flexed, choking her, and she calmed her movements.

Declan's face appeared over her left shoulder. He looked mostly at the cabin, but his scanning told Hutch that the man did not know where they were. On the other side of her head, Declan held a pistol barrel to her temple.

At that moment pushing back the rush of emotion and adrenaline was the hardest thing Hutch had ever done. His head swam, his legs felt unsteady, he wanted to take a step, to brace himself. He knew Laura only through her son. But that connection felt as strong as a metal cable, as though it had been years in the making. He knew it wasn't real, but looking at her now, at the fear in her eyes, at the blood that had streaked down the center of her face, at her lips twisted in pain—panic squeezed every organ, shooting sparks of tingling electricity through him. He had grown to love her son, and it was Dillon's emotions he felt. He knew he could do nothing. Now the shot was not merely impossible and a miss not merely their death warrant. If he did shoot he would likely miss, and if he missed he would likely hit Laura. As much as Hutch believed in a forgiving God, he found it hard to imagine accepting that forgiveness if the last thing he did on Earth was put an arrow in that woman.

Declan pushed Laura toward the cabin, staying close to the side of the Jeep.

"Kyrill, where are they?"

The teen seemed not to hear.

"Kyrill!" Declan repeated. He glanced around. He lifted his chin, calling out to his enemies. "Where are you? I've got the woman! Come out, come out, wherever you are."

68

Behind Hutch, Dillon made rustling sounds, no doubt trying to see if the "woman" was his mother. He wanted to tell Dillon to stay down, to not look, to not move. But even if he were foolish enough to make a sound, Hutch knew if he were Dillon's age and that was his mom, nothing anyone said would stop him from looking.

Hutch closed his eyes and waited for it to come.

More rustling. Then a big intake of breath. A pause, as if the boy was considering doing something other than what he inevitably must do.

"Mom!" he yelled.

"Dillon!" she yelled back, desperate, relieved. "Dillon, honey!"

As Dillon brushed past Hutch, he removed his fingers from the bowstring and grabbed the boy's collar. The sudden stop nearly jerked

Dillon off his feet. Keeping his eyes on Declan, Hutch said in a low voice, "No matter what happens, you have to stay here. If you don't, that man will kill your mother and all of us. We might be able to work out a different ending, but you have to stay here. I need my hand back, Dillon. Can I trust you not to run?"

Out of the corner of his eye, he saw Dillon nod his head. In a weak voice Dillon said, "Yes," and then added, "sir."

For some reason, that one word cinched it for Hutch. Dillon meant what he said. He let go and brought his fingers back up to the bowstring.

Dillon stood at his side, shaking, starting to weep, but holding true to his word.

Phil's head lifted to take in the scene.

In a loud whisper, Hutch said, "Phil, don't move. Not an inch."

Phil's head went down again.

Declan smiled. "Well, looks like we've got—"

Laura's head dropped straight down. The suddenness and power of the movement allowed her to slip out of Declan's grasp. Crouching, she elbowed him in the stomach and then did it again: two quick thrusts. She took off running, not toward Dillon and Hutch, but out from the Jeep, away from the cabin.

Declan stumbled and reached for her. He took several steps, grasping at her. Remembering the gun in his hand, he brought it up.

Hutch let his arrow fly.

It sailed at Declan's chest.

Declan took another step. The arrow passed between his arm and rib cage. It continued into the meadow and disappeared. He must have felt its passing; maybe it nicked him. He jerked his arm up as he pulled the trigger. Laura screamed, spun, and fell.

Running all out, Dillon yelled and ran for his mother.

Hutch darted for the weapons in the dirt near the porch. He stopped when Declan swung the pistol around at him.

Dillon yelled and cried, almost to Laura. She was sitting up, squeezing her arm. Blood gushed through her fingers.

Hutch thought Declan would hold him there while he decided the best, most imaginative way to dispatch them.

Declan fired.

The bullet whistled past Hutch's head. For less than a second he was stunned. Then he saw Declan's finger tightening on the trigger again and he jumped. The shot rang out. A chunk of dirt exploded two feet away. He scampered on all fours, pushing, moving, trying to move faster, faster. The guns were too far away. He would never make it. Thirty feet . . . twenty-five . . .

Declan should have shot him dead, but he had stopped firing. Hutch turned to see the pistol pointed directly at him, Declan's attention elsewhere. He was looking over the Jeep's hood to the corner of the front porch, where Julian stood holding the satellite control device.

"Drop the gun, Declan," Julian said, his voice as tight and shaky as a tightrope.

"I told you not to touch that," Declan said. His voice was more shrill than Hutch had ever heard it. "Julian, bring it to me."

"Just drop it!"

A heartbeat passed. Two.

Declan said, "No."

"You . . . you . . ." Julian was sobbing, hitching in deep breaths to fuel his ragged emotions. Tears streamed from both eyes. He sniffed. "You . . . did all this! You killed people."

"With your help."

"I'm your little brother. You were supposed to watch out for me

Instead you made me . . . you made me part of your . . . your . . ." He shook his head.

"I didn't do anything Dad didn't want me to do. You don't get to where he is by toeing the line, by making nice. He wanted me to show that to you, to make you tough. You got a problem, take it up with him."

"It's you, Declan!" Then sadly: "Just you."

A new wrinkle emerged from the Jeep: Cortland came out of the driver's door, on the opposite side from Declan.

Hutch expected a fervid appeal to Julian, supported by a pistol too large for the girl's hands. Instead her demeanor was timid, her eyes like those beholding a wild lion's fangs as its rancid breath blew across her face. No gun. In fact, she was holding her hands up, chest-high, palms out, as if to show Julian and Declan, and anyone else who might perceive her as a threat, that a threat was the last thing she was. She backed slowly between the two vehicles and continued into the meadow.

Declan took advantage of this distraction to shift the Big Sauer's aim. It moved in a slow arc toward the boy.

Hutch yelled, "No!"

Julian's eyes widened. He glanced down at the device, which sounded a fast, three-tone chime.

The pistol stopped its movement toward Julian. Some emotion flashed on Declan's face—fear or surprise, something Hutch believed was more sincere than had touched it in a long time. His head dropped back and he gazed at the sky.

The laser came down in a flicker of green light. The air rippled around it, radiating heat. The spot where Declan stood erupted. Dirt and burning grass geysered straight up. The Jeep rocked away from the impact. Its side glass and windshield shattered.

Laura screamed. Julian flew back against the front of the cabin and fell to his side.

Hutch turned his eyes on the lump that was a soot-covered Phil He called to his friend. The lump compressed tighter into itself. He called again, and Phil's head came up.

"Cover the guns," Hutch said. "Over here."

Phil nodded.

Hutch rose, started for Laura and Dillon's position. They were lying facedown in the grass a dozen feet from where Laura had been sitting, holding her arm. He ran to them. As he rolled Dillon over, the boy moaned. Blood coated his right ear. His eyes fluttered open.

"Dillon?" Hutch said.

"Mom? Where's Mom?"

Hutch turned to Laura. Gently, he rolled her over. As her son had she moaned and opened her eyes. She sat up. She folded her wounded arm at the elbow and tucked it close to her body. The other arm found Dillon and pulled him close. She squeezed him tightly. Her eyes scanned the area, then turned up to Hutch. "Declan?"

The crater was at least five feet wide and a foot deep. Smoke wafted up from it. Bits of burning grass fanned out from the strike zone. Something near Hutch burned with more intensity. He recognized it as one of the woven bracelets Declan had worn. Here and there, looking like chunks of ash, were the black stones he had strung around his neck.

The Jeep's front passenger door and back half of the front quarter panel were crumpled in the shape of a semicircle, as though the finger had not only poked Declan out of existence but had ground him out for good measure, catching the Jeep in the process. Declan's gun lay on the ground outside the crater. His hand still clenched it. It had been severed at the wrist.

"He's gone," Hutch said.

Laura closed her eyes and nodded. Took a deep breath. "He told me," she said, laughing a little, "that curiosity killed the cat. He must not have known the whole saying: Satisfaction brought it back." Her eyes found Hutch's and she said, "I'm back. At least for my boy. I'm back."

69

Dillon could not get enough of his mother. He squeezed her and buried his face in her neck. He cried. He let loose all the fear and grief and exhaustion that he had so admirably held in since Hutch had first picked him up behind the rec center.

Laura was the mom he needed. She embraced him as would any mother whose dead child miraculously found breath again. She stroked the back of his head and consoled him with promises that everything would be all right. Then her own tears choked her voice, and the two wept together.

Hutch could only imagine the depth of their emotions, the swirling chaos of their grief clashing with the elation of finding each other alive. More quickly than the grief, the elation would fade, or at least distill into something else: most likely, love and appreciation for one another. Dillon seemed like an emotionally stable child, undoubtedly loved. What they had gone through—losing a father and husband, coupled with the very real fear that the other had been lost as well—would strengthen their bond and make them not only mother and son, but best friends for life.

Hutch hoped so, anyway. It would be some kind of redemption for their suffering. Dillon would find a wife someday, have children of his own. He would know how easily they could be taken away, and he would love them deeply and protect them well.

Laura held her wounded left arm out from her body. The sleeve over her bicep was torn and soaked crimson, but little new blood bubbled out; the bullet had not pieced an artery or broken the bone.

He looked around. Phil was a huge lump of coal, sitting on the weapons near the porch. Something about his posture—slumped shoulders, an arm angling back as a prop, legs splayed in front of him—made Hutch very glad to have him there. His presence, his life, was enough.

He walked to where Declan's hand and gun lay in the dirt. He pressed his booted toe onto the wrist, bent, and worked the gun free. Son of a billionaire. More opportunities than most people could dream of in a lifetime, and this is what Declan had chosen to do with them. Boredom, abuse, too many freedoms, and not enough reprisals. Who knew the reason? Hutch was too weary to give it much thought. He kicked the hand into the crater, pushed the gun into his belt, and walked on.

He waded into the sea of ashes. It didn't seem dirty to him. They had immersed themselves in it, and it had saved their lives.

Already a light breeze had softened the evidence of their having been there. The depressions and mounds where Phil and Dillon had lay and he had stood, the miniature peaks and valleys of their footprints, were returning to the uniformity of the ashen surface. Vapors of soot wisped off the few remaining ridges. It lingered over the area like smoke, as though their presence had stirred the memory of heat and flame from the ground. He found the bow, nearly submerged, and lifted it. He shook it gently. Layers of ash fell away, but the blackness he had spread onto the moist, freshly cut wood remained. It was crudely chiseled and stained not only with soot, but with human blood. To Hutch, however, it represented resourcefulness, determination, life. He slipped it onto his shoulder.

He walked to Phil and knelt next to him. He clamped a hand onto his shoulder. "You all right?"

"Fantastic with a capital *V*." He eyed Hutch, seeming for the first time to see how thoroughly the soot had covered them. He looked at his own hands and said, "If cleanliness is next to godliness, I think we're in hell."

Hutch smiled. "More like we just came out of it. Can you get these guns into the car, the Bronco?"

He nodded. "Should I hold one on the kid you arrowed?"

Kyrill sat slumped against the cabin, his hand still clutching the shaft coming out of his shoulder. His skin was the grayish-white of a trout's underbelly.

Hutch said, "He's not going anywhere till we move him." He patted Phil's shoulder and stood. When he stepped onto the porch, he saw a lot of blood had soaked Kyrill's army jacket. The lack of spray and the teen's continued consciousness convinced Hutch he was not in danger of bleeding to death. He knelt between Kyrill and Bad. He felt around Kyrill's waist, under his arms, and around his ankles.

The teen looked up, groggy with pain.

Hutch asked, "Any more weapons?"

Kyrill half smiled. Hutch thought he was going to say something smart, like *I wish,* or *You mean like the one in my shoulder?* But he only shook his head.

"We'll get you to a doctor. You'll be all right."

He checked Bad for a pulse. Found none. He patted him down, found only a knife.

Stepping off the porch, he tossed the blade into the ashes. He approached Julian. The boy was sitting on the edge of the porch, head hung, weeping quietly. The satellite remote was in his lap. Hesitantly, Hutch picked it up. The monitor showed static.

"It's offline," Julian informed him. He sniffed.

"Can we turn it off?" Hutch asked. Then said, "Never mind." He dropped it on the ground and stomped it with his heel. It was evidence, but he didn't want it to cause any more heartache. Not on his watch. When the monitor was shattered, controls broken off, and the housing bent in a shallow *V,* he picked it up again.

Julian peered up at him with red, red eyes. "I killed him," he said.

Hutch knelt, aligning his eyes with the boy's.

"You did the right thing, Julian. You did what you had to do."

"He's . . ." He swallowed hard. A fat tear streaked down his face. "He was my brother."

Hutch squeezed Julian's knee. "He would have killed *you.* Now or over time, he would have. You know that, don't you?"

Julian nodded. After a few moments, he said, "What's gonna happen?"

Hutch thought about it. He had witnessed goodness in Julian: not alerting his pursuers in the forest, cutting him loose on the plateau, stopping Declan here. Discernment told him Julian's wrong decisions had been more about being young than being bad. He hoped the boy would have a chance to prove it.

He said, "What happened here was self-defense, Julian. Clearly. I don't know what else you've done, but considering your age and your brother's influence over you, I think you'll make out okay. Your father might be another story. Sounds like he had a lot to do with this."

Julian shook his head. "Plausible deniability." It sounded like a term he had heard often. Dinnertime chatter. "He's got so many companies and people between him and things like this." He looked at the remote in Hutch's hand, then into the sky. "He'll never take the fall."

"Listen," Hutch said. "No matter what happens, what you did here saved my life, a lot of lives. Thank you."

"I just wish . . . I wish . . ."

"I know."

"Can you . . ." His voice broke. More tears. "Can you and Dillon and his mother and everyone else . . ." His shoulders slumped, his burden of guilt heavy. "Can you *forgive me?*"

Hutch managed a thin smile. "I can, son. I can't speak for the others, but I think they'll see that when you realized what was happening, you tried to make it right or stop it. The real question is, can you forgive yourself?"

Julian dropped his gaze, his head moving slowly back and forth.

"Give it time. When the authorities come, during the investigation, during the trial, be honest. Stick to the truth like it's a life preserver in a storm, and you'll be okay. You will."

Hutch rose and walked around to the back of the Bronco. Phil had opened it and stashed the weapons on the cargo floor. Hutch added the satellite remote and Declan's handgun. He turned.

Phil was twenty paces into the meadow, squinting at the forest beyond. "What about the girl and the camera guy?" he said.

"They can't stay out there long," Hutch said. "The cops will find them, they'll make it to town, or . . . or they won't."

He remembered something and walked around the Jeep. Pruitt'

camera lay in the dirt against the rear tire. It would have been in better shape had it fallen from an airplane. He picked it up, leaving a lens and bits of plastic on the ground. He went back to the Bronco and set it inside. A label on the camera's body indicated it recorded high-definition images directly to an onboard hard drive. No doubt the cops had technicians who could recover whatever data remained in the camera. And Pruitt had probably already dumped earlier recordings onto one of the laptops Hutch had seen at the rec center.

A hand touched his arm. A black marble statue of a boy stood beside him. The whites of Dillon's eyes, his blue irises, stared up at him. Tears had washed away the soot in wide paths from lids to jawline.

Laura stood behind him. She released the grip she had on her wound to push her hair back from her face. Her cheek was smudged with soot where she'd rubbed it against her son. Her hand, her arms, her entire body trembled. She gave Hutch a soft smile. "I can't stop shaking," she said. "Thank you for taking care of my son."

He looked down at the boy. "I think we took care of each other. Right, Dillon?"

Dillon stepped in to hug him. Hutch leaned into it and hugged him back. When their embrace ended, Dillon said, "What are you gonna do now?"

Hutch squared his shoulders. "I'm heading home, Dillon. I've got some kids there who need their father."

"But your wife . . . ?"

"Who is she, next to what we just went through?" He grinned, and to his surprise, he realized that a genuine feeling of hope infused it. *Really,* he thought, *what kind of chance does she have of keeping me from my kids when Declan could not destroy me?*

Dillon frowned. "Will I see you again?"

Hutch pushed his smile wider. "Oh, absolutely." He took in Laura.

"If your mom lets me, I'll come see you, and maybe you and she can come to Colorado. I'll give you a tour of *my* stomping grounds. You and Logan would get along great. Would you like that, to come see me?"

Dillon nodded.

He didn't want to spoil whatever brief respite from the pain they had going on here, but he had to know. He lifted his gaze to Laura's. "Terry?"

She shook her head.

The respite was gone. It would return, he knew. First, the darkness would grow less black. Eventually, over a lot of time, he would notice more light than not, a sort of twilight of the heart. Then, one day, the sun would break through.

He had been too caught up in his own dismal night to recognize that Logan and Macie were braving a bleakness he had helped create. He would remedy that, if he could.

Displaying the impeccable timing Hutch had come to think of as something more than coincidence, Dillon embraced him again. It was a balm to his spirit. He remembered something the child had taught him while they were fighting for their lives: in giving comfort, it was impossible not to receive it.

He pulled Dillon closer and hugged him.

ACKNOWLEDGMENTS

My heartfelt thanks goes to the following people, without whom this story would not exist:

My longtime friend and newfound researcher, Mark Nelson. Years ago he introduced me to the beauty and ruggedness of Canada's backcountry. An early discussion about this story revealed his rich vein of knowledge regarding northern Saskatchewan and roughing it in the wilderness. When I asked for his help in researching this project, he dove in with enthusiasm and astounding aptitude. Where my descriptions of locations and bow hunting prove accurate, he deserves the credit. Where they fail, blame my ignorance and misplaced sense of artistic license.

My gratitude and apologies to the good folks of Stony Rapids, which became the fictional town of Fiddler Falls as I moved it across the river and tweaked its physical characteristics. I hope I preserved Stony's hearty and charming spirit.

Once again, my editor, Amanda Bostic, and publisher, Allen Arnold, for their encouragement and advice. Both possess keen insight into the art of storytelling and the hearts of authors. And the other staff at Nelson—particularly Jennifer, Carrie, Natalie, Lisa, and Mark—whose hard work and talent remind me time and again of how fortunate I am to be part of their team.

LB Norton, my copyeditor. Every author should be so fortunate to have someone like her fixing his literary missteps.

My indispensable agent Joel Gotler and his partners at Intellectual Property Group, especially Josh Schechter. Their friendship and good sense have saved me from myself more than a few times.

John Fornof, Mark Olsen, Mae Gannon—readers, advisors, and best of all friends.

My wife, Jodi, whose love and support have always girded me for long days of writing. She is my first reader, editor, and sounding board. And as my soul mate, she is more precious than rubies.

My children: Melanie, Matthew, Anthony, and our newest blessing, Isabella. Hutch learned the hard way what I've always known time with them is worth fighting for.

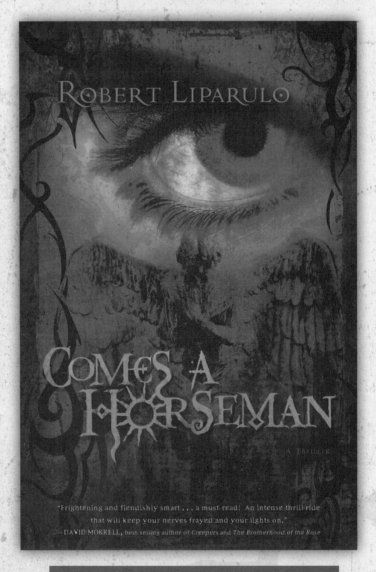

COMES A HORSEMAN

Five years ago
Asia House, Tel Aviv, Israel

He waited with his face pressed against the warm metal and his pistol gouging the skin at his lower back. He thought about pulling the weapon from his waistband, setting it beside him or even holding it in his hand, but when the time came, he'd have to move fast, and he didn't want it getting in his way. He'd been there a long time, since well before the first party guests started arriving. Now it sounded as though quite a crowd had gathered on the third floor of the big building. Their voices drifted to him through the ventilation shaft, reverberating off its metal walls, reaching his ears as a jumble of undulating tones, punctuated at times by shrill laughter. He would close his eyes for long periods and try to discern the conversations, but whether by distortion or foreign tongue, even single words eluded him.

Luco Scaramuzzi lifted his cheek out of a pool of perspiration and peered for the hundredth time through the two-foot-square grille below him. He could still see the small spot on the marble floor where a bead of sweat had dropped from the tip of his nose before he could stop it. If that spot were the center point of a clock face, the toilet was at noon, the sink and vanity at two o'clock, and the door—just beyond Luco's view—at three. Despite the large room's intended function as a lavatory for one, modesty or tact had prompted the mounting of walnut partitions on the two unwalled sides of the toilet. It was these partitions that would allow him to descend from the air shaft without being seen by a person standing at the sink—by his target.

A gust of pungent wind blew past him, turning his stomach and forcing him to gasp for air through the grille. The building was home to several embassies, an art gallery, and a restaurant—enough people, food, and trash to generate some really awful effluvia. When the cooling system was idle, the temperature in the ventilation shafts quickly soared into summer-sun temperatures, despite the nighttime hour, and all sorts of odors roamed the ducts like rabid dogs. Then the air conditioner would kick in, chasing away the smells and freezing the perspiration to his body.

Arjan had warned him about such things. He had explained that covert operations necessitated subjecting the body and senses to elements sane men avoided: extreme heat and cold; long stretches of immobility in the most uncomfortable places and positions; contact with insects, rodents, decay. He had advised him to focus on a single object and think pleasant thoughts until equilibrium returned.

Luco shifted his eyes to a perfume bottle on the vanity. He imagined its fragrance, then thought of himself breathing it in as his fingers lifted hair away from the curve of an olive-skinned neck and felt the pulse with his lips.

He heard the bathroom door open and pulled his face back into the darkness. He held his breath, then exhaled when he heard the click of a woman's heels. Her shoes came into view, then her legs and body. Of course she was elegantly dressed. Not only did the nature of the gathering demand it, but this room was reserved for special guests—the target, his family, and his entourage: people who were expected to look their best. The woman stopped in front of the vanity mirror, glanced at herself, and continued into the stall. Turning, she yanked up her dress. Hooked by two thumbs, her hosiery came down as she sat.

The top of the partition's door obstructed Luco's view of her lap, and during the bathroom visits of two other lovely ladies, he had found that no amount of craning would change that fact. So he lay still and watched her face. She was model-beautiful, with big green eyes, sculpted cheekbones, and lips too full to be natural. She finished, flushed, and walked to the sink, where she was completely out of view. This reassured him that the plan had been well thought through. She fiddled at the sink for a minute after washing her hands—applying makeup, he guessed—and left.

He waited for the click of a latch as the door settled into its jamb. It didn't come . . . Someone was holding the door open. Masculine shoes and pant legs stepped silently into view. Luco's breath stopped.

Watch for a bodyguard, Arjan had told him. *He'll come in for a look. He may flush the toilet and run the water in the sink, but he won't use anything himself. The next man in is your guy.*

He would recognize his target, of course, but getting these few seconds of warning allowed his mind to shift from vigilance to readiness.

He could see the bodyguard in the bathroom now, a square-jawed brute packed into an Armani. The guard stepped up to the vanity to examine each of the bottles and brushes in turn. He dropped to one knee, with more grace than seemed possible, and examined under the countertop and sink. The bathroom had been thoroughly checked once already, earlier in the day, but nobody liked surprises. Luco smiled at the thought.

Standing again, the guard glanced around, his eyes sweeping toward the grille. Luco pulled back farther, fighting the urge to move fast, which might cause the metal he was on to pop, or the gypsum boards that formed the bathroom's ceiling to creak. He imagined the guard's eyes taking in the screws that seemed to hold the grille firmly in place. In reality, they were screw heads only, glued in place after

Luco had removed the actual screws. Now, a solitary wire held up tł grille on the unhinged side.

The guard inspected the toilet, the padded bench opposite tł sink, and the thin closet by the door, bare but for a few hand towe and extra tissue rolls. Every move he made was quick and efficier. He had done this countless times before—probably even did it in b dreams—and never expected to find anything that would validate b existence. He didn't this time either. After all, his boss was the benig prime minister of a democratic country with few enemies. A grud; would almost have to be personal, not political.

Or preordained, thought Luco. *Preordained.*

The guard spoke softly to someone in the hall.

The door closed, latching firmly. Someone set the lock. The targ walked into view. He drained a crystal glass of amber fluid, almc missed the top of the vanity as he set down the glass, and belch(loudly. He fumbled with his pants, and Luco saw that his belly hɛ grown too round to let him see his own zipper, which could present problem with the superfluous hooks and buttons common to fine tailored slacks. The target left the stall door open. He stood before tł toilet with his pants and boxers crumpled around his ankles, his hi thrust forward for better aim, the way a child pees.

A confident assassin may have done the deed right then, jv pulled back and shot through the grille into the target's head. An certainly, he could have hired such professionalism. Arjan would ha done it; had even requested the assignment.

But it has to be me. If I don't do this myself, then it is for nothing.

Given that requirement, Arjan had set about preparing his boss f this moment, arranging transportation and alibis, securing timetabł and blueprints. Arjan had made him train for five weeks with *Incurs(loyalists. They had worked him physically and filled his mind wi knowledge of ballistics and anatomy, close-quarters combat, the arts of vigilance and stealth—at least to the extent that time allowed. Arjan had explained that using a sniper's rifle and scope was infeasible, considering the deadline.

Shooting a man from three hundred yards is a skill! he had snapped. *It's not like the movies, man. It takes years of training to guarantee a kill. And you'll have only one chance, right?*

Right.

So somewhere in Arjan's dark mind, a switch labeled "close kill" had been thrown, sending Luco down a track that led to this ventilation shaft and his hand on the wire that held the grille in place. Slowly, he unwound it from an exposed screw. Then he recalled Arjan's instructions and relooped the wire.

The target's unabated flow told him he had at least a few more seconds. Luco removed a moist washcloth from a Ziploc baggy. He rubbed it over his face, removing sweat and dust from around his eyes, letting the water refresh him. Arjan had told him that countless missions failed because of haste and machismo myths about warriors fighting despite handicaps. "Perspiration in your eyes is a disadvantage you can avoid, so do it!" he had ordered.

Luco dried himself with a washcloth from another Ziploc. His fingers felt clammy inside the tight dishwashing gloves he wore, but that was better than trying to handle the wire and pistol with sweaty hands. Surgical gloves, he had learned, were too thin to prevent leaving fingerprints. And Arjan had been clear about wearing the gloves from ingress to egress—so clear, in fact, that he'd made Luco wear them the entire last week of his training.

The target was tugging his pants up, running a hand around to tuck his shirt. As soon as he rounded the partition to step in front of the sink, Luco whipped the wire off the screw and let the grille swing down.

A string that was attached to the wire slid between his thumb and fore finger until a knot stopped it, halting the grille inches from the wall.

The water at the sink came on.

He used his strong arms to position himself directly above the open ing. His legs pistonned down, and he dropped to the floor. By bending his knees as soon as the toes of his rubber-soled boots touched the mar ble, he managed an almost-silent landing. Still crouched, he pulled th pistol from his waistband. It was a China Type 64, old but especiall suited for the job at hand. Its barrel was no longer than any handgun's but included a silencer; its breech slide was lockable—and was now locked, he noted—to prevent the noises of cartridge ejection and roun rechambering inherent to semiautomatic pistols. With its subsoni 7.65mm bullets, it was the quietest pistol ever made.

He stepped behind the target, who was bent over the sink, splashin water on his face. Perfect. The gun's locking slide meant he had only or quick shot. The next shot would take at least five seconds to prepare— an eternity if a wounded victim was screaming and thrashing aroun and bodyguards were kicking in the door. His goal was instant incapa itation . . . instant death. And that meant the bullet had to sever the bra stem, which was best achieved from behind. He pointed the pistol at th approximate spot where the man's head would be when he straightene

But, still bent, the man reached for a hand towel, knocked it to th floor, and turned to retrieve it. Catching Luco in his peripheral visio he stood to face him. His eyes focused on the gun, and he raised h hands in surrender. His attention rose to Luco's face. Puzzleme made his eyes squint, his mouth go slack.

He knows he's seen me before, Luco realized.

"*Ti darò qualsiasi cosa oppure,*" the man pleaded. *I will give y everything.* His voice was hushed, obviously believing that cooperati would forestall his death.

"*Sono sicuro che lo farai,*" Luco said. *I know you will.* Stepping forward, he touched the barrel to the indentation between the man's lips and nose—lightly, as if anointing him—and pulled the trigger. The man's head snapped back. Brain and blood and bone instantly caked the mirror behind him, as a dozen fissures snapped the glass from a central point where the bullet had struck. Miraculously, none of the shards came loose. The noise had been barely audible above the sound of the faucet. Luco caught the body as it crumpled and laid it gently on the floor.

Then the smell hit him, like meat shoved into his sinuses. He stood, tried to breathe. Something fell from the mirror and landed wetly on the countertop. Vomit rose in his throat. He slapped his palm over his mouth and willed it back down. Hand in place, he forced himself to survey the slaughter—the brain matter on the mirror and counter; the blood there, as well as spreading in a pool under the head, a rivulet breaking away and snaking toward a floor drain near the toilet; the face contorted in terror, mouth open, tongue protruding, eyes wide.

He wanted to remember.

Back below the ventilation opening, he jumped and pulled himself into the shaft. He could have used the bench for a boost up, but the idea was to slow his pursuers, even by mere seconds. It wasn't the time it would take the guards to move the bench into place that mattered, but any confusion produced by not having an obvious escape route to follow. First, they'd call for a screwdriver (or shoot away the screw heads). Then they'd tug at the grille, which the high-tensile wire would hold firm. Ultimately they'd get into the shaft, glance at the false metal wall he would place behind him, and head the other way.

Six minutes after the assassination, he clambered out of the shaft behind a stack of boxes in a storage room. Through the door, two steps down a hallway, and he was descending the narrow and dark servants' staircase, rarely used since the installation of elevators in the 1970s. He came out in a kitchen three floors below. Hands were immediately on him, pulling at his blood-spattered overalls.

"Hurry," a young man whispered in Italian. His head moved in all directions as he peeled the clothes away.

Luco stripped off the rubber gloves, then vigorously rubbed his hands together. He opened a pocketknife and ran the blade over the laces of his boots. The young man—Antonio, Luco remembered—tugged off the boots and pushed on a pair of expensive oxfords to match his suit. Everything went into an attaché case. Antonio scrubbed at his neck, face, and hair with a wet towel.

"Ah," Luco complained, wiping at his eye.

"Dishwasher soap. Nothing better for blood." Antonio tossed the towel into the attaché, produced a comb, and ran it through Luco' hair. "Come." He led Luco to a heavy fire door at the rear of the building and signaled for him to wait. He opened it and slippe through. Fifteen seconds later he was back, beckoning Luco outside

A long alley ran away from the Asia House, cutting a canyon between two tall buildings. The only illumination appeared to be the glow of mercury-vapor lamp on the far street where the alley ended. Everythin else was submerged in blackness. Propping the door open with his foo Antonio pointed down the alley. "The car is parked on Henriata Sold.

Luco gripped the young man's shoulder and gave it a shake. H leaned closer. *"Grazie."*

Antonio whispered back, "Anything for you."

Luco stepped into the dark alley, the click of his heels echoing qu etly. The door closed behind him. He smiled.

It was finished.

And it had just begun.